Wild

The black griffin circled lower, as if he was singling out prey, and soon he could see the strange creatures that moved among the rocks. They were tiny, only about as long as his foreleg, and they stood on two legs like birds, but they didn't have wings. He saw them looking up at him. They did not run, but he heard their calls drifting up toward him, and his heart leapt when he realised that they were speaking to each other.

"Humans," the yellow griffin said. "They are the key."

"Food?" the black griffin suggested.

"No—sometimes, maybe." She fixed him with a steady bright blue stare. "I will give you some advice. If you want to live in this world, find a human. Protect it. Keep it safe. Help it. If you do, you will always be safe. Our magic is not enough for us to survive now. Not alone."

As she spoke—using words he did not know, to express an idea he did not comprehend—the black griffin had a strange feeling in his throat. It wasn't quite pain, but it wasn't quite pleasure, either. It felt as if something was lodged in there, something hard and unyielding and burning hot. It made him want to scream.

The Dark Griffin

THE FALLEN MOON
BOOK ONE

K. J. TAYLOR

ACE BOOKS, NEW YORK

THE BERKLEY PUBLISHING GROUP
Published by the Penguin Group
Penguin Group (USA) Inc.
375 Hudson Street, New York, New York 10014, USA
Penguin Group (Canada), 90 Eglinton Avenue East, Suite 700, Toronto, Ontario M4P 2Y3, Canada
(a division of Pearson Penguin Canada Inc.)
Penguin Books Ltd., 80 Strand, London WC2R 0RL, England
Penguin Group Ireland, 25 St. Stephen's Green, Dublin 2, Ireland (a division of Penguin Books Ltd.)
Penguin Group (Australia), 250 Camberwell Road, Camberwell, Victoria 3124, Australia
(a division of Pearson Australia Group Pty. Ltd.)
Penguin Books India Pvt. Ltd., 11 Community Centre, Panchsheel Park, New Delhi—110 017, India
Penguin Group (NZ), 67 Apollo Drive, Rosedale, North Shore 0632, New Zealand
(a division of Pearson New Zealand Ltd.)
Penguin Books (South Africa) (Pty.) Ltd., 24 Sturdee Avenue, Rosebank, Johannesburg 2196,
South Africa

Penguin Books Ltd., Registered Offices: 80 Strand, London WC2R 0RL, England

THE DARK GRIFFIN

An Ace Book / published by arrangement with the author

PRINTING HISTORY
HarperCollins Australia mass-market edition / February 2009
Ace mass-market edition / January 2011

Copyright © 2009 by K. J. Taylor.
Maps by Allison Jones.
Welsh translations on pages 131, 186 by Janice Jones of Gairynei Bryd.
Cover art by Steve Stone.
Cover design by Judith Lagerman.
Interior text design by Laura K. Corless.

ISBN: 978-0-441-01978-6

ACE
Ace Books are published by The Berkley Publishing Group,
a division of Penguin Group (USA) Inc.,
375 Hudson Street, New York, New York 10014.
ACE and the "A" design are trademarks of Penguin Group (USA) Inc.

PRINTED IN THE UNITED STATES OF AMERICA

10 9 8 7 6 5 4 3 2 1

For Bran.
You'll always be my big guy.

Acknowledgments

Thanks to the following people, who told me I didn't suck: Arthryn, Carnoc, Lord Alexander, Mordacity, Galdor, bl1nk, jumpman1, blahblahwhatever, Cerenthor, Elohim of Death, Skandar Traeganni, Jinx, Fenris, Attack Bunny, Brienne, Irith Omor, Randomdej, Vox, Pegasus, MurtaghRider, Corascant, NammilLumpen, Warthode, Murtagh799, Seithr Arget, StormShade, Texas Sweetie, LadyWater, Sugarquill, Queen Mindi, Beefstew, unconquerableflame, Kazza, Fricai Andlat and many, many others. I apologise to anyone I left out.

Extra thanks to OceanicChick for her helpful suggestions and for listening to and commenting on my ideas in their early stages. Your input was invaluable.

Extra thanks also to Dragonknighttara, a.k.a. Natalie Van Sistine, the great composer. Your talent amazes me. That you decided to use it on a project dedicated to something I created was one of the most incredible things I've ever had happen to me in my life.

Final thanks for Welsh translations to Janice Jones of Gairynei Bryd (A Timely Word), which provides proofreading, editing and mentoring services (camlas@hotmail.com).

Author's Note

The language of the Northerners is Welsh, a very ancient and beautiful language.

Accordingly, in line with the rules of Welsh pronunciation, "dd" sounds like "th."

Hence our protagonist's name Arenadd is pronounced as "Arrenath."

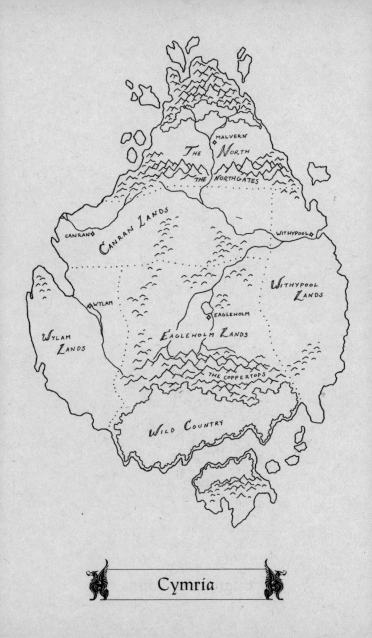

Cymría

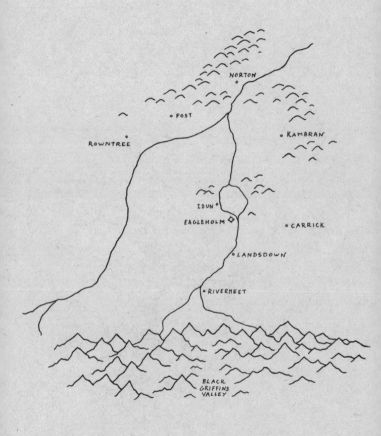

ROWNTREE

FOST

NORTON

KAMBRAN

IDUN

EAGLEHOLM

CARRICK

LANDSDOWN

RIVERMEET

BLACK
GRIFFINS
VALLEY

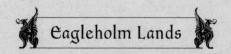

Eagleholm Lands

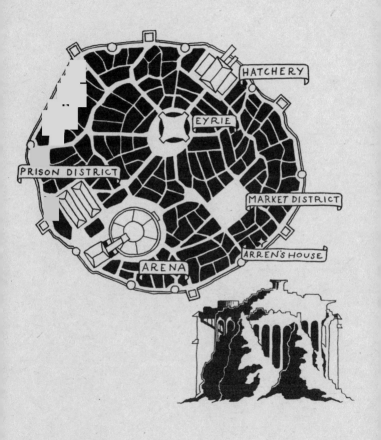

HATCHERY

EYRIE

PRISON DISTRICT

MARKET DISTRICT

ARREN'S HOUSE

ARENA

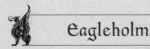

Eagleholm

1

The Black Egg

It all began with the hatching of the dark griffin. A restless day. A grey day. Clouds the colour of lead lay low over the land like a blanket, and the wind that blew over the mountains had the tang of ice in it. Winter was over, but the memory of it lingered.

The valley, overlooked by a trio of craggy peaks, was green and wild, untouched by humans. This was the domain of something else.

From her perch high above the treetops, the great beast who owned the valley had an excellent view of her territory. She lifted her head, the wind ruffling her feathers, orange eyes scanning the area for any sign of movement. All was peaceful, and she sighed and resettled herself in the massive nest she had made for herself. It was supported by the tops of five large trees and woven from the branches she had broken away to make room for it. Normally a griffin was content to sleep on a bare bough or a ledge, but this one had a clutch of eggs to guard. She would not leave her nest once during the three months it would take for them to hatch.

She sighed again and rustled her wings. It had been two

and a half months since the laying, and she had not eaten for two of them. Her stores of fat were running out, and if the eggs did not hatch soon she would be forced to abandon them—or even eat them to save her own life. She lifted her wing and rolled slightly on her side to check on them. There were three eggs, each one about the size of a melon. Two of them had light brown shells, flecked with white. The third was black. Not just dark brown, but pure jet-black, without a speck of any other colour. She had never seen an egg like it before.

She nudged the black egg a little further into the soft curve of her underbelly and crooned deep in her throat, then listened intently. Nothing, and she rolled back onto her chest and refolded her wings. When the eggs were ready to hatch they would start calling back. Until then all she could do was keep them warm and safe.

At thirty years old and as tall at her shoulder as a man, the mother griffin was a well-grown adult. Her front half was covered in glossy grey feathers, and her wings were mottled with black and white. Her hindquarters had tawny brown fur, clawed, padded paws and a long tail whose tip bore a wide fan of rigid black feathers. Her forelegs were bony and covered in grey scales, and her forefeet had long, many-jointed toes tipped with sharp, curved talons. Perfect for grasping and holding. She rested these formidable weapons on the edge of her nest and murmured to her eggs. "Hatch soon. Soon. Do not make me wait longer. Awaken soon and break the shell." It was less real talk than a kind of mantra, and she repeated it several times, letting the sound of her own voice keep her company and stave off her boredom.

After that she slept, woke and slept again, stuck in a kind of half-dreaming twilight as the time dragged by. She wanted to go, wanted to be free and fly away over the valley, but her instincts forced her to stay. She continued to check on her eggs, day after day, waiting for the chicks to begin their piping.

But they didn't. The weeks dragged by and she slowly weakened. Her ribs started to jut through her skin, and her feathers lost their shine. She was starving to death. Yet still she did not leave. Every day she thought of finally giving up and leaving the eggs, but every day she decided to wait another night. Just one more night. Just one more.

And then, at last, nearly half a month late, the chicks began to awaken. She crooned to them, just as she had done so many times before, and finally heard a faint chirping in reply. She nudged the eggs with her beak and called again, and once more the piping voices of the chicks came from inside the shells that imprisoned them.

The mother griffin pushed them forward to rest between her forelegs, and prepared for the final stage of her vigil.

The black egg was the first to begin moving. Tapping came from inside it, and the chick ceased chirping as it began to struggle to hatch. Shortly afterward, the other two eggs began to rock gently from side to side. The chicks were bracing their legs against the inside and trying to push their way out. The hatching began.

It was a slow process. The eggs moved and were still, moved and then stilled again. The chicks had to stop and rest frequently, but they always resumed their struggle, and the tapping grew louder until the black egg started to crack. A hole appeared in the side, and the mother had a brief glimpse of a tiny beak before it withdrew.

At this point, she abruptly stood up. Her chicks would be out of the shell very soon, and they would need to eat almost at once. It was time to hunt again. She stood tall, resting her foreclaws on the edge of the nest, and stretched her wings. They were stiff and sore from disuse, but she flapped them vigorously, forcing the muscles to work. They limbered again after a little while, and without any further hesitation she gathered her hind legs under her and leapt into the air. Her wings struck downward, lifting her, and she flew up and away from the nest and into the sky.

She flew a little clumsily at first, but quickly found her balance and flew in a wide circle over the valley, steering with the feathered rudder on her tail. Wanting to see her territory in its entirety, she circled higher. The valley was thickly wooded and lush, full of vines and lichen and moss. There was a patch of marsh right in the middle, where the trees thinned out, fed by a stream that flowed in from between two of the mountains. There were more mountains and valleys beyond in three directions, but to the north, behind the smallest of the three peaks, the land changed. The trees went only so far beyond it, and after that massive plains stretched toward the horizon. It was strange country, dotted with rocky outcrops here and there but almost completely bare of trees. She had heard that there had been trees there once, but they had all gone now. Taken down by humans. Humans hated trees. They were ground dwellers and preferred flat, clear land for their homes. It was not land for griffins. There was nowhere to perch, nowhere to shelter.

The sight of it irritated the griffin. She circled nearer to the smallest mountain and opened her beak wide to screech. The noise echoed over the valley, and she followed it up with another. She was calling her own name, as every griffin did, announcing her presence and her strength to the world and to any other griffin that could be in the area.

"Saekrae! Saekrae!"

She listened. No reply came. There were no other griffins here to call back.

Saekrae's stomach twinged again, and she flew lower, remembering her original purpose.

She turned back toward her valley and flew low over it, searching for prey. A fully grown griffin needed a lot of food to survive, and she had to feed her chicks as well.

At this time of day there should be a herd of wild goats down by the stream. She had fed on them before, and one would make a good meal now.

But she found nothing. She circled still lower, searching among the trees, but she saw no sign of prey. Nothing she could catch.

Saekrae began to despair. If she did not eat, within a day or so she would be too weak to fly. And if she died, so would her chicks.

That left only one alternative. With a weary flick of her wings, she circled upward again, flew over the mountain and struck out across the plains.

She had never flown over them before, though she had seen them plenty of times from a distance. The valley had become her territory only recently, when the scarcity of food further into the mountains had forced her to migrate. She had come to the valley pregnant and had laid her eggs a few months later, and she was only now finding out how inadequate her new territory was. Perhaps the plains had something better to offer.

She noticed how different they were fairly quickly. The air was warmer and drier, and smelt of bare earth and grass. The lack of trees disturbed her, but she flew on regardless, alert for any sign of prey.

And, after a time, she found it. There were animals wandering over the plains. Not goats. These were much bigger. Four-legged like goats, and standing together in a herd like them as well. They were grazing, completely oblivious to her presence.

Saekrae did not pause to wonder what they were. She singled out one that was on the edge of the group, hovered above it for a while to pinpoint her target, and then dropped out of the sky like a stone. She hit the animal directly in the back, her talons shattering its spine before they hooked themselves into its flesh, and then she swooped straight up again, carrying it with her. The weight of it dragged her down and she lurched in the air, struggling to keep hold of it. It was heavier than she had expected. She held on grimly to the dying animal and turned back toward the valley.

She made it after an exhausting and unpleasant journey, and shot back over the mountaintop very gratefully. She reached the nest and dumped the now-dead animal in the bottom, and then settled down on a branch beside it and folded her wings.

The chicks had hatched by now, all three of them, and were already on their paws and alert. Two of them were grey and brown like herself—one male, one female. The

third was black. The fine downy fluff on its front half was
grey over black skin, and its hindquarters had jet-black fur.
Its big heavy-lidded eyes were silver, and its beak and forelegs were also black. It fell on the prey almost instantly,
tearing at it with its beak, and its siblings were quick to join
in. Saekrae tore into the animal's flank and began to eat . . .
there was plenty for all of them. The animal had a lot of
meat on it; evidently it had been well fed out on the plains.
Its flesh was tender and had a rich flavour, and Saekrae
could feel her strength returning with every beakful.

Once she had eaten and the chicks had had their fill,
she settled down to sleep with her wing spread over them
to protect them. A hard time was beginning for her, but
she was not afraid. She could find food now, and there was
plenty of it. Everything would be all right.

The chicks grew well. The black one was the strongest
of the three, and the most vigorous. Its voice was loud-
est and it had the best appetite. It was more than happy to
bully its siblings, too, and take the best share of the food
Saekrae brought. She did nothing to stop it. It was always
the way for one chick to be stronger than the others.

She did not give the chicks names, either. Chicks as
young as they were rarely all survived to a year old, and it
was bad luck to name them too soon.

Saekrae persisted in trying to find food within the valley for a time, but rarely found anything, and in the end
she took to going out onto the plains to hunt. It was a good
strategy. There was always prey to be found there: big, rich,
good-tasting prey. She quickly regained her health and
strength, and the chicks thrived. They grew and strengthened, their babyish fluff slowly giving way to proper fur
and feathers. The black chick's unusually coloured coat
showed no sign of changing; its coarsening fur remained
black, and the feathers on its front half were metallic silver. The pointed tufts of feathers that grew over its ears
proclaimed it to be male, and Saekrae had no doubt that he

would be a powerful adult some day. But it would be a long time before he or his siblings were completely independent. Still, Saekrae had no doubt that with this new source of food she could rear them to adulthood.

And then, quite suddenly, it wasn't there any more. She flew over the plains again, headed for the spot where the prey always gathered, and it wasn't there. When she ranged further she still found nothing. The landscape began to change: there were patches of trees here and there, and strange outcrops of rock poking up out of the soil. They were oddly shaped and did not look like any rocks she had seen before. Plants grew here that she did not recognise. But there was no food. Eventually, hungry and exhausted, she was forced to fly back. Griffins were not built for long-distance flying, and if she went on she would be too tired to get back to the valley.

Things did not improve on the next day, or the next. She made a few kills, but only sporadically, and the huge herds she had fed on before were gone. She flew far and wide over the plains and did find other herds there, but they were far away, too far for her to carry a kill back to her nest. In the end she was forced to eat what she caught on the spot and carry whatever she could back to her chicks.

It was not enough. Little by little, as the weeks went by and food remained scarce, she saw them beginning to starve. One of the brown chicks—the only female of the brood—weakened very quickly. She had already been the feeblest of the chicks, and now that there was not enough food to go around, the other two were quick to bully and steal food from her. Saekrae knew she would not survive long. But after a time, when Saekrae, too, was beginning to be in danger of starvation, the other of the brown chicks weakened as well. The black chick, still the strongest of them all, did rather better and even began to bully it as well. Saekrae had never seen a chick with so much will to live.

And then, one day, she returned to the nest to find both brown chicks dead.

2

The Emptied Nest

At first when she saw them, Saekrae thought they had died from hunger and exposure. She had been away from the nest for longer than she should have, bent on finding proper food after a week of virtually nothing, and had underestimated the amount of time it would take her to get back. On reaching the place where there had been a herd of animals once before, she found it deserted and flew on beyond it, half-mad with hunger and desperation. Still nothing, and when she had finally headed back to her chicks, a high wind had sprung up, forcing her to land and wait for it to die down. Night came and she slept, curled up in the meagre shelter she had found, and when morning came it was calm enough to fly. She turned for home with a feeling of cold apprehension, and when she finally reached the nest, at midday, she found only one chick waiting for her.

The two dead chicks were not huddled as if they had died in their sleep. One lay on its side, its head thrown back, and the other was on its front, its little limbs curled in under its belly.

The black chick appeared to be in relatively good health.

It had torn open the stomach of one of its dead siblings and was eating at the flesh, chirping enthusiastically to itself.

Saekrae looked down on it, glad that at least one of her young had survived.

It was not until she nudged at the other dead chick that she saw the marks of talons on its back and the deep wound in its throat, the feathers around it stiff with dried blood.

Saekrae looked at the black chick. It ate ravenously, muttering aloud to itself. "Food, food, food, food."

"Yes," Saekrae said softly. "Food."

The black chick lived off its dead siblings for several days. They were thin and did not have much meat on them, but their surviving brother ate everything—skin, organs, fur and feathers—leaving nothing but the bones. During that time Saekrae had gone on trying to hunt, even if she could only feed herself. The herds did not return, but some of her luck did: she began to find prey in the valley again. The wild goats had come back, and she could live off them—not as prosperously as she had lived off the herds on the plains, but it was enough. Still, she continued to explore the plains when she had the chance, and she made a kill there from time to time. It was a good way to supplement her diet.

And the black chick grew. The last of his babyish fluff disappeared, and the stubby wings on his back sprouted long, rigid primary feathers in a handsome mix of black, white and silver. He had more than doubled in size since his hatching and was becoming more and more energetic. Not content to stay in the nest any more, he began trying to climb out of it and explore the tree branches around it, and Saekrae couldn't be there to stop him all the time. He was starting to test his wings, flapping them experimentally to strengthen the muscles and trying little half-flying jumps from the side of the nest. Very soon he would be ready for true flight, and after that he could begin learning how to hunt.

One day, while the black chick was sleeping, Saekrae took the opportunity to leave him and go hunting again. It was a fine, clear day, and she flew up over the valley, feeling the sun on her wings. She liked summer. Hunting was better and the weather more pleasant.

She flew in a leisurely circle, looking for prey as always. The goat herd generally came to the stream to drink at this time of day.

They weren't there today. Instead she found them at the centre of the valley, in the marshy patch, browsing on the lichen that hung from the trees. Saekrae closed in, choosing her target. She selected a large one that was near the edge of the herd and swooped down on it at full speed before it saw her shadow. But she had acted too hastily. The animal moved as she began her dive, and then glanced up. It saw her and bolted.

Saekrae changed direction in midair, angling to head the goat off. It banked sharply to avoid her, and as she turned again, a tree suddenly reared up in front of her. She hit it hard, the branches shattering under the impact of her outstretched forelegs. Unable to recover herself, she ploughed headfirst into the ground. The collision knocked all the breath out of her. She lay in a tangled heap for a few moments and then struggled to her paws. One of her forelegs was sprained, and there was a fragment of wood stuck in her chest. She wrenched it out with her beak and limped away from the tree, shaking her head dazedly.

The goats had fled, and blood was trickling from one of her toes where a talon had been ripped clean away. She took off with a slow, clumsy beat of wings and regained the air. The tree that had robbed her of her prey seemed to mock her with its waving branches, and she screeched her rage.

And she was answered.

Saekrae's head jerked upward as the loud and unmistakeable cry of another griffin echoed over the mountains toward her.

Her fury hardened in her throat. She thrashed her wings,

straining for extra height, and opened her beak wide to scream her name. *"Saekrae!"*

A few moments later the reply came back. The intruder had heard her and was not backing down.

Saekrae forgot about the aborted hunting trip and forgot about her chick. She flew straight upward, making for the peak of the tall mountain that backed her nest. From there she would be able to see a long way and the other griffin would not be able to hide from her. She beat her wings with all her strength, flying as fast as she could, bent on reaching her goal before the enemy arrived.

But as she neared the peak looming overhead there was another screech, and the other griffin soared up over it and into the valley. Even as Saekrae pulled up short, wheeling around to pursue him, something happened that struck fear and confusion into her.

Two more griffins appeared, following on the tail of the first. Both of them were large adults.

Saekrae knew what this meant.

Perhaps she should have fled, but she did not. She would not abandon her young. She rushed at the first of the intruders, foretalons pointed straight at him.

The other griffin—a female a little smaller than her, with pale grey feathers and fur—turned to face her, but instead of flying at her she simply lowered her head and shot past. But then, as the two of them passed close to each other, pain spiked into Saekrae's body. She screeched and bucked wildly in the air, and then the two other griffins were on her. Talons struck her hard in the back, tearing great wounds down over her flanks, and a beak hit her in the neck, at the base of her skull. She turned in the air and latched her claws into the belly of one of her attackers, her beak aimed for her throat. The other griffin tore at her, trying to shake her off, but she would not let go, and the two of them fell from the sky, locked together and ripping at each other.

Mere inches from the treetops Saekrae suddenly let go and twisted free, opening her wings to catch an updraft. It carried her to where the two other griffins circled, and she screamed her defiance and came on toward them, blood streaming down her sides.

It was a futile gesture. Even as she swooped upward, she saw the two of them fold their wings and drop toward her, heads down. Perched on their shoulders, just in front of their wings, the humans that rode them held on tightly.

In midair, one of them unshipped the bow that hung from his shoulder and held on expertly with his knees as he nocked an arrow onto the string. He paused to sight down the shaft at the wild griffin rushing toward him, and then loosed the arrow.

His aim was true. The arrow hit Saekrae in the face, the barb going straight through her eye and vanishing, shaft and all.

Saekrae's neck jerked violently, and an instant later her wings buckled. She fell backward out of the sky and plunged earthward, headfirst, wings and legs flailing aimlessly. She was dead well before she hit the ground.

The three griffins came down to land at the edge of the trees where she had fallen, and the riders dismounted. The one whose griffin had grappled with Saekrae in the air quickly began to examine his partner's injuries. They were deep but not life threatening, and he took a jar of brown salve from inside his tunic and started to dress them. "We can treat you properly when we get home," he said, speaking the harsh language of griffins. "There, is that better?"

The griffin fluttered her wings. "I will be well," she said. "Are you hurt?"

The man patted her neck. "Fine. You fought magnificently. That one was strong."

"Only a common brown," the griffin said dismissively. "But her talons were sharp."

The man's two companions ambled over. "How is she?" one asked.

The man straightened up. "She'll be fine. Just a few flesh wounds. That was a brave thing you did there, Rannagon. I thought you were going to get yourself killed."

Rannagon couldn't help but look proud. "Thanks, Elrick. It took years to learn that, you know."

The third member of the party rolled her eyes. "I told you you couldn't teach him anything about archery. Shall we go and have a look at the beast now?"

"I'm ready when you are," said Elrick. He turned to his griffin. "Will you come with us, Keth?"

Keth clicked her beak. "I will come."

The little group entered the trees, with the humans going ahead, finding it easier to move in the confined space. The ground was boggy here, and they had to pick their way from rock to rock, sometimes using fallen logs or tussocks of grass to avoid sinking into the mud. The griffins followed with less care, keeping their wings tight to their sides to avoid snagging them on the undergrowth.

"Gods, what a dump," Rannagon muttered, extracting his leg from a muddy hole that had claimed it up to the knee.

They found Saekrae lying on her back with one shattered wing crumpled beneath her. Her beak was open toward the sky, and her remaining eye was glazed.

Rannagon walked around her, taking in her size. He whistled. "She's a fine specimen. Twenty-five years old at least, I'd guess. What a waste."

Elrick followed him, noting the arrows poking out of her. "You've ruined the hide."

"That wasn't me," said Rannagon. "Kaelyn did that. I was aiming for the wings."

"I wasn't going to take any risks," said Kaelyn, joining them. "The thing was huge, and I didn't know you were going to use one of your magic shots. Anyway, I'm damned if I'm going to do any skinning out here; it'd take forever. And you can forget carrying a stinking hide through that swamp."

Elrick shrugged. "I'm not blaming you. I prefer the safer approach with these things. Let's just take a few feathers and be gone."

Rannagon had found his arrow embedded in Saekrae.

It had gone in so deeply that only the tip of the fletching was visible among the blood and the vile muck of the ruined eye. He touched it with a fingertip. "By gods, I must have been in perfect form when I loosed that one. Are we just taking the feathers?"

Elrick was already wrenching out the long flight feathers from Saekrae's wing. "If you want the tail or the talons, be my guest. Kaelyn, could you give me a hand here?"

Kaelyn fingered a clump of feathers. "They're pretty rough. I'd say she hadn't been eating so well lately. See how bony the haunches are?"

"Well, those farmers weren't about to let her keep taking their stock," said Rannagon. "They must've moved them far enough to get them out of her range. I wonder why she didn't just move further into the mountains. Griffins aren't usually stupid enough to risk stealing."

Elrick ran a hand through his greying hair. "Unless she had something here to make her want to stay."

Kaelyn glanced at him. "You mean she was nesting?"

"Maybe. We should have a scout around, anyway, just to be on the safe side. Can't let her chicks starve to death."

He finished stripping the feathers from Saekrae's wings, with Kaelyn's help, while Rannagon took out a knife and cut the end off her tail for a trophy. Once they were done and the feathers had been rolled up in cloth the three of them returned to the open, remounted and flew back up to circling height.

Rannagon leant forward to talk to his griffin. "What d'you see, Shoa?"

Shoa scanned the ground for a time. "Nest," she said at length, and circled down toward it. The others had also spotted it and Elrick climbed down off Keth's back and into the nest. He poked through the nesting material while Rannagon and Kaelyn, lacking the room to dismount, looked on.

"Anything?" said Kaelyn.

Elrick straightened up. "Nothing. Just a few bones and some shell fragments."

"Stillborn?" said Rannagon.

"No, they're too well developed for that," said Elrick. "Have a look."

He tossed a small bleached skull to Rannagon, who caught it and turned it over in his fingers. The delicate bone at the base of the skull had been broken, and the dark coating was peeling away from the beak; the whole thing was about the size of his fist. "Hmm. I see what you mean. I'd say it lived for a few weeks at the very least." He dropped it back into the nest.

"There's another one here," said Elrick. "It's in better condition." He pocketed the other skull and a few pieces of shell before climbing into the saddle. "I'll take it back for Roland. He was nagging me to bring him something. All right, let's get going."

Kaelyn sighed. "Poor little things. They must have starved to death."

"Yes, it just isn't good territory here," said Rannagon. "Not with humans so close. Maybe one griffin could've survived, but not with a nest full of chicks. It's almost sad how animals try to breed even when it's just not practical, isn't it?"

"Life holds on where it can," Shoa interrupted. "Humans are the same."

"You're right, as always," said Rannagon, scratching her neck.

She closed her eyes and crooned, but then abruptly turned away and took to the air again, forcing Rannagon to grab hold of the harness on her neck to avoid falling to his death.

Elrick chuckled as Keth followed more sedately, and the two griffins flew up and out of the valley. Kaelyn's griffin paused to poke his beak into the nest. He nosed at the cold litter and the pathetically small bones of the dead chicks.

"What is it?" Kaelyn asked.

He raised his head again and snorted. "A smell. It does not matter." He flew off before she could ask any more questions, and as the two of them soared upward and away

from the nest, neither one saw the pair of silver eyes that
watched them balefully from a branch.

The black hatchling did not move for a long time after
the strangers had gone. Instinct had made him leave
the nest and hide on a branch beneath it, but once the danger had passed he didn't know what to do next. After sitting on the branch for some time, motionless but for the
twitching of his tail, he crawled out along it and climbed
back into the nest. His foreclaws were strong and knew
instinctively where to grip, and he heaved himself up over
the side and tumbled into the bottom of the nest. It was cold
and he could smell the sharp, alien scent of the intruders.
But he curled up amid the soft tufts of fur and feather that
Saekrae had used to line it, and waited.

Night came. After a while the moon rose. The black
chick slept, almost completely invisible in the gloom, his
head tucked under his wing.

He woke up shivering the next morning. Without his
siblings to snuggle up against, the nest seemed a lot bigger
and colder.

The black chick roused himself by flapping his wings,
and looked around for Saekrae. She wasn't there. He stumbled around the nest looking for her, but he could not see
her anywhere. She was neither in the sky overhead, nor on
the branch by the nest where she liked to perch.

"Food?" he called hopefully.

Only silence came back. He continued to call loudly,
expecting Saekrae to appear and bring him food, but she
did not come, and he called and called until hunger and
exhaustion forced him to stop. He slept for a while and
woke when the sun was well up.

"Food?"

Nothing. No Saekrae. No food. The chick found the
bones from the last meal she had brought and pecked listlessly at them. There were a few bits of dried meat still
clinging to them, and he occupied himself for a while with

trying to tear them free. These tiny morsels only increased his hunger, and he called for Saekrae again. This time he gave up more quickly and curled up beside the skull of his dead sister, whimpering softly.

The day wore on and his hunger kept him awake. At last, both bored and distressed, he got up and began to explore.

There was no food inside the nest, so perhaps there was some outside it. He had done this plenty of times when Saekrae was away. A griffin chick is built to climb. He dug his claws into the side of the nest and began to haul himself up and over. His hind legs knew what to do; the claws shot out and his toes spread wide to give him purchase as he thrust upward, foretalons gouging the shattered wood, his tail thrashing determinedly.

He reached the lip of the nest and perched there, peering at the branches near to him. One looked close enough; he stretched out a talon toward it and could nearly touch it. He sat still, judging the distance, and then jumped. His wings opened instinctively in midair and he landed on the branch, claws scrabbling to get a grip on it. He rested there, talons deep in the bark, and clicked his beak triumphantly. Perfect. From here he could go anywhere he liked.

He climbed out along the branch, wanting to see how far it went. It was a long one, and spread out into several smaller branches partway along. The chick stuck to the main branch but it grew steadily thinner the further along he went, until he could wrap his front claws all the way around it. Then it began to bend under his weight, and he had to open his wings for balance. Not liking this, he started to turn back. But he couldn't turn around. The branch was too narrow, and he didn't want to let go of it. He shuffled backward instead, hoping to get to a spot where he could turn, but it was a mistake.

Unable to see where he was going, he snagged a hind paw in a fork. He stopped and tried to extricate it, but it slipped out of its new gripping place and kicked out wildly, throwing him off balance. He struggled to save himself for a brief moment, wings flapping, but then he slipped, sliding almost gracefully sideways off the branch and into space. He hung by his front paws, hind legs dangling, and tried to pull himself back up with his beak, but then the branch broke and he fell.

He thudded into a branch below, but tumbled off before he could grab hold, and for a long heart-stopping instant he was falling, down and down, bouncing from branch to branch and shrieking. He had fallen about halfway down the tree before his flailing foretalons managed to latch onto a branch and halt his descent. He clung to the rough bark for a few moments, quivering with fright.

He was bruised and winded, and his beak hurt from where it had smacked into something. He chirped his distress, calling yet again for Saekrae, but still she did not come.

Fear gripped him. He wanted desperately to go back to the nest, but the branch above him was too high to reach. He managed to shuffle back along the branch to where it joined the trunk and tried to haul himself up by digging his talons into the bark, but it was soft and tore away as soon as he put his weight on it. He tried harder and managed to go a short distance, only to come sliding back down again. He was stuck.

He stayed on the branch for some time, unable or unwilling to go either up or down. He paced back and forth, searching for a way out, but none looked particularly inviting.

Eventually, though, a strange calm came over him. He crouched on the branch, at the thin end of it, and looked upward, toward the sky, showing blue through the forest canopy. There were birds up there, circling casually on the wind. They had wings and they could fly. Saekrae had wings and she flew.

The black chick spread his own wings. They were big and wide, with long feathers. A few wisps of babyish down still clung to the vanes, but the strong feathers of adulthood had finished growing.

He beat them experimentally. They nearly unbalanced him, but he held on tightly and tried again. He could feel them catching the air and lifting him very slightly with each blow. Feeling a little more confident, he flapped them as hard as he could, faster and faster, trying to make them lift him off the branch and into the air. They didn't, and the violent motion threatened to send him tumbling to his death.

He gave up—tired, hungry and frustrated—and ripped strips of bark off the branch, growling to himself.

He calmed down eventually and sat still, thinking. How does his mother do it? She didn't just beat her wings to fly. She jumped. He remembered that now. He'd seen her do it dozens of times, but never really thought about it.

He looked upward again. If he could fly, he could get back to the nest and then Saekrae would come and bring him food. He turned to look toward the end of the branch. Suddenly, it didn't look so daunting. Without another thought or a moment to prepare himself, he braced all four legs on his perch, spread his wings wide, and charged. He ran as fast as he could, claws scattering bits of bark, holding his wings and tail out rigidly as he had seen Saekrae do, and staring straight ahead. As the branch became thinner, it started to bend. He could feel it threatening to break, and for an instant he panicked. Then he jumped.

The branch acted as a springboard, and the black chick launched himself into space. His wings caught the air and held him up, and he went into a clumsy glide. When he realised he was flying, he panicked and began to beat his wings wildly, terrified that he was about to fall. He didn't, but not knowing how to steer with his tail, he lurched crazily around in the sky, unable to go in any particular direction or at any particular height. His wings, still too weak and uncoordinated for true flight, started to falter. He managed to stay up for a while, but his wings finally gave out and he careened toward the ground. It wasn't an outright fall—his wings stayed open and acted as a kind of crude parachute—but he didn't have the strength to pull up again. He screeched, flailing at the air, and then he hit the branches of the tree below him.

Leaves and twigs smacked into him from all sides, lashing at him like whips. He had a confused vision of leaves and sky and brown bark before something hit him hard in the head and lights exploded in front of his eyes.

He did not remember hitting the ground.

The sun was high overhead and it was hot and wet among the trees when the black chick woke up. He lifted his head dazedly, thinking he was still in the nest, and stilled when he realised he was not.

He was lying in a crumpled heap on a patch of muddy ground softened with moss. One foreleg was twisted beneath him, and his head hurt. He struggled to get up; the world seemed to be spinning around him and he cheeped pathetically. But despite the pain in his head and sides and the deep scratch in his foreleg, he was all right. His legs and wings were sound, and he hadn't broken any feathers.

He tottered off over the forest floor, caught up in a sudden need to explore this strange new world. The light was dim and greenish beneath the trees, and the air was full of the scent of leaf mould and damp earth. The trees and rocks were festooned with moss and lichen, and everywhere insects chirped. The black chick wandered here and there, discovering things he had never seen or imagined before, his fear forgotten.

He came across a stream, shallow and perfectly clear, flowing among heaps of moss-green boulders. He stopped to drink from it, throwing his head back to swallow, and dabbed at the water with his foreclaws, fascinated by the way it looked and the soft rushing sound it made. It tasted sweet and cool, and he drank deeply and felt much better for it.

But it did remind him of his hunger, and he moved on in the hopes of finding something he could eat. His instincts helped. He found a rotting log and tore into it with his beak and talons, turning up beetles and wood grubs, which he devoured. The ground beneath yielded earthworms and a small burrowing frog, and he eagerly snapped them up, feeling rather pleased with his own cleverness.

He spent a good portion of the afternoon foraging for more, and eventually returned to the stream to drink again. It left him feeling a lot stronger.

He sheltered under a bush that night, curling up to sleep with his head under his wing, more tired out from the stresses and excitement of the day than he had realised. He woke up several times during the night, disturbed by the cold and the unfamiliar sounds, but by the time the moon had risen he was sound asleep.

He woke up hungry again the next morning, stiff from his exertions on the previous day. This time he did not call for Saekrae.

He tried digging for worms again but was not so lucky this time, and he knew he needed something more substantial. He struck out determinedly, following the stream, intent on finding another way to feed himself.

After a while he picked up a scent that made his stomach gurgle in anticipation: the stench—faint but tantalising—of rotting meat.

The black chick followed it at once, head held high and tail twitching. He lost it several times but always found it again, and it finally led him to the base of a large tree. He sniffed around it and found a hole between two of its roots. The smell was coming from inside. Without a moment's thought he crawled straight in.

The hole led to a little cave just big enough to hold him, and inside there was food. The rotting corpses of birds, lizards and small mammals, all piled up and giving off a wonderful, pungent odour. The black chick plunged in, beak first, and ate. He tore off strips of decaying flesh and swallowed them whole, as fast as he could. He ate until his stomach hurt, until all he could do was lie on his side, eyes glazed, and pant. But he was practically delirious with triumph.

He fell asleep, utterly sated, and slept more peacefully and happily than he had ever done before. When he woke he ate again, and for days he stayed in his new home and gorged himself to his heart's content. Caught up in this new-found bounty, he had completely forgotten about his mother.

It was a solid week before the store of food in the burrow began to run out. The chick grew fat and sleek with all this good food so readily available, and was thoroughly disinclined to wander far from his new home. He hadn't given a thought to where the food had come from; it was just there, and he took all he wanted.

At around the time that the heap of carrion started to run out, the chick was woken one day by an unfamiliar scent. He opened his eyes and realised that the entrance to the burrow was blocked. The smell filled his nostrils, dry, musky and dangerous.

A moment later his eyes, adjusting to the gloom, showed him a brief vision of a huge, snarling muzzle, and then pain tore into his flank. He screeched and lashed out, and his talons hit something soft. The thing withdrew and he pulled himself further back into the burrow, still screeching loudly. There was blood on his flank, hot and clinging, but he had no time to feel sorry for himself. His assailant had withdrawn its head when he slashed at it, but it returned a moment later, teeth bared and snapping for him. He struck back, this time with his beak, and bit it on the nose.

The creature—a pouched, foxlike predator with a striped back—pulled its yellowy head out of its plundered food store and the savage thing it contained and sat back on its haunches, whining. It shook its head and snorted, trying to clear the blood out of its injured nostrils, and then abruptly turned and left. Fighting the thing that had stolen its food simply wasn't worth it.

The griffin chick stayed where he was for some time, panting in his distress. His flank had three deep slashes in it, each one bleeding and painful. He nosed at them with his beak, quivering, and huddled back in the burrow, frightened that the creature might come back.

It didn't, but he barely slept for the next couple of days. His wounds eventually stopped bleeding and scabbed over, and he rested and ate the last few carcasses slowly, to give himself plenty of time to heal. One of the wounds became infected, but he nipped it open and let the muck drain out, and the swelling went down.

The last of the food was gone in a few days, but the wounds on his flank were deep and began bleeding again if he moved. He lay still on his side and felt hunger gnawing at him. If he went into the open now he would be slow and vulnerable. If he stayed here, he would starve.

The black chick was still young and his mind was still simple, but he was more than intelligent enough to understand the situation and how dire it was. But, as he lay there among the damp earth and listened to the sighing of the trees far above, determination hardened in his chest. He would not give up. He would survive. Nothing and nobody would ever take his life away from him. He promised himself this.

The black chick did not forget his resolution. He waited patiently in the burrow for as long as he dared, eating wet earth and insects to sustain himself, and then left it and struck out into the world once more.

And he survived. Against all the odds, he survived. He ate worms; he ate carrion. He taught himself how to hunt small animals, which he did mostly at night, given an advantage by his dark coat. He raided birds' nests and dug mice out of their burrows. Once he even resorted to fishing, waiting patiently by a still pool to snag his prey. He took to climbing into trees to sleep, feeling safer up high, and from these perches he continued his attempts to fly. He only managed a brief unsteady glide at first, and his landings were painful, but he persisted and taught himself how to keep steady and turn by using his tail. After a while he was able to flit from tree to tree and could land neatly on a branch or a rock or on the ground. He began chasing birds on the wing and even started to unconsciously mimic the hunting methods of an adult griffin by dropping out of the sky to snatch up a fleeing animal.

He continued to grow steadily as the months and years went by, his body thickening and his wings becoming longer. From the size of a cat he grew to the size of a goat, then a horse, and he continued to grow until, at fifteen years old, he was the largest creature in the valley.

He was heavier in the shoulders and haunches than his mother had been, and the tufts of black feathers above his ears had become long and pointed to indicate his physical maturity and vitality to other griffins. But there were no other griffins in the valley, and his aggressive screeches every evening went unanswered. He would fly up to the mountains that marked the boundaries of his territory, hoping to see another griffin on the other side. He would look out over the huge plains to the north and scream a challenge at them, not liking their strangeness and the unfamiliar scents the wind carried from them. Nothing ever came to answer him, and he eventually lost interest.

As he grew older and larger, it became harder to find enough food, so he took to ranging further on his hunting trips. The neighbouring valleys were only a little better; he caught enough to avoid starvation, but was not tempted to move to a new territory. For now, the lure of his birthplace was strong enough to keep him coming back.

And that was how he lived from day to day, alone and unthinking, until he was nineteen years old and had reached his full size. He had chosen to live in a cave on the side of one of the three mountains. Less of a cave than an overhang, its semblance of a roof was only big enough to offer partial shelter for him, though the floor jutted out into a rocky ledge that was more than adequate for him to crouch on.

He lay on his belly, basking in the afternoon sun, one wing draped over the rock beside him. From here he could see the remains of the nest where he had hatched; time and weather had left large holes in it, and most of the sides had fallen away, leaving only a crude thatch of rotting plant matter lying abandoned on the cut-off treetops, which were steadily regrowing.

The black griffin, still nameless, yawned and flicked his tail. He was feeling restless just now, though he wasn't sure why. He had eaten well over the last few days, and it was comfortable enough here on the ledge. Perhaps it was just boredom.

He glanced idly at the back wall of his home. There were marks on the rock in shades of red, black and brown. They did not look natural, and he had often puzzled over what had made them. Perhaps they were a kind of moss or lichen, but sometimes when he looked at them in the right light he thought some of the shapes looked familiar. Like animals. And, in the midst of them all, there was one that reminded him of a creature he had never seen outside of a pool of still water during his adult life: a griffin. Its wings were spread wide and its beak was open. Something was coming out of its mouth, but he couldn't tell what it was. It was red, like blood, but it had a shape like a river.

The black griffin had never completely forgotten his chickhood and the other griffins that had once lived in the valley. He remembered Saekrae, his mother. He had never found her remains, but he knew she was dead. He remembered the strange creatures that had come when she disappeared, though the memory was hazy now. They had flown like griffins and made sounds as if they were, he remembered, but they had not been griffins. He wondered what they were and whether they would ever come back.

The thought made him irritable. If they did, he would fight them. This was his land now.

He raised his head and screeched to emphasise the point, a nameless cry that rang out over the valley. But even as it died away it seemed to strengthen suddenly and swing back toward him, higher and louder.

The black griffin stood up, bewildered. He screeched

again, and again the second screech replied. Not an echo. Another voice.

He took to the air, silver feathers shining in the sun, and climbed until he was level with the mountains, looking for the stranger. He screeched again and followed the sound of the reply. It was coming from the summit of the northern-most mountain, and as he flew toward it he could see the creature perched there among the bare rocks.

His heart tugged at his throat. It was another griffin, clear as day, sitting right on the border of his territory. She had seen him coming and was waiting calmly for him. He landed a short distance away and walked toward her.

She turned to watch him. The sun was behind her, making her feathers glow. She was not black like him, or brown, as Saekrae had been. She was . . . gold. Her fur was tawny yellow and her feathers were pale golden brown. Her eyes, though, were blue, as bright as the sky behind her.

The black griffin did not know what to do. He sat on his haunches, wings half-open to make himself look big-ger, and simply stared at her. She had not entered the val-ley. His territory was not violated. But she had suddenly appeared like this, seemingly out of nowhere, and he was completely unprepared for it.

She looked back at him and clicked her beak. "Greet-ings," she said. Her voice was strong and clear and did not sound hostile.

The black griffin knew how to speak. He had talked to himself for most of his life, but did not know many words. Only those he had learnt in the nest. He was silent for some time, trying to marshal his thoughts. "You . . . griff?" he managed.

She chirped at him, evidently amused. He noticed that there were strange bands of yellow and brown metal on her forelegs.

"Where . . . you come?" he persisted.

She looked northward. "I am from the Eyrie, at Eagle-holm."

He knew that word. "Nest?" he suggested.

She chirped again. "Did your mother never teach you how to speak?"

The black griffin just stared at her.

"I have never seen a black griffin before," said the yellow griffin. "Is this your home?"

The black griffin glanced back at the valley. "My land," he said.

The yellow griffin was looking at his forelegs. "Are you wild, then? I do not envy you."

"Wild?" the black griffin repeated.

"You have no human," said the yellow griffin.

"Human?"

The yellow griffin sighed and sat back on her haunches. "By the sky, are all wild griffins so slow?" She spoke again, very slowly, emphasising each word: "You are wild. You have no human. I do."

"What . . . human?" said the black griffin.

"A human is an animal. Small. Weak. But clever. You know, clever? Wise. Cunning. Intelligent."

The black griffin thought suddenly of the things that had taken Saekrae. "Human speak?" he ventured.

"Yes. They speak griffish. They made the Eyrie."

"Human fly?"

"No. Only when we carry them."

The black griffin was appalled. "Carry?"

"Yes. On our backs. Here." She lowered her head and showed him her shoulders. There was a patch of flattened and broken feathers there. "My human sits here."

The black griffin peered at it. "Where . . . you human?"

"He is at the Eyrie," said the yellow griffin. "I came here alone."

"Why you come?"

"I am ready for mating," she said matter-of-factly. "I have come to find a male griffin to father my eggs. I have found you. Do you have a mate?"

The black griffin did not understand. "Mate?"

She was looking at him very closely. "Am I the first griffin you have ever seen?"

The black griffin had a vague idea of what she meant. "This my land," he said. "Me here. No griffin. My mother . . . go." After that he fell silent, almost exhausted from the effort.

"So you have no mate?" the yellow griffin pressed. "No eggs? No chicks?"

"Chicks dead," said the black griffin, remembering his siblings.

"Then you will mate with me?" said the yellow griffin.

"What mate?" said the black griffin. He was desperate to understand, and angry with his own ignorance.

The yellow griffin seemed to sense it. "All creatures know," she said. "I will help you." She came toward him, moving slowly and with grace; he could see the muscles flowing beneath her tawny fur, and the perfect flexing of her limbs. He sat still and let her come to him, and she lifted her beak toward his, tail flicking, and purred deep in her chest.

He scented at her feathers, taking in the sweet, spicy aroma of them, and she chirped and nibbled delicately at the little tuft of feathers under his beak. He lifted his beak and moved his head closer to hers, wanting more. Encouraged, she moved alongside him, pressing her body against his, and began to groom his hindquarters.

He sensed that he should do the same and began to run his beak through the feathers just behind her wing, a hard-to-reach spot. She crooned and circled around him, nuzzling the nape of his neck. He pushed back, and the two of them groomed each other more and more vigorously, growling and crooning by turns.

The black griffin's heart was pounding. He did not understand what this thing was or what it meant, but something deep inside him did. He felt hot and confused, but strangely certain at the same time.

"What is this?" he asked.

The yellow griffin rubbed her head against his. "You like it?"

The black griffin closed his eyes. "Yes. Yes."

"Then do what feels right," she said. "Like learning to fly."

And he did. Part of him was confused, even frightened, but the much stronger part of him wasn't. He pushed and nuzzled at her, growling with a strange almost-aggression, and she turned, tail raised and twitching, beckoning to him. His instincts took over and he dug his talons into her shoulders. She kept still, wings shivering, and they mated, the quick, savage mating of griffins. The yellow griffin screeched and pulled away when the climax came, but she returned shortly thereafter, as the sun went down, and the black griffin was not afraid any more.

The two of them slept curled up together, neither one noticing the cold wind that blew over them.

When morning came both of them sensed that their time was ending. The black griffin wanted to go back to his home, and the yellow female was restless for her own territory. But they stayed together a little while longer.

"I do not envy you," the yellow griffin said. "You are part of a dying breed. One day there will be no more wild griffins left."

"I live," said the black griffin.

"But not for long. These mountains are barren. And places like this are shrinking. Humans always want more land. Soon there will be nowhere left for you or your kind."

The black griffin was silent for a time. "I want . . . see human," he said.

The yellow griffin stood up. "I can show you," she said. "Come with me."

She flew away over the mountain without another word, and after a moment's hesitation the black griffin followed.

The yellow griffin flew out over the plains beyond the valley, calmly and openly. The black griffin did not want to follow. Deep down, he was still afraid of the plains. They were unknown. Alien. But he did not want to look like a coward, so he followed her out over the plains, letting his nervousness fall away from him like an old feather.

The air over the plains was warmer than in the valley

and it smelt different. Drier and mustier, like grass. Now he could *see* grass—miles and miles of it, separated into squares and rectangles by thin brown lines. Animals roamed over it, much bigger than any he had ever seen, and here and there clusters of strangely shaped rock stood out from among the greenness.

He caught up with the yellow griffin, circling over one of these formations, and fell in beside her.

"A human place," she called. "Human nests. This land is their territory. Fly lower if you wish to see them."

The black griffin obeyed. He circled lower, as if he was singling out prey, and soon he could see the strange creatures that moved among the rocks. They were tiny, only about as long as his foreleg, and they stood on two legs like birds, but they didn't have wings. He saw them looking up at him. They did not run, but he heard their calls drifting up toward him, and his heart leapt when he realised that they were speaking to each other.

"Humans," the yellow griffin said again. "They are the key."

"Food?" the black griffin suggested.

"No—sometimes, maybe." She fixed him with a steady bright blue stare. "You were a good mate. So I will give you some advice. If you want to live in this world, find a human. Protect it. Keep it safe. Help it. If you do, you will always be safe. Our magic is not enough for us to survive now. Not alone."

As she spoke—using words he did not know, to express an idea he did not comprehend—the black griffin had a strange feeling in his throat. It wasn't quite pain, but it wasn't quite pleasure, either. It felt as if something was lodged in there, something hard and unyielding and burning hot. It made him want to scream.

3

Arren

Eluna's beak thumping into the wall of her stable woke Arren up.

He stirred and mumbled in protest, but the noise, loud and insistent, wouldn't let him go back to sleep.

"All right, all right, I'm awake. Just give me a moment."

The noise stopped, and he rolled out of his hammock and stretched. His back cracked nastily, and he rubbed it as he padded across the room to the table. There was a bowl of water there; he splashed his face to wake himself up. Eluna, growing impatient, bashed at the wall again. Arren hastily dropped his towel and went to the cage that hung from the ceiling at about head height, near the window. He opened the hatch in the side and reached in. The rats inside scattered in fright, but he trapped one and hauled it out by the tail. He held the wriggling creature upside down in his other hand and caught two more before he closed the cage.

Eluna banged on the wall again.

"I'm coming," Arren called.

He positioned himself next to the door leading into the

stable and lifted the latch as quietly as he could. It swung ajar, and he waited a moment and then burst through it.

"Catch!" he yelled, and threw one of the rats as hard as he could.

Eluna's head shot out and she caught the creature in midair, tossing her head back to swallow it. She turned and gave him a triumphant look.

Arren leant against the doorframe and laughed. "Perfect! I should've known you'd be faster than me."

She chirped at him. "Try again."

This time he threw the rat toward the opposite end of the room. She made a spectacular leap out of her nest of hay and caught it inches from the wall.

Once she'd eaten it, she looked expectantly at him, fluttering her wings. He held up the last rat, as if to throw it. She followed it intently with her eyes, poised to leap again. He jerked it suddenly and she jerked, too, beak opening, but he didn't let go of it.

Arren grinned and did it again, in a different direction. This time she actually did jump for it, and glared at him when she realised he'd tricked her.

"Throw it!"

Arren held out the wriggling, screeching rat. "See if you can catch *this*!" He dropped it.

The rat hit the floor and bolted. Eluna went after it, and chased the animal around the room as it darted here and there, desperately looking for somewhere to hide. It went to ground under her water trough, but she hooked it out with a talon and snapped it up before it could escape.

Eluna sat back on her haunches and gave Arren a slow murderous look. He stared back coolly. Eluna lowered her head and half-raised her wings. Then she charged. She ran straight at Arren, bowling him over, and pinned him down with her talons. He landed on his back, thumping his head into the doorframe in the process. As he lay there, helpless, Eluna brought her beak down toward him. "Perhaps you would taste better than a rat," the griffin said softly.

Arren closed his eyes and braced himself.

She nipped him on the nose and then abruptly pulled away and began to preen her wings. "No, I was wrong," she said. "You taste like old cheese."

Arren got up, dabbing at his nose. "I can't help it. I had mushroom bake last night."

Eluna rubbed her head against his chest. "Try some venison next time and I will reconsider."

Arren scratched her under the beak. "When I can afford it, sure."

She closed her eyes and crooned. "No. Rats are fine for me."

"Well, they're cheaper than mushrooms. Maybe I should be eating them, too."

She chirped her amusement. "They taste best raw and wriggling. Now go and get ready. We have work to do today."

"All right. I'll try to be quick."

Arren returned to his half of the house and opened the window to let some light in. It was only just past dawn, and the light was grey and watery. Arren rubbed the bruise on the back of his head and pulled on a tunic.

He adjusted the tunic and picked up a comb. His hair tended to tangle if he didn't give it plenty of combing, and he hated it to look messy.

Once he had groomed it to his satisfaction and had a quick shave and washed his face, he made himself a bowl of porridge and dried fruit and ate it out on the balcony. His home was right on the edge of the city, and the balcony had excellent views over the countryside. He liked a nice view, but this one just reminded him of how high up he was. Arren stayed close to the wall of his house and ate quickly, watching the bone wind-chimes swing gently in the breeze to avoid looking at the view.

Nearly all griffiners had some sort of official role in the running of the city. Arren had held several assistant positions before being promoted to his current role, that of Master of Trade. It was his job to manage the city's marketplace, and anyone who wanted to set up a stall had to apply to him for a licence. He also had to inspect the goods that arrived in the huge crates hauled up to the mountaintop every day, and there were various other administrative things to deal with. It wasn't the most exciting job, but it meant having some power at least.

Once he'd eaten, Arren went back inside. He filled the empty bowl with water and left it to soak, and then opened a large chest that stood next to the wall by the fireplace. He pulled out a light leather breastplate and strapped it on. Today he had something more exciting than paperwork to deal with.

He found his boots under the hammock where he'd left them and put them on, and then went to the fireplace and lifted his sword down from the wall. He pulled it partway out of its sheath to check on the blade. It was bright and sharp, and he'd kept it well oiled. He slid it back in and strapped the sheath to his back. All ready.

He turned toward the stable door, but Eluna was already there and ready for him. She clicked her beak. "Shall we go?"

Arren nodded.

"Then I will meet you in the city," said Eluna and withdrew her head. There was a door in the back of the stable that led to a platform which jutted out over the city's edge. She pushed it open and stood on the platform for a few moments, then took off, with a graceful flick of her wings, flying out over the farmlands below. Arren watched her through the window, marvelling yet again at how powerful she was in the air. He had flown on her back a few times, but there had rarely been much need for it and griffins weren't built to carry anything heavy a long distance; more than one griffiner had died after their griffin had faltered in midair and dropped them.

Arren shivered slightly at the idea and turned away. He left the house via the front door, locking it and pocketing the key, and walked out into the streets.

The city of Eagleholm was unimaginatively named, but aptly so. Centuries ago people had come across the massive, nearly cylindrical mountain jutting up out of the plains. Not wanting to disturb the gods that undoubtedly lived at the top, these early settlers built their homes around the lake at its base using the chunks of stone that littered the ground, but otherwise they left the mountain alone.

With the rise of the griffiners, the mountain had been selected as the perfect place for the new rulers of the land to build a fortress. Huge trees, selected for their special rot-resistant wood, had been felled hundreds of miles away and hauled to the mountain by teams of slaves. They had had the extremely difficult and dangerous task of carrying the cut and treated timber to the top of the mountain and there using it to build the original Eyrie. Other buildings had sprung up around it over time, and that was how the city of Eagleholm had begun. Later on, during more peaceful times, many more common people had come to live there, and the city slowly grew until huge platforms had to be built out over its sides to make more room. These were constantly being upgraded and expanded, and by now there were at least as many houses on the platforms as there were on the stone of the mountain. Food and other supplies had to be hauled up from the villages below using a massive winching device, and plenty of farmers would come up with their produce and sell it in the marketplace. Other, smaller winches had been built to keep up the supply, and Arren had a team of assistants to help him manage them all.

Of course, more than just food came up with them.

Arren stopped at a crossroads and settled down there to wait for Eluna. Eagleholm had plenty of immigrants and descendants of immigrants living in it, but even so Arren stood out. He was tall and slender, and still had a touch of teenage gangliness about him. He had thick, curly black hair, and the top of one ear was ragged from when Eluna had bitten it a little too hard as a chick. His face was pale and angular, a little stern and unsmiling of expression, and he had black eyes.

He bought an apple from a nearby stall and ate it while he waited. Eluna liked to circle around for a while first thing in the morning, to let her muscles limber up and to enjoy the wind in her feathers.

The streets of the market district were already busy, while the traders set up their stalls. Arren watched idly.

"Morning, sir!"

Arren looked around. "Oh! Hello, Gern. What happened to you?"

Gern fingered the painful-looking cut on his forehead. "I went to the Arena last night and there was a bit of a row. But you should see the other man, sir."

"Gern, I'm only two years older than you. And we're friends. You could just call me Arren."

"Yes, sir. Where's Eluna?"

Arren pointed skyward. "She'll be along in a moment."

"It's a shame you weren't at the Arena last night, sir. You missed a brilliant fight!"

"Why, did you break another nose?" Arren asked sarcastically.

"I mean in the pit, sir," said Gern a little reproachfully. "They've got three wild griffins in at the moment, and they all went in the pit at once. Once they'd killed the criminals they started fighting each other. One of 'em died, sir, it was amazing. And I won a bet."

Arren sighed. "I don't know why people go to those things. It's so pointless. And griffins deserve more respect."

"Not these ones, sir. They're man-eaters."

"So they give them more people to eat," said Arren. "Oh, the logic."

"They're just criminals, sir." Gern eyed him. "Why do you have your sword with you?"

"It's a secret."

Gern's face lit up. "Are you doing another raid today, sir?"

"Maybe." Arren gave up when he saw Gern's expression. "All right, yes. I'll tell you about it later if you keep it quiet. I'm going to go and meet up with Bran once Eluna gets here." He glanced skyward. There were plenty of griffins circling up there, but he thought he could spot Eluna's white wings among them. "Hold on a moment; I'll just call her."

Gern stood back, and Arren cupped his hands around his mouth. He lifted his head and let out a loud, harsh scream. It was an approximation of a griffin's call, and he repeated it several times, completely ignoring all the people staring at him. *"Arren! Arren!"*

After a few moments, Eluna's reply echoed back. *"Eluna!"*

Arren lowered his hands. "Watch out," he said, rather hoarsely.

Bystanders had already picked up on what was going on. They hurried to get out of the way as Eluna came down to land. She hit the wooden planks lightly and came to Arren's side, claws clicking. The people stayed well away from her, openly frightened and awestruck, as if they were looking at a queen. Eluna ignored them. She sat down on her haunches beside Arren, and he stroked her shoulder. "There you are."

Gern came back, moving very slowly and carefully. He kept his eyes on Eluna, who had turned sharply to watch him, and bowed low. She stared at him, sizing him up, and then looked haughtily away.

Gern relaxed. "I'll see you later, then, sir," he said to Arren.

Arren smiled. "I'll be down at the Red Rat tonight, probably. I'll keep an eye out for you."

"Yes, sir, I'll see you then, sir," said Gern. He bowed to Eluna again and left.

Eluna rustled her wings and got up. "Time to go and meet Bran," she said, and set out along the street with Arren by her side.

The two of them moved sedately, keeping pace with each other. People hurried to get out of their way, bowing and greeting Arren with murmured "sir"s. Arren acknowledged them with nods and a cheerful smile. Eluna barely looked at them. Once, when someone ventured too close to her, she lashed out at them, her beak snapping shut inches away from their leg. The unfortunate darted out of the way, to the laughter of the onlookers.

The sun was well up by the time they reached their destination. Another fine day.

The guard tower was right on the edge of the city, not too far from Arren's home. There weren't any direct routes to it from his place, though; the city planners had wanted to discourage too many people from travelling around the edge. The city's platform was extremely strong and was constantly being reinforced, but there was no sense in risking it collapsing. This meant most of the buildings on the platform were built to be lightweight, and those who lived on the very edge, like Arren, were forbidden to own more than two or three pieces of heavy furniture.

The guard towers, however, were too essential to Eagleholm's security to be built anywhere other than on the edge. There were at least twelve of them, spaced around the boundary of the city, and they were constantly manned by lookouts. Cymria was not a united country, not by any yardstick, and neighbouring powers were quite capable of attacking if they wanted to.

Arren's arrival was promptly spotted by the guards on the lookout post at the top of the tower, one of whom immediately went inside to alert the others. By the time Arren reached the tower a group of guards had already come out to meet him.

"Mornin', sir!" said one of them, bowing to Eluna. "Yeh got here early."

"Hello, Bran," said Arren. "Yes, Eluna woke me up. Everything ready?"

"Just about, sir," said Bran. He was a little older than Arren, and three times as heavy. He had broad shoulders and powerful muscles and a square jaw which was only slightly softened by a short beard. Like his colleagues, he wore a red leather breastplate decorated with a black eagle. A short sword hung at his side, and there was a steel helmet under his arm. "How're yeh doin', sir? Nervous?"

Arren laughed. "Me? When I've got Eluna to look after me?"

Bran glanced cautiously at the griffin. "Yeah, of course, I didn't mean—"

"Of course I'm nervous," said Arren. "But if I were that lot I'd be even more nervous. Shall we go?"

Bran put his helmet on. "I hate this thing," he muttered. "Yeah, ready as I'll ever be, sir." He looked at the other guards. "All right, you lot, let's get goin'. Just follow Arren."

Arren nodded to them and left. Eluna walked beside

him, and Bran followed on the other side, keeping well away from the griffin, though he wasn't as afraid of her as other people were. The rest of the guards followed in a neat rank behind them.

"How many d'you think there'll be?" said Arren.

"Oh, probably not too many, sir," said Bran. "There'd be more'n enough of us to take care of 'em even if we didn't have yeh with us. Anyway, they won't be interested in fightin'. They'll try to run off before they try anything like that. I mean, they'd have to be bloody stupid to try and fight a griffiner. An' afterwards"—he grinned, showing a couple of missing teeth—"it'll be rich pickings, I'll bet. Always is with this sort."

Arren nodded. "I hope so. I could do with a few luxuries. I haven't had an orange in months."

"Oooh, a few oranges would be nice," Bran said. "Last time I had one of them was at my sister's wedding."

"We'll just have to wait and see, I suppose," said Arren.

They knew where they were going. The place had already been scouted out, and Arren had seen it several times in the past. It was in the large residential area that backed onto the market district. Thousands of people lived there: traders, craftspeople, guardsmen, anyone and everyone the city needed. Since the house was on the solid part of the city rather than on the platform, it was built out of stone and was significantly older than most of the buildings on the edge, which had to be replaced or repaired much more frequently. This one looked as if it belonged to someone fairly wealthy. The windows were glass, and the doors and frame were freshly painted. There was even a little bit of a garden out the front.

"Huh," said Bran, seeing it. "Bloody bastard thinks he's a lord, does he? Must've had this racket goin' pretty long."

"Yes, and he'd be able to keep it going a lot longer if he hadn't decided to spend some of the profits on his house," said Arren. "Let's go in."

Some of the guards had already detached themselves from the group and moved around to the back of the house, to block any other doors. Arren and Bran made for the front door, not troubling to avoid trampling the flowerbeds. Eluna took up position next to the door, and Bran glanced at Arren. "Yeh goin' in first, sir?"

Arren drew his sword and tried the handle. It turned and he went in. There was no-one in the entrance hall, and he silently beckoned to Bran. The big guard joined him, moving surprisingly quietly, and several other guards came, too. "Spread out through the rooms," Bran told them in an undertone. They nodded and separated, drawing their weapons. Once they had gone, Eluna stepped into the entrance hall. Arren stroked her head. "Will you come with me?" he asked in griffish.

"I will be listening," she said simply and sat back on her haunches.

Arren inclined his head to her and strode through the entrance hall and into the main room of the house.

A man and a woman were sitting there at a table, eating breakfast, and looked up sharply when he entered.

Arren pointed at them. "All right, you two," he said, "don't make any sudden moves. You're under arrest."

The man didn't move, but the woman got up, so quickly she knocked her chair over. "What is this?" she demanded. "What's going on?"

Arren glanced at Bran, who took a set of manacles from his belt and strode forward, pointing his sword at the woman. "Hold out your hands," he said.

The woman tried to pull away, but Bran grabbed her and roughly snapped the manacles shut around her wrists. More guards hurried into the room, one leading a small girl by the hand. "We didn't find anyone else on this floor, sir," he said.

The man at the table still hadn't moved. "I demand to know what's going on!" he shouted.

"Are you Craddick Arnson?" said Arren.

"Yes, what's happening?"

"You're under arrest for smuggling and dealing in stolen goods," said Arren.

The guards were already coming forward to seize him. He made a brief attempt to fight them off, but was over-powered and manacled in moments.

"You can't do this!" he yelled. "I haven't done anything—"

"That's not my problem," said Arren. "That's up to the reeve to decide. But you can make it easier on yourself by telling us where the goods are and whether there's anyone else in the house."

"You're insane!" the woman said suddenly. "This is ridiculous. He hasn't done anything, we're just—"

Arren waved her into silence. "Perhaps you should have had a look in your cellar recently. Could you show me where the door to it is, please? I haven't got all day."

The woman sagged slightly. "Fine. If it'll convince you we haven't done anything, I'll do whatever you say."

The man, Craddick, tried to get to her. "Rose—"

"What?" she said sharply. "You haven't done anything, and the sooner we get this over with the better." She turned to Arren. "It's this way . . . sir."

"Let her go," said Arren to the guards. "Bring him, too. And make sure the child is out of the way."

"Yes, sir."

The woman led them into a back room, where there were a number of barrels and crates stacked. "There," she said, pointing at a large wooden box. "It's under that."

"Why is that blocking the cellar door?" said Arren.

"There was no room for it anywhere else," said the woman. "It's not very heavy."

Bran shoved the crate aside without much effort. There was a woven straw mat on the floor. When he lifted that away, it revealed a trapdoor. In spite of the fact that it had been covered over, it had very clearly seen a lot of use recently; the hinges were new and well oiled, and the door itself was in good condition.

"Right," said Arren. "Get those two out of here. I'm going in." He waited until the prisoners had been hustled out of the room and then hooked the toe of his boot into the iron ring on the trapdoor. He lifted it high enough to get his boot underneath and then kicked it open. One of the guards had handed him a lantern, and he took the covers off and stepped down into the gloom, sword in hand.

The cellar was about half as big as the house above it. Arren caught a brief glimpse of stacks of crates and sacks, and then something cannoned into him, knocking him over. He landed awkwardly on his back, dropping the lantern, and scrambled upright in time to see a man shove past Bran and bolt out of the room. Arren ran after him as fast as he could, with Bran close behind him. The guards in the dining room with Craddick and his wife ran to stop the fleeing smuggler, but Craddick suddenly rose up and shoved one of them aside, giving his friend time to get past. He ran for the front door. Arren tripped over the fallen guard and nearly fell, and then—

Eluna was there. The griffin burst through the doorway, screeching, rearing up on her hind legs. The smuggler screamed and turned to run, but Eluna's talons slammed into his back, knocking him down; before he could even struggle, her beak struck him in the back of the neck, killing him instantly.

There was silence for a moment. The guards hauled Craddick to his feet, thumping him in the stomach to subdue him. Rose was screaming.

"Get her out of here," Arren snapped. The guards obeyed, leading her out of the room as Eluna tore the dead man's arm from his shoulder and threw back her head—swallowing it whole.

Arren strode toward her. "Stop it!"

Eluna turned her head toward him, beak dripping blood, and hissed warningly. Arren put his hand on her shoulder. "Stop it!" he said again. The griffin ignored him and resumed her meal. Arren smacked her in the head. *"I said stop it!"*

Eluna lashed out. Her beak hit Arren in the arm, tearing an ugly wound. He hit her again. "Eluna, no!"

For a moment she stared at him, hissing and growling.

He stared back, ignoring the blood running down his arm and dripping off his fingertips. No-one dared make a move.

But then Eluna looked away and sullenly abandoned the half-eaten corpse. Arren went and crouched beside her, stroking her feathers and murmuring to her. She ignored him for a while, but then turned and nudged him under the chin. He scratched her under the beak. "All right. We're all right now."

Eluna crooned softly, and Arren stood up. "Could you give me some bandages, please, Bran?" he asked calmly.

Bran fumbled in his pocket and handed over a roll of white cloth. Arren bound it around his arm, and then turned to Craddick. For a moment he was still, watching him with a cold calculating expression, just like the one Eluna had worn a few moments before. Then he stepped forward and punched the man in the jaw. Craddick reeled backward, only to be righted by his guards.

"All right," Arren snarled, "how about you start telling us the truth, smuggler? How many other people are down there?"

The last of Craddick's defiance had gone. "There's no-one," he mumbled. "The others don't come here much. Just when—to bring in the new stuff, and when—"

"You will give us their names," said Arren. "And anything else you know about them. But first you're going to show me your cellar and everything that's in it." He picked up his sword from the floor. "And I'm going to be right behind you."

Craddick went with considerable reluctance. He led Arren down into the cellar, picking up the fallen lantern along the way.

He had been telling the truth; there were no other people in the cellar. But there were boxes. Hundreds of them. They were stacked everywhere. And among them were sacks and baskets, and barrels, enough goods to stock a fair chunk of the marketplace.

Once Arren and Bran had explored the cellar and made sure there were no people hiding there, they summoned the rest of the guards down. They came, carrying lanterns and torches, many uttering exclamations of astonishment when they saw the contents.

"Search the place," Bran told them. "We want to know what we're dealin' with here."

Craddick stood by resignedly as the boxes were levered open and sacks were slit. There were all kinds of things in the cellar. Grain, dried meat, fruit and vegetables, clothes, wine and beer, herbs, pots and pans, even a bag of illegal whiteleaf, hidden in a hole in the wall.

"Well," said Arren. "Seems you've got a pretty sweet business running down here. I'm surprised you managed to keep it going as long as you did. Would you care to tell me a little about your methods? I'm always happy to learn. Especially from the best."

Craddick spat. "Go back to the North, blackrobe."

Bran hit him. "Shut up!"

Arren laughed. "I'd rather be a Northerner than a criminal, Craddick. Last time I checked, it was smugglers who went to prison, not blackrobes." He nodded to the guards. "Take him away."

The guards started to haul Craddick away. But as they did, Arren thought he caught something odd. Some expression in his face. Something not quite right.

He froze.

"What is it, sir?" said Bran.

Arren held up a hand to silence him. He was listening intently. Then, suddenly, he turned and crossed the room in two long strides, to a spot in the corner, where there was a box draped in cloth. He pulled it away.

"Oh my gods."

It was not a box. It was a cage. Inside, a pair of yellow eyes peered out at him. There was a rustle of wings, and a beak poked through the bars. "Food?" it said.

Arren turned slowly to look at Craddick. "Craddick Arnson, you're in a lot of trouble."

4

Rannagon

The rest of the raid was fairly straightforward. Once Craddick and Rose had been escorted out and taken to the prison district, Arren helped the guards to empty out the cellar. They carried the goods into the dining room, shoving the furniture out of the way, but in the end there were so many they had to carry a lot of them into the front garden. A crowd of people gathered to watch, and Bran sensibly posted a pair of guards to stop them looting the contents of the crates. Eluna stayed with them, watching the onlookers menacingly. Two other guards bundled up the dead man in a pair of sacks and quietly removed him through the back door. His body would go to the prison district to be searched and then kept safely until his family came to collect him.

The cage containing the griffin chick was one of the last things to be carried out. Arren insisted on taking it personally. The chick looked well enough: undernourished and sensitive to the light, but uninjured. He fed it some dried meat from a sack and watched as it gulped it down. "How long have they been keeping you down there?" he muttered.

Bran noticed the blood soaking through the bandage on Arren's arm. "Yeh should see a healer about that, sir."

"I'll be fine," said Arren. He straightened up. "I'm going to have to take him back to the hatchery, and fast. But I'd better have a look at some of this stuff first."

"Don't worry about that, sir," said Bran. "I'll pick out a few things for yeh and send 'em along to your place, how about that?"

Arren paused, and smiled. "Thanks, Bran."

"I'll make sure there's some oranges," Bran added, grinning.

"Thanks. And if there's any decent leather there, I'll take some of that, too."

"Righto, sir." Bran glanced at the floor, where the dead man's blood was soaking into the wood. "There'll be an inquiry about this, sir."

"I know. Leave me to deal with that." Arren picked up the cage. "But I sincerely doubt anyone will care much about what happens to a griffin thief."

"Doubt it, sir."

Arren left via the front door, carrying the covered cage in his arms. Eluna was waiting for him and silently fell in beside him.

"Where are we going?" she asked.

"To the hatchery."

She fluttered her wings, apparently pleased. "I would like to see Keth again. Why are we going?"

Arren looked grim. "Those men stole a griffin chick. We have to take it back."

Eluna stopped dead. Arren watched her carefully. The griffin nosed at the cage. "I can smell—"

Arren lifted the cloth, revealing the chick. It peered out at Eluna, and she laid her beak against its beak. Then she looked up at Arren. He looked back stonily.

Eluna screamed. The noise was loud and furious, and she reared up and screamed again. *"Thieves! Scum!"*

Arren patted her to calm her down. "I know, Eluna, I know. It's all right, we got them."

"*I* got them," Eluna rasped. "I killed the one who attacked you."

"Yes." Arren pulled the cloth back over the cage and walked on, trying to hold it steady as the chick shifted inside. Neither of them looked at the bloody bandage on his arm.

The hatchery was on the edge, next to the market district. Arren and Eluna both knew the way there, but even if they hadn't, it would have been fairly easy to find. There were dozens of griffins flying over it.

The hatchery itself consisted of a collection of wooden buildings, which were some of the biggest in the city. They had to be. Around them there were pens full of animals—mostly goats—feeding on racks of hay. The griffins circled lazily overhead, enjoying the morning sun. Most of them were young, smaller than Eluna. The air was full of their screeching voices and the bleating of the goats.

Arren and Eluna went along the walkway between the pens. A man paused in the act of refilling one of the water troughs and waved. "Hello, Arren. Nice to see you here again. What's that you've got there?"

"It's a present for Roland," said Arren. "Is he up yet?"

"I think so, yeah," said the man. "He's in the hatchery, or he should be."

"Thanks." Arren made for one of the smaller buildings. It had large windows, which had been thrown open to let in the light, and the doors opened easily when he pushed on them. He backed through, carrying the cage, and found himself in a big open room. Most of it was lined with pens, and in them were the chicks. The place rang with their piping voices and the scuffling of talons on the wooden floor. When Arren came in, the noise redoubled. He smiled to himself. He loved the hatchery. It was where he and Eluna had first met, years ago.

There was a huge griffin there, crouched in the middle of the room. She was old—her feathers greying, her beak chipped and one eye whitened—but she stood up and came toward him at once, tail swishing. Arren stood still and let

Eluna go forward. She loped toward the old griffin, moving confidently, and clicked her beak. The old griffin sniffed at her and then relaxed. "Eluna." She looked past her. "And Arren. Good morning."

"Good morning, Keth. Are you well?"

"I am," said Keth. She sat back on her haunches. "I am pleased to see you, Arren Cardockson. And you, Eluna."

Arren bowed. "We're here to see Roland. Is he here?"

"I will call him," Keth said. She raised her head. *"Keth! Keth!"*

There was silence for a short while, and then a man emerged from a back room. He was short and stocky, and his once-yellow beard was greying. There was a griffin chick nestled in his arms. "Hello, what's this?" he said, speaking griffish. He stopped when he saw Arren. "Arren Cardockson!" he said, and beamed. "And Eluna, of course!"

Arren went to meet him. "Hello, Roland. How are you?"

"In excellent form, thank you, lad." Roland scratched the griffin chick under the beak and put it back into its pen. "Poor little thing has a touch of scale. Should be all right, though, with a little care. So, what brings you here?" He saw the bandage on Arren's arm. "Oh dear, what happened to you?"

"It's nothing," said Arren. "Roland—"

Roland looked at him, and then at Eluna. "Has she bitten you?"

"There was a bit of a scrap this morning," said Arren. "We raided a smugglers' den and one of them fought back."

"Ah, I see," said Roland, relaxing. "A nasty business. So, what have you brought me?"

Arren's jaw tightened. "We found *this* in with the rest of their loot." He pulled the cloth aside.

Roland froze. "Oh, dear gods." He took the cage from Arren and tore the cloth away, looking in anxiously at the chick. It looked up at him and fluttered its wings. "Food?" it said.

Roland looked up. "Where did you find this?"

"In their cellar," said Arren. "With the rest of the crates and things. I checked through it all; this was the only one."

"A red, by the looks of it," said Roland. "Seems to be in good health, thank Gryphus." He opened the cage and lifted the chick out, murmuring to it in griffish to soothe it. It gripped his arm with its small talons and then snuggled up against his chest. "Roland," it muttered.

"One of mine, definitely," said Roland, handing the cage back to Arren. He touched the chick, checking it for injuries. "A bit thin—few bruises—nothing serious. Thank you so much, Arren."

Arren put the cage on the floor. "What were they thinking?"

Roland looked grim. "A griffin chick can fetch a very high price, if you know who to sell it to. Or perhaps they hoped they could win its trust, join the griffiners."

"They must have been idiots," said Arren.

"Quite." Roland found an empty pen and put the chick into it. It sat down amid the fresh hay, still looking hopefully at him. He fed it some goat meat from a pouch tied to his belt.

"Well, we've caught them," said Arren. "We might not find out who stole it, though. Some of the smugglers weren't there, and one of the others was killed trying to escape. Hopefully one of the ones we caught will talk."

"They may as well," Roland growled. "They've got nothing left to lose. I don't condone the use of wild griffins as punishment, but anyone who does what they did deserves the worst Rannagon can offer them."

"One of them already had the worst Eluna can offer," said Arren. "She killed him."

Roland's expression changed. "Ah." He looked at Eluna. She looked back calmly.

"I'd better go. I have to report to Rannagon," said Arren. "He'll want to hear it from me first."

"Don't worry, lad," Roland said gently. "You won't be in trouble for this. The man was criminal scum of the first order. He deserved worse, and he would have had it, too."

Arren nodded. "He attacked me. Eluna saw it."

"Ah. Then the case is clear-cut. I doubt you'll have to do more than explain yourself to Rannagon. He'll believe you. He's fond of you, you know. In fact he told me—no, never mind."

"What?" said Arren.

Roland shook his head and smiled. "No, no, I'll leave you to find out on your own. It's not my place to say. Now, off you go."

Arren bowed to Keth before he left. "See you later, Roland."

"Right you are, lad. And say hello to Flell for me."

"I will." Arren left the hatchery.

Rannagon Raegonson was the Master of Law in Eagleholm, though he was generally referred to as "the reeve," an old word for a judge or sheriff. Where Arren ruled the marketplace, Rannagon was master of the prison district. It was his responsibility to judge and sentence criminals—hard work, and frequently unpleasant. Arren didn't envy him. In fact, he had been offered the chance to work as Rannagan's apprentice but had turned it down. Rannagon was old, and if he died before retiring, his apprentice would be given his position. That was something Arren didn't want.

The prison district was on the far side of the city, but Arren made instead for the very centre of the city. That was where the Eyrie stood. Riona, the Mistress of the Eyrie, lived there, along with many of the more senior griffiners. Arren had visited the Eyrie many times, mostly on official business; he had to deliver completed paperwork there and report anything important that happened in his sector.

The Eyrie was a tall stone building, but it wasn't quite a tower. It had a squat shape to it, and its walls were festooned with large balconies. Each one was attached to the room of a senior griffiner, and there were indeed griffins perched on many of the balconies, haughtily watching Arren's approach. Others were flying overhead.

There were two guards in front of the gate in the stone wall surrounding the Eyrie. These weren't ordinary guards, though, like Bran and his comrades. Each had a griffin beside him and wore a heavy, polished steel breastplate.

Arren nodded formally to them. "Good morning. Arren Cardockson, Master of Trade. I'm here to see Lord Rannagon."

"Is he expecting you?"

"He should be, yes."

The guards stood aside. "Go in, then," said one. "Lord Rannagon should be in his office."

"Thank you," said Arren.

The Eyrie was grandly decorated inside. Fans of dyed griffin feathers hung from the walls, along with fine wooden carvings and painted shields. Lanterns hung from the ceiling, made from glass tinted red and yellow. The corridors were wide, to allow easy passage for a griffin, and the doors, too, were big. Arren and Eluna passed through them without any trouble. They met a few other people along the way, nearly all griffiners accompanied by their griffins; most of them recognised Arren and greeted him pleasantly.

Rannagon's office was on the other side of the building, and the quickest route was to go through the huge chamber at the centre of the Eyrie. It dominated the structure, taking up two storeys. Arren was happy to pass through it. It was almost certainly the grandest room anywhere in the Eyrie, and definitely the grandest in the city: the grand council chamber, where Lady Riona and the elders she led met to discuss affairs of state and diplomacy, and make important decisions. Once these meetings had been open to the public, but not any more. Even junior griffiners, such as Arren, weren't allowed to attend unless it was for a purpose. Arren had often wished to see the chamber when the councillors were in it. As it was, he stopped to admire the lofty ceiling with its painted frieze of stars and flying griffins, and the brightly coloured banners that hung from the gallery. The Mistress' seat was right in the centre.

Today, there was someone in the chamber already.

Arren paused in the doorway. The stranger was sitting

on a couch set up next to the Mistress' carved chair, eating
a bunch of grapes and looking very much at his ease. There
was a griffin crouched beside him.

The stranger looked up. "Hello," he said. "Have you
come to bring me a message?"

Arren came toward him. Eluna went ahead of him to
size up the man's griffin, clicking her beak diplomatically.
The griffin was larger than her, though not enormously,
and had dark-brown feathers and fur. It was female, and
its neck was an extraordinary red colour, unlike anything
Arren had ever seen before. She stood up and sniffed cautiously at Eluna, who bowed her head and chirped.

Arren, meanwhile, was looking at the man. He was
tall and thin, like himself, and his skin was a rich brown
colour. His hair was black and rough, and he had a neat
moustache, sprinkled with grey. He eyed Arren through a
pair of intelligent dark eyes. "Good morning." He had an
accent unlike anything Arren had ever heard before, quick
and slightly nasal.

Arren bowed. "Good morning, my lord. I didn't expect
anyone to be in here. I'm Arren Cardockson."

The man looked at him with renewed interest. "So, you
are the Northerner I have heard about." He stood up. "My
name is Vander Xantho, and this is Ymazu. I am pleased
to meet you."

"I don't think I've seen you before, Lord Vander," said
Arren. "May I ask where you're from?"

"You may. I have come from Amoran to speak with the
Mistress of the Eyrie."

"You're a diplomat?"

"Yes."

Arren thought quickly. "Amoran, that's in the East,
right?"

Vander nodded. "So it is." He was looking at Arren, taking in his sharp features and black eyes. "Forgive me. I
have never seen a Northerner who was not—"

"In chains?" Arren interrupted, more sharply than he
had intended.

"I am sorry," said Vander. "I did not intend to offend you."

"It's all right, my lord," said Arren. "My father was set free when he was a boy."

"I see." Vander rubbed his neck. "It was a strange thing to come here and find no slaves."

"There were plenty here before I was born," said Arren. "Lady Riona sold them all after the famine."

Vander nodded. "Yes, I had heard that story." He smiled slightly. "I am glad to have met you, Arren Cardockson. I have heard a great deal about you."

"You have?" said Arren, surprised.

"Oh yes. The only Northern griffiner in the country, or so they say. And something of a rising star, it would seem. Master of Trade at—how old are you, may I ask?"

"I'll be twenty in a few months, my lord."

"Nineteen years old," said Vander, shaking his head. "Astonishing. I was nineteen when I first met Ymazu here. Tell me, how did you come to be a griffiner?"

"My parents were visiting the hatchery," Arren explained, "to talk with Roland—that's the man who runs it. They took me with them; I was only three. I wandered off while they were busy."

"A small child alone in a building full of griffins," said Vander. "Not a desirable thing."

"No. My parents say they were terrified; they thought they'd find me dead. But they found me in the nursery with the hatchlings. I'd opened up most of the pens and let all the chicks out. And one of them was Eluna. Some of the chicks were trying to bite me—actually, I've still got a scar on my little finger. But Eluna was fighting them off."

"*Xanathus!*" Vander exclaimed. "She attached herself to you when you were a *child*?"

"Yes, my lord. In the end they had to separate us by force."

"They didn't let her go with you?"

"Of course not. But Lord Roland let me keep on visiting her in secret. The Eyrie didn't find out about us until we were both ten, and by then it was too late to separate us."

Vander blinked. "So, after that you were allowed to keep her?"

Arren grinned. "The elders didn't have much choice but to let me become a griffiner. Eluna wouldn't leave me." He put his hand on her head. "And we've been together ever since."

"An astonishing story," said Vander in griffish. "And a remarkable griffin," he added, to Eluna. "I have never seen a white griffin before, nor one as beautiful."

Eluna looked up at him and chirped, pleased. "And I have never seen a griffin like you, Ymazu," she said to the brown griffin. "The red feathers on your neck are not like any I have ever seen."

Ymazu raised her head and half-spread her wings, revealing that their undersides were as red as her neck, edged with dark green. Eluna shivered her own wings, evidently much impressed.

"Tell me," said Ymazu, speaking for the first time, "what is your power, snow griffin?"

Eluna bowed her head. "I do not know."

Ymazu seemed to understand. "There will be time to discover it," she said.

"Thank you," said Eluna.

"And her human impresses me just as much," Vander said graciously. "I have no doubt that you will go on to great things, Arren Cardockson."

"Thank you, my lord."

Vander looked up. "And now I'm afraid our conversation must end."

Arren turned, and his heart thudded hard when he saw Riona herself come into the chamber.

The old woman walked stiffly, leaning on a staff. Beside her was her griffin, Shree, moving with a steady, rolling grace, his grey shoulders humped.

Arren caught his breath and knelt, while beside him Eluna folded her forelegs and touched her beak to the ground. "My lady," he whispered.

Riona looked down at him. "Hello, Arren. Please, get up."

Arren stood. "I'm sorry, my lady, I didn't mean to intrude. I was—"

"He was talking to me, my lady," Vander interrupted, bowing to her.

Riona wore a fine white gown, and her long hair was shot through with silver. Her face was wrinkled and weather-beaten. She was old—nearly seventy—but she was not weak or feeble. An Eyrie Master or Mistress had to be strong. She smiled at Vander. "Greetings, Lord Vander. I am sorry to have kept you waiting. And you, Arren, please leave us. We have matters to discuss."

"Yes, my lady," said Arren. "I hope your talk goes well," he added politely and left.

He passed out of the chamber via a door in the opposite wall and closed it behind him. Once in the corridor out-side, he leant against the wall and slumped. "Phew! Good gods, that gave me a fright."

Eluna was looking pleased. "I liked that griffin. Her human, too."

"They were interesting, weren't they?" said Arren. "I've never met an Easterner before. I wonder what he came to talk to Riona about."

Someone coughed. Arren turned, surprised, and saw a man standing a short distance away. There was a griffin by his side.

"Lord Rannagon!" he exclaimed. "I'm sorry, I didn't see you there."

Rannagon smiled. "Not a problem. I'm glad to see you here, Arren. I was afraid something might have happened to you."

"I'm sorry, my lord, I got held up."

"Well, it doesn't matter," said Rannagon.

Arren bowed to Rannagon's griffin. "I am pleased to see you, Shoa."

Shoa clicked her beak. "And I you, Arren Cardockson." She raised her head, neck feathers shivering, and looked down on Eluna. "And you, Eluna."

Eluna bowed her head, saying nothing.

Rannagon yawned. "Aaah . . . excuse me. I had a rather late night. Shall we go now?"

"Yes, my lord."

They walked off along the corridor and up a flight of stairs into a different part of the Eyrie. This was Rannagon's domain, where he lived with his wife, Kaelyn, and where he did much of his work. The old man opened the door to his office and showed Arren in. "Sorry about the mess. Please, sit down. Can I get you something?"

Arren sat on a chair in front of the desk, which was piled high with papers. There was a fireplace in one wall, and a steaming kettle hung over the fire. "I—" He was about to politely decline, but the sweet smell of stewing herbs changed his mind.

"Yes, thank you."

Shoa took up position next to Rannagon's chair, while he crossed to the fireplace and filled two mugs from the kettle. He gave one to Arren and sat down on the other side of the desk. "Now then, I have had a report from Captain Bran; he tells me the raid went fairly smoothly. But he added that it did not go as smoothly as we would have liked." He looked pointedly at Eluna.

Eluna understood the human tongue perfectly well, even if her vocal cords didn't allow her to speak it. "The man was a smuggler and a chick-thief," she said. "He had attacked Arren and was trying to escape. So I killed him."

"And ate him?" Rannagon said sharply.

Eluna bowed her head. "I was hungry, my blood was up—"

Shoa leant forward over the desk and bit her on the forehead, hard enough to draw blood. "You must learn to control yourself," she said. "You are not a wild griffin, Eluna."

Eluna didn't dare look her in the eye. "I am sorry, Shoa. I will try to be more careful in future."

"And you, Arren?" said Rannagon, looking keenly at him. "What was your reaction to this?"

"He stopped me," said Eluna. "He stood up to me until I calmed down."

Rannagon looked at the bandage. "And?"

"The smuggler injured me," Arren lied. "That was why Eluna killed him."

"I see. Well, that is understandable. So, these smugglers had a griffin chick in their hideout, did they?"

"Yes, my lord," said Arren, hiding his relief.

"I take it you returned it to the hatchery?"

"Yes, my lord. Roland says it's in good health."

"Excellent. It sounds as if you have foiled another criminal operation, Arren. Well done. I will see to it that you receive a commendation for it."

"Thank you, my lord."

"As for the dead smuggler"—Rannagon sighed and shuffled some papers on his desk—"I see no reason for a formal hearing. Your explanations mesh with what Captain Bran told me, and I am disinclined to make much fuss over the death of a criminal."

Relief flooded through Arren's chest. He drank some of the tea. It was sweet and strong, just how he liked it. "Thank you."

"However, the family will have to be compensated," Rannagon added. "You will, of course, be expected to pay."

Arren's heart sank. "How much?"

"Two hundred oblong is the standard amount," said Rannagon.

Arren's heart sank even further. "I—I can't afford that much, my lord."

"Oh. I see. Well . . ." Rannagon looked thoughtful. "As it happens, I do have a way that could help you earn some extra money. But you must keep it to yourself. If anyone asks, I will deny any knowledge of it."

"I understand. What is it, my lord?"

Rannagon rummaged through the papers and came up with a rather grubby-looking scroll. "Ah, here it is. We have received word from one of the villages down in the South. A place called Rivermeet. It seems a wild griffin has been preying on livestock. And now, it seems, people as well."

Arren grimaced. "What does this have to do with me, my lord?"

"There is a bounty on this griffin," said Rannagon. "A substantial one. If you kill it, you will be rewarded with a hundred and fifty oblong. But there is more."

"Yes, my lord?"

"The managers of the fighting pit at the Arena have put in a request for more wild griffins. The bigger and more ferocious the better. If you can capture this griffin alive and without any serious injuries, the bounty will be even higher."

"How much, my lord?"

"Four hundred oblong, I believe. More than enough to pay your debt."

Arren thought about it. "I've never done anything like this before."

"It's straightforward enough," said Rannagon. "I've done it myself more than once."

"Is there a deadline for paying my debt?"

"I'm afraid so. It must be paid within a month at most. Longer than that, and the amount will go up."

Arren cursed under his breath. "How far away is this place?"

"Two or three days' flight. I've been there a few times."

"But how do I catch a wild griffin?" said Arren. "Should I take someone with me?"

"You could, but they would take part of the bounty. Look," Rannagon said kindly, "I promise, it's easy. Here." He reached into his desk drawer and handed Arren a small stone bottle. "This is a special poison. If you soak an arrowhead in it and then shoot it at the wild griffin, it will be knocked unconscious in moments and won't wake up for half a day. How good a shot are you?"

"Quite good, my lord."

"Good, good. I suggest you take it. A bit of excitement for a change, eh? I'll get someone to look after the market-place while you're gone."

"I'm really not sure—"

"Come on, now," said Rannagon, in a jolly kind of way. "Wouldn't you rather be doing something adventurous instead of dealing with paperwork and chasing criminals? I remember when I was younger I was up and about all the time. See." He waved a hand at the wall over the fireplace, where a row of dried griffin tails were hanging up. "Six man-eating griffins. Shoa and I fought them face to face. The local people treated us like heroes."

Arren felt slightly sick. "Can't they just be bargained with?"

Rannagon chuckled. "Bargained with? That's a laugh. They're savage, Arren. Yes, you can speak to them, but they won't listen. They look upon humans as just another kind of food. Trust me; I've seen people try and parley with wild griffins. More than one of them died for their trouble."

"But my lord—"

"We will do it," said Eluna.

Arren stopped, looking at her.

Rannagon looked pleased. "Do you think you can persuade your human to change his mind, Eluna?"

"We will go," Eluna said firmly. "Both of us. We will capture the wild griffin and avenge his victims."

"Excellent," said Rannagon. "I knew I could rely on you." He handed the bottle to Arren, who took it reluctantly. "Here, take this as well," he added, offering him the scroll. "It includes more details about the griffin and a map to help you get to Rivermeet. Can I rely on you, Arren?"

Arren knew he was beaten. "I'll do my best, sir. When should I leave?"

"As soon as possible. Tomorrow."

"Tomorrow? But—"

"The sooner you leave, the smaller the risk you run of failing to make the deadline," said Rannagon. "I will look after things while you're gone."

"Yes, my lord. Thank you." Arren stood up.

"You'll be fine. Oh, yes, take this with you." Rannagon stood to put something into Arren's hand. "For good luck."

It was a small beaked skull. Arren realised with an

unpleasant shock that it was from a griffin chick. The beak and the rims of the eye sockets had been coated with silver, and the entire thing painted with bright patterns and then coated with lacquer. "Thank you, my lord."

"I got it on one of my jaunts," said Rannagon. "With old Elrick. You remember him, don't you? Roland's father. Then I was given this position and couldn't afford to go on wild trips all around the country. Damn if I don't miss it. I'd give anything to come with you." He paused. "Just promise me you won't tell anyone in the Eyrie about it. I don't want people knowing I've been handing out assignments like this. I'll inform Riona and the other officials you're gone, tell them you're on some other assignment. Understood?"

Arren stuffed the grisly trophy in his pocket, along with the scroll and the bottle. "I understand. Thank you for your help, my lord."

"Not a problem at all." Rannagon sighed. "We'll miss you while you're gone. Flell certainly will. And Riona, as well."

"Riona?" said Arren, surprised.

"Oh yes. She's very fond of you, Arren. In fact"— Rannagon smiled—"keep this to yourself, but I spoke to her about you a few days ago. She told me she'd prefer you to move out of that little house of yours out in the city."

"She did?" said Arren, shocked. "Why? What did I do?"

"Oh, nothing. But as an Eyrie official, you should be living in the Eyrie. The Master of Trade is supposed to have a place on the council, after all."

"I know," said Arren, rather sourly.

"Yes, and Riona thinks it's time we acknowledged it. You've proven you're more than capable, and we could do with your help up here."

Arren gaped at him. "Do you really mean that?"

Rannagon nodded. "That's what Riona said, and I agree."

"No, that's not—"

Rannagon grinned at him. "We still have to put it to the council, of course—and I'm sure they'll be more inclined to support you if you come home a hero from Rivermeet. Now, you go and get ready. And don't tell anyone else about what I said, understood?"

Arren managed a nod. "Yes, my lord."

Rannagon returned to his desk and sat down. "Good-bye, then. And good luck."

When Arren and Eluna had gone, Rannagon slumped in his chair and put a hand over his face. "Well, that's that," he mumbled.

Shoa nibbled his hair. "The dark one must be stopped," she said. "We both know this. Trust in me, Rannagon. It will be better for us when it is done."

"I suppose." Rannagon kept his voice neutral; Shoa was annoyed enough with him already.

"And now," the yellow griffin went on, "there is the matter of the bastard."

Rannagon sat up sharply. "Leave him alone, Shoa. He's done nothing wrong."

"The Master of Law cannot be father to a bastard," Shoa said harshly.

"But I am," said Rannagon. "He's my son, Shoa. I won't hurt him. Not for anything."

Shoa turned away, her tail swishing in irritation. "We shall see."

5

At the Sign of the Red Rat

When Arren got back to his home, he found a large crate waiting for him just outside the front door. He lugged it inside before he opened it, and found it full of different goods: cloth, cheeses, sausage, vegetables and—he smiled to himself—a string bag full of oranges. There were also five bottles of mead and two of wine, and a large roll of high-quality thick leather. It was technically forbidden for marketplace officials such as him to do this, but no-one really cared if he and the guards took their pick of whatever items they seized before they handed them over to the authorities. Even Rannagon knew about it but was prepared to turn a blind eye. Stealing from a thief was hardly a heinous crime.

Arren spent some time packing away the contents of the box, while Eluna went to her stable to rest. He found several bottles of salve in among the other things, almost certainly placed there deliberately by Bran. He was pleased about that; his arm was aching savagely now.

He fetched a roll of bandages from a cupboard, sat down at the table and took the lid off the salve. Taking the bandage off his arm was extremely painful, but he gritted his teeth and tossed the bloody cloth into the fireplace. The wound started to bleed again, but he hastily slapped some salve onto it and wrapped it up tightly. The salve did its job quickly, and the pain started to fade even while he was doing up the bandage. He sighed gratefully and sat back in the chair to rest.

After a few moments, he sensed a presence. He looked around and saw Eluna sitting in the door to her stable, watching him.

Arren sat up straight. "Hello," he said carefully.

Eluna said nothing. She looked away and scratched the floor with her talons. Then she came toward him, moving slowly, and crouched by the chair, head bowed.

Arren touched her head. "What's wrong, Eluna?"

She looked up at last. "I . . . am sorry for what I did."

A true apology from a griffin was a very rare thing. Arren got off his chair and knelt by her, resting his head against her shoulder. He could feel her heart beating through her skin, strong and steady, like a drum. "It's all right, Eluna. I understand."

Eluna sighed. "I did not mean to do it. I feel like a fool. To attack you in front of other people—you are my human, and I should not have humiliated you like that. I made myself look like a stupid hatchling."

"Is that why you said yes to Rannagon?"

"Yes. To earn my honour back. And yours."

Arren let go of her. "Do you really think we can do this, Eluna?"

"Yes. You are brave and strong. You can fight. So can I. This wild griffin cannot hurt us if we act together."

Arren remembered the bottle in his pocket. "I suppose I shouldn't be scared. Rannagon has faith in us. And I have faith in you."

Eluna blinked. "You do?"

"Yes, Eluna. I always have done. I let you—" He smiled. "When we were chicks, you bit the top off my ear. But I still trusted you."

She chirped. "And if I bit the top off your other ear, would you trust me even more?"

Arren chuckled. "Maybe. But you shouldn't do it now. Wait a while. If you ever lose my trust, you'll know how to win it back." His confidence grew. "We can do this, Eluna," he added softly. "I know we can. You and me, working together. And we should see something of the world, shouldn't we? Before we're too old and tired for it. Before we—before we become councillors."

"It was just talk," said Eluna. "It may not happen."

"No. Rannagon wouldn't lie to me, and Riona wouldn't lie to *him*. And neither of them would have said anything if it was just talk. Good gods, can you imagine that? Us on the council? A blackrobe advising the Mistress of the Eyrie?"

"Not a blackrobe, Arren," said Eluna. "A griffiner."

Once Arren had finished putting away the last of the goods, changed into a clean tunic and locked his sword up in the chest, he started packing for his journey. He'd never travelled much before, and especially not on griffinback, but he knew well enough that it would mean having to travel as lightly as possible. Eluna would only just be able to carry him and a few light objects.

That meant leaving his sword behind. He unpacked his bow and strung it, testing the string. It was strong and well waxed, and the bow itself was still supple. Arren nocked an arrow onto the string and aimed it experimentally at the wall, drawing back as if to loose it. But he relaxed the string and put the arrow back into the quiver with the others. The bow still had plenty of spring in it. It hadn't seen much use; the only things he'd ever aimed it at were an archery butt and, once, a rabbit. Still, he knew he was a good shot. And a griffin was a big target. He wrapped the bow up in oiled leather and strapped it to the quiver. That would go on his back. There was a packet of spare bowstrings in the chest, and he put that on the table next to the bottle of poison and the skull talisman.

He stopped to eat an orange and think. What else should he take? A clean tunic would probably be a good idea, and some salve and bandages. And a cloak to wear in the air. Food was out of the question, apart from a few snacks to go in his pocket. He'd have to take some money and buy food along the way. People were generally happy to help a griffiner; he'd probably be given it for free. Best not to take too many chances, though. Arren knelt and lifted a loose board out of the floor beneath the table. There was a box underneath, and he filled a small leather pouch with oblong-shaped pieces of metal from it and tied the pouch to his belt. Fifty oblong should be enough to get by on. If the worst came to the worst, he could always ask Eluna to hunt. She wouldn't like it, but it would be better than starving.

Once he'd packed everything into a small shoulder bag and fetched Eluna's harness from the stable, he stacked them neatly in a corner and sat down to have some lunch. Eluna had spent the time dozing by his hammock, but she woke up at the smell of food and gave him an expectant look. Arren got up and took a large wrapped parcel from a cupboard by the window, saying, "All right, I haven't forgotten about you—hope it's still fresh."

He pulled off the cloth wrapping. Inside was a gory lump of meat: a raw goat's leg with half the haunch still attached. Eluna stood up when she saw it, tail swishing. "If you throw it—"

Arren smiled and placed it down in front of her. "No, no. It's a bit heavy for that. Just try not to make too much of a mess."

Eluna tore into it, digging her talons into the floor.

Arren tried to ignore the sound of splintering wood. "How is it?"

"Good," Eluna mumbled.

Arren returned to the table and his own lunch. "It's got to be better than this sausage. I can't believe someone went to the trouble of smuggling it." He ate it anyway. It wouldn't keep while he was gone.

Once they'd finished eating, Arren stood up and brushed

the crumbs off his tunic. "All right. We'd better go and see Flell, and my parents, and let them know what's going on. Are you ready?"

Eluna yawned and stretched. "I will come."

Arren picked up the roll of leather. "Mum and Dad will be glad to get this. There's twelve pairs of boots in it, if I'm any judge. Well, let's go."

He stuffed the scroll in his pocket before he left. They'd probably want to see it.

They visited Flell first. Never politically minded, and lacking an official position, she lived close to the Eyrie in a fine stone house that had once belonged to her mother. Its large windows must have been a help to her because she saw Arren coming and came out to meet him, her griffin following at her heels.

"Arren!"

Arren embraced her. "Hello, Flell!"

They kissed, while Eluna nipped playfully at the other griffin. Flell's griffin was only a chick, as tall as Arren's knee. It rubbed itself against Eluna's foreleg, cheeping.

Arren stooped. "Hello, Thrain. Remember me?"

Thrain fluttered her wings and lifted her beak toward his hand. She sniffed it for a moment, and then bit him lightly on the finger. Arren flinched, but didn't move, and the chick let him scratch her behind the ears. "Food!" she said.

Arren fished in his pocket and found a piece of dried beef. "Well, how are you?" he said to Flell, while Thrain ate it. "I meant to come and see you earlier, but something came up."

Flell smiled and kissed him on the cheek. "I missed you. Come on, come in." She ushered him inside.

They went to the main room and sat down together by the fireplace. Flell made tea for them, and they drank it together in companionable silence.

"What happened to your arm?" Flell asked.

Arren glanced at it. "We raided a smugglers' den this morning."

"Oh!" said Flell. "How did it go?"

"Quite well. We caught two of them, and . . . sort of caught a third. Eluna killed him."

"Oh no," said Flell. "Have you talked to my father about it yet?"

Arren nodded. "It's all right; Eluna was only defending me. But there's a problem . . ."

Flell listened while he explained. She was a little younger than him, delicately built, with a freckled face and light-blue eyes. She looked seriously at him while he told her about the bounty he was setting out to take, though he did not say that it had been her father's idea.

"So, you're going all the way to—where did you say it was?"

"Rivermeet. It's right at the edge of the Coppertops."

Flell looked unhappy. "Arren, you don't have to do this. I can help."

Arren shook his head. "I don't need it, Flell. I can deal with it myself. Anyway, it shouldn't be too hard. I can fight this thing."

"But you've never done anything like this before."

"It sounds pretty straightforward to me," Arren said confidently. "I'll plan it out—set an ambush. Just like catching a smuggler. Find the wild griffin's den, flush it out—"

"But you won't have Bran with you," said Flell. "You'll have a lot of farmers."

"Farmers, guards, what's the difference? They can throw rocks and obey orders. And they want this griffin dead or caught. Its crime is against them, after all." He hadn't added that the thing was a man-eater. He didn't want to upset Flell.

Flell looked wistful. "I wish I could go with you." Thrain, sensing her worry, hopped up onto her lap and snuggled down. She petted the griffin, her eyes still on Arren.

He started to feel slightly uncomfortable. "I'll be fine. Eluna will protect me."

"Do your parents know?" Flell asked.

Arren shook his head. "I was going to go and visit them this afternoon. In fact"—he looked out the window and sighed—"I should probably go soon. I have a lot to do today—got to get my affairs in order before I go. Rannagon said he'd choose someone to look after the marketplace for me, but I have to talk to Gern and the rest, make sure they know what's going on."

"You mean I won't see you again before you go?" said Flell.

"I have to leave at dawn," said Arren. He paused. "Look, tell you what, I promised Bran I'd meet him down at the Red Rat this evening for a few drinks. D'you want to come?"

Flell finished off her tea. "Not if he gets drunk and starts making lewd remarks again."

Arren grinned. "I'll keep an eye on him. Gern should be there."

"All right, I'll come," said Flell. She stood up, lifting Thrain onto her shoulder. "Here, let me help you with that," she added, lifting the roll of leather. "Your arm must hurt."

"It's not too bad," said Arren, but he let her take it to the door for him anyway. There, he gave her a quick hug. "I'll see you in a while, all right?"

She kissed him again as she handed over the roll of leather. "Make sure you're there, Arren."

"I will be." Arren tucked the leather under his arm. "You know . . ."

"Yes?"

Arren paused, and then shook his head. "No, never mind."

"No, what is it?" said Flell.

"I'll tell you when I get back," said Arren. "See you later."

Flell stood at her doorway and watched him go, and he frowned once he was out of earshot. He hated to leave her like this.

Once they were in the street, in a clear patch, he took Eluna's harness from inside the roll of leather where he'd stowed it. "Do you want to fly to my parents' place?" he asked her.

Eluna eyed the harness, saying nothing.

"We can ride the crates down, if you'd prefer," Arren added. "But I thought since we're going to be flying to Rivermeet maybe we should get in practice. What d'you think?"

Eluna cocked her head. "We'll fly," she said at last.

"All right. Hold still."

Arren attached the harness to Eluna's chest and neck. There were straps to hold it in place that crossed over her chest and went around her forelegs. Arren tightened them carefully, not wanting to cause her any discomfort. She shifted irritably a couple of times, but made no complaint. Once he was done, Arren climbed onto her back, settling down between her neck and wings, just over her shoulder blades. The harness had a pair of simple leather stirrups hanging off it, and Arren slipped his feet into them and took hold of the harness in front of him. People had gathered to watch, but he ignored them. He looked down at the roll of leather, lying on the street where he'd left it. "Can you carry it for me, Eluna?"

The white griffin snatched it up in her talons. "Are you ready?"

Arren tightened his grip on the harness. "Yes."

"Then hold on." Eluna tensed and then made a short, hobbling run down the street, wings opening as she went. Arren bounced up and down on her back, cushioned by her feathers, holding on grimly. Her head jerked up and down, threatening to dislodge him, and then, without warning, she leapt. Her wings beat furiously, lifting the pair of them into the air. She was rising, wings lashing, bucking wildly in the sky. Arren lay flat against her neck, eyes closed. He started to panic. Had she done this the last time they'd flown? What if she was about to fall?

The thought terrified him. Even though he forced himself to keep his eyes shut, his brain showed him an image of the ground rushing up to meet him. His stomach lurched horribly. For a moment he thought he was falling, down and down, the wind ripping at him. He bit back a yell, and then Eluna's voice broke through the spell. "Let go!" she shouted.

Arren realised he was nearly strangling her. He loosed his grip as the griffin steadied and flew in a wide circle over the city. When he looked down he realised the buildings were tiny and distant. Vertigo seized hold of him, and he retched. "Oh gods."

"Calm down," Eluna snapped. "Hold still; I cannot balance."

She was listing forward slightly in the air, he realised. He pulled himself together and, to avoid looking down, watched the feathers on her neck moving in the wind. His nausea receded gradually.

Eluna flew away over the city. "You are heavier than I remember," she remarked. Arren didn't reply, and she must have felt how tense he was. "Are you still afraid of falling?" she asked.

"No," Arren lied.

"Arren, it was years ago," said Eluna. "Can you forget it?"

"I have," said Arren.

"But you dream about it," said Eluna. "I have heard you in your sleep. Crying out. Does your back still hurt you?"

"Sometimes."

"I saved you then," said Eluna. "I will not let you fall now. I promise."

Arren calmed down. "I trust you."

But he didn't completely relax for the rest of the journey. They flew out over the edge of the city until they were above Eagle's Lake and the large village built among the hills on its shore. Technically it was part of Eagleholm, but the village went by the name of Idun.

Eluna landed not far from the lake, among some houses built on a hill. Arren slid down off her back, very grateful to feel solid ground beneath him again.

The white griffin dropped the roll of leather and shook herself. Once Arren's head had stopped spinning, he noticed the squashed feathers on her neck and shoulders. "Sorry."

Eluna preened herself wordlessly.

People were already coming to meet them, bowing to Eluna.

"Sir!"

"Sir, can I do anything to help you?"

"Sir, please, can you spare a coin? I have no money for—"

Arren rummaged in his pocket and flipped an oblong toward the speaker. He picked up the roll of leather and tucked it under his arm. "I'm just here to visit someone. No need to be concerned."

Several people followed him as he walked off down the hill, but they gave up and left him alone soon enough. He sensed that some of them just wanted to look at Eluna. Griffiners and griffins didn't come into the village very often. To many of Idun's inhabitants, griffiners were just as unreachably distant as the griffins that circled over their city. Out in the countryside, he could expect even more excitement. In places where griffiners almost never went, they were regarded almost as demigods.

Arren's parents lived at the bottom of the hill, in a modest wooden house. They had seen him coming and hurried out to meet him. His mother threw her arms around him. "Arren!"

Arren hugged her. "Hello, Mum, how are you?"

She let go, bright eyed. "Oh, we're fine. Hello, Eluna."

Eluna sat on her haunches and regarded them with an almost benevolent expression.

Arren held out the roll of leather toward his father. "Here, Dad, I brought you this."

His father felt it and whistled. "This is top-quality stuff. Where did you get it from?"

"Seized it from some smugglers. I thought you'd probably be able to use it."

Arren's mother smiled and waved a hand at him. "Come on, come in, don't stand around out here."

They entered the house, leaving Eluna outside to wait.

Arren sat down at the table in the main room with his parents.

Arren's father, Cardock, stowed the leather away in a corner. "Thanks. There's at least twelve pairs of boots in this if I'm any judge."

"No problem," said Arren. "I'd have brought some other things but I couldn't carry anything else. I'll send them down with one of my assistants. So, how're you doing?"

"We're fine," said his mother, Annir. "Your father's thinking of taking on another apprentice."

"And what about you?" said Cardock. "How are things up in the city, Arenadd?"

"Arren will do fine, Dad," said Arren.

Cardock, who had the same angular features as his son, frowned. "I don't see any reason for you to be ashamed, Arenadd. It's a fine, strong name. A Northern name."

"A stupid name," Arren said flatly. "Things are fine in the city. There was a bit of bother this morning, though. Seems I've—"

"You *are* ashamed, though," Cardock interrupted.

"Cardock, please," said Annir.

"You are," said Cardock, ignoring her. "You don't want to remind people you're a Northerner. Arenadd isn't Southern enough for you, is it? Well?"

"Dad, I've told you before. I changed my name because I didn't like it. That's all."

Cardock shook his head. "I am proud of you, you know. When you first became a griffiner I wasn't happy. After what the griffiners did to us—but there are worthy griffiners, and you're one of them. But you can be a griffiner and a Northerner as well."

"Dad, I've never even *been* in the North."

"But the North is in your blood," said Cardock. "I've seen it, Arenadd. Ever since you moved into that city you've been trying to change. Wearing Southern clothes, using a Southern name. You won't even speak our language any more. What are you so ashamed of?"

"Dad, our ancestors came here in chains," said Arren.

"They were *slaves*. I really don't see why that's anything to be proud of."

Cardock rubbed the livid scar on the side of his neck. "A slave collar can't take away a man's dignity, or his heritage."

"I'd say it does a pretty good job of it," said Arren. He sat back in his chair. "Listen, Dad, there's no point in trying to hang on to the past, so just let it go. I'm sure the North is a beautiful place, but I've never been there and neither have you. This is our home, right here. Forget about the old days. They're done."

Cardock sighed. "I suppose you're right there, Arenadd. But I won't forget who we are, and I advise you not to forget it, either. Because other people haven't."

Arren tried not to think of Craddick the smuggler and his snarling voice. *Go back to the North, blackrobe.* "I've come here to give you some news," he said.

"Yes, what is it?" said Annir, sounding relieved.

Arren recounted the story of the raid, finishing with ". . . so now I have to go down to the South for a week or so, to earn some money to pay it off."

"Where in the South?" said Cardock.

"Oh, nowhere in particular. Some village called River-something. Hold on a bit." Arren fished the scroll out of his pocket; it was badly squashed, and he smoothed it out. "Okay, it says, 'Cattle went missing every night for months before someone finally saw the creature taking them, an enormous griffin with black feathers, which flies out from the Coppertops to steal from us. It became bolder when we locked the cattle away at night, and broke a hole in the roof of a barn in order to take what it wanted. Then, a few days later, a man went missing from out in the fields. He was never seen again. Others also disappeared. We discovered that the griffin was taking them. We beg you to send some of your people to destroy the beast, before it claims any more victims. We are in fear for our lives.'" Arren turned the scroll over and examined the simple map drawn on it. There was a large X over a village by the mountains. "It's called Rivermeet. Probably because two rivers come together there."

"So, they want you to kill a wild griffin?" said Cardock.

Arren nodded. "There's a bounty on its head. If I can capture it alive, I'll get even more."

Annir looked aghast. "But they can't just send you off like that! On your own, when you've never done anything like this before!"

"I can fight," said Arren. "Honestly, Mum, there's nothing to worry about. All I have to do is get close enough to hit it with an arrow. I've got some special poison to coat the barb with. No matter where I hit it, it'll be knocked out in a heartbeat."

"You think you can hit a wild griffin in the air?" said Cardock.

"I've hit moving targets before. And if the worst comes to the worst, Eluna can defend me. And . . ." He paused. "If it turns out to be more than I can cope with, I'll just give up and come back and tell someone else to go deal with it. Maybe try again with someone else helping." In spite of his casual tone, the more he talked about the idea, the less certain he felt about it. But it was too late to back out now.

Cardock, though, looked fairly unconcerned. "I'm sure you can do it. You'll have Eluna with you, after all."

"Well, be careful," said Annir, not quite able to hide her worry. "I don't want anything to happen to you."

Arren embraced her briefly. "I'll be fine, Mum. Really."

Arren hated to leave his parents, but the sun began to sink and he was forced to get back on Eluna and return to the city. This time the flight went a little more smoothly, and he managed to control his fear better. That gave him some hope. Maybe, some day, he would be able to fly without being afraid.

Once he'd arrived home, he took Eluna's harness off and packed a box with a selection of things to go to his parents, including everything perishable in the house. Coming back to a cupboard full of rancid cheese and shrivelled oranges was not a pleasing idea. He nailed the box shut and put it by the door. Gern could come and collect it in the morning.

It was dark by now, and Arren put on his cloak before he left. Time to go and meet Gern, Flell and Bran at the Sign of the Red Rat. He found them there waiting for him; they were sharing a pitcher of beer and called out cheerily when they saw him coming. Arren went and joined them, gratefully accepting a drink from Bran.

"Good to see yeh," said the burly guard. "We were startin' to think maybe yeh'd bailed out on us."

Arren took a mouthful of beer; it was cheap but strong, and he sighed and wiped the foam away from his mouth. "Sorry about that. I had to go and see my parents."

"How'd they like the leather?" said Bran.

"Dad was pleased. Said it was good quality. It was, too. I had a look at it first. Should've kept some for myself, actually. I could use a new pair of boots."

Flell laughed. "That's the weirdest thing I've ever seen, you know, a griffiner who makes boots."

"Well, it's a skill, isn't it?" said Arren. "My dad always said we ought to value our skills above our status. 'Maybe Lady Riona is Mistress of the Eyrie, but she can't make boots, can she?'"

Gern snickered. "He really said that?"

"Yeah. He gets some funny ideas every now and then."

"I saw him in the marketplace the other day," said Flell. "I thought about saying hello, but I decided not to. It's amazing how much you look like him, you know."

Arren frowned. "What was he doing there?"

"Trying to buy something, probably," said Flell. "I almost wish I *had* spoken to him. Maybe I could have got him to tell me what your real name is."

Arren had another drink. "A stupid one," he said, swallowing. "Trust me on this."

"But if you were gonna change your name, why change it to something so plain?" said Gern. "If my name were up to me to pick, I'd go with . . . I dunno, something dramatic. Vercingtorix, maybe."

"Well, Gern," said Arren, once the laughter had died down, "you know why I chose something plain instead of something, uh, dramatic? Because there's a reason why people have plain names."

"Maybe it's 'cause they're plain people," Gern muttered.

"Balderdash. You can be as colourful as you want to be and you can do it without having a name no-one can pronounce—actually, that's not quite true. About me choosing a plain name, I mean. I didn't really choose anything. Arren's just what I called myself when I was three because I couldn't pronounce my real name."

"Ah, so it starts with an A, does it?" said Flell.

"Arthen?" Bran suggested. "Arenthius? Arinu? Arnren?"

"No, no, no and no," said Arren. Beside him, Eluna pecked at the dish of herb-flavoured water she'd been given.

"Arentho?" said Flell.

"Areninan?" said Gern.

Arren threw up his hands. "Good gods, all right, all right, I take it back. There's no way my real name is *that* stupid."

"Well, what is it then?" said Flell.

Arren finished off his beer. "Fine," he said. "But you'll only tease me about it for the rest of my life. It's Arenadd Taranisäii."

Silence.

"'Arenadd'?" Flell repeated. "That's—"

"Stupid, I know."

"Actually, I was going to say it sounds elegant," said Flell. "What does it mean?"

"Oh, it's the name of some old sage from a Northern legend," said Arren. "My dad reckons I'm being pretentious by refusing to use it. Says I ought to be proud of my inheritance, or something."

"Well, yeh should be, mate," said Bran. "Everyone should be, right? An' I don't reckon Arenadd is that bad of a name. Sounds all right to me."

Arren scratched his neck. "Slave scars aren't a proud heritage, and I really wish my father would get that into his head. Arren is fine."

"What was that surname, sir?" said Gern. "Taranisi?"

"Taranisäii," Arren corrected. "It just means 'of the blood of Taranis.'"

"Was that the name of your tribe?" said Gern.

Arren rolled his eyes. "Gern, I don't *have* a tribe. I'm not from the North. I was born in Idun, damn it."

"So, who was Taranis?" said Gern.

"I don't know."

"Yes you do," said Flell. "Come on, Arren. You told me about it before. Taranis the Wolf, son of Tynadd Traeganni."

"It's just an old story," Arren muttered.

She looked at him kindly. "And you say you aren't ashamed. Go on, show them your tattoo. I'm sure they'd like to see it."

"Depends on where it is," said Bran, grinning.

Arren gave up. He rolled up the sleeve of his tunic and turned to let them see the bare skin of his shoulder. There was a tattoo there of a blue wolf's head holding a white globe in its jaws. Inside the globe was a symbol of three spirals joined together.

"That's amazing, sir!" said Gern.

Bran squinted at it. "An' *my* tattoo just says 'MOTHER.' What's it mean, Arren?"

Arren pulled his sleeve back into place. "It's the sign of the Wolf Tribe. The moon is—well, Northerners believe it's the eye of their god."

"Do you?" said Gern.

Arren shook his head. "It's just a tattoo. I thought it would look good. I was a bit drunk at the time."

"It does look good, sir," said Gern. He paused to pour himself another beer. "So, what's all this Flell's telling me about you leaving?"

"It's nothing much," said Arren. "I'm going down South for a while. There's a problem at one of the villages, and they've asked me to deal with it."

"Why, does it have something to do with trading?"

"No. They just need a griffiner. Oh—" He glanced at them all. "I'm not really supposed to talk about it, so just keep it to yourselves, okay? You haven't told anyone else, have you, Flell?"

"No, just Bran and Gern. Why the secrecy?"

"I'm not allowed to talk about that, either."

"So, why are you going South, sir?" said Gern.

Arren took in a deep breath. "Well, it's like this . . ."

6

Rivermeet

The journey southward began the next day, at dawn. Eluna woke him up as usual, and once he had fed her the last of the rats from the cage, he dressed warmly and slung his bow and arrows on his back then strapped them securely in place. Eluna was impatient to leave and shifted around while he put her harness on.

"There," said Arren once it was in place. "We're done. Just wait a moment."

He went back to his half of the house and picked up the box of food. Gern had agreed to collect it some time during the morning, so he left it on the doorstep before he closed the door and locked it from the inside. He'd hidden all his valuables under the floorboards, but he wasn't particularly worried about them. Very few people would risk breaking into a griffiner's house. Nevertheless, he put the shutters over the windows and locked the back door to the balcony before he returned to the stable and passed through it to the second balcony, the one without rails, where Eluna was waiting.

The griffin stretched her wings and flicked her tail, inviting him to get on her back.

Arren climbed on, put his arms through the loops of the harness and braced himself. "All right. Let's go."

Eluna chirped eagerly and stood tall, bracing her paws and claws on the wood. She darted forward with a sudden burst and hurled herself off the edge of the platform and into space.

Arren couldn't hold back a yelp of fright. The wind snatched at his hair and cloak, pulling at him like a giant hand. For a moment they were falling, straight downward, and Arren buried his face in Eluna's feathers and gritted his teeth. She was there, she was solid, she was a kind of solid ground to hold him up, he wasn't going to hit the ground, he wasn't—

Eluna's wings opened. Arren's insides gave a giddy lurch as she pulled out of the dive and swooped upward, shooting into the sky like an arrow. She reached soaring height and levelled out into a steady glide, and Arren breathed deeply.

"Are you all right?" Eluna asked. A griffin's voice carried well, even in flight.

"I'm fine," said Arren.

"Good."

The journey began.

At first Arren did his best to keep still and either looked straight ahead or kept his eyes shut, but as they flew on he found himself fighting the temptation to look downward.

"Look at the sun," Eluna said suddenly.

Arren did, and his heart soared. There were mountains to the east, far away in the distance, and the sun was rising from behind them. Bright golden light was spilling out over the landscape, tinted with pink, and the mountains themselves looked black against the red-and-orange cloud behind them. Above that the sky was pale blue, almost purple. It reminded him of Flell's eyes, and with that thought his fear was suddenly gone.

"It's beautiful," he said, half to himself.

Eluna said nothing, but he could almost sense her satisfaction as she flew on.

His fear did return a little later, when he risked a glance downward. They were flying very high, much higher than they had done the previous day. Idun had already vanished, but when he looked back over his shoulder he could just see Eagleholm shrinking in the distance. It looked like nothing, a tiny black hump on the horizon.

He shuddered and looked away. His heart continued to beat rapidly, and he could feel himself sweating, so he concentrated on trying to remember the precise wording of the letter from Rivermeet. Getting there should be fairly straightforward; he'd shown the map to Eluna, and she had said she could navigate there without any problems. All she had to do was follow the river. There were plenty of villages built along it where they could stop for the night, and some patches of woodland where she could hunt if the need arose.

He and Eluna stopped several times during the day to rest and finally landed that evening in a small town called Lansdown.

It was a fairly nondescript place, built along the banks of the river. Most of the occupants were farmers.

When Eluna landed in the square, there was a crowd of people waiting to receive her and Arren. They gathered around, bowing low, all speaking at once.

"Sir! Welcome, sir!"

"It's an honour, sir!"

Arren stretched. He was stiff and sore after spending so long in the air. "Hello," he said. Beside him, Eluna yawned. His stomach twinged. "I'm passing through here on official business and I was wondering if there was anywhere I could stay here. And I need to buy food for my griffin and myself."

"Sir, anything you want you can have," one of the crowd said promptly. "Food, somewhere to stay—just ask."

"Is there an inn here or something?" said Arren. "I can pay—"

"Oh no, sir! There's no need to pay for anything. Please, come with me."

Arren wasn't about to argue. He followed the man with a feeling of tired satisfaction, in spite of the ache in his limbs. Eluna loped beside him, eyeing the people following them. They were sensible enough to keep their distance. Arren was glad about that. He wasn't sure he had the strength to hold her back if she decided to make a lunge at someone.

They were shown to the local inn, where there was a room for Arren. The horses were removed from the stable so that Eluna could stay there, and people brought meat for her with astonishing speed. Arren accepted the food they offered him with gratitude, especially when he saw that it included plenty of fresh vegetables. Perishable food was expensive in Eagleholm.

He was exhausted when he went to bed that night, but it took some time to get to sleep. It was hard to get comfortable in a proper bed instead of a hammock, without the gentle swinging to soothe him. He'd slept in a hammock for as long as he could remember.

Perhaps it was this vague feeling of unease that gave him an equally uneasy dream.

It was a dream he knew very well.

He was standing in the sky. The wind was icy cold and strong, like a river. But the sun was shining brightly and the sky was blue and dotted with white clouds, and he smiled and reached up toward them, wanting to touch them. And he could, he could—

But then he looked down, and he saw the ground, and it was so far below him, all dark and tiny, and then it was rushing toward him, getting bigger and bigger but never quite reaching him, and he was falling, screaming and screaming, knowing there would be no-one to catch him, knowing he was going to die, and there was nothing but darkness and the howl of the wind and an empty sky mocking him, beyond his reach forever.

* * *

The ground below was dark. It looked like a huge black sea, stretching away into the distance. There was grass down there, shivering and sighing in the wind. Above him a bright half-moon hung in the sky like an eye. Just like his own eye.

He could see the human, walking over the grass toward the village. It was a large one. He'd been watching it for days.

The black griffin circled lower. Up here, he was almost invisible. Anyone looking up might have seen his shadow pass in front of the moon every so often, but only for a moment, and even if they did it would be too late. He was too fast for them.

The black griffin circled lower, intent on the human. It was moving slowly, unable to see where it was going in the dark. Humans had poor eyes. He had thought they were weak, at first. They were so small, so fragile. But they had built this place. They could make their prey obey them. They didn't have to hunt. And there were so many of them, all somehow able to live together without fighting. It was something alien to him. They were too intelligent to be herd animals, like goats, and yet they swarmed together like a herd.

The black griffin tensed. *Now.*

He dived, front talons spread wide. The human never even saw him coming. He passed over it and snatched it up in his talons before he flew upward again with scarcely a sound, taking the human with him.

The human didn't move at first, but as he flew away with it dangling beneath him it started to struggle and cry out in distress. It was calling for help from its fellows, but the black griffin knew it wouldn't be heard. He flew off in a leisurely way over the village and the fields beyond, heading back toward the mountains and his valley. The human continued to writhe in his grip, and he was glad about that. If it could still move around then it probably wasn't badly hurt.

He passed over the tallest mountain and into his valley, and landed in the overhang. There he let go of the human. It tried to crawl away almost instantly, but he blocked its way—not hitting it but simply forcing it to turn back. It found its feet and bolted, taking him by surprise, but he caught up with it in a few quick bounds and dragged it back. It kept on trying to escape, but it was far too slow, and in the end it gave up and huddled in the back of the overhang, whimpering pathetically. The black griffin curled up and watched it. The others had done this, too. He would have to stay awake all night to keep an eye on it, in case it ran again.

When the sun finally rose, the man woke up from the shallow doze he'd managed to fall into and jerked upright almost instantly, terror hitting him in the chest. The light of dawn showed him the overhang and the huge, hunched shape of the black griffin sitting not far away, watching him. The man pulled back as far as he could into the overhang, staring at the beast in terror. He was expecting it to rush at him at any moment, but it didn't. It stayed where it was, perfectly still except for the twitching of its tail, not taking its eyes off him.

The man looked around, searching for a weapon, and that was when he saw them.

Bones. Human bones scattered over the dirt floor of the overhang. There was a pair of pathetically small skulls at the far end, one smashed open by a huge beak. Bits of torn cloth lay with the bones, along with coins and boots and the bits and pieces of things people carried around in their pockets. And there was a smell, a rank, rancid, choking smell.

The man started to shudder. He forced himself to look away, toward the weird shapes painted on the back wall of the griffin's lair. But he could not block the smell from entering his nostrils. His arm and shoulder hurt from where the griffin's talons had cut into him, and he was cold.

He realised that there were tears starting to stream down his face.

"Ee ar kaee?"

The man turned sharply, raising his hands instinctively to defend himself. The griffin had risen to its claws and was moving toward him, tail swishing.

"Stay away from me!" he screamed.

The griffin stopped and sat on its haunches, regarding him threateningly. The man's eyes darted to and fro as he searched for an escape route, but there was nowhere to go. He backed away until he hit the wall and slid down it onto the ground, nearly sick with terror.

The griffin moved closer. It stretched its head toward him, beak opening slightly. *"Ae aa krae ae?"* it said. The sound was a weird, hoarse screech-snarl, low and aggressive.

The man's fingers closed around a bone. As the griffin lowered its head to sniff at him, he screamed suddenly and swung the bone as hard as he could, hitting it on the head. There was a hollow *thunk* as it connected, and he lurched away from the griffin and started to run.

Something hit him in the back almost instantly. He fell hard onto his stomach, and then the griffin was on him, lifting him off the ground and hurling him back into the overhang. He hit the wall and landed on the floor among the bones, winded and gasping.

The griffin rose onto its hind legs, wings spread wide, and screeched. The noise was horrible, harsh and ear-splittingly loud. The man clapped his hands over his ears and curled up, trying to protect himself, but the griffin fell back onto its forelegs and turned away abruptly, lashing its tail. *"Ae ao ak krae ee,"* it uttered, clicking its beak.

After that the man didn't try to escape again. He stayed in the overhang, watched over by his captor, not knowing what to do. There had to be a way to escape.

The griffin did not sleep, and nor did it take its attention off him for a moment. It spent half the day sitting at the edge of the overhang and just watching him. Several times it moved as if to come closer to him, but it always withdrew. And from time to time it would make those strange sounds again. Later, as noon came, it began to pace back and forth, its movements full of easy grace and power.

Gradually the man's terror faded into dull pain and misery. He was hungry and thirsty and cold, but there was nothing to eat or drink and nowhere to run to. After a while he started to wonder how long it would be before the griffin decided to kill him. It was odd that it hadn't done so already. What did it want him alive for? Perhaps it was just doing it for fun. To toy with him, like a cat with a mouse.

Anger rose inside him. "You can't do this," he rasped at the creature. "You monster! You sick piece of—"

The griffin paused in its endless pacing and watched him as he spoke. There was an alertness in its eyes, as if it understood. But it only hissed at him and resumed its pacing once he had fallen silent.

Eventually it seemed to tire of this; it stopped abruptly and looked at him again. He pulled back nervously, and as if this was a signal the griffin came toward him. It cornered him against the back wall, and all he could do was brace himself while it sniffed at him, its beak pressing into his chest. Its feathers smelt dry and musty, and there was dried blood on its beak. He could hear its deep, rumbling breaths.

The griffin clicked its beak and drew back once more, turning away to look out over the valley. Then it lay down and curled up, folding its wings on its back. It yawned. The man dared to relax a little, keeping his eyes on the beast. Was it tired now? Was it going to sleep? Fear was keeping him awake, but the griffin must have stayed up all night. It *had* to sleep sometime, surely.

The griffin was watching him, as if it knew what he was thinking. But then it yawned again and laid its head down on its front talons, tail twitching gently. It stayed like that for some time, as the sun started to go down, and then, at last, it closed its eyes. A short time later it started to purr softly, and the man's heart leapt.

He wasted no time. The instant he was certain that the creature was asleep, he started to edge away from it, toward the end of the overhang where the roof was lower. He'd noticed it earlier and had judged that he could climb over it. Sure enough, the handholds and footholds he had singled out and watched obsessively all evening were enough. He hauled himself up and onto the mountainside above the overhang, stopping every few moments to look back at the griffin. The sun was sinking rapidly, but in the gloom he could still see its great bulky shape on the ledge.

He climbed upward, heaving himself across rocks, ignoring the pain in his arm. Going downward was impossible. That only led deeper into the griffin's territory. The only way out was over the mountain and down the other side. He had to try. It was his only hope.

The sun finally disappeared behind the mountains to the west as he reached the peak, and he stopped there to rest. In spite of the cold, he was sweating. His wounds stung, and dirt clung to his skin. But he forced himself to get up again and headed for the downward slope of the mountain, and home.

The stars started to come out.

Eluna was the first to see their destination on the horizon. "There!" she called.

Arren woke up from his doze. "What?"

Eluna beat her wings a few times and angled her tail, turning herself toward it. "Rivermeet," she said simply.

It took a while longer to complete the journey. Arren watched the village approach. It had taken a day and a half to get here from Lansdown, and by now he found he was much more confident in the sky. He couldn't stay frightened forever. It was simply too exhausting. And he had begun to appreciate how complex and beautiful everything looked from above. He was glad. His fear of heights had always been a secret source of humiliation for him; what sort of griffiner was afraid to fly? It was just good luck that his job hadn't required him to travel much; if anyone had found out about it he would have been a laughingstock. And he knew Eluna didn't like it, either.

Nevertheless, his stomach lurched when they began their descent. He closed his eyes and held on until Eluna's paws hit the ground with a sudden bump, and then he straightened up, sighing in relief.

People were running toward them as he dismounted. Eluna started up instantly, hissing and opening her beak wide. Arren put his hand on her neck and watched the villagers approach warily. But in spite of their fear of Eluna, there was an eagerness about them, and an urgency, too. They stopped at a safe distance and watched him, afraid to come closer.

Arren surveyed the rows of faces. "Who's in charge here?"

Silence, and then a middle-aged man came forward. "No-one, really, sir, but thank gods you've come. We were starting to think—never mind. Welcome to Rivermeet."

Arren nodded to him. "Thank you. I'm Arren Cardockson, and this is Eluna."

The man bowed. "Roderick Kennson. I'm the local reeve. Sir, may I ask . . ."

"What is it?" said Arren.

Roderick looked at him, then scanned the sky. "Sir, why have you come alone?"

The question caught Arren by surprise. "Because I'm all they sent," he said. "Why, is there a problem with that?"

There was another silence, and then Arren noticed a small huddle of people at the back of the crowd. They were trying to comfort a woman who was crying.

Roderick followed his gaze. "I'm sorry, sir," he said in a low voice. "The beast took another victim last night."

Arren went cold. "How many people has it killed?"

"Seven, sir. Two of them were only children."

"Oh gods. I'm so sorry. I would have come sooner, but I only just—well, I was asked to come and deal with it only a few days ago. I flew here as fast as I could."

"It's all right, sir, we don't blame you. Please, come with me. We have prepared rooms for you and your griffin. You can rest from your journey, and then I will tell you anything you want to know."

Arren nodded and started to remove Eluna's harness. "Thank you."

He allowed Roderick to lead him through the village toward his lodgings; the crowd parted to let them through, like water flowing around a stone. He could almost feel their hopeful gazes fixed on him. But he could also hear the soft sobs from the woman grieving for her lost husband. It made anger boil inside him.

His lodgings turned out to be at Roderick's home. Eluna had been provided not with a stable to sleep in but an old storeroom, which had been filled with hay and even decorated with dried flowers and carvings. It almost made Arren sad when he saw it.

His own quarters were equally grand; everything was scrupulously clean and decorated, and the house's occupants surrounded him the instant he appeared, asking him if there was anything he wanted or whether anything was unsatisfactory.

Arren couldn't bring himself to tell them that they were overdoing it just a bit. They probably thought it was a sacrifice for a rich griffiner like him to stay here. It was quite embarrassing, but he did his best to look as grateful as he felt.

He wanted to get down to business straightaway, but Roderick insisted that he get some rest first, and he had to admit that he needed it. He'd spent a very long time in the air and he was still slightly dizzy. His knees kept wanting to fold up.

Once he'd emptied his pockets and put the few things he'd brought with him down on the table in his room, he took his boots off and flopped down on the bed. It was wonderfully soft, and he relaxed almost at once. *I'll just have a quick lie down,* he thought.

A short while later he was asleep.

7

Out of the Blue

"Sir? Sir! Sir, are you in there?"

The shouts and thumping from outside woke Arren up. He opened his eyes and blinked, puzzled. Everything was gloomy, and the shapes around him were unfamiliar.

"Sir!"

The voice recalled him to his senses. He sat up. "Yes? What is it?"

"Sir, can I come in?"

Arren got up off the bed and stretched. "Yes, go ahead."

The door opened and light streamed in. It was Roderick, holding a lantern and beaming. "Sorry to wake you up, sir, but I just had to come and get you."

"What's going on?" said Arren, squinting at him.

"Something wonderful, sir," said Roderick. "The man who was taken the other night has come back. He's alive."

Arren started. "He's—"

"Yes, sir. He walked all the way back from the griffin's lair. You should probably talk to him, sir; he could tell you some things you need to know."

Arren was already pulling his boots back on. He did up

the laces as fast as he could and then snatched up his cloak. "Show me where he is," he commanded.

He woke Eluna before they left the house; she was irritated to be disturbed, but she came with him anyway, hissing to herself.

The man was in the street, not far away from Roderick's home, being embraced by his family. Dozens of people had gathered, and the air was full of their loud, joyful voices. Roderick hurried on ahead, shouting, "Out of the way, everyone, the griffiner's come!"

People moved aside to let Arren and Eluna get to the man, who turned to see them approach. He was pale, his clothes torn and filthy and stained with blood, and he started nervously when he saw Eluna, but he looked well enough.

"Arren Cardockson," said Arren. "I'm so glad to see you're all right."

The man bowed to him. "Thank you, sir. My name's Renn, sir."

Arren was impressed by how in control of himself he looked. "I've come to deal with the griffin that took you. Please, can you tell me anything about it? How did you escape?"

"It kept me in its lair," said Renn. "Wouldn't let me leave. I waited until it was asleep and then ran."

Arren blinked. "What? You mean it just—" He paused. "I'm sorry, I shouldn't be asking questions now. We've got to get you inside and have your injuries looked at. How d'you feel?"

"I'm all right, sir," said Renn. "But if I could just go inside—I need something to drink."

His wife grasped his hand. "Come on, Renn. We'll get you home. If you don't mind coming along, sir, I'm sure you can ask your questions once we're there."

"Not at all," said Arren, glancing at Eluna. She didn't look overly bothered; she was watching Renn curiously, and when they set out she went ahead of Arren, evidently keen to hear what the man had to say.

They were led to Renn's home and Arren went inside; it was a modest dwelling, but clean, and the main room was nicely warm. Eluna had to stay outside, her head poking through the window.

Renn's wife sat her husband by the fire and removed his tunic in order to have a look at his wounds. There were several deep slashes in Renn's upper arm, and his chest was punctured with the unmistakeable marks of talons. Arren had seen plenty of injuries like this in the past and had received a few himself.

"So, tell me," Arren said, while Renn's wife set about cleaning and dressing her husband's wounds, "what happened? Start from the beginning."

Renn shuddered and winced. "Well—" He accepted some water from his wife and drank it in one swallow. It seemed to revive him a little. "Well, I was out in the field seeing about a broken fence, you see, sir, and I knew I had to be careful not to stay out too late, but I lost track of the time. I started heading back, but the sun went down and I couldn't see too well—hadn't brought a lantern with me." He stopped to drink another mug of water. "And—and I was pretty close to the village, I remember, when I heard this noise. Like a sort of rushing, sir. And then the next thing I knew there were big sharp talons wrapped around me and I was—well, flying. I couldn't see much, but I could feel my arm bleeding, and it hurt like mad. I tried fighting back, but the thing was just too strong. It was like being in a vice. I could hardly breathe. Don't know how long I was in the air, sir. A while. The moon was up by the time we got there."

"Where did it take you?" said Arren.

"Into the mountains, sir," said Renn. "Ow! Damn it, that hurt! Sorry, sir. It wasn't very far into the mountains, sir. Right on the edge. The griffin took me into a valley— couldn't see it then, sir, but I saw it the next day. There's an overhang in the side of the mountain; that's where it lives. It just dumped me in there and left me. I tried to run off, but it wouldn't let me. Just dragged me back. I stayed there all night, sir. Didn't know what to do. My arm was hurting and it was cold as anything, and I was stuck there. I think I slept a while. Next thing, it was dawn, and the griffin was still there. Wasn't doing anything. It was just sitting there and watching me."

Eluna nudged Arren's shoulder and muttered to him in griffish.

Arren listened. "She wants to know what it looked like and how big it was."

Renn glanced at the white griffin. "It was bigger than her. Much bigger. It had black fur on the back end, and silver feathers up front. The talons—they were huge. Longer than my hand. It just kept *looking* at me, sir. Like it wanted something. I don't know why it didn't just kill me. It must have been waiting until it was hungry—*oof!*" His wife had suddenly flung herself on him and was embracing him tightly. He held her, a little awkwardly. "It's all right, love. I'm fine. Ouch."

Arren held back a smile. "So how long were you there?"

"Most of the next day, sir. The thing had—there were bones, sir. In the lair. Human . . . bones." Renn shuddered. "I—I recognised some of them, sir. The clothes, I mean. It'd carried them all back there and eaten them. There were just bones, scattered everywhere."

"But the griffin didn't try to kill you," Arren muttered. "Why?"

"I don't know, sir," said Renn. "It just watched me. And once it came up to me and just . . . sniffed at me, sir. Like a dog, almost. Nudged me with its beak a bit, and then backed off. I hit it once. Picked up a bone and whacked it. It screamed at me, but it didn't bite me or anything. Just dragged me back again, sir."

"I've never heard of a wild griffin doing that," said Arren, which was broadly true. He'd never heard about wild griffins doing anything, in fact, but he wasn't going to admit it. "So how did you get away?"

Renn shrugged a little wearily. "It fell asleep in the end, sir. I climbed up over the mountain and got out of there before it woke up, sir. That's when I found out it was right on the edge of the mountains, sir. There were paddocks right on the other side. So I just walked home."

Arren whistled. "You're a lucky man, Renn."

"I know, sir," Renn said quietly. "Oh, I know."

"It's odd, though. I wonder why it did that? I've never known griffins to hoard food." Arren looked at Eluna.

The white griffin paused in the act of preening one of her wings and blinked slowly, thinking. "A griffin does not store food," she said eventually. "We will eat carrion, but a kill is eaten at once. The hunt . . . makes you hungry."

"But could it have just been teasing him?" said Arren. "You know, toying with him?"

"A young griffin might," said Eluna. "But this one is my age, at least. Old enough not to risk losing food by keeping it alive."

"What did she say, sir?" said Renn's wife.

Arren looked at her. "Uh, she said that as far as she knows, griffins don't keep prey alive, and only the very young play with it. Hunting should have made it hungry. It doesn't make any sense."

Renn shuddered and scowled. "You're here to kill it, aren't you, sir?"

"Yes, if I can."

"But is there only one of you here, sir?"

"Yes. I just arrived."

"If—" Renn's brow furrowed. "I'm sorry if this is rude or anything, sir, but where are the others?"

"The others?" said Arren.

"Yes, sir. Shouldn't there be other griffiners here to help you, sir?"

"What makes you think that, Renn?" said Arren. He was beginning to feel uneasy.

"There's been problems with wild griffins here before, sir," said Renn. "The last time it happened I was just a boy, but I remember it. A wild griffin was taking cattle, sir, so the reeve sent a message to Eagleholm. A few days later, three griffiners showed up. They were older than you, sir. They stayed here a while, asking questions and making plans, and then they flew off together one morning, sir. They came back with the griffin's tail for a trophy. Said they'd found it in its territory and killed it, sir."

"I remember that," his wife said suddenly.

"Anyway," said Arren, "I've been assigned to do this and I'll do my best. Now that Eluna has an idea of where it lives, she can track it down."

"We trust you, sir," said Renn.

But Arren wasn't sure if he trusted himself. Now he was here, and hearing about this griffin first-hand from one of its victims, he was feeling less and less certain by the moment. Back in Eagleholm, when he'd told Bran and Gern about his mission they had been impressed and confident. Neither of them had had any doubt that he could do it, and that had boosted his own confidence. Now, though, his certainty was beginning to drain away, and he started to think that perhaps he was in over his head. *What am I even doing here?* he thought suddenly. *I'm an administrator, not a hunter!*

"I'll do my best to make sure your trust is well placed," he said smoothly. "Now"—he stood up—"I'll leave you to rest. I think you'll be fine. You're a strong and brave man, Renn. No doubt I'll be telling your story back at Eagleholm for years to come."

"Thank you, sir," said Renn.

Arren left the house with Eluna. "So, what did you think of that?" he asked her.

Eluna shook her head with a quick, darting motion. "I think that tomorrow we shall find this griffin's territory and fight it, and we shall win."

That cheered him up a bit. "But how will we do it?"

They walked in silence for a time, both thinking deeply.

"I've got a plan," Arren said at length. "How about we find a place to perch, somewhere near to its territory. You call out a challenge, and when it comes flying to attack us

I'll loose an arrow at it. If I time it right, it should be all over in moments. We won't even have to go near it. How does that sound?"

Eluna listened. "It sounds like a good plan," she said. "Have you got the poison?"

"Yes; there should be enough to coat at least three arrowheads. I think I could do it in three tries. And if that doesn't work—"

"If you do not bring it down, I will," said Eluna. "I will fight it in the air."

"You shouldn't."

Eluna's beak snapped shut an inch from his neck. *"Do not tell me what to do!"* she rasped.

Arren jerked away instinctively. "No! No, look, please, calm down, that's not what I meant. I was just—well, it would be dangerous."

She hissed at him. "You think I am afraid?"

"No, no, not at all. I just don't want you to be hurt, that's all."

Eluna looked amused by this. "So, it is not me who is afraid. It is you."

"Yes," Arren said simply. "If you were hurt . . ."

She raised her head proudly. "I am not afraid. I must fight. A griffin who does not fight is worthless. A coward survives, but a coward does not live."

"Yes, but there's a difference between being a coward and just being sensible."

Eluna snapped her beak. "To fight is to live. And I will fight to protect you."

"That's what I'm afraid of," Arren muttered. "I shouldn't have got you into this, Eluna."

"It is not your fault," said Eluna. "I was the one who killed the man. I was the one who agreed to come here. If I must fight, then I will."

"I won't stop you," said Arren, knowing he couldn't even if he wanted to.

"And this wild griffin will learn the meaning of justice," said Eluna.

* * *

Arren ate dinner with Roderick and his family; it was plain but well cooked, and he ate heartily. The journey had given him a very large appetite. Eluna was given an entire side of beef to eat, and she tore into it enthusiastically as soon as it was placed in front of her. When Arren stepped in to visit her before he went to bed he found her sleeping soundly in her nest of hay, surrounded by scattered bones. He smiled to himself and left quietly.

His own bed welcomed him, and he stripped down to his trousers and got under the covers; he hadn't brought a nightshirt with him, and in any case he was used to sleeping in his clothes. His back ached, and when he stretched he felt it crack. Even after more than seven years, it still hurt from time to time. Perhaps it never would completely heal.

He didn't realise he'd fallen asleep until the screaming woke him up.

He jerked awake and climbed out of bed almost before he knew what he was doing. The scream split the air again. It wasn't human, he realised abruptly. It was a griffin's voice.

Arren pulled on his tunic and boots and grabbed his bow and arrows. He found the little bottle of poison on the table and stuffed it into his pocket. The light of dawn was coming in through the window, and he heard the griffin screech again.

He ran out of the room as fast as he could go, tripping over his unlaced boots. "Eluna! *Eluna!*"

She burst into the corridor, all bristling fur and feathers. "Arren!"

The screech rang out again. Eluna flattened herself to the ground slightly. "Come!" She turned and scrambled away. Arren ran after her, and the two of them barrelled through the front door of the house and out into the street.

The sun was rising. Overhead the sky was dark blue, still dotted with stars, and the sun was a yellow line spread out over the horizon. The light was pale, painting everything in unreal shades of grey. Arren barely paused to take this in. He looked straight upward, and his stomach lurched when he saw the dark shape circling high above.

The screech split the air yet again. Everywhere people were appearing, running out of their houses to look up at the distant shape of the black griffin.

Renn was there, and hurried toward Arren, his face rigid with terror. "It's come!" he yelled. "It's come back to find me!"

Arren put his hand on Eluna's shoulders. She was trembling.

"Go back inside," he said harshly to Renn. "Now! All of you!" he added, turning to address the people in the street. "Go inside! Get out of sight! *Now*, damn it! I have to be the only person it can see! Otherwise it can choose who to go after!"

The people obeyed; he watched them run off in a disorderly scramble, doors slamming shut behind them. Overhead, the black griffin continued to circle. It had ceased its calling.

Arren was amazed by how fast his mind was working. "We'll call to it," he told Eluna. "It'll come after us. We'll pull it after us, get it out of the village, out into the fields."

Eluna didn't reply. She lifted her head and screeched. *"Eluna! Eluna!"*

Arren raised his head, too, and screamed his own name at the heavens.

He thought he saw the black griffin pause in its circling. Then it screamed back. There were no discernable words there, just a long, harsh screech, like an eagle's. Arren paused at this; he'd never heard a griffin's cry that sounded like that. But as the black griffin began to descend and he began to run away out of the village, toward the fields, a thought flashed across his mind: this griffin had no name.

The black griffin followed them as they ran. He could

see it flying lower, homing in on him as Eluna had done back in Eagleholm.

Arren vaulted over a fence and ran on, through the dewy grass of an empty field. Eluna leapt after him and ran on ahead, still screeching her name. The black griffin flew lower. It was preparing to dive on them.

Arren stopped when he was well away from the village, in an isolated, open spot where the black griffin couldn't fail to see him. Eluna crouched beside him, and the pair of them continued to call their challenge.

The black griffin took the bait. Arren saw its circles getting tighter as it singled him out. He unshipped the bow from his back and strung it as fast as he could. The cork in the bottle of poison seemed to take forever to come out; once he'd pulled it out and stuffed it in his pocket, he took an arrow from the quiver and dipped it in the liquid. It came out dripping, and he put the bottle down on the ground beside him and nocked the arrow onto the bowstring. His heart was pounding so hard it made his head spin. Would it be enough? It *had* to be enough; it had to—

The black griffin folded its wings and dived. Arren looked up to watch its descent, and his mouth fell open. It was coming so *fast.*

He forced himself not to panic. *Just keep calm; keep still; don't loose the arrow until the moment is right. Think of it as a giant archery butt. Just don't panic.*

The black griffin was getting closer by the moment. Every moment he could see more of it. See the huge front talons, pointed straight at him. See the silvery feathers and the mottled wings, pointed backward like arrows. The beast filled his vision, huge and horrible. Its beak was slightly open, and he could see its eyes, big and silver, staring straight at him.

"*Arren!*" Eluna screamed.

He loosed the arrow.

It hit the black griffin square in the chest, embedding itself among the feathers. The griffin jerked suddenly in the sky, and Arren's heart leapt. But the griffin's dive did not stop. It continued to fall straight toward him, faster and faster. He panicked and ran, dropping his bow, but the black griffin only angled itself to follow him, skimming low over the grass. He could feel its presence looming over him, and terror ripped his chest apart. The poison wasn't working. It was coming for him; it was going to get him.

There was a low, dull thud, and a scream, and then he fell. He was running so fast that he nearly flipped over when he hit the ground. The impact knocked all the breath out of him. He struggled upright almost at once, turning to look, and suddenly realised that the black griffin was not coming after him any more. It had fallen to the ground and was lying there, trying to get up.

Arren looked around for Eluna. And then he saw her, not far away from the other griffin. She, too, was on the ground; he could see her wings flailing as she struggled to recover herself. He ran toward her.

The black griffin had stopped moving. It was lying on its belly, wings and legs limp. Its eyes were still open, but as Arren neared it the beast let out a weary sigh and let its head drop. Its eyes slid closed.

Eluna was still trying to get up. Arren crouched by her side. "Eluna!"

The white griffin's head turned toward him and she lashed out, hitting him in the chest. Arren fell over backward, hitting the ground so hard that his vision flashed red for an instant. He was nearly knocked out, but managed to get up again. His chest hurt horribly. He struggled back toward Eluna, calling her name. The griffin was twisted awkwardly, her hind legs turned sideways as if her back was broken. But she managed to gather them beneath her and tried to lever herself upright. One foreleg pushed at the ground, but the other didn't move, and she fell back, hissing.

As she rolled over onto her side, one foreleg reaching out for something to grip, Arren saw the blood on her chest.

He felt his heart freeze inside him. "Eluna!"

This time she did not lash out when he came to her. She

lay still, making a horrible rasping sound. Her eyes were glazed, and he could see the blood soaking into the ground beneath her, and into her feathers, turning white to red.

Arren knelt by her, reaching out to touch her. "Eluna— oh gods, no."

Eluna tried to get up once again, but flopped back onto the ground. The blood was still coming, more and more of it. Arren touched her chest, very tentatively, and when she only jerked briefly he pulled the feathers aside to look at what was underneath.

"No!"

Eluna's chest had been ripped open, right down the middle. White, shattered ribs were poking through the bloodied flesh, and the wound extended down to her fore-leg, exposing the bone there, too. Blood was pouring out of it. Too much blood.

Arren pulled off his tunic and tried to staunch the flow, but the moment he touched the wound, Eluna screamed. Her head arched back and her beak opened wide, letting forth a loud, awful screech of agony. Her legs and wings trembled convulsively, and then her head suddenly dropped.

"Help me!" she cried, her voice garbled and panic-stricken. "Arren! *Help!*"

Arren grabbed at the wound, pulling the edges toward each other to try to close it. It moved a little, and he snatched up his tunic and tied it around her neck, binding the injury shut as well as he could. But blood began to soak through the fabric almost instantly, and Eluna's movements slowed. She lay on her side, her throat pulsating with each desperate breath, eyes half-closed. "Arren," she whispered.

Arren looked up, toward the black griffin. It lay still, eyes closed, the arrow sticking out of its chest. Its front claws were outstretched toward him, and he saw the blood on them. It was only then that he realised what had happened. Eluna had flung herself in the way.

People were coming already. He was vaguely aware of them running toward him over the field, calling out to him.

Arren sat down beside Eluna, lifting her head. "Eluna, please, Eluna, just breathe, just—"

Eluna's eyelid twitched, but she said nothing.

Arren looked up as people ran past him. They were making for the black griffin. Many of them had knives and sticks.

"Stop!" Arren yelled.

They paused and looked back at him. "What is it, sir?" said one. Renn, he realised. He saw Eluna and came to Arren. "Oh my gods, your griffin—"

"Don't kill it!" Arren shouted at the people. "Leave it alone! I said *leave it alone*! That's an *order*, godsdamnit!"

They withdrew, confused and sullen. "Why, sir?" said Renn. "It's killed people. It's hurt your griffin, it—"

"Go and get some ropes," Arren snarled in a voice that didn't sound like his own at all. "I want you to tie its legs together. And its wings. As many ropes as possible. Don't let it escape."

"But sir—"

"Now!"

They ran away, stung by the rage in his voice. Arren didn't watch them go. He stroked Eluna's face. "Eluna? Eluna, can you hear me?" The wound wasn't bleeding any more, and hope rose inside him. She would be all right. She would survive, she would—

Eluna's beak opened slightly, and she whispered something.

"Eluna?" said Arren. "Eluna, please, just stay awake. Say something."

The white griffin's eyes closed. "Arren," she said, her voice barely audible.

"Open your eyes! Eluna, just—"

Eluna's tail twitched. Her head moved, ever so slightly, and then fell back. Her beak was open, and a little blood trickled out of it. Then, a few moments later, her entire body stilled. She let out a low, soft sigh, and then she didn't move any more.

Arren patted her neck. "Eluna! Eluna!"

Nothing. No response. Nothing but silence. Arren felt for a pulse. There wasn't one.

"Eluna!"

Something wet splattered onto his face. He touched it and realised it was a drop of rain. More of it started to fall. It brought a fresh, green smell with it.

The people had returned. They had brought ropes, and they swarmed over the black griffin, tying its legs and wings and binding up its beak. It lay there, motionless except for the heaving of its sides, not knowing that its freedom was being taken away from it forever.

Arren watched without seeing. He was vaguely aware that there was blood running down his chest, but he felt no pain. He stayed where he was, cradling Eluna's head in his arms, and when people came to him and asked him if he was all right he didn't answer.

8

Taken Sky

The rain helped to wake the black griffin. He opened his eyes—slowly and with a great deal of effort—and found he was lying on his side. He was cold; his feathers were soaked. There was a pain in his chest, and his forelegs hurt. He tried to get up, but found that he couldn't. His legs were tied together, and his wings as well. Thick, strong ropes were holding him down; more ropes bound his beak shut.

Terror shot through him, icy cold and smothering. He began to struggle wildly, pulling on the ropes with all his might, but they would not break. A strange weakness and lassitude filled him and he slumped back onto the ground, gasping for breath. He couldn't breathe properly with his beak tied shut, and the air whistled painfully through his nostrils.

He lay still for a while, taking in his surroundings. He was lying in a field, very close to the human village. There were humans there, standing not far away and watching him. Many were holding sharp objects in their paws. The black griffin hissed warningly at them, and some of them drew back slightly, but they did not run. They knew he was helpless.

The black griffin began to struggle again, trying to move toward them. His legs were still pinioned together, and he began to jerk his entire body, trying to drag himself over the ground. But his hind legs had been tied to his forelegs, and to his wings, and more ropes were attached to stakes driven into the ground. He could not move in any direction, and the more he struggled, the tighter the ropes became. He felt his skin break suddenly; hot blood trickled down over his back paws.

The black griffin slumped back, groaning softly. The rain continued to fall, running in rivulets down his flanks. Dull fear burned inside him. He was trapped. He couldn't fly, couldn't walk, couldn't fight, and the humans were there and watching him, free to do whatever they wanted to him. Would they kill him?

He stretched his neck upward, straining to look ahead, toward the village. The white griffin was lying there, not far away from him. She was dead. He could see the massive wound his talons had torn in her chest. The human was there with her, the one he had chased. It was cradling the dead griffin's head against its chest and staring straight at him.

The black griffin looked back, some of his fear giving way to curiosity. This human was different to the others, in more ways than one. The fur on its head was black instead of brown, and the cloth that covered its body was unfamiliar, too. It had not run when he had swooped on it, but had stood firm and faced him. And there had been a griffin with it. Standing by its side. And when he had chased after it, intent on snatching it up off the ground, the griffin had flown at him. She had attacked him, to defend the human.

And now she was dead and the human was holding on to her body. The black griffin did not understand why. She was dead. What good would it do?

The humans around him were looking toward the one by the dead griffin, as if they were expecting it to do something. The human seemed unaware of them, but then it suddenly stood up and walked away, leaving the white griffin's body lying where it was. The black griffin watched it go, and once again the strange feeling arose in his throat, that feeling of a scream trying to escape. But he could not make a sound.

Arren didn't speak to anyone. He jumped over the fence again and re-entered the village, making for the nearest house. There was a shed attached to it, and he shoved the door open and went inside. He paused a moment to scan the rows of tools, then picked up a shovel and left. People had followed him to the shed and were watching him curiously, but he ignored them and returned to the field where Eluna lay. The black griffin was still there, fighting pointlessly against its bonds. People were poking at it with sticks to torment it, and the creature tried to lunge at them, hissing.

"Leave it alone!" Arren snapped at them. They glanced at him and desisted, though reluctantly.

Arren turned away. He paused a moment, looking down at Eluna's still form, and then thrust the shovel into the ground by her head and began to dig.

People gathered around him.

"Sir?"

"Sir, you're hurt, you should be resting."

"Please, sir, let me do it."

Hands tried to take the shovel from him. Arren jerked it back. *"No!"*

"But sir—"

Arren continued to dig. "Get wood," he muttered. "Build a cage. For the griffin."

"But why, sir? Weren't—shouldn't we kill it?"

"I will take it away," said Arren. "It won't bother you any more. Now get the wood."

"Yes, sir."

Arren didn't watch them go. He continued to dig, not

noticing the splinters digging into his hands, or the pain of the wound in his chest. The rain continued to fall, turning the dirt to mud even as he shovelled it aside. It dripped red off his tunic and turned him cold all over.

He did not stop digging until he had created a large, deep hole, and then he finally threw the shovel aside and returned to Eluna's side. The white griffin's body had gone cold, and her feathers were stained with blood and dirt.

Arren crouched beside her and did his best to smooth down her coat. She wouldn't want to look dirty and bedraggled; she'd always hated rain—

He stopped suddenly, choking back a sob. For a moment he sat still, shuddering, but he managed to control himself again. He lifted Eluna under the shoulders, wrapping his arms around her mangled chest, and began to drag her toward the hole. She came slowly, her wings and legs dragging, head bouncing gently on the ground. Arren fell into the hole and pulled her in after him. She landed on top of him, nearly squashing him, but he struggled out from beneath her and began to arrange her body, gently folding her legs in under her belly and curling her tail around her body. He pulled her wings over her like a shroud, and lifted her head in his hands. "Here," he whispered to her. "You can sleep here, Eluna. You're safe now." He kissed her beak and pulled a feather from her neck. "I'll come back. We'll meet again, Eluna. I promise."

Letting go of her was one of the hardest things he had ever done in his life. He climbed out of the hole, clutching the feather to his chest, and stood there for a time looking down at Eluna's still form. She looked so peaceful. As if she were only sleeping.

Arren's fingers curled around the feather, gripping it so tightly it threatened to snap. He tucked it into his tunic and began to fill in the hole.

Once he was done, he sat down on the mound of earth that marked Eluna's last resting place, wrapped his arms around his legs and put his chin on his knees. Nearby the villagers had dragged some uncut fence posts into the field and were lashing them together into a crude cage around the black griffin. The creature was hissing helplessly at them, its tail thrashing like a headless snake. Arren watched it all through dull eyes, not really taking in what he was seeing. He felt numb and empty, as if reality had fled away from him, rendering him nothing but a mindless shell, unable to feel or think.

People came to him and tried to get him to return to the village, but he wouldn't move or speak, or even look at them. When they gently tried to pull him away by force he shrugged them off, and after that he was alone, in the cold and the wet, listening to the rain drumming on the ground.

He huddled silently on the grave and closed his eyes, but the blackness only showed him a picture of Eluna. Eluna dying in front of him, her blood soaking into the ground and staining his hands. He opened his eyes again and stared blankly at his hands. The blood was still there, ingrained in the skin with the mud and sweat. He tried to wipe it away, but it wouldn't come off. Arren shuddered again and buried his face in his hands.

The cage was nearly completed by now. People had fetched planks and were sliding them under the griffin to create a rough floor. The griffin had given up on its struggling and was lying still, eyes half-closed in a hopeless kind of way. Arren wondered if it had any notion of what awaited it.

He looked away. What did he care?

"Sir!"

Arren paid no attention.

"Sir, look! Sir, look up there!"

The words finally got through to him, and he looked up vaguely. The people building the cage had stopped their work and were chattering excitedly and pointing at the sky.

Arren looked up, the rain splattering onto his face, and saw three dark shapes circling against the grey cloud that had gathered. Winged shapes. Too big to be birds.

Arren looked away again. The three griffins landed in

the field not far away, and their riders dismounted. Arren was woken from his stupor by their voices, and he allowed himself to be hauled to his feet and led out of the field.

They took him to one of the houses and made him lie down on a table, where they took off his tunic and began to clean the wound in his chest. It was deep and ragged and began to bleed again as they carefully removed the dirt. Arren winced and closed his eyes. A hand patted his shoulder. "It's all right, just lie still, you're going to be fine."

Fine! Arren felt like laughing. He kept still as a herbal paste was applied to the wound, and sat up so they could wrap a bandage around his torso.

"There, all done. You'll be all right."

Arren looked up and saw the face of one of the senior griffiners from Eagleholm. "Deanne?"

She clasped his hand. "Arren Cardockson—my gods, you look terrible. Where is your griffin?"

Arren stared at the floor. "She's dead," he whispered.

The three griffiners glanced at each other. "Oh, Arren," said Deanne. "I'm so sorry."

"How did it happen?" one of the others asked.

Arren's hands clenched. "She was . . . trying to protect me."

"From that brute of a wild griffin," the other griffiner finished. "For the love of Gryphus, Arren, what are you doing here? What in the world gave you the idea that you could fight that thing on your own? Are you mad?"

Deanne put her hand on her companion's arm. "Not now, Kryn, please. The boy's in shock. Get him a blanket, would you? And a clean tunic if you can find it."

The third griffiner brought a blanket, and Arren pulled it around himself gratefully. He'd only just realised how cold he was. The blanket warmed him, but his shivering didn't stop. He blinked, puzzled. His hands seemed to be shaking. He tried to make himself breathe deeply, and then before he knew what was happening he had started to gasp for air, his chest heaving. His vision started to go grey around the edges, and lights flashed before his eyes.

He clutched at his chest, wide-eyed. His skin had gone deathly pale and clammy, and the shaking got worse. The three griffiners were there at once. They dragged him to the fireplace and made him lie down in the warmth, laying the blanket over him. Deanne took hold of his hands and squeezed them tightly. "Arren, Arren! Look at me!"

Arren's eyes turned toward her, fixed and bulging.

Deanne patted his face. "Yes, that's right, just look at me. Keep looking. Just breathe deeply. Breathe!"

He started to calm down, and the shaking decreased, but tears were running uncontrollably down his face.

"It's all right," Deanne said softly. "It's all right, Arren. Just keep looking at me. Breathe deeply. In . . . out . . . in . . . out . . . yes, just like that. That's right. You're fine. You're all right. You're all right . . ."

The sound of her voice soothed him, and he slowly relaxed into a faint. When he woke up a few moments later, Deanne gently helped him to his feet.

"There. Careful, steady there . . . All right, just sit down and I'll get you something to eat."

Arren huddled in the chair, letting the fire warm him. He felt a lot better, physically at least. "What . . . happened?" he managed.

"You went into shock," Kryn explained. "It's like a panic. It happens when something very sudden and violent happens to someone. Do you feel better now?"

Arren nodded. "I'm sorry, I didn't mean to—"

"No need to apologise. The same thing would've happened to—well, it's not your fault."

Arren looked at him with a terrible, hopeless expression. "What am I going to do?"

The third griffiner came over, carrying a clean tunic. "Here, put this on. You just rest, all right? We'll take care of everything. There's some more people coming to the village right now by road—we sent them on ahead of us. They'll be taking the griffin back to Eagleholm on a wagon, and we'll all go back home with them."

Arren took the tunic and held on to it as if he had no

idea what it was for. He started to speak and then fell silent and looked away. Deanne brought him some food, but he didn't take it.

She put it into his hands. "Here. Come on, take it. You need to keep your strength up."

Arren started to chew listlessly at the cheese and dried apple. It was poor quality, but he didn't really notice.

"That's better," said Deanne.

Arren looked away and finished his food. It made him feel a little better.

"Now then," said Deanne. Her two companions had left, probably to go and supervise the completion of the cage, but she stayed where she was, her eyes on Arren. "Tell me, what were you doing here?" she asked.

Arren stared into the fire. "I came to fight the griffin. Catch it, if I could. For the reward."

"On your own?" said Deanne. "For Gryphus' sake, Arren, what were you thinking? Do you know how dangerous a wild griffin is? You *never* go after one on your own, even if you *are* a griffiner! Who even told you about it?"

Arren looked up, confused. "It was—" He paused, remembering his promise. "Someone told me about it. He said—well, I have a debt to pay, and someone said I could get some money by catching this griffin, so—"

"Who was it?" said Deanne.

"I—I'm not allowed to say."

She frowned at him. "Why in the world not? Whoever this person is, what did they tell you? Didn't they advise you to take some help?"

"They said I could do it alone," said Arren. "I—I had some poison. To put on my arrows. That's how I caught it."

"What, so this person told you that you could fight a wild griffin on your own, when you're—you've never done anything like this before, have you?"

Arren shook his head.

"But this person persuaded you to do it on your own, without telling anyone where you were going or why, or even asking anyone for advice? Who was it? Was it a griffiner?"

"I thought I could do it. He *said* it was easy, and I—"

"And you just believed him?" Deanne was looking at him in disbelief. "My gods, Arren, I really don't—I never thought you were reckless, but what you did was insane. You're lucky you weren't killed."

A vision of the black griffin flashed across Arren's brain, and he shuddered and felt tears run down his face.

Deanne hugged him. "There, look, just calm down. I'm sorry, Arren, I shouldn't have—here, get up and come with me. You need to keep busy."

"I want to go home," Arren mumbled.

"You will, soon. Just come along and help me, would you? We have to get that cage finished and dragged back into the village. Might need an extra pair of hands. C'mon, up you get."

Arren stood up wearily and let her lead him back to the field. It was still raining. The cage was completed, and the people who'd made it were now busy reinforcing and stabilising it; under the supervision of Kryn and his fellow griffiner. Their griffins were nearby, keeping a close watch on the captive black griffin, not liking being in the rain but refusing to leave their humans unguarded.

The sight sent fresh pain through him, and he gritted his teeth as Deanne helped him over the fence.

"Now, you'd better go and get your bow back," she told him. "Go on, before the rain wrecks it. You'd better take the string off it, too."

Arren felt vaguely irritated by her motherly tone, but he wandered off obediently and found his bow, lying where he'd dropped it. He removed the bowstring and threw it away. The rain had already ruined it. The quiver wasn't too far away; he gathered up the fallen arrows and stuffed them back in, along with the unstrung bow. The work helped; he concentrated on what he was doing and let his mind go blank. It was better that way.

Once he'd slung the quiver on his back, he turned to see what the others were doing. The villagers had finished working on the cage and were now trying to lift it. Arren wondered briefly why they weren't just dragging it, and then realised that the cage would probably come apart if they did. Besides, the ground was now very soft underfoot and dragging anything large and heavy over it would be a nightmare. Lifting it, though, didn't look like a much easier option.

A strange energy filled him. He walked over to the cage. "Can I help?"

They glanced at him. "Shouldn't you be resting, sir?" someone asked.

"Can you lift it?" Arren asked, ignoring him.

"Possibly," said Kryn. He glanced at the people who'd spaced themselves around the cage. There were plenty of them; most of the village's population had come to help. "All right, has everyone got a grip? Good. Now, *heave!*"

They lifted as one. The bars of the cage shifted dangerously, straining against their binding, but it came up out of the mud with a faint sucking sound.

"All right, let's move," said Kryn, pulling it toward the fence. The carriers shuffled in that direction for a short distance before they had to stop and put down the cage so they could rest.

Tamran, the third of the griffiners, stretched and rubbed his back. "Ow. Well, it'll take ages, but we'll make it. Eventually."

Arren had been looking for a spot where he could get a grip and help move the cage, but couldn't find one. In the end he settled for walking on ahead and warning people about unexpected tussocks and other things they could trip on. As they neared the fence he looked over at it and paused—how were they going to get the cage over it?

"Kryn?"

Kryn glanced at him. "Yes, Arren? What is it?"

"How are we going to get it past the fence?"

"I've already asked about that," said Kryn, rubbing his chafed hands. "The nearest gate is all the way back there, so we're going to take out the palings. Arren, can you go into the village and find something to take the nails out with?"

Arren nodded and walked off, glad to be doing something useful. He went back to the shed where he'd found the shovel, and took down a hammer from a shelf. It had a pair of prongs on the back for removing nails—he knew their purpose from the brief time he'd spent helping to replace some planks near the edge back at Eagleholm.

It should do the trick. He took it back to the fence and began levering out the nails that held the palings in place. The nails were old and rusted, and several of them broke in the process, but he got them all out and lifted the heavy pieces of wood out of the way, leaving a large gap in the fence which the cage should fit through. It did, and the bearers staggered their way into the village and finally set it down in a handy barn.

Kryn leant against the cage and wiped the rainwater off his forehead. "Phew! Thank gods that's over. Well done, Arren. And to the rest of you—excellent job. I'll see to it that you're all properly compensated for your time. I hope there aren't any problems with keeping this in here until the wagons arrive to pick it up?"

"It shouldn't be a problem, sir," said the man who owned the barn.

"Good, good. Now, if you don't mind, I'd like to have a word with my friends here."

The villagers left. Arren paused, not knowing if he should go with them, but Kryn gestured at him to join the griffiners.

The three griffins had stationed themselves around the cage and were watching its occupant. The black griffin stared back, unmoving.

"Now," said Kryn, "someone has to keep an eye on it. Keep it fed and watered and make sure it doesn't escape. They'll have to stay here during the night as well. We can't leave it unguarded for a moment."

"Why?" said Tamran.

"Some of those people looked quite angry," said Kryn. "It's been killing their friends and family, don't forget. I wouldn't be surprised if some of them want a chance to take their revenge on it now it can't fight back."

"Oh," said Tamran. "Good point." He glanced at the others. "Who's going to do it, then?"

"I will," said Arren.

They looked at him. "Arren, you really shouldn't," said Tamran. "You've had a nasty accident, and—well, you should be resting. Why did you even come out into the field again?"

"Because I told him to," Deanne interrupted. "His injury isn't that bad, and it won't do him any good to sit around on his own. He needs to keep occupied. It's the best way to deal with stress. If you want to guard the cage, Arren, by all means, do it. I'll ask someone to set up a bed for you in here."

"Just a hammock," said Arren.

"All right, if that's what you want. And"—Deanne glanced at the black griffin—"be careful. Don't get cocky just because it's tied up. And if anyone else comes in here, keep a close watch on them. If anyone killed this griffin they would be guilty of having destroyed the Eyrie's property, and it would be our duty to arrest them. No matter who they were," she added meaningfully.

Arren unslung his quiver and sat down on a bale of hay. "I'll be sure to keep a lookout, then," he said shortly.

He spent the rest of that day sitting in the barn, watching the black griffin. A trough was brought and placed by the cage, close enough for the creature to reach, and Deanne brought a bucket of water to fill it with. "We'll take the ropes off its beak now," she told Arren. "Let it drink."

Arren stood up. "But it might use magic." Griffins used their mouths to cast magic, which was yet another good reason to keep this one's beak tied shut.

Deanne put the bucket aside and drew her knife. "I doubt it. It's probably more interested in a drink right now. And I've added something to the water. It'll make it drowsy."

Her griffin thrust a foreleg through the bars of the cage and pinned the black griffin's head down, and Deanne

reached in and cut the ropes around its beak. She withdrew swiftly, and once she was well out of reach her griffin
released his captive. The black griffin's head shot forward
in the blink of an eye, and its beak narrowly missed the
other griffin's leg. The other griffin hit it in the face with
his talons and returned to Deanne's side, his tail twitching
in a dignified manner.

Arren had restrung his bow with one of his spares, and
he nocked an arrow and pointed it at the black griffin's
head, ready to loose it the instant the creature showed any
sign of using magic. But the black griffin only glared at
him and then dragged itself toward the trough. It poked
its beak through the bars and drank awkwardly, throwing
back its head to swallow. Once it had satisfied its thirst it
laid its head down and sighed. It looked exhausted, and no
wonder, but Arren glanced at Deanne before he relaxed the
bowstring.

Deanne scratched her griffin's neck. "It should have
taken enough. Watch; it's working already."

Sure enough, the black griffin's eyes were closing. It
yawned and clumsily folded its legs under its belly, and a
few moments later its tail ceased its twitching.

"There," said Deanne. "It'll sleep for the rest of the day,
most likely, and when it wakes up it'll still be weak and
confused. Even if you did get close enough for it to attack
you, it won't be able to see properly. That doesn't mean you
should tempt fate, though."

Arren shook his head. "I'm not stupid."

"Good. We'll give it something to eat in the morning.
Everything it eats or drinks from now on will be drugged.
We can't risk it being properly awake. You just stay here
and don't leave unless you have to."

"Yes, my lady," said Arren, suddenly remembering his
manners.

"You don't have to call me that," Deanne said kindly.
She glanced around at the barn's interior. "It may get a
bit boring in here on your own—d'you want something to
read? I brought a book with me."

Arren nodded. Why not?

"All right. I'll bring it along, and some food as well."

She came back with a bowl of hot stew in her hand and a book tucked under one arm.

"Here you go," she said, giving him the stew. "That should warm you up." She placed the book on the hay bale beside him. "It's not a bad read at all, quite interesting. It was a present from my son." The title was *A History of the Peoples of Cymria*.

Arren took the spoon out of the bowl of stew. "Thank you."

"Not a problem. I'll come back later and visit you."

Deanne left with her griffin beside her, the two of them moving together, almost as if they were one being. Never completely alone.

Arren ate the stew. It was mostly vegetables, with some low-grade meat mixed in, but it tasted fine and was hot. He paused between spoonfuls to check on the black griffin. It was still asleep, perhaps lulled by the rain drumming on the roof. Arren was glad about that. He didn't want to see those silver eyes staring at him again.

He finished the stew and put the bowl aside. Now that he was alone and had nothing to distract him, there was nothing to stop him thinking. Nothing to keep him from starting to realise the enormity of what had happened.

Eluna was dead.

Arren stared and stared at the black griffin. It had killed her. It had taken away his partner, his protector, his friend. It had taken Eluna. An image of her danced behind his eyes, like lightning in darkness: the wound in her chest, like a massive eye weeping blood. He saw the black griffin's talons descending on him and heard its screech in his ears. His hands ached for his sword. He imagined bringing the blade down on the black griffin's neck or driving it into the creature's flank.

Arren started to reach for his bow. All he had to do was hit it once, in the eye, or maybe the chest. He could say it had woken up and tried to break out. He could say it had lunged at him and that he'd panicked. He could say all sorts of things.

They wouldn't believe him.

He picked up the bow and took an arrow from the quiver. It was right there, right in front of him, completely helpless. He could kill it in an instant. What did it matter if he got in trouble? He had captured the griffin. It belonged to him now. The owners of the Arena couldn't complain if he chose not to sell it to them.

Arren stood up and walked slowly toward the cage, drawing the bowstring back tight. He pointed the arrow through the bars, aiming the point at the black griffin's eye. He couldn't possibly miss. *Just let go,* his inner voice whispered. *Just let go.*

"Arren?"

Arren turned sharply. Deanne, standing in the doorway, flung up a hand. "Arren!"

Her griffin sprang forward, snarling, and Arren realised he was pointing the arrow straight at the griffiner. He hastily relaxed the string and threw the bow aside. "Deanne, I'm sorry. You surprised me."

The red griffin hissed at him, tail swishing, and Arren bowed low to him. "I am sorry," he said in griffish. "I did not mean to do that."

The red griffin eyed him suspiciously for a few moments and then returned to Deanne's side. She laid a hand on his shoulders but kept her eyes on Arren. "What were you doing?"

Arren went back to the bale of hay and sat down. "I thought it was stirring," he said.

Deanne glanced at the black griffin, which hadn't moved an inch since it had fallen asleep. "No need to be so jittery. It's sound asleep. And you really shouldn't point an arrow at it like that; you could very easily have let go of the string by accident. And don't stand so close to the bars. I already warned you about that."

"Sorry."

She came over and placed a large iron lantern next to him. "Here. For when it gets dark."

"Can I have some blankets?"

"Oh, yes, of course. Sorry, I completely forgot. I'd better see about that hammock, too."

Arren paused as something suddenly occurred to him. "Deanne?"

"Yes?"

"Why did you come here?"

"We came here to deal with the griffin," said Deanne. "We'd been given the assignment about a week before you suddenly disappeared."

Arren stared at her. "You mean you knew about it all the way back then?"

"Of course we did. We don't just rush off on these assignments, you know. They have to be planned first. We left the day after you did."

"Who told you about it?"

"Lord Rannagon, of course. He always handles things like this. What's the matter?"

Arren looked away. "I—nothing. Never mind. I was just curious."

Deanne frowned at him. For a moment she looked as if she was going to say something, but then she turned away, saying, "I'll just go and get those blankets."

Arren stared at the book without really seeing it. His mind was racing. What was going on?

9

To Home

The black griffin didn't wake up for the rest of the day, and by the time night came it was still asleep. It lay very still, its breathing slow and peaceful, its tail twitching from time to time. Plenty of people ventured into the barn to look at it, muttering in astonishment when they saw how huge it was. None of them ventured too close, but Arren kept an eye on them anyway. Some of them tried to talk to him, but his replies were curt and unfriendly, and they quickly realised that he wasn't interested and left him alone.

He became bored with watching them and opened the book. It was a beautiful thing; the pages were high-quality parchment, and the writing on them was neat and done in fine black ink. There were illustrations, too. He turned the pages carefully, skimming through the information on them. There was a section for each of Cymria's regions and their different customs. Eagleholm. Withypool. Wylam. Canran. He turned a page and came across the section about Northerners.

A picture stared up at him. It was of a man, tall and sinewy, with pale skin. He was clad in a long black robe, which was open at the front to reveal a narrow, scarred chest and a pair of black leggings. His hair was black and decorated with feathers and bone discs, and he had long fingers and a thin, angular face painted with blue spirals. He had a small, pointed beard and carried a long spear in one hand. The eyes were black and stared coldly straight at Arren.

Arren sighed and, in spite of himself, started to read the text on the next page.

The people of the North, also known as the "darkmen" or "blackrobes," live in an icy and inhospitable part of the country. They are a primitive race, noted for their savage and heathen ways and for their cruelty in battle. They worship the dark Night God and speak a harsh, crude language, but have neither the wit nor culture for writing or art. Their songs and legends are barbaric and unsophisticated, full of tales of battle and slaughter, and unlike the other people of Cymria, they are not unified but constantly fight amongst themselves.

After the coming of the griffiners and the creation of a united nation under their rule, the blackrobes attempted to make forays into the warmer lands of the South but were driven back. War ensued, and the griffiners led a massive assault on the North which became known as the Blackrobe War. The blackrobes were soundly defeated and their cities destroyed. Most were massacred, but many others were taken back to the South as slaves.

Very few free blackrobes now survive in Cymria, and in fact the very name "blackrobe" has become synonymous with "slave." And yet blackrobes have achieved many great things in the modern age. They were responsible for the building of most of the great griffiner cities, including Eagleholm, Withypool, Canran and Wylam. Woodger's Dam was also the work of blackrobe slaves, and indeed the dam is said to have been named after a blackrobe who drowned in it shortly after the wall was completed.

That was all it said, but there were some other illustrations: pictures of a row of black-robed men and women, their wrists shackled together, slave collars clamped around their necks, carrying heavy rocks to a half-completed dam wall, and another of them hauling huge split logs up a mountainside. He recognised the mountain and the lake half-hidden behind it. They were building Eagleholm.

And there was a detailed illustration of a slave collar, a thick metal band hinged so it could be opened and closed. The inside of it was studded with sharp metal spikes. When the collar was put on, the spikes would be driven into the wearer's neck—not deeply enough to kill or seriously injure, but deeply enough to cause constant pain. Any attempt to remove the collar would only make it hurt more. A perfect device to kill someone's spirit.

Arren slammed the book shut and dumped it on the hay beside him. He couldn't bear to have it so close and finally stuffed it down the side of the bale and out of sight.

He looked up. People were staring at him.

"What are you looking at?" he demanded.

His outburst provoked several shocked looks, but no-one answered. They moved away from him, and most of them left the barn altogether. Arren retrieved his bow and sat down cross-legged with the weapon lying across his lap, glowering at anyone who looked in his direction. Eventually the last of the spectators left, and he was alone with the black griffin, still sleeping in its cage.

The sun was going down, and darkness was gathering in the barn. Arren stayed where he was, not bothering to light the lantern. He had good night vision. Always had done.

His anger didn't last. He looked down at his hands. The fingers were long and thin and sprinkled with black hairs. A blackrobe's hands.

Arren rubbed his eyes. Misery and despair were starting to close in on him, bringing a blackness over his mind as the shadows gathered around him. Eluna was dead. He wasn't a griffiner any more. Now he was . . . what?

Nothing. He was nothing now. With Eluna gone, he felt more alone than he had ever been in his life. For as long as he could remember she had been there beside him, guiding him. She was his friend, but more than that she had defined his very identity.

Without Eluna, Arren felt his world crumbling to pieces around him.

The black griffin sighed in its cage. Arren looked at it. He could just see it, a black, hunched mass in the gloom, moving up and down slightly as it breathed.

The black griffin would never fly again. Not in the Arena. They would cut its feathers and chain its wings together. They even cut the wings off some of the wild griffins they used in the pit, or so some people claimed.

How long would it survive? Some wild griffins lived in the cages under the Arena for years before they finally died—from stress or starvation, or in the Arena. Or from despair. Plenty of people disliked the Arena, particularly griffiners. But there was little chance of it being shut down in the near future. It generated too much money, and people liked it too much. If it was removed, there would probably be riots.

It was too dark to see anything now, but Arren continued to stare at the spot where the wild griffin lay. It had killed humans, and now its punishment would be to kill more of them. In a way, this griffin would soon become a slave just like Arren's parents had been.

Kept alive because it had a use, and fated to die on the day that its usefulness ran out.

"You poor bastard," Arren muttered.

No-one had brought him the hammock he'd asked for, so he slept on the bale of hay. It was uncomfortable, but he was too exhausted to notice much. He slept fitfully, constantly disturbed by brief snatches of bad dreams. Bits of memory replaying themselves in his mind. His chest hurt, preventing him from lying on his side, and when he woke up shortly before dawn he decided to give up the struggle and stop trying to sleep. He sat up and checked on the griffin. It still hadn't moved, but he could see it beginning to stir. The drug had worn off.

Arren sat with a blanket around his shoulders, sagging a little with tiredness, and resumed watching his charge.

The black griffin woke up slowly; he could see it moving its head. The light of the rising sun was coming in through the high window of the barn, all grey and sleepy, making everything colourless. The griffin finally seemed to revive, and made an attempt to get up. The ropes around its legs must have loosened slightly, because it managed to half-stand and turn itself around in the cage. It slumped down again, its head now turned toward Arren. He could see it watching him.

"Good morning," he said in griffish, without really thinking about it.

The black griffin blinked and raised its head a little. "You . . . human?" it rasped.

Arren started a little. It hadn't really occurred to him that the thing could speak. "Yes," he said.

"You . . . kill?" said the griffin.

"I don't understand," said Arren. "Kill what? Kill you?"

The black griffin blinked slowly. It still looked rather sluggish. "Human kill," it said eventually.

"You killed humans," said Arren. "We should kill you, but we won't. You're coming with me. To Eagleholm."

"Eagle . . . home?"

The black griffin spoke griffish slowly and clumsily, as if it was a chick. Arren watched it curiously. "Do you have a name?" he asked.

"Name?" the griffin repeated dully.

"You know," said Arren. "A name. What are you called?"

The black griffin just stared at him.

Arren persisted. He placed a hand on his chest. "Arren Cardockson," he said.

More staring.

"That's my name. My name is Arren. Arren," he repeated, touching his chest.

"Ah . . . rin?" said the black griffin.

Arren could see he wasn't getting through. "Can't you speak properly?"

The black griffin seemed to understand that. "Not speak. Not . . . know."

"You don't know how?"

The griffin started to bite at the ropes holding its fore-legs together. Arren reached for his bow, but it gave up a few moments later and rested its head on the ground in front of it. "Want . . . fly," it said plaintively.

"You can't," said Arren.

The black griffin started up suddenly and screamed at him. *"Want fly!"*

Arren snatched up his bow and nocked an arrow onto it, pointing it at the griffin. "Sit down!" he snapped. "Sit down or I'll hurt you."

The griffin hurled itself at the bars, making the whole cage shake. "Kill!" it screamed at him. "I kill! I kill human!"

Arren got up and came toward it, pointing the arrow at its open beak. "I said *sit down!*"

The griffin ignored him. It jammed its head between two of the bars and started to snap its beak at him, still screaming threats.

Arren loosed the arrow. It hit the griffin in the shoulder, and the creature screamed and reeled, its pinioned wings jerking as it tried to fly away. Arren reloaded the bow. "Lie down, or I'll do it again. *Now!*"

The black griffin stopped abruptly, eyeing him. Arren gestured meaningfully at it with the arrow, and the creature subsided back onto the floor.

"All right," Arren said softly. "I'll take that arrow out of your shoulder. But if you move . . ."

He laid the bow down, moving slowly and carefully, and reached through the bars. The griffin watched him but didn't move, and he took hold of the arrow-shaft and pulled it out with one quick motion. The black griffin screeched and bit him. Arren smacked it in the eye with the back of his hand and then pulled his arm out of the cage. The black griffin hissed and shook its head at him, its eye half-closed.

Arren pointed at it, ignoring the blood dripping from his arm. "I am not afraid of you," he told it in a low voice. "And if you try that again, I will make you sorry."

The griffin couldn't possibly understand all of what he'd said, but the stern voice and steady gaze were enough. It stared back, glaring, trying to scare him, but he held firm and didn't blink or look away. In the end, the griffin looked at the ground in a gesture of defeat.

Arren felt strangely confident. He'd been among griffins all his life, and he knew how to deal with one that was being aggressive. He could deal with this one. "That's better," he told it. "I'll bring you some food. If you're gentle with me, I'll be gentle with you."

"Arren, what's going on?"

Arren turned. It was Tamran, looking rather tousled, with his griffin beside him.

He straightened up. "The drug's worn off," he said, reverting to Cymrian. "It started getting a bit worked up—had to threaten it. Sorry it woke you up."

Tamran rubbed his eyes. "'Sall right, Keea wanted feeding anyway. Did you sleep?"

Arren shook his head. "We should probably feed it now," he said, gesturing at the cage and its occupant.

Tamran yawned. "Yes, yes, I'll have something sent along." He turned and shuffled out.

"Could I please have—" Arren began, but the other griffiner had gone. He returned to his seat.

No-one came until well after sunrise. When the sun was up, the owner of the barn came to check on him.

Arren stood up. "Excuse me, could you help me, please?"

"Yes, sir," said the man. "What can I do for you?"

"I need something to eat. And some food for the griffin."

The man cast a murderous look at the creature. "I don't understand why you're keeping it alive, sir. What use is it?"

"I came here to catch it, not kill it. I have a debt to pay. I'm going to take it back to Eagleholm and sell it to the owners of the Arena. It'll spend the rest of its life disembowelling criminals."

"They really do that with them, sir?"

"Yes. Will you please get me some food?"

"Yes, sir." The man left.

He returned a while later with bread and apples and fresh milk. Arren tucked in very gratefully. "What about the griffin?" he asked between bites.

The man looked unhappy. "Well, how much will it want, sir?"

Arren swallowed a mouthful of apple. "Not too much. One haunch should do it. About this big." He indicated the size with his hands.

The man looked even less happy about this. "I see. Um, I'm not sure. I haven't got a carcass handy right now. But one of my neighbours has got a cow that's on its way out; I could go and ask him."

Arren paused. It hadn't occurred to him that they probably wouldn't have large pieces of meat just lying around. Keeping cows was expensive, and only the wealthy ate fresh meat regularly. Everyone else had to have theirs dried or salted or made into a kind of hard smoked sausage which had to be soaked before eating. "You'll be properly paid for it," he said eventually.

"Yes, sir. I'll see what I can do, sir."

Once the man had gone, Arren bit into the apple again and glared at the griffin. "I hope you know how much trouble you've caused everyone."

The griffin stared back at him. It didn't say anything, but there was a question in its eyes.

Arren looked away. "I should have killed you," he muttered.

The griffin didn't try to speak to him again, but as the day began and Arren continued his vigil, it continued to watch him. A bloody hunk of meat was brought in around noon and dumped on the floor by the cage and the black griffin tore into it at once.

After eating, it drank from the trough and slipped back into a drugged sleep.

The rain had stopped by now, and the sun shone in

through the windows, turning the air gold with suspended
particles of hay. Arren dozed in the warmth. He lay on his
side, one hand curled under his chin, face creasing occasionally in time with his dreams.

It took two days for the wagons to arrive. Arren spent
them almost exclusively in the barn, guarding his charge.
Deanne offered to take over for him but he refused. He
didn't want to leave. Somehow the idea of going out into
the sun again almost frightened him, as if leaving the barn
would mean breaking out of the numbness that had taken
hold of him after Eluna's death. Now that the initial shock
had worn off and his wound had begun to heal, he found
that he couldn't think about her any more. She would slip
out of his mind every time he tried. But it wasn't that he
didn't feel any pain. There was pain, buried somewhere
under the emptiness of his heart and mind. But it stayed
where it was and let him go on living in a hollow, pointless kind of way. All he could really think about now was
home. He wanted to see Flell again, and his parents. And
he had some vague notion that if he could get back to his
house then everything would be all right again.

When the trio of wagons arrived from Lansdown, Arren
helped the bearers load the black griffin onto one of them.
The cage was lashed down with rope and covered with a
large piece of sackcloth, and boxes of supplies were stacked
around it to stop it shaking too much. A second wagon was
reserved for the griffiners; it was covered and contained
bedding for the three of them to sleep on. The third one
was packed with straw and was for the griffins.

There was no room in either of them for Arren. He
elected to sit on the back of the supply wagon, where
there was just enough space for him to lie down, albeit
uncomfortably. Once everything had been loaded up and
the inhabitants of Rivermeet had been thanked and given
money for their trouble, the procession got underway.

Arren sat on the splintery wood at the back of the wagon,

listening to the griffin shifting restlessly in its cage, and watched the village slowly recede into the distance. A small place. Not a particularly interesting one, either. *I'll come back,* he thought. *I swear I'll come back one day. To see you again.*

He could just see the field where he had buried Eluna, visible between the houses. He was leaving her behind, he realised. He was abandoning her.

For a moment he was seized by a wild impulse to jump down from the wagon and run back to the village and beyond it to the field, but he didn't move. It was in that instant that the full impact of what had happened began to dawn on him.

Arren bowed his head and started to cry.

The journey passed miserably. No-one paid much attention to Arren. Even his fellow griffiners seemed to be avoiding him, as if they were embarrassed to talk to him. He didn't try to seek out their company, or talk to any of the wagoners or the mounted guards who rode alongside the procession. It rained for most of the way, and the cover over the supply wagon wasn't quite able to shelter him completely, so his clothes and blankets were constantly damp. When they stopped for the night at various inns along the way, he quietly refused to go indoors and remained at his post. It wasn't that he particularly cared about guarding the griffin, he realised eventually. But the prospect of being with other people did not appeal to him. All his life, people had known he was a Northerner as soon as they looked at him, and he had always hated it. Even when they didn't say anything, he could tell what they were thinking. It was in the way they looked at him. In these places, people didn't know of him. He didn't know how they would react to his presence, and he wasn't interested in finding out.

And then, at last, Eagleholm came into sight. Arren heard the driver of the supply wagon point it out to one of the guards, and stood up to look ahead to where the mountain jutted up from the landscape. They would be there before nightfall. He sat back down again.

The rain had stopped, and the damp ground was steaming slightly in the heat from the returning sun. Arren crossed his legs and scratched his chin. He'd forgotten to take a razor with him to Rivermeet, and by now he'd grown quite a thick thatch of stubble. He hated that. It made him feel grubby and unkempt. But he supposed he would have looked untidy even if he was clean-shaven. At Rivermeet he'd been given some fresh clothes to wear, but they were too large for him and had picked up quite a bit of dirt along the way. *I must look ridiculous,* he thought miserably.

Thunder rumbled overhead. Behind him, the black griffin shifted and bashed its beak against the bars of its cage. It had spent most of the journey drugged, but when it was awake it spent a lot of time thumping on the wood around it. Arren didn't know why. It wasn't vigorous enough to be a real attempt to escape; it was just a mindless action that went on forever. Thump, thump, thump.

It started to rain again.

The thumping went on. Arren was used to it by now and could shut it out, but it filtered through to his brain, mingling with the sound of the rain on the wagon's cover. It was almost rhythmic, really.

As he watched the landscape slowly roll by, he found himself thinking about his childhood. He'd grown up in Idun, living there even after Eluna had chosen him.

Unlike other griffiners, his training had taken place in secret—supported by Roland, who passed on his knowledge whenever his Northern protégé came to visit. After they had been discovered and the Eyrie had been forced to accept the situation, Roland had lent Arren enough money to buy his own house in the city. He was still paying off the debt, which was one reason why he hadn't been able to afford to pay Rannagon's fine.

That made him angry. Most griffiners were wealthy. Even those who didn't have high-paying positions generally had inherited wealth. Supposedly anyone could become a griffiner, but Arren knew that wasn't true. The griffiners currently in power were descendants of griffiners, and some could trace their ancestry all the way back to the ancient warlords who had first conquered their fellow humans and become the ruling elite. The griffins knew this, and so did everyone else. It wasn't so much that commoners were forbidden the chance to win a griffin's respect—more that a griffin was much more likely to be interested in a human who was already powerful and who had, moreover, grown up among griffins. Plenty of new griffiners already spoke griffish, learnt from their parents or grandparents, even though it was technically forbidden for anyone but a griffiner to know the language. Those who made the rules were allowed to break them. That the son of two slaves who spoke no griffish and had no power or status at all had managed to become a griffiner was extraordinary.

Thinking back on those early days made a terrible ache arise in Arren's throat. It made him want to scream or cry, but he made no sound. He started to hum. Then, quietly, he started to sing.

Ar y waun, y diwrnod hwnnw,
Rhoddaist flodyn i mi,
Blodyn cyn wynned â'r lloer

Ond nawr rwyt wedi mynd—
Gwynwood y blodyn,
A'm calon sydd ddued â'r nos.

It was an old song, one his mother had taught him. She said that their ancestors had sung it at night in the slave-houses, when the moon was up and they were alone after a hard day's work. They had been forbidden to speak their own language, but they had continued to do so anyway, among themselves.

The griffin struck the wood harder. Arren stopped singing and got up, muttering to himself. It was probably time to feed the wretched thing again. He took a piece of

dried meat from a bag and sprinkled it with yellowish liquid from a bottle—more sleeping draught. Loading the
cage onto the lifter would be a lot easier if the griffin was
unconscious. He lifted the cloth away and tossed the meat
through the bars. The black griffin stopped striking the
planking beneath it and snapped it up. Once it had swallowed the food it resumed its monotonous beating and
Arren returned to his seat. He listened to the thuds until
they finally stopped, and then sighed in relief. It had disturbed him at night more than once doing that, and he suspected that it was only encouraged to go on doing it when
he gave it more food to shut it up. But he couldn't think of
any other way to make it stop. It didn't respond to threats
any more.

After a while, lulled by the sound of the rain, Arren
slipped into a doze.

He was woken up some unknown time later by loud
voices. As he straightened up and rubbed his eyes, he
realised the wagon had stopped. Their path had ended
between a pair of large stone buildings, the warehouses
used to store supplies before they were taken up to the city
on the massive platform attached to the lifter. They had
arrived.

Arren jumped down from the back of the wagon and
stretched. He was horribly stiff and sore. He winced and
rubbed his back while the guards and the wagoners identified themselves to the workers in charge of the lifter. The
griffiners had already come out of their own wagon and
were busy preparing to fly off. Tamran was putting his griffin's harness on, and as Arren watched, he got on her back
and said something to her. She walked away from the wagons for a short distance before she took off, flying up toward
the city. They were probably going to report to the Eyrie.

"Oi!"

Arren looked up. One of the guards had approached
him. "Yes?"

The guard pointed at him. "Start unloading the wagon,

and hurry up, we don't want anything to get any wetter than it has to be."

Arren stared at him. "I'm sorry?"

"You heard me," said the guard. "Get on with it. You've done sod-all on this trip, and I'm tired."

The curt command in the man's voice irritated Arren. "You *could* say please," he said.

The guard hit him on the ear. "Who d'you think you are—a griffiner?"

The insult stung him more than the blow did. He was about to argue, but then dull depression settled over him. What was the point? He lifted a box down from the wagon. It was heavy. "Do I just put it on the platform?" he asked.

"Yeah, now move it."

Arren changed his mind. He put down the box and glared at the guard. "Excuse me, but what d'you think you're doing?"

The guard hit him again. "I'm *telling* you to get to work before I thump you in the nose, blackrobe."

Arren snapped. He pulled his dagger out of his belt and pointed it at him. "If you call me that again, I swear to gods I'll kill you."

Instantly the guard darted forward and struck him on the wrist, making him yelp and drop the dagger. The guard flicked it away with his foot and punched Arren in the face, so hard he knocked him off his feet. Arren hit the back of the wagon quite hard and landed in the mud, but he rolled when he hit the ground and was upright in a moment. He nearly attacked the guard, in spite of the man's armour and sword, but at that point Deanne came running up.

"What in Gryphus' name is going on?" she demanded, reaching for her sword.

The guard bowed his head to her. "I'm sorry for the fuss, my lady, but your slave needs to be disciplined."

Arren started forward. *"I—am—not—a slave!"* he roared.

"Well, you bloody look like one," said the guard, unmoved. "Where's his collar, anyway?"

Deanne covered her face with her hand. "Oh gods—just get out of here, please."

"Yes, my lady."

Arren snatched up his dagger from the ground and stuffed it into his belt. "Thanks," he muttered.

Deanne sighed. "I'm so sorry, Arren. It never occurred to me that we hadn't told any of them who you are."

"Oh, I think they already know who I am," said Arren, unable to stop himself. "Nobody. Should I—" He glanced back at the cage. "I should probably go to the Arena with it. I caught it, after all."

"Yes, you should," said Deanne. "And after that you should go to the Eyrie. They'll want to hear your account of what happened."

In other words, he was going to have to try to explain himself. But he didn't intend to be the only one.

10

The Arena

Arren had to wait while the supplies were unloaded from around the black griffin's cage, which took some time. He briefly considered going to visit his parents while he was in the area, but he couldn't bear the thought of having to tell them what had happened. Right now he felt a shaky kind of strength, and he was going to need it. He did his best to sustain that feeling as the last of the crates were taken down and carried to the lifter. Now that the wagon had nothing on it but the griffin's cage, the wagoner got back onto his seat and urged the horses onto the narrow road that led around the side of the mountain. There was another lifting device directly under the Arena, used for no other purpose than lifting newly caught wild griffins into their prison. Arren sat by the cage and watched the rain dripping from the underside of the city's platform. It was astonishing, really, that something so huge had been built and then maintained for such a long time. The platform needed constant repairing and reinforcement, though; thousands of wooden and metal struts had been placed between it and the side of the mountain to help hold it up. Arren thought of the slaves who had put those first few planks into place. He couldn't imagine how they had done it. He wondered how many of them had fallen to their deaths from the mountainside. Hundreds, probably.

Arren shivered and turned away.

Someone, probably Tamran, must have gone ahead and alerted the winch operators, because the platform had already been lowered, ready to receive the cage. A group of large, hefty men were waiting on it. The wagon stopped alongside, and Arren got down and went to meet them.

One of them bowed to him. "Evening, sir. You're the griffiner who caught it, right?"

The wagoner turned sharply in his seat. "You're a *griffiner*?" he said.

Arren ignored him. "I'm Arren Cardockson." He gestured at the cage. "I'm not sure you'll be able to lift it; it's a big one."

"Not a problem, sir," said the man, going to inspect it. "We know how to deal with this sort of thing." He climbed up onto the wagon with several of his colleagues and lifted the cloth away.

Several of them uttered exclamations of astonishment. "Dear gods, look at the *coat* on that thing!"

"I've never seen anything like it," said one of them. "Where'd you catch it, sir?"

"Rivermeet," said Arren. "Near the Coppertops."

The man grinned at him. "Well done, sir. It's a magnificent brute. People'll queue up for days to see this." He glanced at the griffin again, which hadn't moved. "Drugged, right?"

Arren nodded. "Just a sleeping draught."

"Good idea, sir. It looks pretty healthy—got any injuries?"

"Two arrow wounds, but I've treated them. They're healing. Oh, and some scratches on its face there, just above the beak, but they're nothing serious."

"Good, good. You're going to get a handsome price for

this one, sir. All right, just stand aside and we'll get it down off the wagon."

Arren went to stand by the platform while they spaced themselves around the cage and lifted it down. They were strong and well organised, and got it onto the platform with surprising speed. Once it was on, the apparent leader said, "All right, sir, you an' me will ride up with it, an' my mates will wait until the platform's sent down again for them. Can't afford to overload this thing. Up you get."

Arren stepped onto the platform, and the man tied the rope barriers into place at the front to stop either of them from sliding off. This done, he tugged sharply on a rope that dangled by one of the thick cables that disappeared into a hole in the city platform high above. A few moments later the cables went taut and the platform slowly started to rise. Arren sat down beside the cage and concentrated on watching its occupant.

The man was also watching the griffin, with considerable admiration. "I've never even heard of a black griffin before. Have you, sir?"

Arren shook his head.

"I saw a green griffin once," the man went on. "Well, it was sort of dark brown, but it had green on its neck. Belonged to an ambassador from somewhere in the east. It brought its human to the Arena to watch a fight. I talked to him. The griffiner, I mean. He said the griffin could make plants grow. Now, that's a kind of magic I'd like to see."

"How do you stop the griffins using their magic in the Arena?" said Arren.

"Oh, it's simple enough, sir. We drug 'em. There's a potion you can use that suppresses their magic. We put it in their food and water. Some of 'em figure out what's going on, but they have to go on taking it or they starve. After a while they get so they can't use magic at all any more. When I was a lad there was a griffin that managed to get its magic back somehow. It set half the damn Arena on fire— excuse me, sir. They had to kill it in the end. Still"—he watched the sleeping griffin—"I can't help but be curious. What would a black griffin be able to do?"

Arren eyed it with unconcealed hatred. "I'd rather not find out."

Arren had met the owner of the Arena, a man named Orome, once before, and astonishingly enough he was a griffiner. Orome walked around the cage, examining the black griffin while his own griffin, Sefer, looked on.

He whistled. "Well, damn me. The thing really *is* black."

"How much will you give me for it?" said Arren.

Orome scratched the long scar that went across his forehead. "The standard price for a good-sized wild griffin is about three hundred oblong, but for one this big and in such good shape, and with that coat, I'd be willing to raise the price to, say, five hundred. I won't go any higher than five hundred and fifty."

"Five hundred and seventy and it's yours," said Arren.

"Fine," said Orome. "Just you wait a bit while I get it into a cage and see if it's in as good a shape as it looks, all right?"

Orome nodded to a couple of assistants who were standing by. They came forward and cut through the ropes holding the bars on one side of the cage in place. The crude wooden bars fell away and were quickly removed, and the two of them entered the cage and snapped a set of heavy iron manacles into place around the black griffin's wings, preventing them from opening. They put more manacles around its front legs, chaining them together, and finally put a steel collar around its neck. The griffin, which had woken up by now, tried feebly to lash out at them, but it couldn't do anything to save itself. Once the manacles were on the men cut the ropes and dragged the griffin to its paws. It stood after several attempts, swaying and confused by the after-effects of the drug, and the two handlers took hold of the chains attached to either side of the collar and tugged it forward. Sefer, Orome's red griffin, bit at the creature's haunches until it started to move. The handlers slowly marched it to the far side of a large enclosure and shoved it into another cage, this one much larger and furnished with a trough and several iron rings driven deep into the walls. They attached the chains to two of these on opposite walls, and then withdrew, slamming the heavy iron door shut behind them. The griffin slumped where it stood for a time, and then abruptly started up and hurled itself at the bars. The chains went taut, stopping it in its tracks an arm's length from the barrier. The griffin nearly fell, but recovered itself and reared up on its hind legs, screeching and wrenching at its bonds. The chains rattled and shook, and dust rained down from the rings, but they held firm.

Orome watched the screeching, struggling beast and shook his head. "Magnificent," he said. "Just look at the muscles on it. Thing could break a man's back with a kick." He glanced at Arren. "How did you catch it?"

"Poison," Arren said. "On an arrow."

"Oh, yeah. It's a tricky method, that. I've used it myself. Problem with it is, it doesn't work straightaway, and if the thing's too far off the ground when it kicks in, it can fall to its death."

"Can I have my money now?" said Arren.

Orome looked at him. "You're in a bad mood, aren't you? You don't look so good—why are you such a mess?"

"I have to be somewhere soon," said Arren, ignoring the question, "so could you please just pay me now? I need the money."

"All right, all right, I understand. C'mon." Orome walked away, while Sefer stayed to watch the black griffin. The enclosure they were in was round, and the planks underfoot had been reinforced with metal plates and then covered with sand and sawdust. There were dozens of large cages set into the wall, and several of them contained griffins, stirring in their chains to watch the two humans pass. There was a large archway leading out, which Orome went through, with Arren in tow. "We're going to have to give it a name," he said. "Something impressive. Draw the crowds in."

Arren had seen the posters advertising fights at the Arena featuring popular griffins. Plenty of people had a favourite. The names were chosen to sound melodramatic and exciting, things like Hammerbeak and Bloodrender.

"What d'you reckon, lad?" said Orome, pausing at the door to his office. "Got any good suggestions?"

"Blackgriffin?" said Arren.

Orome took a moment to spot the sarcasm. "Very funny." He unlocked the door and they went into the office. It was a large space dominated by a battered desk. Woodcuts of fighting griffins hung on the walls, along with a notched sword and a shield with a star design on it. Orome edged around the desk and slid aside a secret panel in the wall, revealing a heavy iron box. He lifted it out onto the desk and began to flick the row of levers set into the lid, arranging them in a precise order. "Silvereyes?" he mused aloud as he worked. "No, too girly. Blackwings? Darkstar? No, doesn't quite fit." The last lever clicked into place, and he opened the box and lifted out a leather bag. "All right, give me your money bag."

Arren detached it from his belt and handed it over. Orome began counting out the oblong with practised case, still running through a list of names. "Mooneye? Hmm, gotta be something that relates to the coat. That's what everyone will remember. Blacktalon? That's got some potential—c'mon, help me here, would you?"

"They're not real names," said Arren. "They're just labels."

"Of course," said Orome. "That's what people want. Labels. Something to set the blood afire. Something you can tell stories about. We're not just here to punish criminals, you know. We're here to entertain people. It's a performance. Always has been. Thunderbolt? Nightwish? Night-something has got possibilities. Nightwings? Nightsky? Night—four hundred and fifty, four hundred and seventy, four hundred and ninety, five hundred, five hundred twenty, five hundred seventy. All right, all done." He tied the pouch shut and handed it to Arren.

It was heavy, but he stuffed it into his pocket.

"Thanks."

"My pleasure. I'll just show you out."

They left the office and passed through a draughty corridor that went under the high wall of the Arena itself. Up ahead was the huge iron door that led to the pen where the griffins were held before a fight, until the gate was lifted and they were let into the Arena. Orome took a right turn through a heavy iron gate set into the wall, and they followed a second passage that went around the edge of the Arena, beneath the spectators' gallery. It ended at a small but heavy door which opened onto the street that circled the Arena. Orome stood aside to let Arren through. "There you go. If you want to come and watch your griffin fight, I'll let you in for nothing."

Arren rubbed his eyes and blinked in the sudden light. "Thank you. Oh—" He started to leave, but then stopped and turned back. "You're not going to cut off its wings, are you?"

"What?" said Orome. "Oh, good gods no. That went out years ago. No, we just keep 'em chained together."

"You don't clip the feathers?"

"Not usually, no. We need to have them still able to fly."

"Why?"

"What, you don't know? Sometimes we put a cover over the pit and take the chains off, let 'em fly. People like to see 'em attack from the air."

Arren remembered seeing the black griffin falling out of the sky toward him. It made him feel slightly sick. "Well, just—I mean—" He sighed. "Good luck with it. I'll see you around."

Orome nodded. "Take care." He retreated back into the Arena, and Arren left.

Nothing had changed during Arren's absence. He passed out of the Arena district and went through the marketplace in order to get to the Eyrie, almost bewildered by the sameness of it all. The stalls were set up and people were everywhere, buying and selling. He had to weave his way through the crowds, his ears full of the shouts of the traders advertising their wares. The air smelt of frying onions and fresh bread and the mingled sweat of hundreds of people. For him, this was the smell of home.

But one thing had changed. No-one moved aside for him. No-one even looked twice at him. There were no muttered "sir"s. Without Eluna beside him, he was nobody.

"Sir! Sir, stop!"

At first he only just heard the voice and didn't really pay much attention to it, but then someone grabbed his arm. He turned.

"Sir, I—oh my *gods*."

"Hello, Gern," Arren mumbled.

Gern looked horrified. "What happened to you, sir? Where were you all this time? We expected you back days ago. Flell's scared sick and Bran's talking about going to look for you. What were you doing? And why are you all . . . ?"

Arren looked at the boy's honest, friendly face and suddenly felt ashamed. "I was . . . I caught the griffin," he said at last. "We had to—we brought it back on a wagon. I had to stay with it."

Comprehension dawned in Gern's face. "Oh, I get it! Of course! So, you caught it? That's amazing, sir! Have you taken it to the Arena yet?"

"Yes." Arren started to shove his way through the crowd again.

Gern followed him. "I can't wait to see it fight. How big is it, sir? Is it really black? Ow! Damn it!" Someone's elbow had caught him in the ear. "This is ridiculous," he said, pushing his way through to catch up with Arren. "Look at the bastards! They're not even getting out of your way!" He managed to get back to Arren's side and was nearly knocked over by someone running past. "Godsdamnit!"

They had neared the edge of the marketplace now, but the crowds hadn't thinned much. Arren ignored all the bodies thumping into him and forged on, stone-faced.

Gern, though, had other ideas. "Out of the way, godsdamnit!" he roared at the people in their way. "This is a griffiner!" Several people turned to stare at him. "You heard me!" he resumed. "The Master of Trade is trying to get through, so get out of his way!"

It worked; as Gern continued to shout, many people did move out of Arren's path. He could see them staring at him, and it made him crumble inside.

"There you go, sir, that's a bit better. Oi! Move it, you, you're in the griffiner's way!"

Arren grabbed him by the shoulder. "Please stop it, Gern."

Gern stopped and looked at him. "Why, sir? What's wrong?"

Arren started to speak, and then shook his head and stared at the ground. "I just—not now. Please."

"Sir? Are you all right?" Gern looked upward, and then at the surrounding buildings. "Where's Eluna, sir? Sir?"

But Arren had let go of him and was walking away. Gern tried to run after him, but he vanished into the crowd, leaving Gern to search for him in vain, frowning and confused.

Arren could see the Eyrie looming overhead, and he sped up. Would they be expecting him?

When the guards on the door saw him they instantly came forward to stop him. "Excuse me, but what do you want?" said one of them.

Arren made an attempt to straighten his tunic. "I'm here to see Lord Rannagon."

"Is he expecting you?"

"Yes."

"That's news to *me*," said the guard. "Because the last thing I heard, Lord Rannagon was in the council chamber taking part in an important meeting which can't be disturbed."

"I can wait," said Arren. "He told me to report to him as soon as I arrived."

"What for?"

"That's between him and me."

"I see." The guard didn't sound particularly sincere. He looked Arren up and down. "And you're intending to go in there looking like that, are you?"

Arren growled and barged past them into the Eyrie. One of the guards followed him for a short distance, but gave up and returned to his post. When Arren reached the doors leading into the council chamber, though, he found them shut and guarded by two more guards, these ones accompanied by their griffins. He stopped at a respectful distance, and one of the griffins came forward to sniff at him. It turned away with a contemptuous flick of its tail and returned to its partner, who lifted his spear slightly and said, "What are you doing in here?"

Arren bowed his head slightly. "Arren Cardockson, Master of Trade. I'm here to see Lord Rannagon. Will he be long?"

"Don't know, but you can't see him now," said the guard. "He's busy talking to the Mistress of the Eyrie. I couldn't say how long they'll be; it's been a while already."

"What are they talking about?"

"I don't know."

"I think *I* know," the other guard broke in. "He's arguing with her again. Trying to make her change her mind."

"About what?" said Arren.

"Didn't you hear?" said the guard. "It's all over the place."

"What?"

"Lady Riona's thinking about retiring and naming someone as her replacement. Obviously Lord Rannagon thought it'd be him, what with him being her brother and all. But she said no."

"It's because of that bastard of his," said the other guard. "It's got to be."

"What, you mean that boy who showed up claiming to be Rannagon's son?" said Arren.

"Yeah, that's him. Erian, I think he's called. Rannagon gave up and admitted he was the boy's father. He didn't have much choice; he's the spitting image of him. Anyway, there went his chances of being Master. You can't have a Master of the Eyrie who goes around fathering bastards."

Just then they were interrupted by a loud screech and a thump from inside the council chamber. The guards' griffins started to hiss, and one of the guards opened the door behind him in order to look through and see what was going on. Arren looked over his shoulder and saw Rannagon and Riona. They were trying to restrain their griffins, which were snarling and snapping their beaks at each other. The two guards entered and approached warily. Arren hesitated a moment and then followed.

"My lady?" said one of the guards, stopping and bowing. "Is there anything you want us to do?"

Riona and her griffin looked up sharply, but then relaxed. Shree sat back on his haunches, tail lashing, and Riona carefully let go of his wing. "No, thank you," she said. "We're fine."

Rannagon had a bloody tear on the front of his tunic, but he glared at the guards. "I told you not to come in here."

"Sorry, my lord. We'll just leave."

Arren stepped around the guards. "Lord Rannagon."

Rannagon looked at him, apparently noticing him for the first time. His face fell. "Arren?"

Arren paused and then bowed. "Lord Rannagon, I—"

Riona came toward him. "Arren Cardockson, explain yourself."

Cold dismay bit into him. "My lady, I—"

Riona waved at the guards. "Get out and close the door. Don't come back unless we call you."

They bowed and left. Once the door had closed behind them, the Mistress of the Eyrie confronted Arren. Her griffin, Shree, stood tall with his wings half-open, still savage with anger. Riona looked a little more composed. "Where have you been? Answer quickly."

"I—I was at Rivermeet, my lady."

"So I heard," said Riona. "And what were you doing there?"

"I was sent there to catch a wild griffin," said Arren.

"I caught it. It's at the Arena now. I—" He took the bag of money from his pocket and showed it to Rannagon. "I've got the money, my lord. I can pay you now."

Neither Rannagon nor Riona touched it.

"Arren, why did you do it?" said Riona. "I don't understand."

Arren blinked. "Why did I do what, my lady? I was following orders, that's all."

Riona pointed at the couch next to her seat. "Sit down."

Arren sat. It was soft and comfortable, and he resisted the temptation to lie down. "I'm sorry I'm such a mess," he said. "I only just got back."

Riona seated herself on her own chair, and Shree crouched by her hand. Rannagon remained standing, his hand on Shoa's shoulders. The yellow griffin's tail was swishing, and she looked restless.

"Now," said Riona. "Tell me everything. Start from the beginning."

Arren took in a deep breath. "I came here to report to Lord Rannagon after the raid on the smugglers' den on Tongue Street. He told me I would have to pay compensation to the dead smuggler's family, and when I said I couldn't afford it he said he knew a way I could earn some money. He said there was a wild griffin out near Rivermeet that had started killing people, and that if I caught it I would be paid. I said I didn't think I could do that because I'd never done it before, but he said he thought I could do it and it was easy. He gave me some poison and said that if I put it on an arrowhead it would put the griffin to sleep, and he gave me a map to the village. I didn't want to do it, but Eluna—" He paused a moment, wincing. Just saying the name made him feel a sudden thump of pain in his chest. "She—she agreed to do it for me, and I couldn't argue with her. Lord Rannagon said I should leave the next day and that he would take care of my affairs while I was gone. I had doubts, but I went anyway, and the day after I got there Deanne arrived."

Riona had listened closely to this, expressionless. Beside her, Shree started to hiss.

"So, that's your story, Arren?" she said once he had finished.

"Yes," said Arren. "If you ask Lord Rannagon, I'm sure . . ." He looked appealingly in Rannagon's direction, but Rannagon only stared back impassively.

"You're sure that's everything?" said Riona. "There's nothing else you want to tell me? Remember," she continued, even as Arren opened his mouth to speak, "I am your friend. I can understand that there were mitigating circumstances. Obviously, you are not well-off money-wise, and you were upset over what happened in the smugglers' home. And I can understand that you have a thirst to prove yourself—you're young, after all."

Arren clasped his hands together, his long fingers entwined. "I—yes, my lady, I didn't think it through properly. Eluna pushed me into it, and Lord Rannagon asked me not to tell anyone else about it."

"You're right. You didn't think it through," said Riona. "I knew you were impetuous, Arren. You're young. It's only to be expected that you would be overconfident. However, that does not mean I can forgive you for what you've done. Lord Rannagon told me everything."

Arren looked up.

"Indeed I did," said Rannagon. "Arren, do you really think you can lay the blame for this on me? I suggest you tell the truth. You're in enough trouble as it is."

"But I already did tell the truth," said Arren.

"You told the truth, did you?" said Riona. "That's strange. Because the story I have been told is that Lord Rannagon offered you the opportunity to go with Deanne and her companions to Rivermeet and claim a share of the bounty, but that you, apparently thinking you could be a hero and take all the money for yourself, stole the map and a bottle of poison from his desk, abandoned your duties and ran away to Rivermeet the very next day, without asking for leave or permission or even taking the time to appoint someone to stand in as Master of Trade during your absence."

"What?" said Arren, bewildered. "But I never—"

He broke off. Shoa had moved closer to him, and now she settled down behind the couch, very close to him.

"That's *a lie*," said Arren. "Who told you that?"

"I did," said Rannagon.

"And several of the Eyrie's guards saw you hide the letter inside your tunic as you were leaving the office," said Riona, "although Lord Rannagon didn't notice it was missing until the following day, after you had already left."

"But—"

Shoa nudged him in the back of the head with her beak. "Do not argue," the yellow griffin said, her voice barely audible. "You will not be believed. If you accuse Rannagon of anything, I will kill you."

Arren glanced at her. She stared back, her blue eyes cold.

"I—" he began. Immediately, the yellow griffin hit him with her beak—not hard, but just enough for him to feel the sharp point at the base of his skull. If she decided to strike hard now, he would die instantly.

Arren bowed his head and said nothing.

Riona sighed. "I am very disappointed in you, Arren. You were an excellent Master of Trade, and I had hoped to see you go far. But I cannot ignore what you have done. I have no choice but to relieve you of your post. Consider yourself unemployed until further notice. You will not be allowed to act as Master again until you have satisfied me that you have learnt your lesson."

Disbelief showed in Arren's eyes. Shoa had returned to Rannagon's side, and the two of them were watching him, showing no sign of guilt, or even recognition. "How could you?" he asked in a small voice. "How could you do this to me? You've—I've—oh gods—" He bowed his head, fighting back tears.

Riona paused. "Arren? Are you all right?"

Arren looked up at last. "Eluna's dead," he said.

Rannagon and Riona both looked deeply dismayed.

"Oh no." Riona came forward and put her hand on Arren's shoulder. "Oh, Arren, I'm sorry," she said, her voice losing its stiff formality.

Shree nudged Arren in the side. "I am sad for this," he said. "Eluna was a fine griffin and a strong warrior."

"Arren, how did this happen?" said Rannagon.

"The black griffin killed her," said Arren.

Rannagon let go of Shoa's neck and put his hand on Arren's other shoulder. "Oh, Gryphus—Arren, I'm so sorry."

Arren punched him in the face. Rannagon yelped and fell over backward. Instantly Shoa leapt straight at Arren, knocking him violently to the ground. Her talons went deep into his flesh and she screeched at him, beak opening wide, threatening to snap shut on his neck. Arren struggled wildly, striking the griffin in the chest. The words burst out of him. *"Kreeaee! Liar!"*

Rannagon rushed forward and hauled Shoa off him. It was a hard struggle and she fought every step of the way, her yellow wings thrashing in his face and threatening to knock him over. Arren struggled out of the way and managed to get up, blood soaking into his tunic. Shoa broke away from Rannagon and ran at Arren again, but Shree threw himself in the way. The two griffins scuffled briefly before Shoa retreated, hissing and bristling.

Arren's shoulders had been punctured by the griffin's talons, but he barely registered the pain. He started toward Rannagon, raising his hand to point accusingly at him. "You lied to me!" he roared, speaking griffish. "You tricked me!"

Riona called for the guards. They ran in and grabbed Arren by the arms, restraining him as he tried to get at Rannagon.

Riona stroked Shree to soothe him. "Arren Cardockson, control yourself," she snapped. "And Rannagon, even if this was not your fault, apologise. You put this idea in his head, even if you didn't intend to, and I hold you partly responsible for what happened."

Rannagon dabbed at the bruise forming on his chin.

"Arren, I really am sorry," he said. "More than I can say. You're like a son to me, and I never intended for anything like this to happen. Yes, perhaps I led you on without meaning to, and for that I'm sorry. There's nothing I can do to take away your loss, but if there is ever anything I can do for you, just ask and I will do everything in my power to see it done."

Riona looked slightly mollified. "Good. However"—she looked at Arren, who had stopped struggling and was staring at Rannagon—"my brother cannot take all the blame for this. You are ultimately responsible for your own actions, and Eluna's death is your own fault. I was wrong to think you were trustworthy enough to be promoted so young. I will choose a new Master of Trade. You are banned from the Eyrie. You are not a griffiner any more, and you have no place among us now."

"But I—" Arren began.

Riona nodded to the guards. "Please show him out."

Arren didn't resist. He walked between the guards as they led him out of the building, unable to say a word. They took him to the front door and ushered him through it.

"Off you go," said one, giving him a slight push.

Arren said nothing. He walked away without looking back.

It seemed to take a long time to get home. The bloody patches on his tunic stuck to his skin. He felt as if he hadn't slept in over a year. The ground lurched beneath him, and he staggered and nearly fell, but managed to stay upright. He reached his own door at last and half-collapsed against it. Recovering, he fished the key out of his pocket, unlocked the door and entered.

His house was cold and musty, and full of shadows. He shut the door behind him and pulled the bar into place.

Everything was exactly how he'd left it, though there was a coating of dust and cobwebs over the furniture. The blanket was still draped over the hammock, and the pillow was on the floor underneath. His porridge bowl was on the table, and the water in it had a coating of mould on the surface.

He dropped his belongings on the floor by the door and wandered into Eluna's nest. The hay had gone musty, and there was a little mound of dry dung in one corner.

Arren walked forward as if in a dream. He picked up a loose feather and clutched it to his chest. It was soft and downy, white as snow, the edges tinged with silvery grey.

He held it in one hand and lay down in the hollow left by Eluna's body. Her scent still lingered in the hay, strong and musky and fierce. It was so powerful that when he looked up, he half-expected to see her there, glaring at him for taking her spot.

The sun began to go down. Darkness slowly gathered, and torches were lit in the city streets. The moon rose, bright and full, silvery-white against the black sky. The day was over, and people returned to their homes or went to the taverns, to drink and relax and talk to their friends. But Arren stayed where he was, staring at nothing, and did not move at all.

A loud thump woke him up. He sat up sharply, his heart pounding. There was another thump. Someone was in his home.

Arren got up and made for the door leading out of the stable. Someone had lit the lamp in the next room. They were there, waiting for him.

It was Rannagon.

The griffiner was sitting at the table, holding something in his hands. He was clad in his usual fine clothes, yellow-brown to match Shoa, who was crouched in the corner, preening her wings.

Arren stood in the doorway, frozen in astonishment. "Rannagon?"

Rannagon stood up. "Ah, Arren, there you are. I hope you don't mind the intrusion." His voice was as cordial as always, and his look friendly.

"What are you doing here?"

Rannagon held out something toward him. "You left this behind at the Eyrie."

It was the bag of money Orome had given him. He took it, weighing it in his hand. "Did you take the money I owed you?"

Rannagon shook his head. "No, I paid the compensation myself. You don't need to pay me back."

Arren stuffed the bag into his pocket. "I don't need your charity."

"It wasn't charity," said Rannagon. "Consider it a favour. Please, sit down."

He didn't. "Do you want anything, or can I have my home back now?"

Rannagon sat down at the table, his head in his hands. "I came here to apologise to you, Arren, though I don't know how much good it will do."

"You think you can *apologise*?" said Arren. "After what you did to me? You betrayed me! I don't even understand *why*. Why me? What did I do? I wasn't a threat to you, was I?"

"It's not like that," Rannagon said abruptly. "You have to believe me."

"Why should I? You already lied to me once."

"Yes, and I've come to explain why," said Rannagon. He looked, Arren thought, utterly miserable. "Listen to me, please. It was not my intention for this to happen. I didn't want either you or Eluna to be hurt. I thought that Deanne would arrive before you tried to fight the griffin alone. She'd arranged to leave only a day after you, and I knew she would be able to travel faster. All I wanted—I don't hate you, Arren. I never did. What I did was intended to help you."

"*Help* me?" Arren repeated.

"Yes. Please sit down."

Arren dragged a crate to the other side of the table and sat on it, watching Rannagon closely. His hands itched for his sword.

Rannagon glanced at Shoa, and then looked at Arren again. "I won't pretend I didn't set out to get you into trouble, Arren. That was my intention. But that was *all* I intended. I didn't want you to be hurt or killed; I just wanted you to be disgraced. Temporarily."

Arren leant forward. "Why?" He paused. "No. I know why. It's because Riona told you she wanted to put me on the council, isn't it?" He could feel a terrible hatred bubbling up inside him. "And you couldn't bear the idea, could you?" he added, his voice becoming louder. "The thought of a *blackrobe* on the council was too much for you, wasn't it? Blackrobes are supposed to scrub floors and build dams, not run cities. Isn't that right? Well? So, you thought you'd get me out of the way before that happened."

"No!" Rannagon half-shouted. "It's not like that! Calm down, for Gryphus' sake, or the whole neighbourhood will hear you. But you are partly correct. Many of the senior griffiners were horrified by Riona's plan. I myself argued against it. And it's not because I don't trust you, Arren. I know you too well for that. But I agreed that we couldn't risk your being placed on the council. Something had to be done. Some of my colleagues wanted to have you assassinated or banished, but I couldn't allow that to happen, so I decided to act before they did. I arranged matters so that you would be disgraced and demoted rather than killed. By the time you were back in Riona's favour she would already have retired and a new Master or Mistress would be in power. The danger would be over. That was all I wanted."

Arren listened. "But in all that time it never occurred to you to talk to *me*, did it? Didn't you consider finding out what *I* thought about all that? I didn't even *want* to be on the bloody council."

Rannagon's contrite look faded. "Don't play innocent with me," he snapped. "We both know perfectly well that you would have taken it. You've always been ambitious, Arren, and so was Eluna. Even if you had said no, she would have pushed you into it. She was always embarrassed by your lack of standing at the Eyrie. The other griffins laughed at her for choosing a Northerner in the first place, but if that Northerner became a councillor . . . No, we could not risk it happening."

"So you killed her," Arren said softly.

"No. The black griffin did that, and if you want revenge on anyone I suggest you buy him back and kill him yourself. But you have to understand"—Rannagon looked at him intently—"I don't have any ill will toward you. What I did was for the good of the city. Can you imagine what would have happened if you had become a councillor? The entire country knows the nature of your people. If you were put on the council, our neighbours would consider it tantamount to an act of war."

"Then why did Riona even consider it?" said Arren.

"Riona believes that the way to make peace with the Northerners is to foster better relations with them," said Rannagon. "She believed that putting you on the council would show the world that Eagleholm, at least, believes that Northerners have worth. You could have been an inspirational symbol and a good example. But she's naïve. It never would have worked. If Northerners ever attacked here, what would you do then, Arren? Would you be able to fight against them? And what if you had been sent into the North or asked to track down runaway slaves?"

"I would have done my duty," said Arren.

"But your duty to whom?" said Rannagon. "Blood is thicker than water. You may have been born in the South, but you're still a Northerner at heart and you always will be. You can't control your nature forever."

"Lord Rannagon, I am not a Northerner," said Arren. "I know I look like one, but I'm not. I've never been in the North. I don't want to go to the North, and I never have. I only ever wanted to live here and . . ." He trailed off.

"And what?" said Rannagon. "Be like us? No. It doesn't

work like that. You live in the South and you speak the Southern tongue, and you act like a Southerner, but sooner or later your true nature will emerge. When that day comes, it'll be better that you aren't a councillor or a griffiner."

Arren slammed his fist onto the table, so hard the porridge bowl rattled. *"There's nothing wrong with me!"* he shouted. "My true nature? What in the gods' names do you think you're on about? You killed Eluna because you think I've got some sort of dormant *something* inside me? You did this to me because of—because of *this*?" He grabbed a lock of his hair and yanked it violently, nearly pulling it out.

Rannagon started when Arren began shouting, and put his hand on the hilt of his sword. "No," he said, drawing back slightly. "I did what I did because of this." He gestured at Arren. "Northerners are violent at heart and always will be. I have seen them in battle. They fight like wild animals."

Silence. Arren looked down blankly at his fist. It was still resting on the table where he'd slammed it, and he suddenly realised that it hurt.

Rannagon stood up. "I've said all I have to say. You'll be left alone from now on. I have no wish to persecute you after what you've already gone through. I hope that one day, perhaps, you'll forgive me for what I did."

Arren stood, too. "I didn't ask to be born the way I was," he said.

"None of us ever do," said Rannagon. "All we can do is try to make the best of it. You are a worthy man, Arren. I never thought otherwise."

There was another silence as each man regarded the other, waiting for him to make a move.

Finally, Arren lost the battle with his rage. He spat. "I will not forget," he promised, speaking griffish, and thumped a fist against his chest. "I will not forgive. And if the chance comes, I will have revenge."

They were ritual words only ever used by griffiners or griffins, and Rannagon stiffened when he heard them.

Shoa suddenly rose from her corner and advanced on Arren, head low and shoulders raised, hissing softly, backing him up against the wall. Rannagon stood behind her, hard-faced. "You will regret that," he said. "And if you ever breathe a word of this to anyone else, no matter who, you will suffer the consequences. You will tell everyone the same story I told Riona, and you will not deviate from it. Believe me when I tell you that I have my methods of finding things out. If you accuse me to anyone, they will die. And so will you. Do you understand?"

Arren, flattened against the wall, looked away from the hissing griffin. "Yes . . . my lord."

11

Darkheart

The black griffin was terrified. He could see light ahead of him, showing through the bars of the strange cave he had been put into, and he lunged toward it, again and again. The thing around his neck would not let go. It dug into him with every lunge, but he continued to fight as hard as he could, pitting his full strength against the chains. The skin at the base of his neck was one massive bruise, and the feathers had begun to wear away. When he finally subsided, exhausted, he could feel blood trickling down over his shoulders.

He bit at the chain holding his forelegs together. His beak left a shallow groove in the metal, but it would not break. He tried again, tilting his head to move the chain to the back of his beak where his bite would be more powerful. It tasted cold and unpleasant on his tongue, like a rock, and it was as hard as a rock. The base of his beak started to hurt, and he heard it make an ominous cracking sound. He spat out the chain and began trying to pull the manacles from his ankles. They would not budge.

"They will not break," said a voice.

The black griffin looked up. The voice had come from somewhere to his left, but he couldn't see anyone there. He got up and made a lunge in that direction, only to hit the rock wall of his prison. The collar drove into the tender flesh around his neck again, sending fresh waves of pain through his body. He screeched his rage and despair, and slumped down onto his stomach, tail twitching convulsively.

"They will not break, fool," the voice resumed. "You cannot escape."

The black griffin looked up. "You . . . griff?" he managed.

There was a weary chirp from the other side of the wall. "You chick?" the voice mocked.

The black griffin didn't understand. "Where you?" he said.

"I am in the cage beside yours," said the voice. "My name is Kraee."

The black griffin listened. "What this place?"

"The Arena," said Kraee. "We live here."

"I want . . . fly," said the black griffin.

Kraee hissed. "You will not fly again, black griffin."

The black griffin got up suddenly and hurled himself toward the door at an angle. The chain snapped tight again and he fell hard, sending up a cloud of dust. *"Want fly!"* he screamed, struggling to get up. The chain on his forelegs had tangled itself up in his talons, and he fell again and rolled onto his side, thrashing wildly to get free. His wings jerked clumsily, unable to unfurl properly because of the manacles holding them together. His hind legs, still free, scrabbled at the dirt, the claws scraping on the iron plate beneath. He began to screech, again and again, his rage reverberating out into the enclosure beyond his cage. It roused the other griffins, and they began to screech back at him, their voices high and mocking. They only encouraged the black griffin; he found his feet and reared up, screaming as loudly as he could. He kept on and on, while the others continued to scream, too, by now half-hysterical with pent-up rage.

There was another screech, barely audible above the

cacophony, and Sefer arrived. The red griffin entered the enclosure via the archway, opening the gate that now blocked it by lifting a lever with his beak. It closed behind him and he came to the centre of the enclosure and screeched again. The sound cut across the others, and many of the caged griffins fell silent and sullenly lay back down. Others, though, continued to screech, and many threw themselves at the bars as the black griffin was doing, their chains clanking loudly.

Sefer looked around sharply, and quickly identified the black griffin as the main source of the disturbance. He darted over to the cage and bit him through the bars. The black griffin lashed out, nearly hitting him, but Sefer darted back out of the way. He lowered his head, hackles raised and tail swishing. "Be quiet, or you will suffer," he warned.

The black griffin only paused a moment before he resumed his struggle. "Kill! Bite! Tear!" he threatened.

Sefer screeched at him. "Idiot humanless beast! I will rip out your eyes!"

"*Kill!*" the black griffin replied, eyes mad. There was blood all around the edges of his collar, but he didn't seem to notice.

"He will not listen," Kraee volunteered. "He does not know griffish."

Sefer paused, apparently deep in thought, and then opened his beak and breathed a beam of red light. Where it struck, flames erupted. It hit the bars of the black griffin's cage, turning them red-hot, and burned the feathers on his face. He screeched again, this time in pain and fear, and lurched toward the back of the cage. Sefer closed his beak and the fire disappeared, but the black griffin stayed where he was, hissing to himself and rubbing his beak on the ground, trying to dispel the heat.

The screeching had stopped, and all was quiet in the enclosure. Apparently satisfied, Sefer turned and loped back toward the gate. He poked a foreclaw through a gap in the bars and hooked the lever. It moved, and the gate swung open with a faint creak. Sefer slipped through, pulled it shut behind him and was gone.

Silence reigned for a long time after he had left. The black griffin continued to hiss, but it seemed his defiance had been knocked out of him. Eventually he got up and drank deeply from the trough of water provided for him. That made him feel a little better.

As he lay down, sides heaving, he felt the strange feeling in his throat again. It was even more powerful now than it had been before, heavy and burning and awful, fighting to escape. This time he breathed in deeply and tried to let it out, but it would not come. His voice died inside him, leaving him mute and exhausted, and his head slumped to the ground.

"I told you that you could not get free," Kraee said in weary tones.

The black griffin said nothing.

"What is your name, black griffin?" another voice asked, this one from the cage on his other side.

The black griffin raised his head slightly. "No . . . name," he mumbled, and let it drop again.

"My name is Aeya," said the other griffin, who sounded female. "Do you not have a name?"

"No name," the black griffin said again.

"Why can he not speak?" Aeya said.

"Perhaps his mother died," Kraee answered. "Where is your mother, black griffin?"

"Mother die," said the black griffin. "When chick. Human come kill."

Aeya shifted in her chains. "Humans killed your mother?"

"I live in mountain," the black griffin managed. "No—chick die."

"I had chicks once," said Aeya. "Humans took them. So I killed them. Until the griffiners came for me and brought me here."

"Want fly," the black griffin said again, in a hopeless kind of way. "Want . . . home. Want hunt."

"We all want that," Kraee interrupted. "But we cannot have it. We cannot leave here. But we can hunt."

"Hunt human!" another griffin yelled. "Kill human!" it screeched, and bashed its beak against the bars in front of it. Others hissed and snarled their agreement, but the sound died down before it became another bout of savage hysteria.

"Kill human?" the black griffin repeated.

"Yes," said Aeya. "In the pit. We kill them. Make them die." Her voice became low and bloody. "Break their bones. Tear them apart. Make them bleed."

The black griffin hissed. "Want human."

"And you shall have human," said Kraee. "They give us that." He hissed to himself. "I want to taste their blood again."

There was silence, broken only by a savage muttering from several of the griffins who were within earshot. The black griffin lay with his head on his talons and thought about one human in particular. The tall one with the cold black eyes and the black fur on its head. The one called Arren. That human had run from him in fear at first, but later—later it had spoken to him. None of the others had, but it had, and it had shown no further fear of him, only hatred. When he had attacked it, it had fought back. It had conquered him.

He hissed to himself and dug his talons into the dirt.

"I am bored," Aeya said suddenly. "Black griffin?"

The black griffin moved his head slightly in her direction. She must have heard the rattle of his chains, because she went on, "I want someone new to talk to. If you would like, I shall teach you griffish as your mother would have. Do you wish me to do that?"

"You . . . teach?" the black griffin said blankly.

"I will teach you how to speak," said Aeya.

Comprehension of a kind dawned on the black griffin. "Want speak," he said eagerly.

"Then I will help you," said Aeya. "Listen . . ."

She spent much of the rest of that night teaching him

new words, saying them slowly and making him repeat
them. He quickly grasped this notion and recited strings
of new words over and over again until he could say them
properly. It was so strange, but he found he liked it. He
liked talking to her, and he liked learning.

He spent the next few weeks in his cage, unable to move
far or stretch his wings. The black-eyed human did not
come to give him food any more, but now other humans
did instead. They brought meat, plenty of it, and he ate it
voraciously even though it tasted unfamiliar. It helped to
restore some of the strength he'd lost during the journey.

He made several more attempts to escape, and whenever a human ventured too close to his cage he rushed at
them to attack. But the chains always pulled him back, and
the bars were in the way. Infuriatingly, the humans seemed
to know this would happen and passed insolently close to
him, barely even bothering to glance in his direction, let
alone show any fear.

Once every few days he was taken out of the cage and
forced to walk around in the enclosure, pulled along by
the chains around his neck. The first time, he immediately tried to fly away, but his wings wouldn't open and the
chains weighed him down. And even if he had been able
to take to the air he would not have got far. The enclosure
was open to the sky, but a huge net of steel cables had been
stretched over it, preventing anything as big as a griffin
from flying in or out.

In the end his spirit died down and he stopped trying to
attack or run. He would lie in his cage, eyes dull, and thump
his beak on the wall over and over again, not even fully
aware of what he was doing. His mind slowly turned into
a blank sea in which he was unable to think about anything
much or even really be aware of his situation or his surroundings. Sometimes he would doze and remember his old
life, back in the mountains, when he had still been able to fly.
The dreams were so vivid that he would believe they were
real, before he was woken up by the pain in his wings and
realised that he had been trying to beat them in his sleep.

The only relief he had from the monotony and despair was Aeya. She talked to him often, teaching him new words and phrases, and when he was bored he would mumble them to himself, trying the sounds. It helped him to get by.

One night, when his speech was a little better, she told him a story.

"Long ago," she said, her voice soft but clear, "the eagle and the lion were enemies. They lived together in the land, and both of them wanted to rule it. They fought day and night, but neither one could win. The eagle could fly but he could not run, and the lion could run but could not fly. The eagle had powerful sight and a sharp beak and talons, but the lion could climb and he had strong teeth and talons of his own. One day the eagle swooped down on the lion and carried him away. He wanted to drop him into the sea and make him drown, but the sea was a long way away and he soon became tired.

"He began to fall from the sky, but he could not let go of the lion because his talons were tangled in the lion's mane. They fell very far, because in those days the eagle could fly as high as the sun. They fought as they fell, trying to kill each other, and when the eagle tried to fly away, the lion bit his tail and held on to him. But when they fell, they fell into a great hole in the ground. The hole was very deep, so deep it had no bottom.

"The lion and the eagle fell into the shadow that lived there, and both of them were afraid, when they were not afraid of anything else in the world. They clung to each other like chicks in a nest, and they could not see each other then, or the sun or the moon or the sky. They fell for years and years and did not stop, until they reached the light that was on the other side of the darkness in the hole. The light took them, and it wrapped itself around them until they were both flaming with it. After that they were lifted out of the hole together, and when they flew up and into the sky they saw that they were not themselves any more. They had become one. The wings and the talons of an eagle, the paws and tail of a lion. One creature with the strength of both. They were the first griffin, and they flew and screamed with the eagle's voice and proclaimed that they were lord over the land and would be forever, for the light had given them magic and wisdom, and no creature would ever be stronger or wiser than they."

The black griffin listened. He understood only part of the story, but he took it all in anyway, occasionally repeating the odd fragment.

"My mother told me that story," Kraee remarked. "It was almost the same."

"What did you think of it, black griffin?" said Aeya.

He concentrated. "I . . . like . . . it."

"Well done," said Aeya. "You are quick to learn."

"Why do you teach him, Aeya?" said Kraee.

"Because I am bored," Aeya said. "And because . . ." She trailed off, unable to express what she was really thinking, which was that, to her, the black griffin's clumsy speech made her think of him as a chick. Like those she had lost. And a chick needed teaching. Yes. He needed to be taught. She sat back on her haunches and rustled her wings. "I have nothing to do. I may as well teach him."

The next day they were visited by Orome. The black griffin knew him by sight; he'd come to the enclosure several times, always with Sefer beside him, and had shown a fair amount of interest in the black griffin. Now the human approached his cage and stood a short way back from the bars. The black griffin stood up and started to walk toward him, but then changed his mind and lay down again, watching him listlessly.

Orome scratched his chin. "Seems you're starting to lose interest in living," he said in griffish. "Don't worry, you'll be able to leave there soon. It's time for you to go into the pit. We have some people for you to chase."

The black griffin said nothing. None of the griffins ever did speak to Orome or his fellow humans, except to scream curses and threats at them.

"I have a name for you," the man went on. "Sefer thought of it." He moved a little closer, taking in the black griffin's silver feathers and black fur and his mottled wings. "We're going to call you Darkheart," he said. "Darkheart, the black griffin. Be proud of it. Your name is all over the city. Hundreds of people are coming to see you."

The black griffin looked up at that. "Dark . . . heart?" he said, puzzled.

Orome nodded. "Your name: Darkheart. I give it to you. Soon you'll have humans to hunt again."

After he had left, the black griffin lay and thought for a while, and then got up to have a drink. "Aeya?"

"Yes?"

"What is Darkheart?"

"You are," said Aeya. "That is your name now. The human gave it to you. Darkheart—a strange name. Not a griffish one."

"Darkheart," the black griffin said again. He repeated it several times. It sounded strange, but he realised eventually that he recognised it. It was two words, not one. "Dark . . . heart. What . . . dark heart?"

"It means a heart that is dark," said Aeya.

He couldn't remember what a heart was. "What . . . heart?"

"Your heart is inside you," said Aeya. "In your chest. You can feel it inside you, clicking its beak."

The black griffin had a vague idea of what she meant. He touched his beak to his chest, and felt his heart thudding gently beneath the feathers. "Heart," he said, half to himself.

"Your heart is where your magic lives," said Aeya. "It is precious."

"Magic?"

Aeya sighed. "Magic is our power. Humans do not have it. Every griffin has their gift. You would have found yours one day. Mine was to create the wind. My breath could make a tree fall. Who knows what you could have done, Darkheart."

He felt the imprisoned scream again. "Magic."

They were silent for a time.

"So, you will go into the pit," said Kraee. "I hope I will go with you, Darkheart. I want to hunt."

Darkheart perked up at that. "We hunt?"

"Yes. Hunt humans. Sometimes three of us, sometimes more."

"We . . . hunt human?"

Kraee's chains clinked. "Yes. Many humans."

Darkheart lay down to think. Did that mean he was going home? Were they going to let him fly back to his valley, where he could fly and hunt again?

Joy flooded into him. He was going home. He was going to hunt again. He knew it. And he had a name now. It was all his, all his own, just for him.

"Darkheart," he said. And then, again, "Darkheart."

He looked up at the sky. It was evening, and the sun was sinking below the horizon. Time to fly, time to hunt. Time to call. He remembered his valley. The wind in the trees, the rich scent of the earth, the icy wind that blew over the mountains in winter, the snow and the rain. He stood up clumsily, the chains dragging at his limbs. The other griffins were lying down, either asleep or simply doing nothing. They were silent except for the occasional rustle of a wing or clink of a chain.

The black griffin lifted his head toward the sky and screamed. It was the call, his call, and this time it was a true call. *"Darkheart! Darkheart!"* He called it again and again, breaking the depressed silence of the cages. It made his heart beat faster and put a wild and wonderful energy into him, which freed him from his lethargy and despair.

This time no-one came to silence him, and he continued to call until he was hoarse. He drank deeply from his trough and lay down to rest. Night was falling. The collar still hurt him, but he did not care. He was going home.

The next day came, and Darkheart spent it sitting on his haunches, watching expectantly for them to come and let him out of the cage.

No-one did.

They brought food at noon, as usual, but they did not give him any. Kraee and Aeya also went hungry and had to watch while the other griffins tore into the freshly killed goat meat provided.

Darkheart began to get angry. "Want food," he huffed. "Want to hunt."

"Be calm," Aeya advised. "This is a good sign: If they do not feed you, it means you will go to the pit very soon. And Kraee and I will go with you. We can hunt together."

"You come?" said Darkheart, perking up.

"Yes. Three of us together, hunting humans. You will see."

That made him feel better. He waited out the rest of the day, hunger gnawing at him, and when sunset eventually came he called his name again. He imagined calling it from his cave in the mountainside. *Soon,* he promised himself. *Soon.*

And then it was morning, and he was woken up by the sound of human voices. There were many humans in the enclosure, more than he had ever seen there before. Orome was there, with Sefer. The red griffin looked wary but confident.

He could hear scuffling, thumps and clinking chains from Aeya's cage. A few moments later several humans emerged into his line of sight. They were pulling a griffin along by the chains connected to her collar, and she was following them meekly enough, though she kept tossing her head and flicking her tail.

Darkheart stood up to watch. The griffin was grey, and older than him. Her eyes were blue, and there were hints of blue on her wings and throat as well. He realised that she was Aeya. He had never seen her before now, only heard her voice. He called her name but she didn't look at him. The humans led her away from the enclosure and out through the gate, which had been opened to let them through. Others were already opening Kraee's cage. He proved to be brown and quite old. He put up no resistance at all and walked with a slight limp as they took him out after Aeya.

Now it was Darkheart's turn. He watched closely as a pair of humans came forward and opened his cage door. It swung outward with a loud creak and groan, and suddenly there was nothing in the way, nothing standing between him and freedom. He threw himself forward at once, and screamed when the collar jerked him back yet again. Escape was so close, not even a tail's length away—

The humans put themselves in the way. He screamed again and lashed out at them, but they were beyond his reach. They carried long sticks in their paws. One of them poked its stick into the cage. Darkheart tried to grab it at once, but the other human smacked him smartly in the face with its stick. He started trying to seize the stick instead, and while his attention was on it, the first human unhooked the chain connecting one side of his collar to the wall, dragged it out and held it. The second human unhooked and seized the other chain, then two others came to help, and between them they dragged Darkheart out of his cage. At first he resisted, but then, realising the chains were no longer holding him to the walls, he rushed at them.

But they were ready for that. They darted out of the way, pulling the chains tight. When he tried to attack the humans on one side, those on the opposite side would pull him back. Others had run around behind him and were striking his hindquarters. He lurched forward to get away from their sticks, and the humans holding the chains immediately began pulling him toward the arched entrance. He went, fighting every step of the way, his instincts screaming at him to fight and kill.

They got him through the archway, and the gate was instantly slammed shut behind them. Up ahead there was light, and they headed toward it, bit by bit, hitting him in the sensitive spot under his beak whenever he tried to attack. The gate blocking the end of the tunnel was just large enough for him to fit through. They opened it and lodged him in the opening, which pinned his wings to his sides. There they took the manacles off his forelegs and removed the chains from his collar, and then pushed him forward into the open space beyond. He instantly turned and tried to attack them, but the gate had already clanged back into place.

And then . . .

A roar filled the air. It came from above and from all sides at once, loud and rushing, almost like wind. Darkheart turned, peering around in confusion, and he saw them.

Humans. Hundreds and hundreds of them. They were sitting above him, lining the walls of the strange round cave he was in, and all of them were calling. Their voices had mingled together into one sound, like that of a giant beast.

Darkheart ran around the edges of the pit, looking for a way to get at them. His legs were free now, but there was no way out of the pit. There were more steel cables here, forming a huge net between him and the humans. It was too high for him to reach, and he knew he could not fly. He tried all the same, struggling pointlessly against the chains holding his wings together. It hurt, and he screamed his frustration.

Aeya and Kraee were there already, pacing back and forth expectantly. Darkheart ran to them and sniffed cautiously at Aeya's feathers. She stopped her pacing and raised her head, looking down on him aggressively. "Do not expect me to help you," she hissed, her voice suddenly hostile. "I will take what I can, and I will fight you for it."

Darkheart hissed at her. The presence of the humans had filled him with rage and fighting will, and he suddenly wanted to attack her. "I want human," he rasped.

She ignored him and loped toward the centre of the pit. Kraee had barely looked at him. The old griffin's feathers were fluffed up, and he was striking the ground with his tail, over and over again.

Darkheart left him where he was and ran around the edges of the pit again, looking for a way out. There were other gates, but they were all shut, and when he tried to break through them they proved too strong. And overhead the crowd continued to roar. They knew what to expect.

A few moments later one of the gates opened, and a human staggered through. He was followed by several others. Three other gates opened, and more humans entered, many of them carrying long sticks like those wielded by the humans who had taken Darkheart out of his cage. They scattered as soon as they emerged, running away into the pit, keeping close to its walls. Some tried to get back through the gates they had emerged from, but were forced out again.

Kraee acted immediately. He rushed at the nearest group of humans, beak open. They didn't stand a chance. He killed three of them with one blow and knocked down a fourth. Before it could get up again, he ripped its head off and swallowed it. Aeya, too, was quick to go after them. Some of the humans, overcoming their panic, began to strike at her and Kraee with their spears, but the two griffins paid little attention. The slaughter began.

Darkheart watched for a few moments, bewildered. He had never attacked humans on the ground. But then one passed close to him, and he lashed out at it by instinct, bowling it over. His hunger took over and he pounced on it and tore it open with his beak. Blood spurted into his mouth, hot and sticky and wonderful, and he pulled the limbs off and swallowed them. It tasted delicious. Human meat was not like goat or cow or any other kind of animal he had ever eaten. It was rich and sweet, and he loved it.

He finished his meal quickly, aware that there were still others there to catch. If he could kill a few of them, he could store them somewhere to eat later.

Ignoring Kraee and Aeya, he spotted a pair of humans by the wall. They were trying to help each other climb up it. He galloped toward them, wings raised as high as they would go. They, seeing him, turned and tried to run. But he darted first one way and then the other, blocking their escape. He killed one with an easy blow of his talons, but as he bent to finish it off with his beak he suddenly felt a sharp pain in his shoulders. He turned and saw the other human. It was already running, but he lashed out and caught it around the torso with his foreclaws. He dragged it toward him, struggling and screaming, and pinned it to the ground. It lay there, injured but alive, unable to get up.

Darkheart brought his beak down toward it. "You fight?" he asked it.

There was no recognition in the human's eyes, only fear. It snatched up a rock from the ground and smashed it against the joint of one of Darkheart's toes. He screeched and pressed down as hard as he could, crushing the creature into the ground. There was a crunch and a wet tearing sound, and when he raised his claws he saw that the human's torso had been mashed into a pulp. The head lay on the sand, connected to nothing but red mush, and he peered curiously at it. The eyes were still open, but they weren't looking at anything now.

He lost interest a moment later and turned his attention to the rest of the humans. There were still plenty left. Most of them just ran away. Others, cornered, tried to fight back. They died. Darkheart dragged their bodies to a spot by the wall and kept an eye on the pile. The other two weren't stockpiling their kills. They paused to eat parts of the humans they killed, but left the bodies lying on the ground and ran on to kill more. Darkheart began taking these, too, until he had a sizeable collection.

It was all so easy.

After a while, as the killing went on and his beak and talons turned red with blood, a strange madness came over him. His killer instinct, left unsatisfied for so long, rose up inside him with a vengeance, blotting out all thought and all semblance of rationality. He was barely aware of what he was doing. All he could see were the humans, dying, and all he could hear were the screams, the snarls and the roar of the crowd over the dull thud of beak and talon in flesh.

And then, at last, there were no more humans left.

Darkheart ran here and there, looking for them, but they were all dead. The madness receded somewhat and he withdrew to his heap of corpses and began to wolf them down. His exertions had made him hungry again, and the madness put an insane greed into him.

He saw a beak flash past him to snatch one of the bodies, and turned, snarling. Kraee had come and was eating, too. Darkheart did not think. Nor did he pause. He threw himself at the other griffin, smacking bodily into him. Kraee staggered away but then turned, rearing up on his hind legs. Darkheart rose, too, and the pair of them started to lash out at each other with their talons, screeching and rasping. Darkheart dived in under Kraee's beak and sank his own beak into Kraee's throat. It tore through the feathers and left a deep gash, which started to bleed profusely. Kraee screamed again and hurled himself at the black griffin. His front talons struck him in the shoulders and sank in deeply, puncturing the thick muscle. Darkheart howled in agony and began to strike wildly, hitting Kraee in the face, neck and chest. His beak clacked against that of the old griffin with a sound like falling rocks. Then it hit Kraee's in the eye.

Kraee's scream was indescribable. He let go and reeled away, still screaming, blood pouring from his ruined eye. Instantly Darkheart sprang forward, foretalons outspread. His hind legs gathered beneath him, kicking away from the ground in a great burst of powerful muscle. His wings spread partway and beat just once, clumsily. It was enough. He leapt at Kraee with all his strength. His front talons hit the other griffin square in the neck.

There was a crack and a thump, and Kraee fell, writhing on the ground. Darkheart did not pause over the dying griffin. He hit him again, in the back of the neck, and shook him violently until he stilled. Then, ignoring the yells of the crowd, he began to eat.

In the end it took twelve strong men to fight him into submission. They threw a net over him and pinned him down, and then wrenched his beak open and poured something bitter-tasting into it. A few moments later, exhaustion and weakness enveloped him, smothering his will to fight back. He could only just stand up when they reattached the chains to his collar and tugged him back to his paws, and the journey back to his cage passed in a haze. When he woke up there later, he wondered if it had all been a dream. But there was still blood on his talons, and his wounds ached savagely.

And there was no answering voice from Kraee's cage.

12

Visions

The Red Rat was bustling. Flell stood uncertainly in the doorway; she'd never seen the place so busy before. Every table was full, and the sheer volume of talk was deafening.

Thrain, perched on her shoulder, shifted nervously. "There are so many of them," she said. "What do they do here?"

"They're talking and drinking," Flell explained, wincing slightly as the griffin's talons stuck into her. "Can you see them anywhere?"

Thrain was silent for a time, scanning the room with her violet eyes. "Yes," she said at length. "They are there. By the fire."

Flell looked in that direction, and sure enough, there were Bran and Gern, sharing a drink. There was no-one else with them, and her heart sank. But she went toward them anyway, practically wading through the mass of people crammed into the tavern. It was so crowded that barely anyone noticed she had a griffin with her, so she didn't attract too much attention. She managed to get to their table and sat down next to Gern, somewhat awkwardly. He and Bran stopped their conversation and looked at her with surprise.

"Hello, Flell," said Gern, raising his voice over the hub-bub. "What are you doing here?"

"Looking for you," said Flell. "What's going on?"

"Not much," said Bran. "Gern's been tellin' me about this new griffin they got at the Arena."

"You mean Darkheart?" said Flell. "I heard something about that. Is it really black?"

"Yeah!" Gern half-shouted. "Black and silver! Arren caught it!"

"So, he *is* back," said Flell. "Gern, where is he? Have you seen him?"

"No," said Gern. "Well, once. Where've you been, Flell? I haven't seen you in ages."

"I had to go to Lansdown," Flell explained. "Father sent me to see about something—it's not important. Look, where's Arren? I can't find him."

"Have yeh checked his house?" said Bran.

"Yes. Haven't you?"

"Yeah, but there wasn't anyone home. Windows shut up, no-one answerin' the door."

"We've both been," said Gern. "If he's there, he's not coming out."

"Well, haven't you tried to find anything out?" said Flell. "What if something's happened to him?"

Gern looked grim. "Something *has* happened to him," he said. "Haven't you heard?"

"No, what's going on?"

"Eluna's dead," said Gern. "I heard it days ago."

Flell froze. "What? How?"

"It's all over the city," said Gern. "Arren didn't have permission to go to Rivermeet. He just heard about it from your father and ran off on his own."

"But why?" said Flell. "He wouldn't do something like that!"

"But he did," said Gern. "Or that's what I've been told.

He fought the black griffin on his own, and he caught it, but Eluna got killed. He came back here and Lady Riona sacked him for disobeying her. No-one seems to have seen him since then."

"We've been to his house dozens of times," said Bran. "Never saw a sign of him. His neighbours ain't seen him, either. We've got no idea where he's gone."

"I've heard all sorts of things," said Gern. "Someone said he's left the city. Gone to the North, to find his people."

"His people are *here*," Flell snapped. "You know he doesn't think like that, Gern."

"Yes, yes, I know," said Gern, holding up a hand as if to shield himself. "I didn't believe it. And someone else said he's killed himself, which I don't believe, either. That's rubbish. He'd never do something like that. And someone else said he's been locked up."

"What for?" said Flell, aghast.

"It's said he went crazy when Riona told him he was disgraced and tried to kill Lord Rannagon. If that's true, then it's a pretty serious crime. They could execute him for that."

Flell jumped up. "What? No—for the gods' sakes, tell me it's not true!"

"It ain't," Bran snapped. "Shut up, Gern. Yeh've got no bloody idea what yer goin' on about. Sit down, Flell."

Flell sat. "What's going on, Bran? How d'you know it's not true?"

"I've been moved to a different squad," said Bran. "I'm workin' in the prison district now, and I promise yeh that if Arren was in there I'd know about it. All right?"

She relaxed a little. "Well, if he's not at home and he's not in prison, where is he?"

"I think he's probably gone to visit his parents down in Idun," said Gern.

Flell shook her head. "I went to see them before I came up to the city. They haven't seen him. They don't even know about Eluna. I don't like this. He wouldn't just run off again, not after what happened last time."

"I saw him right after he got back," Gern said. "He looked terrible. He was dirty and he'd grown a beard, and there were bruises on his face, like someone'd been hitting him. I couldn't understand what was wrong with him. He wouldn't talk to me—just disappeared. It must've been right before he went to the Eyrie. I've never seen him look like that before. It scared me."

Flell stood up. "Well then, we've got to find out what's going on," she said sternly. "Come on."

"Where to?" said Gern, putting down his drink.

"To Arren's house," said Flell. "I know where he keeps the spare key. Even if he's not at home, there could be a clue there. Come on, let's go."

"What, now?" said Bran.

"Yes, now. Come on, damn it! What if he's in trouble? He's our friend, and he needs our help."

Bran and Gern got up and went with her without much argument, abandoning their drinks and following Flell as she left the tavern and walked toward the market district at high speed. Thrain jumped down off her shoulder and ran ahead, her claws skittering on the wood beneath her.

When they reached Arren's house they found it cold and still. The front door was closed and the windows shuttered. Flell, though, lifted Thrain over her head, holding her as high as she could. The griffin chick, balanced on her partner's hands, rooted around among the thatch over the door with her beak, as if looking for worms. Eventually she gave a triumphant chirp and pulled out a small oilcloth pouch. Inside was a key. Flell put it into the lock and turned it. But the door wouldn't open. She pushed hard, but it refused to move more than an inch. "It's stuck," she said.

Bran reached past her and shoved on the door, but without result. "Must be blocked from the other side," he said.

"Then someone must be in there," said Flell. She put the key back into the pouch and hid it among the thatch. "What do we do now?"

"Shouldn't be a problem," said Bran. "I've done this sort of thing before. Outta the way please, miss."

Flell stood aside and the big guard drew his sword. He poked it through the gap at the edge of the door, and then lifted it hard and pushed. There was a thud from the other side, and the door swung open.

"There yeh go," Bran said triumphantly.

It was gloomy inside the house. Some light was coming in through the back windows, but there were no candles or lamps burning. The air smelt stale and there was a layer of dust on the furniture. But it was plain that it had been lived in recently: there were dirty dishes on the table and a fire smouldering in the hearth. The hammock had been slept in, and there was a stained tunic hanging on the back of the chair.

There was also a large bowl on the table with a cloth over it. Flell wandered over and lifted the edge of the cloth, and the bowl proved to be full of water. "What—" she began.

"Don't touch that!"

They turned. Arren had appeared in the entrance to the stable. He was grubby and dishevelled and his face was obscured by an unkempt beard. Never particularly tanned, he now looked as if he had just climbed out of a tomb.

Flell stared at him, horror-struck. "Arren!"

He stood there, swaying slightly. "Hello, Flell."

She started toward him. "Arren, for gods' sakes, are you all right?"

Close up he looked even worse. There were faded bruises on his face, and his hair, normally obsessively neat, was matted. He peered at her, looking slightly bemused, and then shook his head. "No, no, not really. I mean, I've been better. I mean—" He made a half-laughing, half-coughing sound. "Eluna's dead. I'm broke, I'm unemployed, and also—excuse me a moment." He walked past her and lurched away through the door leading to the balcony. They heard him vomiting, and then he returned. He almost fell over in the doorway, and Gern and Bran took him by the shoulders and led him to the table. He sat down in the chair and slumped forward onto the table, groaning.

"I've also—also—also, I've drunk enough cheap wine to kill a horse," he added, to no-one in particular.

Flell had found a jug of water by the hammock and poured some into a mug. She had to put it into his hands for him. He downed it and then dropped the mug on the floor, where it broke.

He stared at the pieces and then suddenly started to cry. "Oh gods, I'm s—I'm sorry, I—I didn't mean, I—" He huddled down in his chair, face in his hands, sobbing brokenly.

Flell put her arms around him, and he clung to her pathetically, shuddering all over. She could smell the alcohol on his breath. "Arren, it's all right, it's all right, I've got you."

Bran patted him awkwardly on the shoulder. "It's all right, mate. We're here for yeh. I'll just—" He glanced at Gern. "I'll get some more water."

They kept their distance, both embarrassed, and Flell held on to Arren until he started to calm down, which took a while.

"I'm sorry," he said, between sobs. "I re—I really—I didn't want anyone to see me like this. Gods, I'm so pathetic, I—I'm an idiot, I'm a stupid gods—godsdamned idiot."

Flell didn't let go of him. "It's all right, Arren," she said, again and again. "It's all right. You're not an idiot."

After that his sobs died down, and he drank some more water. "I need to lie down," he said eventually.

Flell helped him to his hammock. He slumped into it, legs hanging over the sides, breathing heavily. He tried to shuffle himself further toward one end, but then slid back, wincing. "Thanks, Flell."

Flell crouched by him and touched his forehead. It was hot and clammy. "Gryphus—Arren, you're a mess," she said.

He turned his head slightly to look at her. "Am I?"

She couldn't help but laugh at the innocent inquiry in his voice. "Yes," she said. "You're a mess."

Arren closed his eyes. "I suppose so. I've been . . . drinking too much. I ran out of food, and—and—and . . ."

Flell took his hand in hers. "It's all right. Just rest."

His hand moved slightly. "I don't . . . I don't feel . . . well."

"I'm not surprised," she said, standing up carefully. She turned to Gern and Bran; they were watching silently and gave her imploring looks. Flell took her money pouch from her belt. "I need you two to help me," she said. "Go and buy some food."

"Won't be many places open right now," said Bran, taking the pouch.

"I know somewhere," said Gern. "C'mon."

The two of them departed. Flell closed the door behind them and sighed unhappily.

Arren had fallen asleep. Flell touched him lightly on the forehead, brushing away a few loose curls. He stirred slightly, his face creasing, and she covered him with a blanket and set about cleaning his home. She left the bowl of water untouched and found another one in a cupboard, filled it from the rain-barrel out on the balcony and used that to wash the dishes. After she had dried the dishes and put them away, she went into the stable, where she found that all the hay had been removed, leaving it bare and rather depressing to look at. A keg of wine stood against one wall. It was indeed cheap, and half the contents were gone. She carried it onto the balcony and poured the rest of it over the edge. Then she returned to the house. The floor was covered in dirt, and the shattered pieces of the broken mug were still lying by the table. She found a broom and cleaned it up as well as she could, and then opened the front windows to let in some fresh air. It was an improvement, at least.

Thrain had been exploring the corners, and now she wandered back. Flell bent and scratched her head. "It's much better in here now, isn't it?" she said, keeping her voice low.

Thrain lifted her beak, wanting Flell to scratch the

spot underneath it, which she did. Satisfied, the little griffin sat down by her foot, purring. "Arren is sick," she said suddenly.

"I know," said Flell. "He's very unhappy. Eluna died."

"He is hurt," said Thrain.

Flell paused. "What d'you mean, Thrain? Where is he hurt?"

"I smell blood," said Thrain. "Blood, there." She stood up, but instead of walking toward Arren she made for the table. She paused there a moment, sniffing, and then snatched at the tunic hanging over the back of the chair. It fell down, landing in a sad little heap at the chick's foretalons, and she started to peck the fabric, twittering to herself.

Flell came over and crouched to look at it. "Can I pick it up?" she asked.

Thrain nodded and withdrew, and Flell picked up the tunic.

There were bloodstains on it. Several of them. Flell dropped the tunic and almost ran toward the hammock. When she pulled the blanket away, she noticed for the first time that there were also stains on the tunic Arren was wearing now, over his chest and shoulders.

He woke up when she undid the fastenings on the front, and tried to push her hands away. "No, don't—that hurts—*aah*!"

His chest was thin and pale, scattered with black hairs and the faded scars that all griffiners had. There were several puncture marks on his shoulders and a partly healed slash just above his heart, and nearly all of them were red and swollen with infection.

Flell knew a few things about medicine. She felt the wounds carefully; they were hot to the touch, and Arren cringed at the slightest contact.

"*Ah!* Ow! Please, stop it, you're hurting me. *Flell!*"

She withdrew her hands. "Arren, for gods' sakes, why didn't you go to a healer?"

He closed his eyes. "I thought they'd get better on their own. I couldn't *afford* it."

There was a thud from behind them. Flell turned to see Bran and Gern arrive. They were carrying several parcels.

Flell went to them. "How did you do?"

Bran put down his burden on the table and gave her back her money pouch. "Not too bad. I owe yeh five oblong."

"Don't worry about it," said Flell. "Did you get food?"

"Of course we did," said Gern, gesturing at the parcels. "What d'you think that is, the Mistress' jewels? We caught a couple of stallholders as they were packing up. Got cabbage, cheese, bread and some smoked fish. It was cheap, too. Always is at the end of the day." He looked toward Arren. "How's he doin'?"

"Not well," said Flell. "He's got some infected wounds on his chest. Thrain smelt them out."

"I'm all right," Arren called. "They don't hurt much now. They'll get better."

"I'll be the judge of that," Flell said grimly. "You two, could you give me a hand?"

There was nothing for it but to clean the wounds as well as they could. Bran held Arren down while Flell used her knife to cut away the scabs and then cleaned the pus out. Once each wound was as clean as she could make it, she daubed on some ointment Gern found in a cupboard and then covered it up with a crude bandage.

Arren didn't enjoy the process one bit. He yelled and struggled and mouthed abuse at them when they refused to let him go. It was an ugly scene, but Flell only gritted her teeth and worked on. When she had finished, she tied the last hastily made bandage into place and pulled him to his feet. He stood, trembling slightly, but didn't try to make good on any of the threats he'd made.

"There," said Flell. "That's better. Now, try not to touch them. They need a chance to heal. How d'you feel?"

"My head hurts," Arren volunteered.

"I'm not surprised. How does your chest feel?"

"Like I've been stabbed by a girl with a dagger," said Arren.

"Har har, very funny. How did you get those injuries in the first place?"

"Shoa," said Arren. "She—she—she knocked me over and stuck her talons in me 'cause I . . . called your father a liar to his face."

"You did what?" said Flell. "Arren, what were you thinking?"

"Well, he is a liar," said Arren, slumping back into his hammock. "He said—he said—said—he told me to go, and then when I got back he said he didn't, and Riona wouldn't listen to me, and I called him a liar, and Shoa said—" He broke off suddenly and glanced toward the door with a slightly fearful expression. "Never mind. It doesn't—it's not important. I just n-need to rest a while, till I'm better."

"Good idea," said Bran. He stood up. "Sorry, everyone, but I gotta be off home. Early start tomorrow." He nodded to Arren. "G'night, sir. Hope yer feeling better in the—well, all right, not in the morning. By lunchtime, maybe. I'll come back an' see yeh later."

Arren had closed his eyes again. "Right, right," he mumbled.

Flell put the blanket over him, careful not to touch the bandages. "Just get some sleep now, Arren. I'll come back in the morning, all right?"

He yawned and covered his face with one arm. "If—don't tell anyone. Lock the door."

"I will, Arren," said Flell. "Goodnight."

She hustled the other two out of the house and locked the door behind her with the spare key. The moon was up by now, and the torches in the street were lit.

Gern leant against the wall of the house and wiped his forehead with his arm. "Phew! That was horrible!"

Bran shook his head. "I've seen him drunk before, but never that bad. He's really lost it, hasn't he?"

"Who can blame him?" Flell snapped, lifting Thrain into her arms. "And if either of you two had any sense you'd have put a bit more effort into finding out if he was all right. That's how people die, you know, because no-one bothers to check on them. I've heard about people who've killed themselves, and no-one found them for months just because they lived alone. What if that'd happened to Arren while I was away and you were off worrying about yourselves?"

"I just thought he wanted to be left alone, that's all," said Gern, shamefaced. "I mean, he's always been pretty solitary."

They walked off into the city.

"Everyone needs other people," said Flell. "And that includes him. And tomorrow I'm going to go and have a word with my father. I can't believe he and the Mistress just let Arren go like that and didn't do anything to help him. It's outrageous."

"Well, they've always been a bit off about that," said Gern. "Arren being a griffiner, I mean. I mean, he's not a noble like you. He's not even a Southerner."

"Yes, he is," said Flell. "He was born in Idun, just like you were."

"He's got a Northern accent, though," said Gern.

"So? It doesn't matter."

They stopped at a crossroads, and went their separate ways. Flell walked back toward her home on the other side of the Eyrie, with Thrain riding on her shoulder.

She knew perfectly well that other griffiners privately disapproved of her relationship with Arren. She didn't care.

She still remembered the day they had met, in the great council chamber at the Eyrie, when they had both been inducted as new griffiners. Thrain had only been a tiny hatchling then—half the size she was now—but Eluna had already been close to her adult size.

Flell had noticed the tall boy with the black hair during the ceremony and had watched him curiously. She'd never seen a Northerner before that day, although she had heard stories about them from her father, who had owned Northern slaves during his youth and had fought others during a rebellion in the North itself. She had already heard about how one of them had become a griffiner, but she hadn't seen him in person until that day. He had seen her looking at him, and she had been frightened when he looked back. His eyes were black, and it was hard to tell where they were looking or what the mind behind them was thinking. She had looked away nervously. But after the ceremony, during the celebrations that followed, he had come to find her.

"I'm Arren," he'd said in forthright tones. "I saw you looking at me."

He'd laughed at her stammering apology.

"It's all right. Everyone always looks at me. They all want to know why there's a blackrobe in the Eyrie."

That had given her confidence, and she'd introduced herself and Thrain. They had talked about their homes and their families and how they had become partnered with their griffins, and Flell had started to like him almost immediately. So solemn and serious, but with such a sweet smile. Handsome, too, in a cold kind of way.

Now she reflected on him as she had just seen him— barely recognisable under the beard, his chest cut up and infected, mumbling in his drunken despair—and her fists clenched.

A rren slept badly that night. He heard Flell leave, and some part of him wanted to call her back, but he couldn't seem to do anything other than lie on his back and mumble. He fell asleep a short while later. Half-formed dreams kept flicking in and out of his mind, and he couldn't stop sweating. He woke up again a while later—not sure if he'd slept at all—and tried to sit up. Instantly the hammock tipped over sideways, dumping him onto the floor. He lay there for a while, groaning. His head was still spinning, and his chest hurt so badly it felt as if Shoa's talons were still embedded in the flesh.

He managed to gather his arms beneath him and climbed laboriously to his feet, wincing. He staggered a little and nearly fell over again, but managed to reach the chair and sit down in it. It was midnight, and bright moon-light was shining in through the back windows. It fell over the table, turning it silvery grey. It also shone on the bowl he had left there. He stared at it blankly, trying to remember why it was there. Oh, yes.

He removed the cloth and put it aside. The water gleamed. The bowl was made of copper, but in the moon-light it looked like gold.

Arren stood up, steadying himself on the table, and shoved the chair out of the way. He stared down into the still water, watching the light play over its surface, and tried to think.

He spread his hand over the water and moved it in a gentle circling motion, counting under his breath. "One, two, three, four . . ."

When he reached thirteen, he held his hand just above the water, fingers spread, and started to chant softly.

> *Plentyn yn tyfu'n ddyn,*
> *Gorffennol ddaw'n bresennol,*
> *Rhaid i amser fynd rhagddo*
> *Arglwydd tywyll y nos, gweddïaf*
>
> *Cwyn len y nos, rho i mi ond trem*
> *Yn y nen, tair lleuad lawn ar ddeg,*
> *Pob un yn fywyd blwyddyn,*
> *Llygad y nos, agor led y pen,*
> *Dangos fy njynged i mi.*

He repeated the words several times, staring intently at the water until it became still.

Nothing happened. He withdrew his hand without taking his eyes away from the water, and continued to watch it as closely as he could, barely even blinking. Waiting.

After a while, the lingering effects of the wine mingled with his exhaustion made his vision start to waver. He was swaying slightly where he stood, though he didn't realise it, and as a cloud covered the moon and its light faded, he started to see things.

Shapes moved on the surface of the water. They were grey and very faint, but he leant closer, squinting at them, trying to make them form into something.

Two shapes. One light, one dark. Griffins, that was it. Two griffins, fighting. One white, one black. Eluna and the black griffin, locked together. Then the white shape faded away, leaving only the black griffin, which wandered away over the water, alone.

And then . . .

Visions flashed across his brain. He saw a line of people clad in black robes, each one carrying a heavy burden and wearing a shining collar. He saw Eluna lying in the muddy field, her eyes looking into his as she died. He saw Rannagon looking at him, his old face sad as he said something indistinct. And then the black griffin was there, rushing at him, wings spread wide, beak open to scream. Its talons hit him in the chest, and he was falling, down and down . . .

He didn't feel himself hit the floor. The visions vanished abruptly, but as darkness closed over him he saw one last thing. He saw himself, lying on dark ground beneath a silvery moon. His eyes were open . . . but they were blank and empty.

13

Cursed One

Flell went to visit Arren the next day, as promised, late in the morning. This time when she knocked on the door, he opened it.

"Good morning," Flell said awkwardly.

Arren looked at her for a moment and then stood aside, gesturing at her to come in.

The inside of the house looked a lot better now; the back windows and door were open, and sunlight was shining in, though Arren winced when it touched his face.

"Sit down," he mumbled. "I'll just—I'll be back in a bit."

He retreated into the stable and returned carrying an empty crate, which he put down next to the table and sat on. Flell noticed that, though he wasn't lurching now, he moved with a slight limp.

"Are you feeling better now?" she asked kindly.

Arren rubbed his face. He hadn't shaved off the beard, though he'd obviously done his best to neaten it up, and he'd made an attempt at combing his hair. He was still pale, though, and his eyes were bloodshot. "I feel like I've been run over by a cart," he said.

"So, would that be an improvement?" said Flell, setting Thrain down so she could wander off as she chose.

"A bit, yeah. Look, I'm sorry about last night. You didn't deserve to see me like that."

Flell put a hand on his shoulder. "It's all right, I understand. But you need to look after yourself, Arren. I care about what happens to you, and so do the others. You're not alone."

He reached up and put his hand on hers. "I know," he said. "I know. I just—I just miss her so much, Flell. I couldn't stand it. I mean—I thought there was something wrong with me. The whole way back here from Rivermeet I just . . . didn't feel anything. Like nothing was really real. And then when I got back home, it was like—like it all just hit me at once. I kept turning around and expecting to see her there, and when she wasn't, I felt lost. I still feel lost. Like there's something that used to be inside me and now it's gone, but I can still feel where it used to be."

"You should have come to see me," said Flell. "Or Bran, or Gern. We were worried about you."

"How could I?" said Arren, looking up at last. "I couldn't face you any more, not like this. The whole city knows I'm in disgrace. I kept expecting someone to come and arrest me, and then when no-one did I realised it was because no-one even cared. I'm not a griffiner any more, Flell. I'm nobody."

Flell laughed softly. "Oh, Arren, listen to yourself. Don't be ridiculous. We don't care about whether you're a griffiner or not; we care about *you*. You're our friend, aren't you? And to me—" She lifted his chin with her other hand so that their eyes met. "I love you, Arren. You do know that, don't you? And I'll go on loving you no matter what you do or what happens to you."

His face softened. "I know. I've always known. But what can I do now, Flell? Where can I go? I've *looked* for other jobs, but no-one will give me one. I'm too skinny to be a guard or a lift-loader, and I don't know anything about carpentry or metal or making bread. I mean, I know how to make boots, but what good does that do me? There's already five bootmakers working in the marketplace and none of them needs an assistant. I'm not good enough to do it on my own, and besides, I wouldn't have the money to pay for my own stall."

"Don't be silly; there has to be a job for you somewhere," said Flell. "You can read and write, can't you? There must be dozens of people out there who'd give anything to employ someone with your education."

"Oh yes?" said Arren. He slumped. "Flell, look at me. What do you see?"

She paused. "I see Arren Cardockson, who's grown a beard and looks miserable. Why, what did you expect me to see?"

Arren ran his fingers through his hair. "You can see *this*, can't you? And these?" He pointed at his eyes. "And these." He flexed his long fingers. "Well, so can everyone else, Flell. They see a Northerner."

"Well, you're not one," Flell snapped. "You're as Southern as I am."

He snorted. "Don't be ridiculous. I can't be a Southerner by pretending. My father keeps telling me that. Maybe I don't wear a robe or have spirals on my face, and maybe I'm not a slave, but I'm still a blackrobe, and everyone knows it as soon as they see me. I'm not just Arren Cardockson. I'm Arren Cardockson, the Northerner. And nothing can change that."

"So what?" said Flell. "It's nothing to be ashamed of. You didn't have any choice about what you were born as, any more than I did. Why should anyone care? You're still human."

"You're sheltered," Arren said bluntly. "I'm sorry, but you are. You don't live among ordinary people like I do. And I'm telling you, it matters. It's always mattered. Ever since I first came here people have said things. Treated me differently. They didn't dare make it too obvious, not while Eluna was there. But I could tell that nearly everyone who turned me away for a job was thinking: why employ a Northerner? It'd only make the customers nervous, and besides, there's plenty of other young people looking for work. Ones with proper brown hair and everything." He said this quite matter-of-factly; the bitterness was in the words rather than the tone.

"You're just being paranoid, Arren," said Flell.

He was silent for a time. "You know—do you remember how I fell off that roof when I was twelve?"

"Yes."

"It wasn't an accident," Arren said in a low voice. "Someone pushed me off."

Flell started. "What? Who? Why didn't you tell anyone?"

"I did. They didn't believe me, and anyway, I didn't see who did it. I was on an errand to fetch something, but someone grabbed my bag. I ran after them and they threw it on the roof of a building. I went and picked it up, and then someone shoved me from behind. Eluna was flying overhead, and she swooped down and put herself in the way, so I hit her instead of the ground. I probably would have died or been crippled if she hadn't. But I was knocked unconscious, and a while later Bran came along and found me lying there and carried me back home. That was how we got to be friends."

"Arren, that's—but why would anyone do that?"

"Because I was a Northerner," said Arren. "Other children were always picking on me when Eluna wasn't there. In the end she started staying with me all the time, and they left me alone then. But I knew they still hated me. And now Eluna can't protect me any more."

Flell stiffened. "Arren, you don't think—you're not in danger, are you?"

"No, no. I'm all right. They aren't going to kill me. But they can still make trouble for me. At this rate they won't need to push me off another roof; they can just wait for me to starve to death."

Flell paused. "Have you eaten anything yet?"

He shook his head. "Too sick."

The parcels of food were still on the table. Flell found

a plate and started opening them. "You've got to eat," she said, pulling out a loaf of bread. "Go on, Bran and Gern went out especially to get all this for you."

Arren accepted the plate of food she offered him and started to eat, chewing listlessly. "I don't deserve this," he said.

"Nonsense. Eat up, you've got a big day ahead of you."

He gave her a cynical look. "Oh? Why, what's happening today?"

"We're going to get you a job," said Flell. "And possibly something else, too."

Arren swallowed. "You're not going to ask your father to help, are you? Because I really don't think—"

"No. How's your chest, by the way?"

He let her open his tunic and carefully peel away the bandages to inspect the wounds. They looked much better, though it was difficult to tell yet whether they would begin healing. At least none of them looked as if they were filling up again.

"Ow. How do they look?"

"Not too bad," said Flell, "but we'll have to change the bandages tonight. Have you got a clean tunic anywhere?"

Arren picked up a piece of cheese. "Yes, in the chest over there."

She fetched it and a fresh pair of trousers, and when he'd finished eating she gave them to him, saying, "You'd better wash yourself first. And you look like you need a shave, too."

The bowl of water was still on the table. Arren found a small bar of nasty-smelling soap and gave his face a wash, beard and all. Once he'd dried off he combed his hair, carefully reordering it until it had begun to resemble its old neat self again. After that he combed the beard as well.

"Aren't you going to shave it off?" asked Flell.

He shrugged. "I can't find my razor. Can I have that now? Thanks." He took the tunic and put it on, along with the clean trousers and the pair of heavy leather boots he seemed to wear everywhere, even on official occasions. "There," he said once he was done. "How do I look?"

"I can't say I like the beard much," said Flell. "You look completely different now, you know."

"Oh? How?"

"Older. And a lot scruffier."

He scratched it. "Maybe I'll have it trimmed once I can afford it."

"Why not just get rid of it?"

Another shrug. "So, where are we going?" He was playing along with her now, but evidently curious.

"To the hatchery," said Flell, scooping up Thrain. "We're going to go and see Roland."

Arren's face fell. "Flell, you don't really think—"

"Get your cloak and come on," Flell said firmly. "It's cold today."

He obeyed and they left the house together. Flell walked ahead, her expression determined, and in spite of his long legs Arren nearly had to run to keep up with her. "Flell, you don't honestly think I could find another griffin, do you?"

"Why not?" said Flell. "You never know until you try."

He sighed. "I really don't know."

When they arrived at the hatchery they found it bustling as always. Roland, along with two helpers, was in the huge space that housed the adult griffins, replacing the soiled straw and refilling the water troughs. They were working hard and didn't look around until Flell called out to Roland. Thrain, made nervous by the presence of so many much larger griffins, huddled against her partner's chest.

Roland came to meet them, wiping the sweat off his forehead. "Hello, hello! Good morning, lass, how are you?" He paused. "Dear gods—Arren, is that you?"

Arren nodded, shamefaced. "Hello, Roland."

Roland looked concerned. "Well, I must say it's a shock to see you like this, Arren. I'm not entirely sure that beard suits you. But"—he placed a large freckled hand on Arren's shoulder, nearly engulfing it—"I heard about what happened," he said softly. "And I can't possibly express how upset I am. Eluna was—well, she was an extraordinary griffin, just like her partner."

"Thanks," said Arren. "I—thanks, Roland."

Roland straightened up. "All right, you two, you finish up here," he bellowed to his assistants. "If anyone asks, I'm in my quarters." He turned to Flell and Arren. "If you'd care to join me, I think I may be able to rustle up some tea from somewhere. Shall we?"

Flell took hold of Arren's hand as she nodded. "Yes, thank you, Roland."

They followed him to the main building of the hatchery, and through into the back room that served Roland as a home. He gestured at them to sit at the table, and put down a bowl of strayberries and a pot of tea.

"There you go," he said. "Some mint tea and strayberries. Nothing better to cheer you up, I always say." He sat down opposite them and poured out the tea. "It's not quite as hot as I'd like, but it should do."

Arren drank gratefully. The sharp flavour of the mint helped to remove the dry, unpleasant taste in his mouth. "Thanks, Roland."

"Well, well, it's the least I can do," said Roland, watching him with concern. "So, how are you holding up, lad?"

"I'll be all right," said Arren, reaching for a strayberry.

"I hear you did a magnificent job in catching that griffin," said Roland. "Darkheart, they're calling it."

Arren snorted. "So I heard. Gods, those people annoy me. Darkheart. What sort of a name is that? And they're *happy* about how the damned thing crushes people's ribcages? It's pathetic."

Roland sipped at his own tea. "Yes, I can certainly see where you're coming from there. But it does bring in a great deal of, shall we say, *revenue* for the city, and it creates jobs. People have always been fascinated by violence. It comes of spending so much time around griffins, probably."

"Violence doesn't bother me much," said Arren. "You fight when you need to. But using it as entertainment . . ."

Roland shrugged. "It *is* thrilling, in a way. So, what can I do for you, Arren? I mean, beyond offering you a few strayberries."

Arren knew he'd already guessed. "Well, Flell thinks— that is, *I* think—that maybe I could show myself to the griffins here. You know, in case one of them . . ." He shrugged, trying to hide his embarrassment.

Roland looked grim. "Well, it's not for me to say yea or nay, but I won't pretend it isn't a stretch. Griffins tend to— well, try if you must. You never know."

"There's something else," Flell interrupted.

"Yes?"

"Arren needs a job," said Flell. "And badly."

"Oh!" said Roland. "Well, I think I can help you there, lad. One of my assistants has moved on to better things— possibly worse, I didn't ask—and I'd be more than happy to take you on here. Mind, it wouldn't be very glamorous. Sweeping floors, fetching and carrying, that sort of thing."

"I don't mind," said Arren. He was pleased by this. It hadn't occurred to him to ask Roland for help, but he was grateful to Flell for coming up with the idea. If another griffin didn't choose him—or even if one *did*—working here wouldn't be so bad.

"That's excellent to hear," said Roland. "I admit we've missed you here. Haven't we, Keth?"

The old griffin had wandered over to the table to inspect them. She sniffed at Arren. "You smell of sickness," she commented.

Arren ducked his head slightly. "I'm sorry. I haven't been well."

"Death is a poison, to the living," Keth remarked enigmatically. She yawned and went to Roland, who scratched her under the beak.

"Are you well, Keth?" said Arren, privately thinking that her words were the most ridiculous thing he'd heard all day.

"I am well." The answer was courteous enough, but there was something about the way she looked at him that suggested she didn't think he was. And not just because he was hungover.

Roland took another swallow of tea. "You know," he said, "I doubt this will be any comfort to you, but do you know I used to be a griffiner, too?"

"You still are," Arren pointed out.

"Oh, I suppose so," said Roland. "In a way. But no, what I mean is that when I was younger a griffin chose me. Just a little chick. His name was Rakee." He smiled, his old face creasing. "He was a wonderful griffin. So tiny, but so full of life. He was yellow. Had golden eyes, as I recall."

"What happened?" said Flell.

Roland put down his mug. "He died," he said briefly. "Sickness. Egg-scour. There was an epidemic. It killed dozens of young griffins, and my Rakee was one of them. I had to give up my job as Rannagon's assistant and come to work at the hatchery. Luckily my father owned it, so I was put in charge of it. And after my father died, Keth attached herself to me. Not the most likely of pairings, but we work together well enough."

Arren listened, with a sad little chill. *Imagine having your dreams snatched away from you just like that, so suddenly and so senselessly,* he thought, and then realised, miserably, that he didn't have to imagine what that would be like.

"Anyway," said Roland, "if you've finished your tea, we may as well get on."

Arren swallowed the last of it and put down his mug. He stood up, heart pounding. "I'm ready."

Flell abandoned the rest of her own tea and followed them as they went to the nearest pen. Roland opened the gate at the front of it and gestured at Arren to go in.

There was a griffin chick in there, about the same age as Thrain, curled up in the straw and watching him warily.

Arren crouched and held a hand out toward it, keeping his movements slow and careful. "Hello, little one," he said, speaking griffish.

The chick got up and sniffed his hand. "Food?"

"My name's Arren," said Arren. "What's yours?"

It peered up at him for a while, realised he wasn't offering it any food, and lay down again. It yawned dismissively and closed its eyes.

Arren got up and left the pen, and Roland closed the gate behind him. "Not to worry," he said cheerfully. "We'll try the next."

The next chick was awake and immediately tried to charge out of the pen when the gate was opened. Roland gently nudged it back with his foot, and Arren slipped through.

When he reached toward the chick it bit his fingers. "Food! Food!"

Arren forced himself not to flinch. "I'm Arren," he said.

It paused and peered at him, and then flicked its wings and walked past him, toward the gate. Arren turned awkwardly and watched as it tried to climb out. "You can't get out that way," he told it.

The chick paid absolutely no attention. It stood up on its hind legs, looking up at Roland. "Food! Food!"

Roland gave it some dried meat, and Arren vaulted over the gate and landed beside him. "It's no good," he said. "They're not interested."

"It's a tad early to be saying things like that, lad," said Roland. "Go on, move on. Never say die—well, until you're actually about to die, I suppose," he added, half to himself.

The next chick was equally dismissive, and so was the next. There were literally dozens of them in the hatchery, and Arren spent what felt like half a day going from pen to pen, trying to coax the chicks into speaking to him. Some bit him, some ignored him, others cheekily called out curse words they'd picked up, and one tried to use him as a ladder to get out of its pen.

By the end of it Arren was grubby and exhausted, and both his hands were covered in scratches. Leaden depression had settled into his chest. "I told—" he began, and then stopped and shook his head. There was no point in being bitter at Roland and Flell. It wasn't their fault. And besides, they already knew.

"Well then," Roland said resignedly, "it seems there is no other choice but to move on."

Arren knew what that meant. He almost started to protest, but then gave up and joined Roland in the next room. Keth followed them silently.

The adult griffins had just been fed, and most were lying in their stalls, dozing. Others were flitting among the massive rafters in the ceiling, or were wandering here and there as they chose, or talking or mock-fighting among themselves.

Without being prompted, Keth stepped forward and screeched loudly, cutting across the racket. Every griffin's head turned toward her at once. Some of them called back, but most of them stopped what they were doing and came toward her in silence. They formed themselves into an untidy group in the middle of the floor, all looking toward Keth with considerable respect.

She stood by Roland's side, tail swishing. "A human has come for you to see," she told them. "Do not leave until it is done."

Arren came forward at Roland's prompting. He was horribly aware of all the eyes now on him, sharp, fierce, intelligent griffin eyes. Some of them chirped or clicked their beaks at the sight of him, and one or two lay down on their bellies and rested their heads on their claws, openly bored.

He knew what to do now. He'd seen it dozens of times, when young would-be griffiners had come to present themselves. He and Eluna had always found it amusing. As he came forward and stood where they could easily see him, he almost thought he could see the white griffin sitting in the rafters overhead, mocking him with a griffish snigger.

"Who are you?" one griffin asked.

Arren looked up. "I am Arren Cardockson," he said, keeping his voice loud and clear. "I am nineteen years old. I can—"

"So this is he," a brown griffin interrupted. "The Northerner. I remember him."

"You fed me when I was a chick," said another griffin. "I remember. You were hardly older than a chick yourself. You had a griffin with you then. Where is she now, human?"

"She is dead," said another. "Shree himself has told me this. Darkheart the mad griffin killed her, and the black-robe fool did not protect her."

There was a hissing from the assembled griffins.

Shame burned inside him. "Eluna was my friend," he answered. "She chose me when I was only three years old, and she told me she would not have any other human as her partner."

"And yet you let her die," said the brown griffin. "Why is this so, Northerner?"

"It wasn't my fault," said Arren. "She persuaded me to fight the black griffin. When he attacked us, she died to save me from him."

"I knew her," said a grey griffin. "We were chicks together. She was a fool to choose you."

"What griffin would want to tie herself to someone such as you?" said the brown griffin, coming forward slightly. "I see nothing about you to make you special. You have no noble blood, or power. Are you wealthy?"

Arren paused, but he knew what would happen if he lied to a griffin. "No. Eluna didn't choose me because of those things," he said. "She chose me because she believed I was brave and intelligent."

"And perhaps you are," said the brown griffin. "But those qualities do not change the fact that you are a black-robe. And a blackrobe cannot and should not be a griffiner."

Arren bit down on his anger. "That's for you to decide," he said, bowing his head to them all.

That pleased them. He heard them muttering among themselves in approval.

He didn't look up, but waited silently where he was.

After a while, a griffin came forward to inspect him. She looked at him closely and scented at him, and then turned and went back to her place. A few moments later another came. This one scented him and then backed away. The griffin paused a moment, and then suddenly reared up, hissing. Arren looked up sharply but didn't move. He stayed where he was, braced for an attack, and stared defiantly up at the griffin. The griffin lashed out at him with his claws, narrowly missing Arren's face, and then screeched. The noise was deafening and utterly terrifying to anyone who did not know griffins. But Arren refused to back down.

The griffin dropped back onto his foreclaws and clicked his beak, evidently impressed. "Courage, indeed," he said, and returned to his spot.

None of the other griffins came forward, but the contempt in their gazes had lessened noticeably.

No-one moved or spoke for some time, and then there was a scuffling from among the griffins and a third one came forward. This one was female and had vivid silver feathers. She crouched a short distance from him, watching him closely. She seemed uneasy and kept shivering her wings, the feathers rustling.

At last she rose and stretched her head toward him, half-closing her eyes as she sniffed. Then, suddenly, she started and backed away, hissing. *"Kraeai kran ae!"* she rasped, opening her wings.

The other griffins hissed and began to stir at this, some backing away.

The silver griffin raised a forepaw and held it out toward him, talons spread. *"Kraeai kran ae!"* she said again. *"Kraeai kran ae!"*

Arren had never seen or heard anything like this before. "What does that mean?" he asked nervously.

The silver griffin snapped her beak at him. "You are cursed," she snarled. *"Kraeai kran ae!* Cursed one!"

Keth started forward. "Okaree, stop this! You know nothing about curses."

"A silver griffin smells magic!" Okaree snarled, eyes blazing. "I smell it on this man. He is *Kraeai kran ae*. He is cursed. Beware!"

There was silence, and the silver griffin turned away and flew up into the rafters and through one of the huge open windows in the roof, into the sky beyond.

No-one spoke for some time after she had gone, but then the griffins began to chirp. They were laughing, and they broke up and wandered back to their stalls without another glance at Arren. The brown one stopped on her way past him, though. "Do not listen to Okaree. She is a fool. But perhaps she should have chosen you. You are as mad as each other."

"Don't insult me," Arren snapped back. "I'm still a griffiner."

The brown griffin paused, looking at him. Then she leapt. She knocked him onto the floor and pinned him down, much as Eluna had once done, and brought her beak toward his face. "Not just a blackrobe, but an arrogant blackrobe," she hissed, and bit him on the ear.

Keth darted forward to intervene, but the brown griffin removed her claws and walked off, tail swishing.

Roland and Flell helped Arren to his feet. His ear was bleeding, and Roland took a rag from his pocket and gave it to him, saying, "Here, quickly, cover it up before you get any on your tunic."

Arren folded it up and clapped it over his ear, which was hurting quite badly. "I think she took a piece off it," he said through gritted teeth.

Flell took him by the arm and steered him back into the chicks' room. "That cursed thing," she muttered venomously. "She had no right to speak to you like that."

Roland looked unhappy. "I'm terribly sorry for that, Arren. Okaree has always been a little peculiar, and Senneck—well, she's always been like that. Are you all right, lad?"

"I'll be fine," said Arren. He took the rag away from his ear and felt it carefully. "She's bitten a piece off the top. Well, at least it'll match the other one," he added bitterly.

"I don't know why griffins always seem to bite people's ears," said Roland. "I asked Keth once, but even she either didn't know or wouldn't tell me." He sat Arren down at the table and pushed a mug of the now-cold tea into his hands. "I really am very sorry, Arren."

"It's not your fault," said Arren, taking it. "I didn't expect them to be pleased to see me."

In fact, he had guessed from the outset that they would be unsympathetic, and that they would dislike him on principle given that Eluna had died as a result of being partnered with him. But the rejection had still hurt, even more so than his torn ear.

"Well," said Roland, ever cheerful, "there's no cause to despair just yet. Consider yourself my assistant from now on. You can come in here every day to help me keep the place up and running, and I'll see to it that you're well paid. And who knows, perhaps things will change for you. We've always got more chicks hatching. They'll get to know you better if you're here all the time, and I don't see why one of them won't change its mind."

Arren nodded. "Thanks, Roland. This means a lot to me."

"It's the least I can do," said Roland.

Flell scratched Thrain's head. "You'll be all right," she said. "Don't listen to those overgrown chickens next door. Ow!" Thrain had bitten her on the ear. "I didn't mean *you*, silly." She took Arren's hand. "Will you be all right?"

He nodded again. "Thanks for your help, Flell."

Flell lifted him to his feet and embraced him. "I'll always be there when you need me, Arren," she said. "Always. Just as you've always been there for me."

The embrace, and her words, lifted some of his black despair. He hugged her back tightly, ignoring the blood soaking into his hair. "I love you, Flell," he murmured.

She let go and punched him playfully on the arm. "Do you, now? Well then, next time there's a problem, you come to me. No more locking yourself away, understood?"

Arren dabbed at his ear. "I'll try to remember that."

"Good," said Flell. "Now, I'm afraid I have to go and see my father. But come and visit me soon and we'll have dinner together, all right?"

"I'll be there," Arren promised. "Roland, d'you want me to start work today?"

Roland shook his head. "No, no. You've had quite enough excitement for one day, I think. Go home and get some rest and be back here tomorrow as early as you can. If I'm not here, just go to Alisoun or Landry. I'll let them know about the situation so they'll be expecting you."

"Thanks, Roland." Arren drank the cold tea out of the mug. "I'd better go home and do some tidying up."

He and Flell parted just outside the hatchery, and Arren made for his home, shoulders hunched. He'd put on a brave face for Flell and Roland, but he knew they hadn't been fooled. They knew what he was really feeling. They'd always been able to read him, especially Flell.

He tried to look on the bright side. At least he had a job now, even if it was a menial one. It would help him get by until . . .

Until what? Until another griffin chose him?

He sneered. There was no chance of another griffin choosing him, not now. It had been a freak chance that had led him to become a griffiner in the first place, and the likelihood of it happening again was extremely poor, if not nonexistent. No, he was not a griffiner now, and he never would be again. That dream was over, and there was nothing left for him to do but get on with his life.

He reached into his pocket and felt the tiny object in there. He'd almost forgotten about it. Perhaps it was time now . . .

He reached his home, lost in thought, and unlocked the front door. Some food and sleep would do him good, after he put a dressing on his ear.

But when he entered the house, he found someone already there.

14

Accusation

It was Lord Rannagon.

Arren started toward him. "What are you doing here?"

Rannagon was alone this time, but he had his sword with him. He stood up. "Good evening. Don't worry, there's no need to be alarmed; I'm just here to say hello."

Arren closed the door. "I'm not doing anything wrong, all right? I haven't told anyone anything. They wouldn't believe me anyway. I'm just trying to get on with my life, understand? So you can leave me alone."

Rannagon nodded, "Yes, yes, understood. Have you found another job yet?"

"Yes. With Roland, at the hatchery."

"That's good," said Rannagon. "Roland's very fond of you. He'll be a good employer. Flell told me she was helping you get back on your feet."

Arren stuffed the key back in his pocket. "I suppose you want me to stop seeing her."

"No. That's her own choice. I don't entirely approve, but I can't stop her. Go on seeing her, by all means. I've been keeping an eye on you, and I'm very pleased to see you're doing so well. But if there's anything you still need—"

Arren sneered at him. "D'you honestly think you can come in here and pretend you're my friend? You betrayed me, Rannagon. Don't think I'm going to forget that."

"I don't think that," said Rannagon. "I'm just making sure you're all right."

Arren pointed at the door. "And now you know. So you can leave me alone."

Rannagon nodded and made for the back door. It was open, and Arren could just see Shoa crouched outside. "Understood. Goodnight, Arren."

Arren stood by the table, arms folded, and watched him go without saying a word.

Rannagon paused in the doorway. "I'll be in touch."

Arren just stared at him, unreadable, and the old lord shrugged and was gone.

Once he'd left, anger boiled up inside Arren again. He slammed the back door and locked it, then sat down heavily at the table. The chair was still warm.

So, Rannagon was still watching him. And probably other people were, too. If he did anything—tried to tell someone the truth—what then?

"No," he muttered. "No, I won't put up with it any more. I'm going to . . ."

To do what?

The next day, Arren's new life began. He put on his plainest and toughest clothes and went to the hatchery first thing in the morning. There he was met by Alisoun, another of Roland's assistants, who gave him his first task for the day, feeding the chicks. After that he had to clean out and replace the straw in the pens, help round up some goats so they could be slaughtered and fed to the adult griffins, carry some heavy crates from the nearest lifter to the storeroom and then sweep the floor.

It was hard work, and boring, but he didn't mind. He worked steadily, not speaking to anyone, his face a cold, impassive mask.

At noon he broke for lunch, which he ate with Roland and the other assistants, and after that it was back to work. He left that evening with a sore back and aching hands, but Roland had given him a small bag of coins. It wasn't much to show for one day's effort, but it was enough. He only needed to feed himself now.

Flell was waiting for him that evening.

Her home was only large enough to need two servants, who had already finished preparing the meal. She and Arren sat together in the dining room and ate, enjoying each other's company.

The food was good, much better than his usual fare. Arren ate heartily, savouring the rich flavours of roasted meat and fresh vegetables, and the fine wine Flell had had brought out.

Flell watched him a little anxiously. "How's your ear?"

Arren touched it carefully. "It's all right. The bleeding stopped in the end. It should heal."

"And your chest?"

"It still hurts, but I think it'll be fine. I've been keeping an eye on it and I think the infection's gone."

"That's good. So, how was work?"

"Hard," Arren said. "My back is killing me. I had to carry a lot of crates; I didn't ask what was in them, but I'd swear it was lead. I don't mind, though."

Flell nodded. "But how are *you*, Arren? And I don't mean are you healthy; I mean, are you all right?"

"There's no need to worry about me," said Arren, in a tone of forced casualness.

"Isn't there?" said Flell.

Her direct gaze was unsettling, and he drank some more wine to hide his uncertainty. "What d'you want me to say?" he said, putting down his cup. "I mean, no, I haven't forgotten about . . . what happened. But life goes on, doesn't it? I can't sit around feeling sorry for myself; you already made that quite clear, and you were right. And—" He tried not to think about Rannagon, or Shoa's icy stare.

Flell hadn't dropped her gaze. "What did happen out there, Arren?" she asked. "Why did you run off like that? It doesn't make any sense. It's not like you to do something like that. What were you thinking?"

Arren was silent. He looked at Flell, at her light-blue eyes and freckled face. He couldn't bear the thought of lying to her. Surely . . . surely Rannagon wouldn't kill her? Not his own daughter. "I—"

His eyes flitted toward the door. Flell's housekeeper was standing there, watching him. She saw him look in her direction and quietly vanished.

Fear ran down Arren's spine. "I made a mistake," he said, a little too loudly. "I was stupid." And it was true, he thought. He wasn't lying to her.

"But why didn't you ask anyone else before you left?" said Flell. "And you lied to me. Why, Arren? I just keep wondering why you didn't tell me the whole truth. Was it because you were afraid I'd tell someone else?" She was looking at him not reproachfully, but with hurt bewilderment. "I'm not angry with you," she said. "I just want to know why."

Arren couldn't look her in the eye. "I don't want to talk about it," he said.

"Please, Arren," said Flell. "Just tell me. I'll understand."

"Because I wanted it to be a surprise," Arren said at last. "I wanted—I was trying to impress you."

"*Impress* me?" said Flell. "Arren, for gods' sakes, you don't need to impress me! What on earth gave you that idea?"

"It's just—well, I've always felt—you know, that I didn't deserve you," said Arren. He was speaking the truth now, at least in part. "And I know people don't approve of you seeing me. I thought maybe if I did it—if I proved I could be brave, it would—"

"Arren, disobeying orders and abandoning your duties

so you could put yourself in danger does not impress me," Flell said sharply.

Arren bowed his head. "I know. I know. I told you I was stupid. I can't forgive myself for it, but—I'm sorry, Flell. What I did was selfish, and I'll never stop paying the price. I know that now."

Her expression softened. "It *was* brave of you, though. But you didn't need to prove that to anyone. You've always been brave."

Arren looked up. "I have?" he said, genuinely surprised.

"Yes," said Flell. "You went into a griffin's territory when you were just a child, didn't you? You impressed one before you could read. And you became a griffiner when everyone said it should be impossible. And you lived in the South when you're not a Southerner, when you knew people would never stop treating you differently, but you never let it change you, did you? I know your father. He looks like you, but he's not you. He's bitter. Your mother is, too. But you're not."

"Oh, I am bitter," said Arren. "I've always been bitter."

She smiled at him. "You don't show it."

Later on, once they had finished eating, they sat together by the fire in Flell's study and shared some mulled wine. Thrain dozed at her partner's feet, her stomach bulging with goat meat.

"I don't care that you don't have a griffin any more," Flell declared. "You'll always be a griffiner to me."

That made Arren smile. "Well, if I'm a griffiner to you, that's enough for me." It wasn't, and both of them knew it, but for now it didn't matter.

"It really is stupid, you know," Flell said suddenly. "What people say about Northerners."

Arren took another mouthful of wine. "I know."

"I mean, look at you," said Flell. "It's really quite—it's very strange, in a way. I've seen pictures of Northerners in books, and you look exactly like them. But you're *not* them. You're nothing like the ones in the books, or the stories people tell. You're not wild or savage, you don't worship the moon, you can read and write, and you're a griffiner. D'you know, someone said to me once that Northerners can use magic?" She laughed. "Even some of the books say that. It's the silliest thing I ever heard. Humans, using magic? Next thing they'll be saying you can fly."

Arren smiled. "It's true, though, you know," he said.

Flell looked up. "What?"

"We can—oh, nothing. It's nonsense."

"No, go on," said Flell. "What is it? You're not saying you really *can* use magic, are you?"

"No," said Arren. "But my mother *did* teach me a spell."

Flell stared at him. "What? A spell? What does it do?"

"Well, she said that, supposedly, every Northerner can call on the power of the moon. Every phase has a power. The crescent moon means protection. The half-moon means destiny. And the full moon means a time for magic. Anyway, my mother said that every Northerner can use the full moon to divine their future. It only works once, but what it shows you is always true."

Flell gave an incredulous laugh. "Have you ever tried it?"

Arren paused. "Yes. That's why there was that bowl of water on the table when you came to see me. I'd had some stupid idea about trying it, to see what I should do next. You know how you get these ideas when you're—well, when you've drunk a bit too much."

Flell nodded. "Yes, of course. So what happened?"

Arren tried to remember. "Not much, really. I think I fell asleep while I was waiting for the vision to appear. I woke up a while later on the floor."

"So, you didn't see anything?"

"Well . . . maybe."

"Tell me, then," said Flell. "What was it?"

Arren laughed. "It's stupid. It's just nonsense. Humans can't use magic, and the moon can't do anything except shine. Nothing happened. I fell asleep and had a dream."

"Yes, but what did you see?"

Arren's smile faded. "I shouldn't tell you. It'll just make you nervous for no reason."

It was the wrong thing to say. "Just tell me, silly," said Flell. "If it's stupid, it won't mean anything."

"Well . . ." Arren looked into the depths of his drink. It was dark and the light gleamed off it, just like the water in the bowl. He looked up. "I saw myself dying," he said at last.

Flell stifled an uncomfortable half-laughing sound. "What?"

"I saw the black griffin fly at me," Arren recalled. "And then I was falling, and then I saw myself lying on the ground somewhere. It was night-time."

Flell paused and took a drink. "That's—I don't like that."

"It was just a nightmare," said Arren. "I told you it didn't mean anything. I always have dreams about falling. And the black griffin—" He sighed. "I haven't stopped having nightmares about it. Not since Eluna died. I keep waking up and thinking it's there, waiting to kill me."

Flell scowled. "I've seen that griffin," she said. "Gern talked me into going to the Arena this morning. It killed seven men and then started eating them. None of the other griffins would go near it; someone told me the first time it went into the pit it killed one of them. And then it tried to eat it."

"I should have killed it," said Arren. He stared into the fire, black eyes gleaming in the light. "I nearly did. I had it right there in front of me, tied up in a cage. I wanted to kill it; I was about to kill it. I had an arrow pointed right at the thing's eye. But I just—maybe he was right," he added, half to himself. "I should buy it back and kill it."

"Orome would never sell it to you," said Flell. "Never. Haven't you heard? That griffin is famous. It's only been in the Arena twice and everyone's talking about it. Darkheart, the mad black griffin. People are writing *songs* about it. In fact—oh, never mind, it's not important."

"What is it?"

Flell shook her head. "No, no, forget about it."

Arren smiled. "I told you something I didn't want to, so now it's your turn."

"Well, there's a song about you," said Flell. "About how you caught the black griffin."

"There is?" said Arren, surprised. "Really? How does it go?"

"Uh . . . I don't really know it very well. It just says something about how the black-eyed boy fought the black-furred griffin until the griffin gave in and said you were its master, or something."

"Oh." Arren was a little pleased by this.

Flell finished off her wine and stared at the empty cup. She wished she hadn't said anything about the song, and she hoped Arren wouldn't get to hear it in its entirety. The song was far less complimentary than she had implied, and when she had first heard it she had come close to shouting at the person who'd sung it. People were cruel and ignorant sometimes.

Arren finished his wine and put his cup aside. He yawned. "Oooh, I'm tired."

Flell glanced out the window. It was quite late, and she put her own cup down. "I think it's bedtime for me," she said.

Arren looked at her. "I'd better get going, then," he said, standing up.

"Leaving so soon?" Flell asked, smiling.

"Well, if you'd prefer—"

She stood, moved closer and kissed him lightly. He paused, and then kissed her back. Flell took his hand. "Come on, you," she said, and the two of them dashed up the stairs, giggling like children. They reached Flell's room, where one of her servants had already lit the lamp.

Flell closed the door and kissed Arren again. "You're so rough with that beard," she giggled.

"Sorry."

"Don't be."

They embraced tightly, their hands in each other's hair, suddenly breathing hard. Flell said nothing. She undid the fastenings on Arren's tunic, and he shrugged it off, letting it slide onto the floor. His hands slid down the neck of her gown and onto her shoulders, massaging the soft skin and muscle, and she undid the fastenings on the back and let it fall down over her hips and to the floor. They pressed themselves together, whispering each other's names, until there was no more need to speak. They knew all they needed to know, and always would.

Flell slept deeply that night, her head resting on Arren's chest, undisturbed by dreams.

When she woke the next morning she moved carefully away from him, not wanting to disturb him, and stretched. Sunlight was coming in through the window, and she could hear birds chirping. She could also hear Thrain. The griffin had climbed onto the roof and was calling, albeit not very loudly or impressively. Flell smiled to herself and looked down at Arren.

It was strange how different people looked when they were asleep. Flell had seen dead people, but they weren't the same. Someone dead always looked empty somehow, as if they weren't really a person any more but just a thing. Which they were. A dead person's soul fled their body the moment their heart stopped beating, and took their memory and personality with it. Someone asleep, though they were often just as still as a dead person, didn't look like that. In sleep, Arren still looked like Arren. His personality was still there. But his troubles weren't. He looked utterly peaceful and content, as if nothing had ever hurt him or ever would. Once again she noticed how much older he looked with a beard. She made a mental note to ask him to get rid of it. Kissing him was much less pleasant now that he had hair all around his mouth.

As she watched, Arren's face twitched. His eyebrows lowered slightly and his lips moved, as if he was trying to speak. Then he started to mumble, making vague half-speaking sounds that were almost words but not quite.

Flell watched him. She wondered if she should wake him up, but curiosity got the better of her and she listened, trying to understand what he was saying, if anything. His mumbling became a little clearer, and she lay down with her head next to his, listening.

". . . falling . . ."

It was only just discernable, but even as she registered this he suddenly started to speak coherently.

"Help me, I'm falling. Help me . . . falling . . . help me . . . I'm falling . . . falling . . ."

The words were spoken in an emotionless monotone, but for some reason they scared her more than yelling or screaming would have.

Flell nudged him awake. He stopped talking and opened his eyes.

"What?" The irritability in his voice was so normal it made her feel almost ridiculously relieved.

"Good morning," said Flell. "Did you sleep well?"

Arren blinked a few times and yawned. "Ooh, sorry. Quite well, thanks. I can't normally get to sleep in a real bed, you know. But yours is"—he grinned—"pretty comfortable."

Flell grinned back. "Remember when we tried to share your hammock?"

"It was fun," said Arren. "Not for very long, but it was fun." He looked over at the window and sat up. "Godsdamn-it, I have to get going. Roland will be expecting me."

They got up and dressed and shared a quick breakfast before Arren left for the hatchery. Another day of work began.

15

Entrapment

Darkheart lay on his belly in the cage he had now occupied for nearly a month and knocked his beak on the wall beside him, over and over again. He'd been doing it for weeks now. Not for any particular reason. He was hardly aware that he was doing it any more. It had become a mindless reflex.

Things had changed since his first visit to the Arena. Since then he had been in the pit several more times and had killed two more griffins. Aeya, though, was not one of them. They hadn't been in the pit together since Kraee's death, as she had taken a wound that day and was still recovering from it. The other griffins in the cages had come to fear the black griffin, and with good reason. He had a habit of attacking his fellow griffins as much as he attacked the humans in the Arena. Humans were easy to kill, but other griffins—he hated them. They mocked him for his dark coat and slow speech, and enjoyed his helpless anger and threats. It was the only sport they had when they weren't in the pit. But it was in the pit that Darkheart would take his revenge on them. He attacked the other griffins indiscriminately, even the ones that hadn't joined in the taunting, and besides the two he had killed outright he had wounded many others, one of whom died a few days later from an infection. Some of the more cowardly griffins had started to leave him alone, but others didn't. They were too proud to succumb to their fear of him, and when he attacked in the pit, none ran away. They always stood and fought. It was the griffish way.

Darkheart had noticed that the humans who came to the cages paid extra attention to him. They gave him more and better food than the others, and after his second visit to the Arena they tied some strips of brightly coloured cloth to his wings and daubed a strange-smelling substance on his throat which turned the feathers deep red. He had no idea why. The colour wore off after a few days, but they renewed it every time they took him out of his cage.

When they were removed from their cages and taken to the pit, most of the other griffins went passively enough, now accustomed to the knowledge that they had no hope of escape. Darkheart did not. He continued to try to break free at every opportunity, and would lunge at every human he saw, even if he was still chained.

It took a toll on him. The collar wore away all the feathers from around his neck, and the flesh underneath became permanently raw and bleeding. The manacles on his forelegs rubbed away the scales and bit into the skin beneath, which swelled and hurt. In the end his lunges tore one of the rings out of the wall, and the humans had to drug him so they could reattach it. He tried to chew away the chains, until his beak became chipped and cracked. He dug his talons into the dirt, until he had made a deep ditch just in front of the spot where he lay, exposing the metal plates underneath, which he scratched at pointlessly.

Eventually, though, his strength failed him and he took to lying still with his talons outstretched, only rising when he needed to drink, or striking the wall with his beak until the noise ground itself into his head and put him into a kind of trance.

His eyes became dull and lifeless, his fur rough and his
feathers bedraggled. He lost interest in talking to Aeya, or
in eating, and became steadily thinner. It was only in the
Arena that he came to life. There he was more than alive;
he was wild, savage, magnificent, caught up in a killing
frenzy that took away his pain and his despair. That was
where he lived now, in the Arena. There he was more than
a mindless nothing that lived in a cage. There he was Darkheart, the mad griffin, the one the crowds screamed for.
There he was alive.

He stopped hitting the bars and laid his head on his talons, feeling the warmth of the evening sun on his face. He
tried to remember his valley. Had there been sunsets there?
Had he basked in the sun there? He couldn't remember.
The images kept slipping away from him like fish wriggling between his talons.

"Darkheart?"

It was Aeya's voice. Darkheart raised his head slightly.
"Aeya?"

"How did you come here?" said Aeya.

She had asked him this question before, but he hadn't
answered it. Not properly. He had learnt more speech from
her since then, though. "I live . . . on mountains," he mumbled. "Tall. Cold. Three. Three mountains."

"Was it in the South?" said Aeya. "I came from the South."

She had taught him about the four directions. He looked
up at the sky and tried to remember. Which way had he
come? The journey had passed in a haze. Now, looking back on it, it felt like a dream or like something that
had happened to some other griffin in another place and
another time. "South," he said eventually, hoping this
would be enough.

"I lived in the Coppertops," said Aeya. "On the edge. I
had a nest. But I built it too close, too close, too . . ." She
trailed off. "I built it too close," she said again. "Humans
saw it. When my chicks went to the ground, they took them
away. I could not stop them. I chased them; they were fast. I

looked for them for days, but I never saw my chicks again. So I killed the human chicks. And the adults. Killed and ate them. They were good. Good food."

She had told him this before. It was a kind of litany she recited when the mood took her, and she said it as if she had said it so many times that she didn't even remember what the words meant any more. Darkheart half-listened.

"Why did *you* do it?" Aeya asked suddenly. "Why did you kill humans?"

Darkheart tried to think. "Was looking," he said slowly. "For human."

"For human? What human?"

"I wanted—a griffin told me she had human. One who spoke. I looked for one. I speak. They not speak. So I killed them. Then saw a griffin. White griffin. Calling me. Griffin with . . . with human. Dark human. I chase human. The griffin . . . want . . . stop. Kill her. And then . . . could not fly. Went to sleep. Dark human there. Speak. Dark human speak. He speak, I speak. He wanted . . . dark human want kill. Smell it. Watch me. Always watching. Come here, with him. Dark human. Arren."

"Arren Cardockson?" said Aeya.

Darkheart almost didn't hear her. He had been concentrating so hard on his speech that it had exhausted him, but the sound of the name caught his attention. "Arren . . . Card . . . k . . . son?" he ventured. "What that?"

"The human's name," said Aeya. "I have listened to Sefer and Orome talking. Arren Cardockson. The human who caught you and brought you to this place."

"Dark human?" said Darkheart.

"He is a blackrobe," said Aeya.

"What . . . blackrobe?"

"I do not know. Something bad. But you must surely hate this man. He put you in that cage. It is his fault you are here and not free."

"Arren Cardockson," Darkheart repeated. "Arren . . . Cardockson. Blackrobe. Cardockson. Dark human." He remembered the eyes. Black and cold, and full of hatred. Not like other humans' eyes. The memory made him shiver slightly.

A rren sat at his usual table in the Red Rat and waited. He'd arranged to meet Flell, Bran and Gern, but they were late.

He rubbed his ear. It had taken a while to heal, but it was all right now. It was ragged, though, just like the other. The wounds left by Shoa's talons had more or less healed, too, but they had left scars, which still ached from time to time.

Arren took a mouthful of cheap mead. Well, it didn't matter. No-one but Flell was likely to see them, and she didn't mind.

It had been nearly a month since he had returned from Rivermeet, and by now his life had settled back into a kind of normality. He continued to work at the hatchery every day and was doing fairly well. He'd requested to work only in the hatchery itself, with the chicks, which Roland had agreed to without argument. Whenever he went into the adult quarter now, he was greeted with mocking screeches from Senneck and some of her fellows. The brown griffin was positively gleeful over having put him in his place and would snap her beak at him every time she saw him. Only Keth was able to keep her out of the chicks' quarter, and there Arren could have some peace and quiet to get on with his duties. The chicks, at least, had grown used to him, and would happily start up a raucous chorus of "Food! Food! Food!" whenever they laid eyes on him. That always cheered him up a little.

"Hey, you."

Arren looked up. He'd been approached by a pair of heavy-set young men, both of whom were standing uncomfortably close to his table. "Yes?"

"Are you the Master of Trade?" one of them demanded.

Arren picked up his drink. "No."

"But you used to be, didn't you?" said the man.

"Who cares?" said Arren.

"You're Arren Cardockson," the second man interrupted. "You're the blackrobe bastard who used to be Master of Trade."

Arren drank deeply and put down his mug. "And you're the idiotic loudmouth who comes up and shouts at people in bars. Pleased to meet you."

The first man flicked the mug off the table with the back of his hand and grabbed hold of the front of Arren's tunic. "Listen to me, you snobby little shit," he snarled. "You talk to either of us like that and we'll break your kneecaps, get it?"

Arren looked pointedly at the hand holding on to his tunic. "Yes, I think I can grasp that idea. What do you want?"

The man let go of him. "D' you know the name Norbit Tamson, blackrobe?"

"I can't say I do, no," Arren said carefully.

"You killed him," the man said.

Arren looked at him, bewildered. "No, I didn't. I've got no idea what you're talking about. I've never heard of him."

"You son of a bitch!" the man roared, so loudly that people turned to stare at him. "We got him back with one of his arms torn clean off! And a bag of money. *Compensation*. You murdered my brother, and you give us *money*? You think you can *pay* us not to say anything, you piece of shit?"

Arren stood up. "Your brother's death was an accident," he said calmly. "He was caught in a smugglers' den and was killed when he assaulted me and several of the city guards and then tried to run away. I'm sorry for what happened to him, but it was out of my hands."

The man hit him in the face. Arren fell backward, knocking over his chair. As he scrambled to get up, the two men advanced on him. The foremost of them kicked him, knocking him over again. "That's for Norbit," he snarled, ignoring the shocked stares of the onlookers. "You're gonna pay for this, blackrobe. You think that just because you had a griffin you were special? That you were as good as us? That you weren't a blackrobe bastard howling at the moon like a dog? You thought *that*?" He spat on Arren's tunic. "You think you can live like us and wear our clothes an' that makes you one of us. Riona shouldn't've taken your collar off, slave."

It happened in a heartbeat. One moment Arren was lying on his back and the next he had hurled himself straight at the man with a wild scream.

He hit him hard in the chest, and in spite of his light frame, caught him by surprise and bowled him over. The man landed hard on his back, and Arren's long fingers closed around his neck.

The man hit him as hard as he could, in the face and chest, but Arren did not let go. He held on with all his might, squeezing the man's windpipe until his knuckles went white. His face, once impassive, had twisted itself into an insane, animal snarl.

The man's friend came to his rescue after a moment's frozen shock. He seized Arren by the hair and dragged him off. Arren screamed, half in pain and half in fury. His hand went to his belt and pulled out his dagger, and he whipped around and buried it up to the hilt in the man's leg, just above the knee. The man bellowed and fell over, blood soaking into his trousers, and Arren turned and kicked the first man in the face, knocking him over again. Then, utterly heedless of the shouts and the people running over to intervene, he started to rain blows down on the man's face, hard and fast, shouting incoherent curses at him all the while. The man's resistance quickly gave way in the face of that, and he started to drag himself away, but Arren scrabbled after him and slammed the heel of his boot into the man's groin. As the victim curled up, screaming, Arren picked up a fallen chair and raised it over his head, ready to strike.

Someone grabbed him from behind and snatched the chair out of his hands. He twisted in their grip and swung a punch at them, but a hard blow caught him on the chin, stunning him, and he sagged to the ground.

A pair of strong hands dragged him away; he tried to break free and resume his assault, and received a stinging blow to the top of his head for his trouble. After that he calmed down a little and allowed himself to be taken out of the tavern.

He was led to a nondescript corner in an alley, and his captor sat him down on a crate.

"There," said a voice. "Are yeh gonna calm down, or do I have to hit yeh again?"

Arren blinked. He had the strange feeling of having just woken up, and he squinted vaguely at the bulky shape in front of him. "Bran?" he managed.

Bran was still wearing his uniform and had his arms folded. "Yeah, that'd be me."

Flell and Gern appeared behind him. Both of them looked horror-struck.

"Arren!" Flell exclaimed. "What in the gods' names?"

Arren rubbed his head. "Who hit me?"

"That was me," said Bran. "Hope I didn't hurt yeh."

"I think I'm all right."

"Good. Now what in Gryphus' name was that all about?" said Bran.

"That was *incredible*, sir," Gern interrupted. "I had no idea you could fight like that! You would've killed that man if Bran hadn't pulled you off him."

Bran thumped him on the ear. "Shut up. Arren, what were yeh playin' at?"

"I'm sorry," said Arren, suddenly embarrassed. "I—well, he hit me first. He was saying things, calling me a black-robe. I don't know what happened. I just snapped."

"Well, I could see that," said Bran. "It was a bit hard to miss." He exchanged an uneasy glance with the others.

Flell laid a hand on his arm, somewhat hesitantly. "Arren, I—"

Arren stared at the ground. "I'm sorry, Flell. I don't know what came over me." They were silent, but he knew what they were thinking. "It wasn't my fault," he insisted. "I was defending myself. You *know* I'm not like that."

"I thought I knew," said Bran.

"To be honest, sir, I thought you were a bit of a—well, not a fighter," said Gern. "I've seen people insult you before, but you never said anything. You just ignored them. Some people reckoned you were violent because you're a Northerner, but I always said, 'No, Arren's not like that. He's too nice for that sort of thing. Wouldn't hurt a fly.' But you—I got your dagger back, by the way. That poor sod pulled it out of his leg and I picked it up." He was holding it wrapped in a corner of his tunic and removed it rather gingerly, holding it between two fingers. "It's—uh, it probably needs a bit of cleaning, sir."

Bran waved him into silence. "Yeh ain't been yerself lately, Arren. Flell said—"

"I told them I had a feeling you weren't as well as you kept saying," said Flell. "I knew you couldn't be. Not after what happened. I know you had to be depressed and feeling guilty, but . . . you're so *jumpy* all of a sudden. Haven't you realised it? You keep looking at corners and doorways and things, and you won't talk about what happened at Rivermeet. I've seen you walking around. You've got a—well, a *hunted* look. What is it, Arren? Have people been harassing you or something? You know we can help you with that sort of thing."

Arren shook his head. "It's nothing."

Flell paused to restrain Thrain, who was looking rather jittery. "No, it's not," she said firmly, almost sternly. "There's something going on, and I want to know what it is. You're hiding something."

Arren said nothing, but his eyes darted toward the alley's entrance.

"I'm here, Arren," said Flell. "There's no-one there."

"Please, sir, you can trust us," said Gern. "We trust you, right?"

"Course we do," said Bran.

"I *can't* tell you," Arren blurted. "Please, just believe me. If I tell you, something awful will happen."

Bran touched the hilt of his sword. "Arren, for gods' sakes, if yer in danger—"

"I'm not," said Arren. "But I will be if I tell you, and so will you."

"Did someone threaten you?" said Flell.

Arren hesitated. "Yes. They said that if I told anyone, I would die and so would the person I told. No matter who they were."

"Who was it?" said Bran. "Can yeh tell us?"

"No."

Flell took hold of his hand. "But Arren, for gods' sakes, you can't let someone get away with this! It's criminal! My father has to know about it, I'm sure he can do something."

Arren grabbed her by the shoulder and pulled her into his arms. As he held on to her, he laid his head on her shoulder and whispered, "It *is* your father." He spoke griffish and kept his voice so low that even he could scarcely hear it, but he felt Flell stiffen as he said it and knew she had heard.

He let go of her and she pulled away, staring at him. She opened her mouth to speak and stopped, half-reached toward him and then turned abruptly and left the alley, carrying Thrain under one arm.

"Flell, where are you going?" Gern called after her, but she didn't look back.

Arren got up. "I should go home," he said.

"But Arren—"

"No, Bran," said Arren. "I can't. I won't. And it doesn't matter any more. It's too late for anyone to do anything. If you ask me about this again, I'll pretend I don't know what you're talking about. Goodnight." He left the alley at a quick stride, and as soon as he was back in the street he broke into a run. He didn't stop until he reached his own home, and then he slammed the door behind him. But he didn't relax until he had locked and barred it, and blocked up the windows.

* * *

Arren spent the next two days in agony. Every moment he expected someone to come after him, at home or at work or out in the street. No-one did. He didn't see Flell, either; he avoided her, and she was probably doing the same. He avoided Bran and Gern as well, and when he wasn't at work, he spent every moment barricaded in his house. He began carrying his sword with him wherever he went and wore his leather breastplate under his tunic. When nothing happened, his tension didn't decrease—in fact, it worsened.

Roland was quick to notice the change in his demeanour. "What's the matter, lad?" he inquired. "You look terrible. And why do you have your sword with you? I'll admit it's a rather nice one, but why carry it around all day? Isn't it a tad heavy?"

"There's a problem with muggers," Arren lied. He'd prepared this excuse beforehand. "I don't want to be attacked on the way home."

"Ah, I see," said Roland. "Fair enough, I suppose, but there's no need to keep the thing on your back all day. Just put it over by the door until you leave, why don't you? I wouldn't worry about anyone stealing it. The chicks will yell loud enough to wake the dead if they smell anyone they don't know come in here."

Arren hesitated a moment before he obeyed, but he quickly saw that Roland was perfectly correct. No-one would attack him in here. Not with so many witnesses. He undid the straps holding the scabbard onto his back, and put the sword down by the door, leaning it against the wall of the pen beside it. Then he picked up his broom and resumed sweeping the floor.

Roland wandered over to inspect the sword. "I can see you've been taking good care of it," he said, pulling it out of the sheath and examining the blade. "That's good. My father was very fond of this sword. He told me it was used in proper warfare by his grandfather. Against Nor— oh, I'm sorry, Arren."

Arren shrugged and pushed a heap of dust toward a hole in the floor. "I'm not all that good with it, but I'm very proud to own it. I keep thinking I should get someone to teach me proper swordplay. I mean, I know the basics, but that's about it. I practise, though."

"Well done," Roland said approvingly. "Truth be told, when Rakee was still alive, I never took much of an interest in fighting. In fact, for a while I considered joining the priesthood."

"You did?" said Arren, surprised. The priesthood was highly respected, but the only griffiners that ever joined it were the ones who had been deemed to be useless or undesirable in some way.

"Oh yes," said Roland. "I was very religious back then. But my mother wouldn't hear of it. 'Wait until you're old, if you really must,' she said." He chuckled. "Of course, by the time I'd started to go grey I'd already lost interest in that idea. I never could settle down to anything when I was your age. Or when I was twice your age, come to that. No, the priesthood is holy and everything, and learned, of course, but nowadays I think they were rather out of touch with the rest of the world. Always looking back when they should be looking forward."

Arren had seen the city's temple from the outside plenty of times but had never been inside it. "I don't think I really believe in any gods," he said, turning to sweep out a particularly stubborn corner. "I've always liked the idea of religion, but I never really could *believe*. Not properly."

"Didn't your parents pass their beliefs on to you?" said Roland.

"No. They taught me about it, but, well, they're not very religious. I know that—" He paused, almost embarrassed to say it. "Well, Northerners never had priests, as far as I know. They worship on their own. You know, in private. So it's just between them and their god."

Roland gave him a quizzical look. "*They*, Arren?"

"That's what I said."

Roland paused a moment and then shrugged and made for the door to his home. "Well, I think we've done about enough for today. You can be off home once you've finished with the floor. Just wait a moment and I'll get you your pay."

He disappeared into his home and returned to put a bag of coins on the table before bidding Arren goodbye and going back through the door.

Arren finished sweeping the floor and put the broom back on its hook. He yawned as he pocketed the money. It had been another long day. He'd had to help Roland with a recalcitrant chick that didn't want to swallow its medicine, and the thing's talons had left a large hole in his tunic. He'd have to sew that up before he went to bed.

He picked up his sword from its spot by the door and strapped it back on, then left the hatchery. It was sunset, and the horizon was bright orange and gold. He sighed when he saw it, and turned for home, walking quickly and keeping to places where there were plenty of people.

He turned the corner into his street and reached the door to his home. He unlocked it and went inside, and the moment the door closed behind him he relaxed. Back in his own territory.

He unfastened the sword from his back and put it down on the table, and that was when he noticed that something was different. The door leading out to the balcony was hanging open. When he went to close it, his eyes adjusted to the gloom and he finally saw what was wrong.

His home was ruined. The furniture was smashed; the cupboards were hanging open with their contents strewn all over the floor. Someone had slashed his hammock to ribbons, and his clothes had been thrown over the balcony; he could see a solitary tunic hanging forlornly on the railing like a banner.

Arren swore. He looked for his lamp, but it was lying in a corner, broken into three large pieces, and he swore again and made for the stable. There should be another one in there.

He passed through the doorway, and froze. There were people in there, shrouded and anonymous in the gloom. They stood up and came forward to meet him. Arren turned to run back through the door, but someone had already moved to block it. He lashed out and managed to hit them on the chin hard enough to knock them aside. As Arren dived for the gap, someone grabbed him from behind. They dragged him back into the stable and threw him onto the floor, and in an instant he was surrounded.

A hand hauled him upright, and suddenly he was being struck from all sides. Blows rained down on his head and shoulders, so hard they made stars explode before his eyes. He made an attempt to fight back, but someone thumped him in the stomach and he doubled over, yelping. He staggered backward and hit the wall, and then they were on him. Arren curled up, trying to protect himself, but they continued to hit him, kicking him in the chest, stomach and groin. Helpless and close to blacking out, he started to shout at them.

"Stop it! Stop it! Help me! *Help!*"

They jeered and began to hit him even harder. Something that felt like a falling tree hit him in the chest, and sharp pain shot through him. His head hit the wall so hard it blinded him for an instant. For a moment he tried to get up, groping at the wall behind him, but then he slid down it and landed in a crumpled heap at its base, moaning softly. Hands grabbed his arms and shoulders to hold them still, and someone else seized him by the hair and yanked his head backward. He heard them laughing, and one of them said something he couldn't make out.

There was a sharp metallic *click* just below his ear, and then pain stabbed into his neck, like a dozen knives. He cried out, but then the hands let go of him. "Try and forget now, blackrobe," a distant voice sneered, and then something hit him hard in the head and the world was snatched away from him.

16

The Collar

Eluna was calling him. He could hear her. He could *see* her, too, just there in front of him. The white griffin loomed out of the darkness ahead of him, her silver eyes bright. *Arren. Arren.*

He reached toward her. *Eluna? Where are you?*

She just stared at him. *Arren,* she said. *Arren.*

It hurts, Eluna, he said. *Why does it hurt? Eluna. It hurts, Eluna. It hurts.*

Arren.

I don't want—I don't want it . . .

And then Eluna was gone and he could see something else. Himself, lying on the ground, while the moon drifted overhead, looking down on him like a great silver eye. A griffin's eye. He lay still, staring up at it, but his eyes were empty and sightless. There was blood on his face, and more on his clothes. A tear slid slowly down his cheek. But it was thick and dark, and red. A shape loomed above, unmoving. Watching.

And then the world came back.

The first thing he felt was pain. It was everywhere, all

over him. He heard himself cry out, and the noise sent red-hot agony through his head. He lay still, gasping, wanting to escape back into unconsciousness, but he couldn't. He stayed awake, and the pain consumed him. His back ached. His stomach and groin felt as if they had been crushed under a rock, and his chest . . . he couldn't feel anything in his chest. It had gone numb. His neck hurt, too, and badly. But his head was worse. It made him want to scream, but he couldn't make his voice obey him. His entire body was out of his control. All it would do was lie still on its side, and hurt.

He managed to open his eyes, but his head hurt so severely that his vision was blurred. Everything was grey around the edges, and red flashed behind his eyes with every heartbeat.

Some perverse inner strength made him try to get up, and now he really did scream. The instant he moved, agonising pain crackled through his chest. He fell back down again, and the impact made it a hundred times worse. It made him black out briefly, and when he woke up he couldn't move at all.

But the pain faded gradually, and his resolve hardened. *Try again,* he thought.

Very carefully, he moved his free arm. It was fine. The wrist and elbow were uninjured and his hand intact, though the shoulder hurt. He could cope with that.

He touched his chest, gritting his teeth in readiness for a resurgence of the pain. But nothing happened. His chest felt strangely . . . *hard* under his tunic, and it took him some time to remember that he was still wearing his breastplate. That was a relief, he decided, the thought moving very slowly through his head. It would have protected him a little.

He checked his other arm. It was also fine. His legs, too, still worked and were more or less pain free.

He paused to prepare himself, then pushed on the ground with his lowermost arm and very gently rolled onto his back. To his surprise, this didn't make the pain come

rushing back. It did surge a little, but not too badly, and he
let his head drop. Instantly, pain stabbed into his neck. He
winced and reached up to feel the spot.

His hand touched cold metal.

He stopped, bewildered, and started to run his fingers
over the surface of it, trying to discern the shape of it. It
was smooth and slightly rounded, like a ring, and it went
all the way around his neck.

The realisation hit him slowly and coldly, like ice moving down into his brain.

It was a collar.

And, on the skin below it, blood had flowed and dried
into a thick crust. When he slid a finger under the collar,
he could feel the spikes that lined its insides, embedded in
his flesh.

Panic took hold of him. He grabbed the collar in both
hands and started to pull at it, trying to make it come off.
But it stayed firmly in place, and his efforts only drove the
spikes further in. There was a wet tearing sensation and a
burst of pain, and fresh blood started to trickle down over
his fingers.

Arren let go of the collar and lay still on his back, not
daring to move.

He realised, eventually, that he was sobbing.

Wild rage and terror flooded into him. He forgot everything and rolled onto his side, pulling at the collar with all
his might, wrenching it upwards, trying to get it over his
head. It would not come. He didn't even notice the agony of
his ribs; he jammed his fingers under the collar and pulled
outward with all his might. The spikes cut his fingers, and
more blood ran down over his wrists. He started to scream
and swear, not even knowing he was doing it, thrashing
around on the floor in a haze of pain, tears streaming down
his face. But nothing he did would make the collar come
off. It stayed where it was, its spikes biting into him, its
surface becoming sticky with blood. In the end he slumped
back onto the floor, sobbing weakly, every fibre of his
being screaming out.

"No . . . no . . . oh gods, no . . ."

His head pounded and his chest was agony. His neck continued to bleed, weighed down by the collar. Part of him wanted to call for help, but he knew in his heart that no-one would hear him. And if they did, what then? What would they do when they saw him?

Gradually, though, his terror gave way to rage. Burning, terrible rage, the same rage that had made him attack the two men in the tavern. It took hold of him, overwhelming his senses, blotting out the pain and giving him strength.

Slowly, very slowly, he got up. Broken bone grated together inside his chest; he could *feel* it, and hear it. The collar shifted on his neck, sliding down and settling into place just above his shoulders, the spikes tearing grooves into his skin. But he could stand up. His legs were still sound; the pain was all in his neck, head and torso. The collar unbalanced him, and he staggered sideways and hit the wall. More pain blossomed inside him, but he grabbed hold of one of the roof supports and managed to stay upright. Once he had rested, he turned himself around and began to make his way toward the door, staying close to the wall to hold himself up. Walking was painful, and he had to move very slowly and place each foot carefully. If he trod down too hard, it sent pain shooting up his spine.

He reached the door after what felt like an age and rested there again. It was daytime, but the light coming in through the broken windows was dull and grey, and as he stood in the doorway, lightning turned everything pure white for a heartbeat. Thunder rumbled a few moments later.

In daylight, the ruin of his home was much easier to see. Everything was destroyed: the cupboard doors had been ripped off, the shelves were broken, all the food had been stamped into the floor, and his clothes chest had been tipped over and the contents were either wrecked or missing. They had even found the secret cavity under the floorboards, and he knew without looking that they'd stolen everything in it.

They'd taken his sword, too, along with his bow and arrows, and every plate, bowl and cup was in pieces on the floor.

Arren put a hand over his face. One side of it was badly swollen, and he winced. He'd probably lost a few teeth as well, he thought.

He breathed deeply, trying to keep himself calm. All right. One thing at a time. He couldn't stay in the doorway forever. It was just a few steps to the table, and that was still intact. He could make it.

He braced himself, took in a deep breath, and set out. He reached the table in a few lurching steps and grabbed on to it before he collapsed, gasping for breath. There. He'd made it.

The chair had been reduced to a heap of shattered wood, but the crate was still there. He managed to shove it into place next to the table and then sat on it, resting his elbows on the table. Sitting down was difficult. It made his back and chest hurt—not horrendously, but continuously, to the point that he considered standing up again. But he couldn't summon the energy for that and instead slumped over the table. The collar dragged his head downward, and he had to prop his chin on his hand to hold it up. There was blood in his beard. He tried absent-mindedly to clean it off while he waited for the pain to subside, which it eventually did.

His head felt a little better now, and he found it easier to think. Strangely, his first thought was that if he could walk, then that meant he would be all right. He wasn't too badly hurt. He'd survive, even if he wouldn't be as flexible as he used to be. They hadn't killed him.

Fear suddenly intruded on him. He tried to remember what his assailants had looked like, but he had no idea. He'd only caught a brief glimpse of the one in the doorway, not enough to be sure of anything. But his first thought was that Rannagon must have sent them. Somehow, he'd found out that Arren had told someone the truth. But how? Who had told him? Bran? Gern? Flell? How much did they know? Had there been a spy listening in on him in that alley? Had the others been arrested, or were they dead?

He started to feel cold all over. In his head, images spiralled, each one worse than the last. Bran and Gern, assaulted like himself, either dead or badly hurt. And Flell, what would Rannagon have done to her? He wouldn't kill her. There was no way he could do that. Not his own daughter. But the others . . . if anything happened to them, it would be his fault.

He had to do something, but what? He couldn't get to them. Just walking across a room had exhausted him. And he couldn't go outside. Not like this. Not with a slave collar clamped around his neck. If he was still being followed, they would know where he was going. They'd stop him. Maybe kill him. Or maybe they only knew that he'd told, but they didn't know *who* he'd told, and now they needed him to lead them to his accomplices. Maybe if he went to Gern's house or Bran's, it would mean bringing danger right to their doorstep.

He realised, dully, that there was nothing he could do. If something had happened to them, it had happened already. If he went to their houses and found them safe, perhaps he could warn them—but they already knew they were in danger. He'd already put them on their guard, surely.

But what if the attackers came back for him? What if the assault had just been a prelude to his murder?

No. He calmed down slightly. No. They weren't going to come back and kill him. If they'd wanted to kill him he would be dead already. This had been something else. A warning. If, mere days before being killed, he was seen in this condition and talked publicly about what had happened, people would get suspicious. If he wanted to keep himself safe, he had to do what they would want him to do: hide, say nothing, do nothing. Just recover and go back to work. Make it clear that he wasn't going to try anything. Maybe then they'd leave him alone.

Miserable, helpless anger consumed him. Was this how he was going to spend the rest of his life, looking over his shoulder every day, constantly frightened? How long would it take before they finally killed him? They had already taken Eluna from him, and now they had taken his belongings and his dignity as well. What did he have left that they could take, other than his life and those of his friends?

Arren's fists clenched. No. They wouldn't. He wouldn't let them. There had to be something he could do. He had to fight back. They weren't going to make him be silent forever. "I'm going to make them pay, Eluna," he whispered. "I swear it."

It took nearly a week for him to recover sufficiently to leave his house. The bruising and swelling slowly went down, and he found it easier to move, but when he moved he could feel something crack inside him.

And then there was the collar.

It plagued him constantly, unbalancing him and weighing him down. He couldn't lie down properly, and every time he leant in any direction the collar pulled him down and made his wounds start to bleed. Though his other injuries began to heal, the gashes in his neck stayed open. Every time they scabbed or sealed partway, the slightest movement tore them open again.

But he persevered. He forced himself to eat the food that his assailants had ground into the floor, and he drank as much as he could from the rain-barrel outside. He felt tired and hungry all the time, but little by little he regained some of his strength, and he decided that he was well enough to go out. He had to find out if the others were all right.

He picked up a strip of blanket and wrapped it around his neck, covering the collar. He couldn't let people see it. He'd also tried stuffing rags underneath it to stop it moving around, but it fitted too tightly for that. Putting anything underneath made him feel like he was choking.

He left the house without bothering to lock the door behind him. There was nothing left to steal or break. Almost without thinking, he headed straight for the Red Rat. It was evening, and one of them had to be there.

The tavern was bustling, as always. When he entered, many people turned to stare at him, and most moved away, casting nervous glances in his direction. He supposed, vaguely, that he must be less than pleasant to look at by now.

The owner had seen him and came toward him at once. "Are you going to start trouble in here again, blackrobe?"

Arren shook his head, very carefully. "No. I'm here looking for someone."

"Who? And what in Gryphus' name is that around your neck?"

"I'm looking for Bran. Or Gern."

"What, Branton Redguard? He's just over there. Go on. But I've got my eye on you."

Arren ignored him. He could see Bran sitting at a table with some of his fellow guardsmen. Gern wasn't there and neither was Flell, but the sight of him made Arren's heart soar with relief. He was all right. He was alive.

"Bran! Bran!"

Bran looked up, and his face fell. "Arren?" He got up, ignoring his friends, and hurried toward him. "Arren, good gods, what happened to yeh?"

Arren grabbed his arm. "Bran, are you all right? Has anything happened? Where's Flell? And Gern? Are they safe?"

"I'm fine," said Bran. "I ain't seen Flell, but I would hear if somethin'd happened to her. Arren, where've yeh been? I've been lookin' for yeh here every night—what's wrong with yer neck?"

Arren glanced around quickly. "I can't say here. Come on."

The two of them left the tavern. Outside, Bran said, "Look, Arren, I dunno if yeh've heard about it yet, but—"

"What?" said Arren. "What is it?"

"Gern's dead," Bran said in a low voice.

Arren went cold. "What? How? When?"

"It was an accident," said Bran. "He got caught up in another fight at the Arena and fell down a row of seats. Broke his neck."

"Oh no."

"I know," said Bran. "His mum was distraught. Poor kid—"

"This wasn't an accident," said Arren. "They got him. Oh gods, I've—I've killed him. They found out."

"Who did?" said Bran.

"I told you!" Arren hissed. "There's people watching me. We're all in danger. Bran, for gods' sakes, where's Flell? Has something happened to her?"

"She's fine," said Bran. "Arren, calm down—"

"No!" Arren half-shouted. "I can't! It's my fault, don't you see? Gern died because I told him—Bran, you've got to get out of here. Go into hiding somewhere, before they kill you, too. I've got to warn Flell!" He turned and started to run away.

Bran dashed after him and pulled him up sharp. "Arren! Stop!"

Arren tried to break free. "Let go!"

"Arren," Bran said sharply, "stop it. Yer babbling. There's no-one after yeh."

"Yes, there is. Bran, are you stupid? *Look* at me! D'you think *this* was an accident?"

"Arren, I—after what yeh told me, I got a couple of mates on street duty to follow yeh. They kept an eye on yer house; they was tailin' you for a couple of days. They never saw nothin'."

"You think I'm losing my mind, do you?" said Arren.

"No, Arren, I just think yer scared of somethin' ain't real."

"So, I'm mad," said Arren. "Is that it?" He reached up to his neck and started to unwrap the strip of blanket. It fell away and the collar gleamed dully in the torchlight. "Does *this* look like something that isn't real?"

Bran's eyes widened. "Gryphus, that's not a—"

"It's a slave collar," said Arren.

"But how—"

"Someone broke into my house," said Arren, hastily covering it up again. "They've wrecked everything. They stole everything I owned, and when I got home they attacked me. I've got broken ribs and I think there's a crack in my skull. And when I woke up, I found they'd put this on me, and I can't get it off."

"But Arren, why didn't yeh—"

"I *can't*," said Arren. "They'll come back and kill me. I can't let anyone see me wearing this, they'll—I don't know what to do, Bran."

"Well, yeh can't keep that thing on," said Bran. "There ain't—oh my gods, you're *bleedin'*. We've got to find a blacksmith to take it off."

"I can't afford it," said Arren. "They took all my money."

"I'll pay," Bran said firmly. "C'mon." He took Arren by the arm and dragged him off.

As they walked rapidly toward the part of the market district where the craftspeople lived, Bran asked questions, speaking in a quick, clipped voice, as he would to any other crime victim. "When did it happen?"

"A week or so ago."

"Who were they? Did yeh get a good look at 'em?"

"No, it was dark. I didn't see their faces. There were about six of them, I think. They didn't talk much."

"So, they got in through a window?"

"Yes, one of the back ones. They must have climbed onto the balcony; one of the back windows was broken."

"And they beat yeh up?"

"Yes."

"So, once yeh were down they put the collar on and then left yeh."

"Yes. One of them hit me in the head afterwards—knocked me out. I didn't wake up until the next morning."

"And yeh ain't told anyone else about it?"

"No. I couldn't even leave the house."

"Well, I'm gonna find out," said Bran. "I'm gonna find those sons of bitches and get them thrown into the Arena.

And after that yer going to tell me who threatened yeh, and I'm gonna to tell Lord Rannagon about it."

"But—"

"Shut up. Yeh wanna wait until yeh get yourself killed? Well, I ain't lettin' yeh. I already lost one of my mates; I ain't gonna lose another one."

They had reached the craftspeople's quarter, and Bran led the way to a low-roofed stone building, built near the centre of the city rather than on the platform, as building regulations dictated. The windows were lit up.

"Knew he'd still be open," Bran said in satisfied tones. "Let's go have a word with him."

They pushed open the door and went in. It was a fairly typical blacksmith's workshop; there was a long workbench against one wall, and various tools hung on the walls. The forge itself was in the middle of the floor, its coals glowing brightly. The blacksmith was standing by it, clad in a large leather apron, busy repairing a chain-mail shirt with a pair of pliers, but he looked up when the door opened.

"Yes? How can I help you?"

Bran pulled the strip of blanket away from Arren's neck, exposing the collar. "We need yeh to take this off."

The blacksmith reached for his hammer. "What's this all about? Who is he?"

"He's a mate of mine," said Bran. "Look, what'll it cost to take it off?"

"I'm not going to help you hide a runaway slave, if that's what you're trying to do. I'll take the collar off, but I'll have to report it as well."

"He ain't no slave!" Bran roared. "He's Arren Cardockson, the old Master of Trade. Godsdamnit, yeh probably bought yer bloody licence off him!"

The blacksmith peered at Arren. "I don't think I've seen you before."

Arren strode forward and slammed his hand down on the brick top of the forge. "Can you see a brand anywhere? Well, can you?"

The blacksmith backed off slightly. "All right, all right,

you're not a slave. I'm sorry. But why are you wearing that collar?"

"Someone put it on me by force," said Arren.

"Well, I never heard of anyone who'd put on a slave collar by choice," said the blacksmith. "All right, sit down and I'll have a look at it."

Arren sat down on the anvil, gritting his teeth at the pain this caused him, and the blacksmith examined the collar. He tapped it gently with his hammer and felt around the edges, looking for the join, frowning in concentration.

"Well," he said when he was done, "I'm really not—" He sighed and sat down on the forge, apparently not noticing the heat it was giving off. "I've only ever seen a slave collar once before, but—I'm really not sure what I can do."

"Can't you saw it off or something?"

"You see, the problem is that these things aren't *designed* to be taken off," said the blacksmith. "They have a locking mechanism inside and once it's snapped shut and the mechanism is engaged there's no way to unlock it. You're supposed to wear it for life. They made them so that the only real way to get one off was by cutting off the poor bastard's head. If it had a lock I could pick it, or if it was a different kind of hinge I could take out the pin, but it's made from very hard metal, you see. Normally I'd heat it up before I cut it, to soften it up a bit. But I can't do that without giving you a very nasty burn. If I chiselled it off, it'd drive the spikes right into your neck—it could kill you. I really wouldn't want to risk it."

"So, what can we do?"

"The only thing I can really think of is to saw through it, but I'd need a better saw than the one I've got, and even then it would take a long time. We'd have to do it in instalments—once every week."

"Why?" said Bran.

The blacksmith looked grim. "Well, you'll probably bleed to death if I keep it up too long. We'd have to wait for you to heal."

"But you could get it off?"

"Yes. It'd tear you up pretty badly, though."

"I don't care," said Arren. "I want this thing off me."

"All right, then," said the blacksmith. "But I'll have to send off for a better saw first. The nearest place I know of that makes them is Norton; I know someone who's about to go there, so I'll send him along with a note."

"How long before it gets here?" said Bran.

The blacksmith sighed. "At least six months."

Arren groaned. "Don't any of the other smiths around here have one?"

"I doubt it," said the blacksmith. "There's three other smiths in the city, and I know all of 'em. A few months back one of us had a tricky bit of cutting to do and was asking for a better saw to do it with, and he came to me last. Said the others hadn't been able to help. But I can ask them anyway, if you'd like."

"Yeah, do that," said Bran. "What d'yeh reckon, Arren?"

"Well, it doesn't look like we have any other choice," said Arren, carefully getting down off the anvil. "How much is this going to cost?"

"I'm not sure," said the blacksmith. "But the saw won't be cheap, and I'll have to pay the courier . . ."

"I'll borrow money," said Arren. "I'm not letting you pay for this, Bran."

"We'll see how it plays out," Bran said diplomatically. "Now"—he looked at the blacksmith—"yer gonna keep this to yerself, got that?"

"Can I ask why?"

"No."

"Fine. But can you tell me where the collar came from? Who put it on you . . . sir?"

"I don't know," said Arren. "Someone."

"I just want t' know *why*," Bran said later, when they had left the blacksmith's workshop and were walking back toward Arren's home. "Why'd they do that to yeh? Who were they?"

"I know why they did it," Arren said bitterly. "They wanted to humiliate me. Break me. Make me give up."

"It's them smugglers again," said Bran. "Must've been."

Arren turned the idea over in his mind, and then dismissed it. "I would have recognised them. This was someone else. Bran, I—you're wrong. It's not my imagination. There are people trying to hurt me, and they did this to me. And I'm afraid—I'm afraid they'll do worse. I'm afraid for you. What if they go after you? I mean, Gern can't have died by accident. It can't be just a coincidence. They had him murdered because they know I told him something I shouldn't have."

"But why?" said Bran. "What are yeh hidin' that's so important?"

"I can't tell you," said Arren. "I already told you why. But you've got to protect yourself. Don't go anywhere on your own."

Bran touched the hilt of his sword. "I can look after myself. But look, is there anyone else who could've done it?"

Arren remembered the two men from the Rat. Maybe it *had* been connected with them. "I—I don't know."

"Look," said Bran, "I can't do nothin' unless I got more. Unless I know where t' look, who t' question, I'm out. If yeh really need protection, then for Gryphus' sake, just tell Lord Rannagon. He can help yeh."

Arren said nothing.

"Well," said Bran, "meantime, I'm takin' yeh to a healer."

"No," said Arren. "I don't need it. I'm fine."

Bran gave him a slightly irritated look. "Arren, yeh look like yer half-dead. Don't tell me yer all right; I wasn't born yesterday."

Arren stopped and leant against a wall, covering his face with his hand. "Bran, please, I can't. I can't let people see me like this. I'm—I only left my house at all to make sure you were all right. I thought someone had come and killed you while I couldn't walk properly; I had to know you were alive. But if—I can't stand it, Bran. I just can't. People staring at me. Calling me things. They don't treat me like I'm human. Since Eluna died I've—I've been thinking about killing myself."

Bran grabbed his arm. "Arren, for gods' sakes!"

"Don't make me do it, Bran," said Arren. "Being called a slave everywhere I go—I just can't cope with it. Not now. I have to go home and rest. I'll be fine."

"Arren, yer *sick*. If yeh don't get help . . ."

"I'm going to get better," said Arren. "I really am. The bruising's gone down, and there's no way to treat broken ribs anyway. They heal up on their own. As long as I take it easy for a bit, I'll be fine. If I went to a healer, she'd just poke me for a while and then say I have to take it easy for a few months."

"Look me in the eye an' say that."

Arren looked him in the eye. "I'll get better on my own. Honestly. And if I *don't* start getting better, then I'll go to a healer. All right?"

"Well, fine," said Bran. "But I'm gonna come by tomorrow and visit yeh. I'm goin' to keep an eye on yeh till I'm sure yer all right. Go ahead and say no if yeh want to, but I ain't listenin'."

"I won't," said Arren. "That would be—well, I'd appreciate it."

17

Unspeakable Crime

True to his word, Bran came to visit next day around noon, and brought a large box of food with him. He looked horrified when he saw what was left of Arren's home.

"Oh holy gods, I never thought it'd be this bad. There's not a damn bit of furniture left!"

"It's been tidier," Arren said dryly. "Come in."

"I brought food," said Bran, putting the box down on the table. "Ain't much, but I figured yeh could use it. How are yeh feelin'?"

"Not too bad," said Arren, who'd spent half the night lying awake, trying to find a position to lie in that wouldn't make his neck hurt.

There was fresh bread and dried meat in the box, along with some apples, carrots and cheese, and some wine. Arren took a large helping and ate ravenously. After days of virtual starvation, it felt like the most delicious thing he'd ever tasted in his life.

Bran left him in peace and began trying to clean up some of the mess, muttering swearwords under his breath when he saw the slashed hammock and broken windows. "Gods damn them, those sons of bitches, if I could get my hands on them . . ."

"Bran?"

"Yeah?"

"You don't really think I'm mad, do you?" said Arren.

Bran paused. "No, not really, but I can't say I—well, I'm a little worried about yeh, I'll say that. I mean, yer changing, yeh know. Yeh ain't like yeh used to be."

"How d' you mean?" said Arren.

Bran took some time to think about that. "Well, yer . . . I dunno, just different. I just keep hopin' . . ."

"Hoping what?"

"Hoping that one day we'll get our old Arren back," said Bran, with touching sincerity.

For some reason that gave Arren a pang of guilt. "I'm sorry. I don't know what—I don't know how I'm changing. But I can't help it. Now Eluna's gone, I just feel . . . lost. I haven't stopped feeling lost since the day she died. She wasn't just my partner; she was part of me. And now I don't know what to do any more."

"I know," said Bran. "Everyone knows." He looked grim. "After she died, that's when yeh stopped bein' the Arren I knew. An' now I don't think that's ever gonna change."

Arren shook his head and stared at the floor. "You're right, Bran. Eluna was everything to me, you know that. But she's gone, and she isn't coming back. I have to accept that. I know I have to move on, and I'm trying."

"Yeh'll manage," Bran said encouragingly. "What about Flell? Have yeh been to see her yet?"

"No. I want to see her. More than anything. But I don't want to go anywhere near the Eyrie. You couldn't—you couldn't take a note to her for me, could you?"

"Sure," said Bran. "I'm off-duty today. Yeh got any paper?"

"Uh . . . no."

"Well, use a bit of the wrappin' off the bread," said Bran.

Bran couldn't write and could read only a few words. He watched with a kind of fascination while Arren carefully wrote a message on the scrap of cloth, pausing occasionally to sharpen the piece of charcoal on the edge of the table.

Flell,

How are you? I am not very well. I had an accident a few days ago. I can't come and see you just now; can you come and see me? I need company, and miss you.

I love you very much.

Arren

"I'll take it to her," Bran promised once it was finished. "What are yeh gonna do today?"

Arren sighed. "I really should go to work."

"*What?* Are yeh mad?"

"Apparently. But I've already missed a week. If I don't go in today I'll be sacked, assuming I haven't been already. Don't worry, Roland will probably send me home again when he finds out why I didn't come in sooner."

Bran rolled his eyes. "Yeh really don't believe in lookin' after yerself, do yeh?"

"Maybe, but I *do* believe in being practical. It's not that far to go. We probably went that distance last night, and I managed that." Arren finished eating and stood up. "May as well make a start now. Could you pass me that piece of blanket?"

He covered up the collar again, and he and Bran left together.

"Be careful," Bran said before they parted. "I'll come and see yeh again tomorrow."

"Thanks, Bran."

Arren walked to the hatchery, taking back streets and alleys and staying away from crowds as much as possible. Inevitably, though, plenty of people saw him. He pretended not to notice them staring and pointing.

Roland was out the front of the hatchery, helping to feed the goats, and ran to meet Arren as soon as he saw him. "Arren! There you are, thank Gryphus! I was beginning to be very worried. Where have you been? And what's that around your neck?"

"I'm sorry, Roland," said Arren. "I've been . . . sick."

"Sore throat?"

"You could say that. Have I—I haven't lost my job, have I?"

"No, no, not at all. We've been coping well enough. I'm assuming you've recovered enough to come back to work?"

Arren started to say no and then changed his mind. He needed the money too badly for that. "Yes, I think so. But I can't do any heavy lifting for a while."

"That's all right. You can just help with the feeding for now. I won't push you too hard."

"Thank you," Arren said, and went inside.

Nothing had changed much. The moment he entered, the chicks started shrieking for food, and he crossed the room to the cage of rats.

W ork that day wasn't too strenuous. He fed the chicks and changed the straw in the pens and went home that evening with his pay, tired and sore but feeling oddly relieved. Work took his mind off his troubles, and being paid cheered him up. It would take a long time, but he'd be able to buy some new furniture in the end.

Roland had agreed to let him work for only half the day for a few weeks, and the next day Bran came to visit again shortly before he was due to leave. He'd brought more food, and some blankets, a pillow and a new tunic. He'd also brought news.

"Took the note to Flell. She wasn't at home, but I gave it to her housekeeper. So how are yeh? Better?"

"I will be, Bran."

And he was. As the days and weeks slowly passed, he recovered. The broken ribs grew less and less painful as they healed, and his headaches went away altogether. Only the collar remained and it was a constant torment.

Bran kept on bringing him food and also supplied him with a new hammock and a chair. There were no more problems; no-one attacked or threatened him, and he slowly lost the feeling of being watched. And, gradually, he started to relax. Maybe it was all over now. Maybe.

Flell, though, still hadn't contacted him. He went to her house several times, only to be told she was out, and she hadn't sent a message. But other people who'd seen her assured him she was well.

Deep down, Arren knew she was avoiding him. But he tried to convince himself that it was better this way. She deserved better than him. She always had. All he could do now was be grateful that she was safe, and hope that she might decide to contact him again.

At the end of two months he was able to go back to working all day. His ribs had completely healed, though they still twinged occasionally, and he was putting on weight.

But the collar still would not leave him alone. It was always there, hurting him, a constant, secret reminder, humiliating and degrading, even though he kept it covered. Roland started to ask him why he kept his neck wrapped up, and looked suspicious when he evaded the question; other people kept staring and saying things. "Why're you wearing a scarf?" "You're not in the North now, blackrobe." "Covering up your collar, are you, blackrobe?" "Hey, blackrobe! When you've finished wrapping your neck up, come and clean my floor." "I could use a slave to help around the place." "What are you looking at, blackrobe?" "I don't sell to blackrobes, get lost." "Go back to the North, blackrobe."

Stupid things. Mindless things. Cruel things. But they went on and on, every day, all the time, following him everywhere like a disease.

Arren's face became gaunt, his eyes cold, his mouth set into a hard, bitter line. He stopped talking to people unless it was necessary. He stopped smiling. He forgot how to laugh. Not even Bran could cheer him up any more. He stopped caring that Flell had abandoned him. Perhaps she was ashamed to be seen with him.

Roland noticed. "What's wrong, Arren?" he asked in kindly tones, about three months after the assault. "You're not yourself any more."

Arren paused in sweeping the floor and leant on his broom. "Aren't I?" His voice was flat and dull.

"No," said Roland. "You're not. What's happened to you? I've never seen you so . . . depressed."

Arren was silent for a time. "I'm sure I shall be fine," he said eventually, and resumed his sweeping.

"What is it?" Roland said again. "Have you had an argument with Flell? Is someone bothering you?"

More silence. Then Arren stopped again, automatically putting a hand to his neck to hold the collar in place. "Roland?"

"Yes, lad?"

"What are you supposed to do when someone hurts you?" said Arren.

"How d'you mean, Arren?"

"When they're cruel to you. If they lie to you or hurt you. What's the right thing to do?"

"Well, I'm not sure how I would be expected to know," said Roland. "Why do you ask?"

"You know about the gods," said Arren. "What do *they* want us to do?"

"Oh, I don't think I'm the right person to ask. The only god I know is Gryphus. And Gryphus is . . . well, he's . . ."

"Not my god," Arren said shortly.

"Why do you ask, Arren?" said Roland.

"I was just curious. That's all."

Roland paused, and then put the griffin chick he was holding back into its pen. "There's something wrong, isn't there?" he said, coming closer. "Something's troubling you. What is it, Arren?"

As Arren moved away, the broom fell out of his hands. He bent to pick it up, and the collar moved. He cried out without meaning to, and his hand went to his neck.

Roland stopped. "Arren, what's wrong with your neck? You're—oh my gods, you're bleeding!"

Arren tried to pull away, but Roland was too quick for him. He grabbed the strip of blanket and pulled it off, revealing the collar underneath. Blood was crusted on the skin above and below it, which was red and swollen, and a thin trickle of fresh blood was slowly weaving its way over Arren's collarbone.

Roland went pale. *"No!"*

Arren tried to grab the strip of blanket, but Roland tossed it aside and grabbed him by the shoulder. *"How long have you been like this?"*

"I . . ."

"Answer me! How long have you had this on?"

"Three months," Arren almost whispered.

Roland's expression was horrified. "Arren, who did this?"

"I don't know."

"What d'you mean?"

Arren's shoulders slumped. "They broke into my house. I came home and they were waiting. They beat me up and put the collar on me. I can't get it off."

"Is that why you didn't come to work for so long?"

"Yes."

"Arren, why didn't you tell me? For gods' sakes, why did you just—you've been wearing that thing for three months and you never told anyone? You could have died!"

"I didn't know what to do," said Arren. "I was afraid."

"Yes, but not *stupid*. This is—well, this is an outrage! The whole city should be up in arms!"

"Why?" Arren said sharply. "Why should they care?"

"Care? Arren, you're a griffiner! You're not a slave. Yes, I know you don't have a griffin any more, but you still deserve respect! If Riona knew about this she'd be furious. Lord Rannagon would—"

"I can't *tell* anyone, Roland," said Arren.

"Balderdash!" Roland snapped, in a voice such as Arren had never heard him use. "Come with me right now; we're going to go and see Lord Rannagon this instant."

"No!"

Roland stopped. "What?"

Open fear showed in Arren's face. "No, please, don't."

"Don't what?"

"I can't go to Rannagon. I can't tell people about it. I can't let them find out . . ."

"Find out what?" Roland was looking at him with concern. "Arren, what are you afraid of?"

"I—I can't tell you."

"Why not?"

"I just can't."

"No." Roland seized him by the shoulders and forced Arren to look him in the eye. "I am not going to stand idly by and let this happen. You're going to tell me what's going on, right now, or I'll take you to Lord Rannagon anyway."

Arren glanced toward the doors. There was no-one there, but . . .

Roland noticed. "Come with me," he said, and hustled Arren into the back room. His home consisted of a solitary but large and very comfortable-looking room, and most of the furniture was well made and expensive, as befitted a griffiner. Roland sat him down at the table and poured some wine into a cup. "Here, drink this."

Arren drank deeply. It was strong and richly flavoured, and he relaxed a little.

Roland closed and locked the door and then came back. "All right," he said firmly. "Tell me what's going on. Start from the beginning."

"I can't."

"Why not?"

"Because—" Arren stopped, and then suddenly felt his resistance cave in. "I've been told that if I tell anyone, they'll be killed, and so will I. One of—a friend of mine, I told him I'd been threatened, and . . . he died a few days later. They said it was an accident, but—"

"Who was this?" said Roland.

"Gern. You know, the tailor's son. Bran told me he died in a fight at the Arena, but—"

"He did," Roland interrupted. "Alisoun was there and

saw it happen. It was a complete accident. He wasn't even pushed; he tripped over something. Arren, who threatened you?"

"But if I tell you—"

"I will be fine," said Roland. "I have a hundred griffins living here with me, and if anyone showed the slightest sign of attacking me they'd be torn to pieces. Now tell me, who threatened you?"

"Lord Rannagon," Arren whispered.

Roland froze. "What? Arren, that's—that's not funny."

Arren looked up. "It was Lord Rannagon," he said again. "Him and Shoa. They came to my house. Rannagon said that if I didn't keep quiet I'd be killed. He said people would be watching me."

"But . . . *Lord Rannagon*? Why? When?"

"Eluna," said Arren.

"Eluna? What about her?"

"She—it was a lie. The story they told about why I went to Rivermeet. It wasn't *true*. I didn't steal the map. Lord Rannagon gave it to me. I went because he told me to go."

"What? Arren, I don't understand."

"I went to him that morning," Arren went on. "I told him about the raid and how the smuggler died. He said I had to pay compensation. I said I couldn't afford it, and he said I could earn the money quickly by catching a wild griffin. I said I didn't know how to do it, but he gave me the poison and the map and said I could. He talked me into it. He said it was easy and he'd done it on his own dozens of times. He said—he made it sound like a big adventure. And I believed him and said I'd go. He told me to leave the next day and promised he'd take care of everything for me while I was gone. He made me promise not to tell anyone in the Eyrie. So I went, and—and Eluna died.

"And when I got back, Rannagon had told everyone that I lied and ran away. He'd got other people to support him. And when I tried to tell Riona the truth, Shoa stopped me and said she would kill me if I accused Rannagon of anything. I had to go along with what he said. And then later

on, Rannagon and Shoa came to my house and told me if I
didn't keep it secret I'd be killed."

Roland was looking at him in disbelief. "But why would
Rannagon act like that?"

Arren stared at the tabletop. "Because I'm a blackrobe,"
he mumbled. "Blackrobes can't be griffiners."

"Arren, this—this can't be *true*," said Roland. "I refuse
to believe it. I've known Rannagon since I was a child; he
isn't *like* that. I've never met anyone kinder and more just
than him. He wouldn't do something like that to you."

"He said he didn't want to," said Arren. "But he did it.
I swear, he did it."

"But why?"

"Because—because when I went to see him, he also
told me a secret. He said Riona wanted to put me on the
council."

"She *what*?"

"I didn't believe him, but he said it was true. And later
on Riona said it was true, too. Rannagon said—he said
the other senior griffiners knew, and they didn't want
me on the council because of what I am. So he sent me
to Rivermeet to get me into trouble, so I'd be disgraced
and Riona wouldn't go ahead and make me a councillor.
He said he didn't want Eluna or me to get hurt, but it went
wrong."

Roland stood up. "I'm going to go and talk to him," he
said. "I'll get to the bottom of this. You stay here. Don't
leave until I come back, understood?"

Arren stood, too. "But Roland—"

"Stay here," Roland repeated. "That's an order, Arren."

"I—yes, my lord."

"Good. You just finish your wine and rest a bit. I'll be
back by evening."

Roland unlocked the door and opened it. Arren hurried
after him as he left the room, but the old man moved surprisingly fast. He crossed the hatchery floor, arms swinging gently by his sides, making straight for the doors. Keth
got up from her corner and followed him. As she passed

Arren, she paused and looked at him. "Guard the hatchlings, Arren."

"I will," he promised.

Keth nodded briefly to him and loped away after Roland, and the two of them were gone.

Arren stayed where he was for a while after they had left. His heart was pounding, and he felt light-headed and dizzy. He swallowed hard, trying to suppress his sudden nausea, and then snatched up the broom and began sweeping fiercely, trying to distract himself. But he couldn't stop his mind from racing. What was going to happen now? Would Rannagon deny everything and persuade Roland that he, Arren, was a liar? Or would Roland expose him? He touched the collar again, trying to shift it around so it would hurt less. It didn't work.

"You!"

He turned. Someone else had entered the hatchery. It was a boy, a few years younger than himself. He had straw-coloured hair and blue eyes that looked very familiar, and though he was plainly clad there was something proud and confident about the way he stood. When Arren just stared blankly at him, he strode forward, pointing at him. "I'm talking to you."

Arren sighed and leant on his broom. "Yes?"

"I'm looking for Lord Roland. Have you seen him?"

"He's just left for the Eyrie," said Arren. "He should be back later."

"Damn! How long will he be?"

"I'm not sure. What do you want? I could be able to help you."

"I sincerely doubt that," said the boy. He paused to look him up and down. "I have to say I'm a little surprised to see you here. I'd been told there weren't any slaves in Eagleholm nowadays."

"There aren't," said Arren.

"But you stayed behind, did you?"

Arren started sweeping again. "This is my home. I don't have anywhere else to go."

The boy laughed. "You've got some nerve, slave. Is Roland your master? I didn't think he was the sort to keep slaves."

"And *I* didn't think Lord Rannagon was the sort to father bastards, but you live and learn, don't you?" said Arren, without looking around.

He derived a great deal of satisfaction from the shocked silence that followed. "How dare you?" the boy demanded. "Who d'you think you are, talking to me like that, slave?"

Arren turned. "Why, would you like me to introduce myself?"

The boy glared at him. "By Gryphus, Roland must be soft on you."

"Pleased to meet you, I'm sure," said Arren. "I'm Arren Cardockson."

The boy's expression changed. "What, you mean the Northerner who used to be a griffiner?"

Arren gave him a look so cold it was barely human. "And you'd be Erian, the bastard who never was one. Charmed."

Erian looked a little puzzled at that, as if he hadn't encountered sarcasm before. "But if you're not a slave, why are you wearing a collar?"

"It's the latest fashion, farm boy. Is there anything I can help you with, or are you just here to ask stupid questions?"

Erian drew himself up. "I am *here*," he said coldly, "to present myself to the griffins."

"Is that so?" said Arren. "I hope you're ready. They eat the rejects, you know."

Erian hesitated a moment. "Are you joking?"

Arren rolled his eyes and put the broom aside. "Fine. I'll lead you through it."

"I'd really rather wait until Lord Roland gets back."

"You'd have to wait for a long time," said Arren. "There's nothing to it. I've done it before dozens of times."

Erian glanced around at the pens. "What am I supposed to do?"

"It's simple. Just go to each chick in turn and see if you can get its attention. If it takes an interest in you, and not just because it wants food, try to pick it up. If it doesn't bite you or run from you, that means it likes you. And after that it's more or less done."

"What, is that all?"

Arren shrugged. "They have an instinct for these things. It's uncanny."

Erian went to the nearest pen and looked over the side at the chick sleeping in it. "I thought they'd be bigger."

"Well, the adults are next door if you'd like to see them."

Erian took a moment to think about it, and nodded. "I think I should probably see them first."

Arren started to speak, but then stopped and smirked. "All right, if that's what you'd prefer, come with me and we'll see what we can do."

"All right." Erian followed him across the room to the doors leading into the adult quarter. As they neared them, they could both hear the screeches and hissing of the griffins on the other side. Erian started to look nervous. "Uh, they won't attack me, will they?"

Arren paused with his hand on the nearest door. "Oh, no. Not if I'm there."

"Are you sure?"

"Of course. Don't you trust me?"

Without waiting for an answer, Arren opened the doors and strode through into the next room, with Erian trailing behind him.

The adult griffins looked around sharply the moment the two humans entered. Arren stopped in the middle of the floor and waited, with Erian beside him.

Almost instantly, the shouts started. The griffins, seeing him, began to jeer in their own language.

"Blackrobe!"

"Ragged ears!"

"Northern brat!"

Arren winced, very glad that Erian couldn't understand them. He nodded to the boy, who was looking slightly pale. "Well, go ahead. Talk to them."

Erian glanced at him. "What, just . . . talk?"

"Yes, go on. Introduce yourself."

"All right."

Erian moved forward a few paces. The moment he did, Arren darted back the way they'd come and took shelter in the open doorway. When Erian looked back at him, he gestured encouragingly and then settled down to watch.

Apparently reassured, Erian turned his attention back to the griffins. Many of them had come down to the floor and were coming closer to inspect him, their tails twitching as if they were stalking prey. For a moment Erian did nothing, either confused or, more likely, frightened. And then he started to speak. In griffish. "Griffins!" he shouted. "I have come to show myself to you! I am Erian, son of Rannagon! I have noble blood in my veins—the blood of griffiners— and though I was raised as a farm boy, I am strong and brave and a natural leader! I am worthy! I have come all the way to Eagleholm to show myself to you and prove that I am deserving of your mighty company! If there be any griffin here who would choose me, I would consider it the greatest honour and privilege of my life, and I would spend every day henceforth in that griffin's company, as his friend and servant, always ready to fight against the forces of darkness and preserve the light of peace and justice!" He raised a hand high, fingers spread. "I am Erian Rannagonson! I am worthy!"

Arren's gleeful expression changed to one of deep dismay.

The griffins had fallen silent while Erian spoke, and now they were gathering around him in a great bustling flock, all fluttering wings and clicking beaks. Erian stood still and watched them, his demeanour almost bewilderingly calm and collected as the griffins began to come forward, one by one. They sniffed at him and looked at him closely, and some touched him, but one by one they turned away and returned to the flock.

And then a large brown griffin came forward. She scented Erian's tunic and his hands, and then she sat back

on her haunches and looked him in the face. He looked
back, unmoving. Then, slowly, he reached toward her.

Arren caught his breath. This was insanely dangerous.
Anyone who touched a griffin that was not their partner
was liable to lose their hand, if not their entire arm.

Erian laid his hand on the brown griffin's forehead,
right between her eyes. For a time there was absolute stillness between them, and then she sighed and bowed her
head. Erian withdrew his hand and she abruptly stood up.
She nudged him very gently in the chest and then quietly
moved to stand beside him.

Deathly silence fell. Erian stood proudly, with the brown
griffin beside him. Then he raised his head and screamed.
"Erian! Erian!"

The brown griffin opened her beak toward the ceiling
and added her voice to his. *"Senneck! Senneck!"*

The other griffins took up the cry, screeching their own
names as loud as they could, until the whole room rang
with the sound. Standing frozen in the doorway, Arren was
seized by a powerful urge to do the same. A scream rose
in his own throat and whispered in his ears, pleading with
him to release it. *Arren, Arren, Arren.*

"Eluna," he whispered.

Erian and Senneck turned and began to walk slowly out
of the room, keeping pace with each other. Arren saw them
coming toward him and was suddenly afraid. It was as if he
was watching Rannagon, a younger, taller Rannagon, but
with the same hard blue eyes, the same yellow hair. And
the griffin—the griffin's eyes matched his. Light blue. Sky
blue. So bright, so perfect.

Arren backed away into the hatchery as they came
through the doors, but neither of them so much as glanced
at him.

Erian put his hand on Senneck's shoulder and looked
at Arren. "Tell Lord Roland what happened. I am going to
find my father. I mean"—he glanced at Senneck—"*we* are
going to find my father."

Arren couldn't bear to look him in the face. "I will."

Erian took his hand away from Senneck and came toward him, moving slowly. There was an odd expression on his face; it made him look slightly mad. "That's *Lord* Erian, blackrobe," he sneered, and shoved him in the chest. Arren fell over backward, hitting the wall of the pen behind him. His collar struck the wood, driving the spikes deep into his neck, and he yelped.

Erian returned to Senneck's side and the two of them left without looking back, but as they passed through the doors and into the sunlight a word drifted back toward him: ". . . blackrobe . . ."

For a long time, Arren did not move. His neck was aching savagely, as if a griffin's talons were embedded in the flesh. He got up slowly, cringing and clutching at the collar. Once he had got his balance, he glanced upward. The sun was going down, and the light through the windows was tinted with orange. It was time for him to go home.

Arren looked into the pen behind him. The chick that occupied it stared back. It was a red griffin with orange eyes. "Food?" it said.

He never quite knew how it happened. Moving slowly and deliberately, his hand rose and took hold of the bolt on the gate. He watched with fascination as his fingers wrapped around it, gripped and pulled. The bolt came out with a soft *thunk*, and he pushed the gate open and stepped into the pen. The red chick came toward him, cheeping. "Food! Food!"

Arren knelt in front of it. "Will you help me?" he whispered in griffish.

The chick stopped and peered at him. "Arren?"

"Yes," said Arren. "Yes, that's me. Will you help me, little one?"

"Help?"

Arren reached out toward the chick, and his hands closed around its body, pinning its wings to its sides. Instantly, it stabbed its beak into the back of his hand.

He didn't even feel it. He straightened up, holding it

tightly, and backed out of the pen. There, he stopped and looked quickly around. There was no-one there. Just the chicks, chirping in their pens.

The red chick started to struggle, squawking in protest. Arren tucked it under his arm and clamped its beak shut with his hand. He found his cloak hanging by the door where he'd left it and draped it over himself, hiding his wriggling burden from view. Then, watching all the while for the slightest sign of another person, he turned and stole away into the gathering night.

18

A Thief in the Night

Even as he reached the edge of the goat pens and entered the market district, Arren heard the sound that came from the hatchery. A high, piercing shriek rose over the rooftops of the city, followed by another and then others, louder and louder. The adult griffins had noticed the missing hatchling.

Terror gripped him and he broke and ran, not even noticing the collar dragging at his neck. The chick struggled, its claws digging into him, but he kept hold of it and ducked into an alley. There was a stack of old barrels there; he huddled down behind them and lifted his cloak away from the chick. It immediately tried to pull free, but he took off his cloak and wrapped it up tightly in the coarse fabric, pinning its legs and wings. The chick screeched in protest, and he grabbed it by the beak. "Quiet!"

The chick looked up at him, and Arren suddenly realised it was trembling with fear. He stroked its head. "It's all right. I'm not going to hurt you. I'm your friend."

There was a screech from overhead. Arren looked up sharply, and his face twisted with dread. Griffins. Dozens of them, flying over the market district and screeching. The sky was darkened, but he could see their black shapes moving over it, wings beating, tails held out rigidly behind them as they called. They were hunting for him.

The chick heard them and started to struggle even harder, letting out muffled cries. Arren stood up and tucked it under his arm, covering its head with his cloak and holding its beak shut with one hand. The screeches were getting louder, and he ran. He left the alley and sprinted down the street, turned left through another alley and ran on. The griffins were circling overhead, flying so low he could hear the sound of their beating wings.

People were gathering in the streets, staring and pointing at the sky. He did his best to avoid them, but when he turned a corner into a crossroads he found it packed with people. There was no other way through. He ran forward, shoving past them. Some of them shoved him back, but most of them were too distracted to pay much attention to him. He got through the crowd and ran on. As he went, he heard someone shout after him, "Hey, why is he wearing a—"

Arren did not stop. He left the words behind and fled straight toward his home.

"We're going," he muttered as he ran, diving into a side street to avoid a low-flying griffin. "We're going to leave the city. We'll hide until they're gone, and then we'll—"

He stopped dead. Up ahead was the block where he lived. Griffins were circling above it, but they were not the only thing in the sky.

There was a column of smoke rising from the rooftops.

People were running ahead of him, shouting in panic, and Arren ran after them, his heart pounding so hard he thought it would burst. His street was clogged with people, but he ploughed his way through until he reached the centre of them all. They were standing well back from the source of the smoke, all talking at once, and some were already turning to run away.

Arren broke through the crowd, but he already knew what he would see.

The door and both of the front windows had been broken open, and flames were billowing out. The thatch had already caught and, even as he watched, his house turned into a fiery inferno.

Arren couldn't move. He stood rooted to the spot, frozen in horror.

Behind him, he could hear people yelling. "Get water!" "Wet next door's roof, for gods' sakes, before it catches!" "Someone run and warn the—"

Too late, Arren realised the danger. The burning house was a beacon. The griffins started to gather, and the crowd looked up and began to back away. Several griffins came down to land, scattering them in fright. Arren ran. A griffin swooped down directly in front of him, so he turned and ran back toward the burning house. The heat hit him in the face and he stopped and turned back, looking desperately for somewhere else to flee. He could feel the chick fighting even more fiercely to get away. He glanced down. It had shredded the cloth over its head, and now it freed one front talon and ripped his hand away. The instant it could, it opened its beak and called out to the other griffins.

The crowd had fled, and now the street was virtually deserted. And the griffins began to land. More and more of them, their talons thudding down onto the wooden street. And Arren had nowhere to run. They were advancing on him, hissing and snarling.

He held up a hand. "No! You don't understand—"

The chick freed its paws and wrenched itself out from beneath his arm. He made a grab for it, and in an instant it twisted around and struck him in the face, just under his right eye. Its beak ripped downward, tearing a deep gash from his eye to his mouth. Arren screamed and dropped the chick, and it ran away from him, toward the nearest of the adult griffins, taking shelter behind its foreleg.

The griffin lowered her head and stalked toward him. "Thief!" she snarled.

Blood was running down Arren's face like tears. "No! I didn't mean—"

The griffin leapt. An instant before she struck him, a dark figure darted in and shoved Arren out of the way. He landed in a tangled heap, and as he pulled himself upright he saw his rescuer draw a sword and point it at the enraged griffin. She made a rush at him, but veered away at the last minute, intimidated by the sword. Guards were coming, dodging around the edge of the flock to surround Arren, protecting him with their swords.

The griffins backed away, hissing, and the man who had led the charge pushed through his colleagues and pulled Arren to his feet.

"Bran!"

Bran said nothing. He grabbed Arren by the arm and snapped a pair of manacles on his wrists.

Arren stared dumbly at them. "Bran, no—"

Bran turned away and nodded to two of his colleagues. "Get him out of here."

They came forward and took Arren by the shoulders. "To the prison district, sir?"

"No. The Eyrie."

Arren did not try to resist. He walked silently between the guards as they led him away. A group of them went ahead, swords drawn, fending off the griffins that were still trying to get at him. Some of them had taken to the air and were trying to swoop down on him, and the guards suddenly broke into a run. They hustled Arren away from the flock and into the nearest building, and there sat him down on a table.

"We wait here until someone comes and gets them to calm down," said a voice from the doorway. "Keep an eye out. I wouldn't be surprised if they started breaking the roof."

It was Bran, grim-faced and wearing his uniform. Arren tried to get up and go to him, but the guards pulled him back. "Bran, please!"

There was no recognition in Bran's face. He looked at

Arren for only a moment, then went to the door and peered out. "They're here now. They'll get it under control."

"Bran, I didn't do anything!" Arren shouted. "Someone set my house on fire, don't you see, they're trying to—*aah*!"

One of the guards had struck the side of the slave collar, making pain explode in his neck.

Bran turned to look at Arren, and the hard look on his face faded. "Arren, how could yeh?"

"Bran, it's them, they're trying to kill me! You've got to—" He broke off, crying out as the guard hit him again, this time striking his torn face.

"Stop it," Bran snapped. "Someone get him a cloth."

One of the guards by the door fished a bandage out of his pocket and gave it to Arren. "Here. Cover it up with this."

It was too short to wrap around his head, so he folded it and held it over the wound, keeping his arm up with difficulty under the weight of the manacles. "Bran, please, you've got to help me," he said.

This time Bran ignored him. He stood in the doorway, watching the scene outside. Arren could hear screeching mingled with commanding shouts. Griffiners had arrived to break up the flock.

They waited in tense silence until Bran turned around. "All right, it looks like it's been sorted out. Let's get goin'."

Arren was pulled to his feet and the guards set out, taking him with them. They left the building and marched through several blocks and onto the main street, heading straight for the Eyrie. As Arren walked, the manacles and the collar weighing him down, blood soaking into the bandage on his face, he could see people crowding around to watch him pass, all staring at him with expressions of horror and amazement.

Quite suddenly, a wild urge came over him to break free of the guards and run at them. He wanted to hit them, hurt them, scream at them, make them feel some tiny part of the agony inside him. He wanted to burn their houses and take their belongings, clamp slave collars around their necks and twist them until they screamed. He wanted to kill them.

He made no move, but his wounded face twisted with hate.

A shadow passed over him. Griffins, these ones with riders, had come and were following from above. Others brought up the rear and more went ahead. They were guarding him, still wary of the unpartnered griffins from the hatchery, some of which had decided to follow the column. But none of them tried to attack, and most were leaving. They were satisfied that he had been caught and would not escape.

The group reached the Eyrie, and Arren was taken inside and down into an old part of the building, a part dug into the rock of the mountain itself. There were storerooms down here and rooms where slaves had once slept. And there was a dungeon. It wasn't very large, and the cells were small and dank. The guards took Arren to one of them and threw him inside. He landed hard on the floor, crying out as his collar struck the stone; the door slammed behind him, leaving him in utter darkness.

His eyes adjusted after a while, and he could see faint light filtering in under the door, but it only just allowed him to see the walls of the cell. The floor was damp and filthy, and there was water dripping from the roof. There was no food or water and no furniture except a jar meant to serve as a toilet.

Arren groped his way to the corner and sat down, shivering in the cold. He couldn't see anything or hear anything except the dripping water and the faint sound of the guards moving on the other side of the door. His cheek was throbbing and so was his neck.

After a while the cold seeped into the collar and the manacles as well, until they felt like ice pressed against his skin. He rubbed his hands together, trying to keep them warm, but it didn't do much good. Water had soaked into his clothes, which stuck to his skin, cold and clinging.

As he sat there, blind and trembling, a strange thought occurred to him. *Now I know what it was like for them. Now I know.*

It was impossible to track time in the cell. He slept fitfully and woke up hungry and thirsty. When he went to the door and called to the guards, asking for food and drink, no-one answered. In the end he resorted to sucking the water out of his tunic. It tasted of dirt and blood, but he drank it anyway, glad to have something to take away the stickiness in his mouth.

He was too cold and anxious to sit down again, so he started to pace back and forth in the dark, his chains rattling. All he had to do was wait. They would take him out of here eventually. They had to. They'd take him out of this place, and then—

The door opened and light flooded in. It was so bright it hurt his eyes, and he backed away, raising his arm to cover his face. He heard footsteps as someone entered the cell, and a voice said, "All right, time to go. Hold out your hands. No funny business."

Arren stood with his back to the wall and held his arms out, closing his eyes to blot out the light. The guards took him by the elbows and shoved him toward the door, and he went meekly enough. There was no point in fighting back.

"Where are we going?" he asked as they took him back out along the corridor.

One of the guards struck the collar. "To the council chamber."

Arren cringed. "Why?"

"Well, I'd have expected them to just throw you in the Arena and be done with it, but Lord Rannagon insisted you get a fair trial," said the guard. "Move it."

They climbed a flight of stairs that led to the upper levels of the Eyrie and thence to the doors leading into the council chamber. There were guards there, clad in ceremonial armour. They opened the doors immediately and Arren was taken through and into—

His heart seemed to pause in its beating.

They were all there.

The councillors' seats were all occupied. The gallery was full of people and griffins sitting together, the humans finely clad and the griffins adorned with their own kind of formal outfit: forelegs decorated with bands of gold, silver and copper, some decorated with jewels, and their heads crowned by plumes and tassels. The place was brightly lit by fine glass lanterns, and light also filtered in from the windows in the roof. But the banners had been taken down and there was a formality, even a coldness, to the room.

In the centre of the floor a kind of wooden pen had been set up, about chest height and open at the back. The guards led Arren toward it.

The pen was facing Riona's seat, but Riona was not sitting there. Rannagon was. He stood up as Arren entered the chamber, and watched as the guards made their prisoner stand inside the pen, facing him. His wife, Kaelyn, was by his side, and their griffins flanked the pair, staring balefully at Arren.

Arren stood in the pen, holding on to the front of it, and stared around at the chamber, scarcely able to believe what he was seeing. Surely every griffiner in the city was there, and every griffin as well. He recognised dozens of faces. Roland was there, and Flell, watching from a seat in the gallery just behind her father, and Deanne, and Tamran. People he had known. Some he had been trained alongside; some he had just spoken to briefly on official occasions. Even Vander was there, with Ymazu, his dark eyes watchful.

The moment Arren entered the chamber, the mutterings started. Human and griffish voices filled the air, low and ominous, and there were a few shouts, though he couldn't catch the words.

He stood in the dock, his eyes on Rannagon, and terror paralysed him. The guards silently took up station on either side of him, and then Rannagon stepped forward and raised a hand for silence.

Almost instantly, the chattering stopped.

Rannagon said nothing. He was wearing a tunic made from yellow velvet trimmed with blue and silver, and there were red lines painted on his forehead, the ancient signs of justice and authority. His sword was strapped to his back, its hilt gleaming.

For a moment, the Master of Law regarded Arren, his expression not hostile but a little sad. And then, at last, he began to speak.

"Arenadd Taranisäii," he said, his voice echoing in the huge space, "also known as Arren Cardockson, of Idun, you have been accused of abducting a griffin chick. You have been brought before me, in the company of your fellow griffiners, for the chance to defend yourself and perhaps win your freedom. What do you have to say for yourself?"

Arren looked at him and then at the gallery. They were all watching. Waiting. "I . . ."

"Go ahead," said Rannagon. "It's your right."

"I didn't do it," said Arren. "I didn't steal the chick. It chose me."

There was a muttering from the gallery.

"Indeed?" said Rannagon. "Then why did you run away? And why did you restrain it? And why did a dozen witnesses see it break free and tear your face?"

"It was frightened," Arren replied. "The fire scared it, and it panicked. Hasn't your griffin ever bitten you, my lord?"

Rannagon's eyes narrowed. "Don't presume to speak to me like that. You have not answered my other questions. Why did you run and hide?"

"Because . . ."

"Answer me."

"Because I knew I had to," Arren said loudly. "Because I knew no-one would accept it. I knew I had no chance to be a true griffiner again, and so I decided we both had to leave."

"Why?" said Rannagon. "What were you afraid of, Arenadd?"

"You know the answer to that, my lord."

"Speak plainly," said Rannagon. "Speak the truth."

Arren was silent. He looked down at the wooden edge of the dock, where his hands rested. Long, pale hands with black hair scattered over the knuckles, the manacles resting just behind them. He could see his reflection, faintly, on the surface of the metal. See his own eyes, black and cold as steel.

"Speak," Rannagon commanded. "Speak now or I will presume that you have waived your right to do so, and I will pronounce sentence on you."

Arren looked up. "I was afraid of you," he said.

There was more muttering from the crowd, louder this time.

Rannagon waved them into silence. "Why would that be?"

"You already know," said Arren. "You *know*. You knew from the beginning."

"What did I know, Arenadd?" Rannagon asked steadily.

Arren straightened up. "Griffiners! Listen to me!" he shouted, and pointed at Rannagon. "This man is a liar and a traitor! He drove me to do what I did! He betrayed me!"

The guards grabbed his shoulders to hold him still, as the listeners reacted with a flurry of shouts and screeches.

"Silence!" Rannagon roared. He came toward Arren. "Tell me what I've done," he said, raising his voice above the noise. "Tell them."

"You killed Eluna!" Arren shouted back, provoking further consternation. "It was your fault! You lied to me and sent me to my death! And then you lied to Riona as well! You told them it was *my* fault, you said I was a liar and a thief, you said if I told anyone you'd kill me, and then you murdered my friend because he knew the truth! You sent people after me, made them put this collar on me and destroy my house, and then you set it on fire! You took my life!"

This time there were not mutterings or muted exclamations. This time there was an outburst of shouting and screeching, deafeningly loud and terrible with rage.

Arren ignored them completely. "You can't do this to me!" he half-screamed. "Murderer! Traitor!"

"Shut him up!" Rannagon snapped at the guards.

They took Arren by the elbows and dragged him back from the front of the dock, and one of them clamped a hand over his mouth, silencing him. Arren bit him, and the other guard hit him in the neck and then grabbed him by the hair, dragging his head sideways. He tried to fend them off, but they only hit him harder; he subsided, fists clenched, unable to speak, the guard's hand once again firmly in place over his mouth.

Rannagon was busy trying to silence the crowd, but without much success. Then Shoa stood up and screeched. Her voice cut across the babble; as it started to die down, she reared up, opening her wings, and screeched again. The crowd went quiet.

Rannagon watched them sternly then turned back to Arren, and the look on his face was not angry or accusing but full of terrible sadness. "Arren, I'm sorry," he said. "I didn't want to have to do this."

He turned to address the gallery again. "I had been expecting something like this to happen," he said, "though I hoped it wouldn't. I take no pleasure in saying it. I've known the accused since he was a boy and considered him a close friend. I was always proud of him for having risen so far from such beginnings, and I cannot express how miserable I was when I learnt of Eluna's fate. I have been doing my best to help him since then, out of sympathy. I have kept an eye on him for the last few months and have tried to help him recover. As some of you already know, I asked favours of certain people to give him a job if he ever asked for one. I have also spoken to his friends and his employer and some of his neighbours and acquaintances. And, unfortunately, it would seem that he did not recover from the trauma of Eluna's death. I had hoped that he would improve, but as you can plainly see, he has not."

There was near-silence, broken only by a few curious voices.

"I can say with complete sincerity," Rannagon went on, "that I have never in my life held prejudice against Arenadd because of his heritage. I have fought his kind in the past, and I know their history in detail, but I never thought of Arenadd as what some call a blackrobe. To me, he was a friend first, and a Northerner second, as I hope it was with all of you. I saw him not as an upstart raised to our status by some outrageous twist of fate; I saw him as a symbol, and an example. An example of the fact that, no matter what his origins and blood, a man may always rise above his past and become something better.

"It is said—indeed, it is known—that all Northerners have a madness in them. I have seen it myself. It is in their blood to be this way. But Arenadd was not like that. All those who knew him agreed with me. Although he looked Northern and was born of Northern parents, he did not act like them. Few men his age were as civilised and intelligent. Some even called him gentle. However—" Rannagon bowed his head, his demeanour full of weariness and pain. "However, I have now been forced to face the truth. Others have told me about his erratic behaviour recently—his violent outbursts, his paranoia and secrecy, and his wild appearance—and only yesterday I received confirmation. Arenadd cannot be blamed completely for his actions. He cannot help himself. My lords and ladies, the boy has lost his mind."

Arren's mouth fell open.

The crowd started to mutter again. He scanned the rows of faces, trying desperately to tell what people were thinking. Most looked surprised or contemptuous. Some looked angry. Others merely looked sad or disgusted. He saw Roland, but the old man's head was bowed. He saw Flell, and her eyes were on him. There were tears on her face.

Rannagon sighed and resumed. "I had hoped that it was not true—that there was some other explanation for his behaviour—but I cannot close my eyes to it any longer. The evidence is overwhelming. Every single person I have spoken to who has associated with him over the last few months has told me that they feared for his sanity. Yesterday his employer, Lord Roland of the hatchery, came to me with a story that confirmed it. Apparently, Arenadd told him a wild tale in which he blamed me for Eluna's death and claimed that he was being followed and threatened with death if he should ever reveal it. He told a similar story to other people. His delusion is so complete that he blamed the accidental death of Gern Tailor—which took place in daylight and was witnessed by dozens of people—on some secret group of spies that had been following him around and listening to every word he said."

"What about the collar?" someone shouted from the gallery. "Where did that come from?"

"Ah," said Rannagon. "Yes. I am afraid that, most likely, he put it on himself."

"How?" the same person demanded.

"There are plenty of slave collars left in the city," said Rannagon. "Mostly kept as ornaments or conversation pieces. As it happens, one went missing from a house on Tongue Street . . . at around the same time as Arenadd was seen in the area. But it seems to have woven itself in with his delusions; I wouldn't be surprised if he didn't even remember stealing it.

"However," he went on, "while insanity is not a crime, what followed is unforgivable. After he had confessed his delusions to Lord Roland and sent him here to bring me the story, he took advantage of the fact that he had been left to guard the hatchlings, abducted one of them and fled the hatchery, obviously intending to leave the city and find a place to hide with it. Fortunately, by coincidence, his house had caught fire because of an unattended candle— an investigation of the ruins has confirmed this—and he was caught by the adult griffins from the hatchery, who had noticed the missing chick and had gone looking for it. There is no doubt whatsoever that he committed this crime. More than thirty people have already testified to having seen him attempting to escape, and the hatchery griffins confirmed that he was the only person in the hatchery when the chick went missing and that they saw him holding it captive. Therefore, I have no choice but to hand down the sentence of death."

The crowd roared. It was not a shout, not a scream—it was a deep collective *bellow*, full of rage and hatred and pure, unrestrained bloodlust. Many of the griffins in the gallery rose up, wings spread, and began to snap their beaks, stretching their heads out toward him as if they wanted to tear him limb from limb.

Arren started to struggle, trying to pull away from the hand covering his mouth. The guards restrained him again, but then Rannagon turned toward him and said, "Arenadd Taranisäii, have you anything more to say before you are removed?"

The hand was taken away. *"Liar!"* Arren screamed. "You godsdamned *liar!"*

Once again the rage rose up inside him, filling him with terrible strength. He shrugged off the guards as if they were nothing and lunged forward, trying to climb over the wall between him and Rannagon. Shoa darted forward to defend her partner, but Arren managed to hook a leg over the edge of the dock and started to pull himself over. The guards hauled him back, but he slammed into them, heedless of any pain, and began to shout, *"I'll kill you! I'll kill you!"*

More guards came running. They dragged him bodily away, and he fought every moment of it, lashing out wildly at their faces and screaming. "I am not insane! *Liar!* You can't do this to me! *Liar! Murderer!"*

But there was nothing he could do. The guards took him out of the chamber, to the jeers and screeches of the crowd, and he kept his eyes on Rannagon until the doors slammed on him. Once they had him out of sight of the

crowd, the guards beat him into submission. Not laughing
or jeering or taking any pleasure in it, but simply hitting
him in places calculated to hurt, in a methodical, almost
bored way, until he finally stopped fighting back. Once he
had fallen silent and gone limp and passive, they hauled
him upright and led him away. They left the Eyrie by a
back door and travelled a short distance through the city,
accompanied by other guards who had been waiting for
just that purpose. Arren already knew where they would
be going. The prison district. It was very large. Once it
had housed nearly a hundred slaves. Now, though, it was
virtually empty. Now that the slaves had gone, the only
people kept there were criminals waiting to be punished
then freed or to be put to death, either by execution or in
the Arena, at the claws of wild griffins.

Arren was taken to a large wooden building and there
handed over to the prison guards. They checked him for
weapons and then took him to a room where there was a
row of huge wooden cages resting on sealed trapdoors. The
cages were attached to the ceiling by thick ropes threaded
through pulleys and wrapped around a series of large wind-
lasses. His new guards removed the manacles and bundled
him into one of the cages, tying the door shut behind him.
Then they opened the pair of latches that held the trapdoor
beneath it shut. It swung open with a loud bang, revealing
nothing but empty air underneath. The floor of the cage
was made of wooden slats, the gaps between them almost
as wide as Arren's hand. He yelled and hurled himself at
the cage door, trying to force it open, but it would not move.
The guards ignored him. They went to the windlass and
began to turn the handles, and the cage jerked and began to
move downwards, through the trapdoor and into the void.
It went down and down, swinging gently from side to side,
the mountainside passing in front of him. It drew level with
a platform that jutted from the rock and came to a stop.
There were more guards on the platform, and they hurried
forward and snapped a set of wooden holders into place at
the base of the cage, to secure it.

Arren tried not to look down, but he couldn't help it. Through the slats he could see the ground so far below, right under his feet.

His whole body went cold. He stood absolutely still for a heartbeat, and then he ran forward and started to wrench at the door which faced the platform. "Let me out! Please, I can't stay in here! No!"

The guards paid no attention; they returned to their posts without even looking back at him. Arren yelled until he was hoarse, but went utterly unheeded.

He slumped into a sitting position, his arms wrapped around the bars in front of him, gripping on as if they were the only thing holding him up. He could feel himself trembling violently all over. The wind tugged at his hair and he closed his eyes. He was going to fall . . . The floor was going to break and he was going to fall . . .

His eyes had gone wide and staring, bulging with terror. He looked toward the other cages that hung alongside his, and then at the guards, beseeching them. "Help me," he whispered. "Someone help me."

19

Hanging

" . . . Arren? Arren?"

Very slowly, Arren looked up. There was a strange, fixed look on his face, and he squinted at the person looking down at him as if he had no idea what he was seeing.

Someone nudged him in the shoulder. "Arren? Arren, say somethin'."

The blankness in Arren's face receded slightly. "Bran?"

Bran looked relieved. "Thank gods, I thought yeh didn't recognise me. Arren, listen, there's someone here to see yeh."

Arren looked past him. There was a woman standing behind Bran. She was holding a piece of paper and a stick of charcoal, and was watching him without much interest. Seeing him looking at her, she came forward. "Arren Cardockson?"

Arren nodded vaguely.

"I understand you've been condemned to death," said the woman.

Arren said nothing, and the woman glanced at Bran, who nodded.

"Well then," she said, "I've been sent to make you an offer."

Arren looked up at her and listened silently.

The woman took that as her cue and went on. "You have two choices facing you at this point," she said. "You can either accept the immediate death sentence or you can volunteer to fight in the Arena tomorrow. Now, if you choose the Arena and you win the fight, you'll be set free. If you're interested, put your mark on this piece of paper and everything will be arranged. You will be allowed a weapon in the Arena, and you will be given better food beforehand. Make your choice."

Arren was silent.

"Should I take that as a refusal?" said the woman.

The sound of her voice seemed to recall him to his senses. "Which one would I be fighting?" he said.

"I'm sorry?"

"Which griffin would I be fighting?"

"There would probably be more than one," said the woman. "Why do you ask?"

"I want to fight the black one," said Arren. "I want to fight—I want to fight Darkheart."

"That shouldn't be a problem," said the woman. "Darkheart is very popular at the moment. He goes into the Arena nearly every week."

"Alone," said Arren.

"I'm sorry?" the woman said again.

Arren's grip on the bars tightened. "If you let me fight the black griffin on my own—just him and me—I'll say yes."

The woman looked thoughtful. "I've never had anyone make a request like that before."

"Promise me," said Arren, hauling himself up on the bars. "Promise me I can fight the black griffin, and I'll do whatever you want."

The woman hesitated a moment, then nodded. "I don't

see why not. I think Orome would like the idea. Yes, I
agree. Just give me a moment." She knelt, placed the piece
of paper on the wooden decking beneath her and scribbled
away with the stick of charcoal, adding a few extra lines.
This done, she offered the charcoal to Arren. "Just put your
name here, or an X or whatever you like. Just as long as it's
your mark."

Arren stared at the blank spot on the paper for a few
moments and then gripped the charcoal stick and drew a
crude picture of a wolf's head holding the moon in its jaws.
The woman took it from him and said, "Excellent. I shall
go and tell Orome at once. Good luck." She inclined her
head briefly and left.

Arren watched her go and then sighed, almost with
relief.

Bran had been watching all this in silence, keeping well
back from the cage. "Why'd yeh do that?" he asked now.

Arren looked at him as if seeing him for the first time.
"I'm going to die, Bran. I want to die fighting. If I can have
revenge before then, I'll take it."

"Yeh'll be killed," said Bran. "The thing'll tear yeh to
pieces."

Arren sneered at him. "What a tragedy."

"Stop it," said Bran. "This ain't my fault, an' yeh know it."

Arren turned away. "Well, that's nice. Now I'll feel a lot
better when my head comes off."

"Don't blame me for this," Bran snapped. "I was just
doin' my duty. Yeh think that just because we're friends I
can let yeh get away with what yeh did?"

Arren looked back at him, suddenly ashamed. "Bran,
I—"

Bran's anger disappeared, and he came closer to the
bars. "Arren, why'd yeh do it?"

Arren bowed his head. "I couldn't help it. I tried to put up
with it for so long, but I couldn't. I just couldn't. It was too
much for me. I wanted back what Rannagon took from me."

"Arren—" Bran hesitated. "Arren, yeh know it ain't
true, don't yeh?"

"I know what's real, Bran," Arren said coldly. "I know that every word I told you was the truth."

Bran sighed. "Gods, Arren, how did it come to this?"

"Bran, Rannagon killed Eluna. He *told* me he'd done it."

Bran turned away. "Stop it. Just stop it."

"You've got to believe me!" said Arren, coming as far forward as he could and grabbing hold of the bars. "Please, just listen to me. I'm *not* insane."

Bran looked back at him, his face full of misery. For a moment he looked as if he was going to speak, but then he turned and walked away, head bowed.

"Bran! Bran, come back! Please!"

But Bran did not look back. He went back to his post at the entrance cut into the mountainside and did not return, and Arren was left alone with his terror and his despair.

At noon food was brought to him. It was plain but solid and plentiful, and he ate ravenously. Afterward he felt a lot better. His wounded cheek had scabbed over, though it hurt every time he blinked or moved his mouth, and his neck had returned to its usual dull pain. Neither of them would stop him from fighting the next day. He would face the black griffin again, and this time he would kill it, and he didn't care if he himself died in the process. After all, what attraction did life have left for him?

He put aside his plate and settled down to rest, keeping his eyes on the rock wall in front of him to avoid looking at the drop below, and wondered vaguely if there really was an afterlife. Would he meet Eluna there? And Gern?

Movement from the doorway made him look up. Bran and his fellow guard had turned to greet someone who had just arrived on the other side, and now Bran came toward Arren's cage, bringing them with him.

Arren stood up, and the two people came to meet him. "Mum! Dad!"

Annir stared at him for a moment and then rushed forward, reaching through the bars to hug him tightly. "Arren! Oh gods, Arren, no . . . no."

Arren held on to her as best he could, the bars pressing

into his chest and making the scars throb. "Mum, I'm sorry. I really—*ah!*"

Annir pulled away, staring at the collar. "Arren, what in the gods' names—"

Cardock started forward. "Who did this?" he roared. "Who put that on you?"

"I don't know—Dad, I'm sorry. I'm—" Suddenly, Arren started to sob. "Dad, I'm sorry. I'm—I'm such an—you were right. You were right. You were always right. I couldn't pretend forever. I couldn't be one of them. I couldn't be a griffiner. They've—they've killed Eluna. They burned down my house; they put this collar on me and I can't get it off and it hurts all the time. It—I—I just couldn't—"

Cardock reached through the bars and took him by the shoulder. "You shouldn't have stayed," he said. "You should have come home."

"I thought I *was* home," said Arren. "I thought—I thought it didn't matter. I thought I was a Southerner, but I'm not, I'm not. I'm a blackrobe. I don't want to be. I kept trying not to be, but they—I couldn't help it. I couldn't stop it. They took everything away and now they're going to kill me."

"Arren, it's not your fault," said Annir. "It never was. Never let anyone tell you that. You didn't ask for this."

"We're going to the Eyrie as soon as we leave here," said Cardock. "We're going to talk to the Mistress. I'm going to demand your release, or at least stop them killing you. Don't worry, Arenadd, you're not going to die. I'll save you."

Arren shook his head vaguely. "It won't work. I did it, Dad. I stole that chick. I'm guilty."

Cardock ignored him. "We've brought something for you," he said, showing him a bundle he was carrying.

Arren looked at it. "What for?"

"What for?" said Annir, with a kind of forced cheerfulness. "Arren, don't you know what day this is?"

"I don't . . ."

"It's your *birthday*," said Annir. "Your father and I were

coming to see you, and then someone told us you'd been arrested, and—"

"And we came to bring you your present," said Cardock, holding it up. "Your mother and I put a lot of work into it."

It was made of black cloth and looked like a piece of clothing. "What is it?" said Arren.

Cardock unfolded it and held it up by the shoulders. It was a long black robe with wide, full-length sleeves and silver fastenings that stopped halfway down, so that the wearer's legs would be visible and free to move.

"What's that for?" Arren said blankly.

"To wear, of course," said Cardock. "Here, feel it. It's the best-quality material I could get. Warm and tough. It could just about stop an arrow."

Arren reached through the bars and pulled the robe into the cage. It was woven from wool and was indeed thick and strong, though a little coarse. "Why did you make it for me?"

"Because it's part of who you are," said Cardock, almost fiercely. "Take it. If you go into the Arena tomorrow, wear it."

"Why?" said Arren.

"Because you're a Northerner," said Cardock. "When we went into battle, we always wore robes just like this. Let them see you wear it, Arenadd. Let them see you're not ashamed of what you are."

Arren bowed his head. "But I am ashamed," he said.

"Arenadd Taranisäii, don't you *dare* say that in front of us. You are a Northerner, and you have no reason to be ashamed of it. It's part of you and it always will be."

"And I don't want it to be!" Arren shouted. "I never did! What godsdamned good did it ever do me? When did it ever make me happy? Everywhere I go people look at me like I'm some kind of animal! And now they're calling me insane. They're saying—" He broke off suddenly, wide-eyed with helpless dread. "They said it was my blood coming through. The Northerners' madness. And—" He looked out at them, almost pleading with them. "And I can feel it," he whispered. "I can feel it in me. Someone called me a blackrobe and I tried to kill him. I tried to kill Lord Rannagon. I couldn't stop myself. I'm going mad."

"No," Cardock rasped. "Arenadd, no. Stop it. You're not mad."

"Well then, what am I?" said Arren, his fingers tightening on the robe until the knuckles whitened. "You tell me, then."

"Every Northerner is a warrior at heart," said Cardock. "It's your spirit coming through. You were born to fight. Why else do you think they made us wear those collars? They had to. It was the only thing that could subdue us. A Northerner is like a griffin. Nothing can ever break his spirit, and he will never stop fighting back until he dies. That's what my own father told me, and it will always be true."

Arren gripped the robe in both hands and pulled, as if trying to tear it apart. Then he threw it away. "The blackrobes are savages," he snarled. "And I won't let myself become one. Not now, not ever. No matter what happens."

Cardock looked at him, shocked and hurt. "Arenadd, please—"

Arren turned his back on him. "Leave me alone, Father. If you want, you can come to the Arena tomorrow. See how a blackrobe dies."

"Arren, please, don't do this," said Annir. "Please."

But Arren did not turn around. As she began to cry, shame bit into him, but he forced himself to look away. Finally, he heard them start to leave.

"Dad!"

Cardock almost ran back. "What is it?"

Arren couldn't look him in the eye. "I wanted to ask . . ."

"Yes? What is it, Arenadd?"

"When—when they give my body back to you, I want you to take it to Rivermeet. Bury it in the field, where Eluna is. The locals can show you the spot. Can you do that for me?"

Cardock's face creased in pain, but he nodded. "Yes, Arenadd. I promise I'll do all I can."

"Thank you," Arren whispered.

Annir looked as if she wanted to stay, but Cardock took her by the arm. "Come on. We have to go and see the Mistress." He looked at Arren. "We'll see you again, Arenadd, I promise. I swear you'll get out of there alive and we'll take you home."

Arren managed a weak smile. "Goodbye, Dad."

He watched silently as they left and then sat down again, miserable with guilt. The words he had spoken to his parents repeated themselves in his head, and they sounded even more bitter and cruel than he had realised. But they were the truth, and they always had been.

The robe lay crumpled in the corner where he'd thrown it, and some part of him wanted to hold it again. But he left it lying where it was and didn't look at it for the rest of that day, and then night came and it was too dark to see it anyway.

The moon rose, appearing over the distant mountains, faint and dull at first, until it passed through the clouds and soared up into the sky. It was a fat crescent, nearly a perfect half, and Arren kept his eyes on it as it rose higher and higher. In the darkness, he couldn't see the ground below him or even the mountain in front. Everything was utterly black, as though he was standing in space. Alone in the world, hanging in the air with the moon and the stars. The stars glittered brightly, and he remembered the Southern belief that they wove the future.

But they were all outshone by the moon. Pure white light shining on his upturned face, he walked slowly to the other side of the cage, not noticing when it shifted and creaked against its supports. The moon, huge and silent, like a cold sun, filled him with awe and a strange sense of humility.

He stared up at it, speechless, and then bowed his head and started to murmur under his breath, speaking not griffish or the Southern tongue but another language: a harsh, lyrical, cold language, one he had not spoken in front of anyone but his parents for as long as he could remember.

One he had spent most of his life pretending he did not know.

"Help me," he whispered. "Please help me. I'll do whatever you want. Please, I don't want to die. Help me."

Arren was not the only one watching the moon.

Darkheart lay in his cage in the darkened enclosure and stared up at the glowing disc. Hunger was burning inside him, and thirst as well. He had not eaten in four days and had not taken any water in nearly two. There was water in his trough and a joint of meat just beside his beak, but he ignored them.

His captors had tried to make him eat and had even attempted to force food into his beak, but they had failed. He had only hissed and cursed at them, and tried to attack. When he caught one of them with his beak and ripped a deep wound in its side, they had finally left him alone.

"You must eat," Aeya said softly. "You will weaken and be unable to fight."

Darkheart didn't answer her. He hadn't spoken to anyone in nearly a week. He had even stopped bashing his beak on the bars, and he had ceased his evening call. He lay on his belly, making no sound or motion other than the slow in-out of his sides, and the faint rumble of his breathing. His eyes stared straight ahead, not turning to follow movement as they normally would, as if he had gone blind.

Now they were fixed on the moon. He could just see it over the wall of the enclosure, shining out of the darkness. The light reflected in his eyes and he blinked slowly, just once. There was a strange feeling inside him, and it was not hunger or fear or pain, or even despair. It was in his throat, ice-cold, burning hot, powerful and maddening. The imprisoned scream was resting just behind his tongue, trapped and striving to be free and yet refusing to come out. Unable to emerge from his beak, it spread back into the rest of his body, filling him with its energy. Strange mutterings and whisperings sounded in his ears, and vague visions flitted before his eyes. He thought he could see the shape of a human standing there, and a griffin as well, and a pale mist. His eyes ached, and still the feeling stayed with him. It was like the hunger in his stomach, but he knew food would not make it go away. It infused his fur and feathers, and the skin and muscle beneath, not painful and yet so powerful that it made his vision waver.

He started to tremble. The feeling turned and gnashed in his throat until he felt as if he was suffocating, and he opened his beak wide, trying desperately to rid himself of it. But it would not leave him and he kept his neck arched, head held out rigidly, beak wide open, until saliva slowly started to drip from its tip.

But still the feeling would not leave. It grew and grew until he began to feel nauseated and then, quite suddenly, he started to bash his head against the wall of his cage. Stars exploded in his eyes, but he kept on doing it, harder and harder, until his beak cracked and he slumped back, panting. The feeling slowly faded away, and he sighed a deep, exhausted sigh and slipped into a fitful sleep.

A rough hand shook Arren awake.
"What?"

"C'mon, get up," said a voice. "Time to go."

Arren sat up. He was stiff and sore, shivering in the cold wind. He didn't even remember having fallen asleep, but he found himself lying in the middle of the cage floor with a pair of guards standing by and watching him impatiently.

He got up, supporting the collar with his hand. "What— what's going on?"

"It's nearly noon," said a guard. "They're expecting you."

"Who are?"

"The people at the Arena, idiot. Want something to eat before you go?"

Arren's insides started churning. "No—can I have some water?"

The guard picked up a jar of water that was sitting by the door and gave it to him, saying, "Hurry up."

Arren drank deeply, not caring when the water spilt out over his face and soaked into his beard. It made the wound on his face sting a little, but he didn't bother to dry it off. He gave the jar back to the guard, who tossed it aside and produced a pair of manacles. "Hold out your arms."

Arren obeyed, and his wrists were chained together once more. "I'm not going to try and run away," he said.

The guard ignored him. He and his colleague took him by the shoulders and shoved him out of the cage and onto the platform, and he walked stiffly between them toward the guard post. Bran was not there any more—his shift must have ended—and Arren was taken through the stone entrance and into a small cave. It was fairly dry inside and well lit by torches. Arren had expected there to be a staircase in there, but there wasn't. Instead there was a wooden platform, like a miniature version of the lifters all over the city. The guards walked him onto it and then one of them pulled a hanging length of rope. A bell rang from somewhere in the darkness above them, and a few moments later the platform jerked once and began to rise.

Arren, seeking desperately for something else to occupy his mind, decided that this system must have been devised to make it harder for prisoners to escape. The cages were utterly exposed, with no secret crannies where things could be concealed and no way of hiding from the guards. And even if a prisoner managed to get out, he would be trapped on the platform with no way up or down except for this small lifter, which, when Arren and his escort reached it, turned out to be very well guarded at the top. There was a room carved into the rock, manned by several attentive guards and sealed off by not one but two metal gratings, both of which were locked from the outside.

A guard was waiting for them, and once he had examined them briefly he unlocked the grate and let Arren and his two comrades come through into the chamber. The grate was locked behind them, and one of Arren's guards showed a piece of paper to those in the chamber. One of them glanced at it and then nodded and let them go toward the second grate, which led out of the chamber. The pair of guards on the other side also checked the paper, and then let them through.

After that there were stairs, which took them up to the level of the city. From there they passed through the main building of the prison district. There were more checkpoints and locked gates to pass through, and the document—no doubt some kind of official form stating the reasons for Arren's removal—was displayed several more times before they finally reached a large pair of wooden gates studded with nails, and passed through them into the Arena. There, Arren was placed in a small cell under the stands, one that was rank with terrified sweat.

There was a bench there, at least, and he sat down and tried to breathe deeply as the guards departed, leaving him alone. Food was brought to him a short time later, but he didn't eat it. From somewhere far above him, he could hear the noise of the crowd.

He was not left alone for very long. After a while he saw movement on the other side of one of the two cell doors, and Sefer arrived, followed by Orome. He was clad in red and looked a little sombre, but excited as well.

"Good morning, Arren. How are you?"

Arren only stared at him.

Orome sighed. "I'm sorry about this, Arren, but it was your choice. Now, you requested—actually, *demanded*, from what I'm told—to fight Darkheart in the Arena today, on your own. Well, I've come to tell you that we've decided to go ahead with it. All the arrangements have been made. It'll be just you and him in the pit."

"Good," said Arren.

Orome nodded. "Okay, I'm fairly sure that's all I had to say. We're ready to take you out of here. Is there anything you want to know before we go ahead?"

Arren thought it over. "What happens if I kill it?"

If Orome thought the question was ridiculous, he didn't show it. "Well, the standard procedure then is to let you go free. It's a little silly, now I think about it—we certainly won't be setting the griffin free if he kills you, but there you go, I suppose. Is there anything else?"

"What weapons will I have?" said Arren.

"A spear," said Orome. "It's the best thing for fighting a griffin; you can keep well away from the thing's talons while you're stabbing at it." He looked past him, at the door on the opposite side of the cell. "They're here. Good luck, Arren."

A pair of Orome's assistants had arrived, both armed and armoured. Arren stood up and walked across the cell to the door, without looking back at Orome, and waited while they unlocked and opened it.

They looked wary, as if they were expecting Arren to attack them, but he stood passively and let them lead him out of the cell and along a short corridor. It led to a small anteroom, unfurnished and gloomy, with a dirt floor. A narrow iron gate was set into the opposite wall, and sunlight shone in through it, casting shadows of the bars onto the floor.

One of the guards took off Arren's manacles and handed him a long wooden spear. Arren took it and clutched it tightly, while the other guard went to the gate and opened it.

He didn't wait for them to push him through it; he took the spear in both hands and stepped forward, without glancing at them, and they stood by and let him through, into the open air of the pit.

The instant he emerged, the roar of the crowd hit his ears. He looked up and saw hundreds of people sitting high above him on the rows of seats. There were even a few griffiners there. They were so close to him, separated only by the high wooden walls of the pit and the net of steel cables stretched between them. He could see their faces hanging above him.

A man was shouting over the noise of the crowd, from

the podium where Orome had taken up position with Sefer by his side: "Arren Cardockson, the Mad Blackrobe, condemned for abducting a griffin chick, famed for his insane bloodlust! Darkheart the black griffin, killer of man and griffin alike! They fought once before, and today they fight again, to the death!"

Arren barely heard him. He looked around quickly, taking in his surroundings. There was no sign of the black griffin yet, or anyone or anything else. The pit walls were bare wood, marred by deep scratch marks and dark stains. Underfoot there was sand, brought up from the shores of Eagle's Lake. And there was nothing else. Nowhere to run. Nowhere to hide. Overhead, the crowd was shouting. Some were chanting. Chanting a name. "Darkheart! Darkheart! Darkheart!"

Arren looked at the spear. The shaft was about as long as he was tall, and made of cheap, splintered wood. The head was worn and a little rusty but sharp enough, broad and well barbed. He could kill a griffin with it, in theory at least.

"Darkheart! Darkheart! Darkheart!"

Arren looked up at them, and a feeling of fierce rage overcame him. He lifted his head and screamed. *"Arren! Arren! Arren!"*

"Arren!"

"Arren!"

The shouts were faint, but they hit him almost as if they were physical blows. He scanned the crowd, trying to see where they had come from. The voices continued to shout his name, and then he saw them. They were in the front row, standing up, calling to him.

"No," Arren whispered. "No, please, don't do this."

But he knew they could not hear him, and that they would not obey even if they could. Annir and Cardock had come to watch their son fight for his life, and their voices chanted his name, a solitary counterpoint to Darkheart's name.

Arren moved toward them, wanting to call to them, but

then a loud metallic thump made him turn sharply, raising the spear.

A gate had opened in the wall on the opposite side of the pit, and even as he turned, the huge shape of the black griffin charged through it, beak open wide to screech. *"Darkheart!"*

Arren gripped his spear. "Come to me," he snarled softly. "I'm ready."

The beast had seen him. Darkheart started to run toward him, but then horror and disbelief thudded into Arren's stomach as the black griffin spread his wings wide and leapt into the air.

20

Pact

They had unchained the griffin's wings.

The realisation shot through Arren's brain as he watched Darkheart fly up and over the pit, flying clumsily but with growing confidence. There were no chains on his forelegs, either. The only thing left was the collar, embedded among the feathers on his neck and gleaming in the sun, and Darkheart was plainly well aware of that. He flew as high as the net would allow him, screeching his name, while above him the crowd reacted with amazement and wild excitement.

Rage and hatred followed quickly on the heels of Arren's fear. He ran toward the centre of the Arena, pointing his spear upward, preparing himself for when the griffin swooped. But Darkheart showed no interest in him at all. In fact, he seemed completely oblivious to his presence. He flew around the pit, silent now, head turned upward to stare at the crowd. As Arren watched, he turned on his back and latched his talons onto the net, biting at it. The steel cables would not break, but he wedged his beak into one of the gaps and tried to squeeze through it, even though it was hopelessly small. When that didn't work he thrust a foreleg through and groped at the empty air above the net, as if hoping to find something he could grab. A few moments later, he let go and dropped. His wings unfurled and he resumed his circling, looking for a place where the net was weak or irregular. Arren watched him as he grabbed another part of it and tried to break through, letting out a deafening screech when it held firm. Next he tried the edges, where the net joined the wall of the pit, digging his talons into the wood. But there were guards stationed all around the edges of the pit, and they thrust downward with long spears, forcing the black griffin to retreat. He persisted for some time, snarling, and then suddenly let go and resumed his circling.

Arren's rage only increased as he watched him. That great dark shape, with its mottled black-and-silver wings and its black legs hanging beneath it, dragged his mind back to that day at Rivermeet, when he had stood in the field with Eluna and seen what he did not yet know was the agent of his own destruction, soaring high above.

And now, as then, he steeled himself and called out a challenge. *"Darkheart!"* he screamed in griffish, raising his spear over his head. *"I have come for you!"*

Darkheart looked down at him, and Arren continued to shout, hurling threats and curses at the black griffin with all his might.

Darkheart suddenly appeared to forget his bid for escape. He circled lower, and Arren could hear him hissing as he closed in, his circles becoming smaller as he targeted him, as he had once targeted his prey. Arren rammed the spear-butt into the ground beside him, pointing the blade straight at the griffin, and braced himself, his breathing a low rasp. All he had to do was wait. When Darkheart swooped down on him, he would wait until the last moment and then duck, leaving the creature to impale himself on the spear.

Darkheart flew still lower. Then, without warning, he folded his wings and dropped.

Arren heard his mother scream from above. For a

heartbeat he stood utterly still, looking up at the raging monster falling toward him, and then he prepared to throw himself flat on the ground, holding on to the spear as tightly as he could.

Darkheart's talons lashed out, wrenching the spear from Arren's grip and hurling it aside. He landed with an almighty *thud*, right on top of him.

Arren felt pain rip into his leg as he was knocked backward, landing hard on the sand. One of Darkheart's talons had caught him a glancing blow and sent him flying, but Arren did not stay down for long. His body took over and seized control of his brain, and he rolled, vaulted upright and ran without a moment's pause. As he ran, he heard the thump of paws and talons hitting the sand and knew that Darkheart was chasing after him.

The spear was there, ahead of him, stuck in the sand. He grabbed it as he ran past, wheeled around and then turned, pointing it at the oncoming griffin.

A griffin would not run onto a sharp point willingly. He had seen it dozens of times. They would charge, but then wheel away at the last moment. As long as he had the spear, he could defend himself.

Darkheart ran straight at him, without even slowing down. When Arren swung the spear toward him, his beak shot out, catching it just behind the point. The griffin snatched it out of his grasp, so hard and so suddenly that it bowled him over. As Arren struggled to his feet he saw the griffin advancing slowly, his eyes burning with bloodlust. He was still holding the spear in his beak, but as he advanced he bit down on it, shattering the wooden shaft into splinters.

Arren turned and ran.

Darkheart pursued him with awful speed, his wings spreading wide. As Arren tried to dodge him, he beat his wings hard and launched himself into a glide, talons outstretched. They hit Arren hard in the shoulders, and he felt them try to grab hold of him as he fell forward. But they failed to get a grip, and Darkheart shot past him and collided with the wall of the pit. He landed in a heap, hissing

furiously, and Arren got up and ran back the way he had
come, running as he had never run before in his life. Up
ahead he saw the spearhead, glinting among the sand, and
he bent and snatched it up.

That brief delay was more than enough. Before he had
even straightened up, Darkheart was on him. His beak shot
out, and Arren only just managed to dodge it. The blow,
which would have taken his head clean off if it had hit him,
slashed straight through his tunic and left a deep cut in his
shoulder.

A redness closed over Arren's senses, and the pain vanished completely as the fighting madness took him. He
threw himself straight at Darkheart, screaming, and hit him
bodily in the chest. It took the griffin completely by surprise.
He staggered back a few paces, and Arren stabbed the spearhead into him again and again, piercing his chest and shoulders. It hit the griffin's collar and bounced off with a loud
clang, and then Darkheart recovered himself and swung his
head sideways, sending his attacker flying. The spearhead
flew out of Arren's hand and was lost in the sand, and as he
tried to get up, Darkheart leapt. One huge forepaw slammed
down on Arren's chest, pinning him to the ground, the talons
entrapping both his arms. The barely healed breaks in his
ribs turned into white-hot agony, and he screamed.

In the crowd above, Annir, too, screamed. *"Arren! No!"*

Arren struggled wildly, trying to wriggle out from
under the griffin's crushing weight, but Darkheart brought
his other front paw down, trapping him. He could see the
griffin's face looming above him, the eyes cold and savage, the features angular, the beak chipped and sharp.
Darkheart's breath smelt of death and decay, and the collar
shone around his neck.

Arren's wounded face twisted. "Kill me," he snarled.
"Finish it!"

Darkheart stared at him, unmoving for a moment, and
then he brought his head down toward him. His eyes and
beak filled Arren's vision, so close he could hear the air
whistling through the creature's nostrils.

Cold, crushing terror came into him, paralysing him, and he screwed his eyes shut and turned his head away, bracing himself for the end.

"Arren Cardockson."

Arren's fear turned to bewilderment. He opened his eyes and turned his head back again. Darkheart had not moved. He was still there, above him, his talons pressing down.

"Arren Cardockson," the griffin said again.

Arren just stared.

Darkheart's eyes were wide, almost . . . frightened. "Arren Cardockson."

Arren tried again to break free, to no avail.

"Arren," the griffin repeated. "Arren. Arren."

Arren stilled. "Darkheart," he said, not knowing what to do.

"Arren."

Arren turned his head away. "Kill me," he said again.

"Arren," said Darkheart. "You . . . Arren."

Arren closed his eyes. "Yes."

Darkheart paused, and then brought his head down still lower, until they were almost touching. "Arren," he said. His voice was deep, slow and rumbling, like distant thunder. "You . . . Arren. You . . . human. You want . . . die?"

Arren could feel himself shaking uncontrollably. *Yes.* He wanted to say it. He wanted to shout it for them all to hear. *Yes. Kill me. I want to die. Kill me.*

"No," he whispered.

The talons tightened around him. "Free . . . me," the griffin's voice rumbled.

Arren looked up, uncomprehending.

"Free me," Darkheart said again. "Let me fly away. Free me, Arren Cardockson. Free me or I kill you."

"Free you?" Arren said.

"Promise," said Darkheart. "Promise free me. Promise and I not kill. Promise, Arren Cardockson."

He could see the look in the griffin's eyes. He could see it as clearly as he could see the cracks in his beak and the raw flesh around the edges of the collar. It had been there all along. "I promise," he said softly. "I will set you free, Darkheart."

Darkheart was silent for a moment. "Dark human," he whispered. "Dark human, dark griffin. Promise me, Arren Cardockson."

"I promise," Arren said again. "I swear it. I swear."

Silence reigned in the pit. Even the crowd had gone quiet.

Then Darkheart let him go. He lifted his talons and backed away, and Arren struggled upright and staggered away from him, blood streaming from beneath the collar and soaking into his torn and filthy tunic. He was gasping for breath and his chest was agonising, and he stumbled toward the wall and collapsed at its base, unable to move.

But Darkheart made no move to go after him. He watched him briefly and then turned away and began to groom his wings, apparently oblivious to the baying crowd above him.

Arren could hear them, but their voices seemed to be coming through a kind of curtain. He lay on his side, feeling as if a great weight was dragging down on his limbs, his senses dulled by pain. The wound on his face was bleeding again; he could feel the hot liquid trickling over his cheek like tears. More blood was coming from his neck. Too much blood. It was making him dizzy and confused. He made a brief attempt to get up, but then slumped back. A short time later, he blacked out.

The crowd had watched it all. They had seen the black griffin pounce on the prisoner and knock him down, and they had waited expectantly, knowing what would come next. Waited for the wet crunch and the blackrobe's brief scream as his chest was crushed to a pulp. Waited to see him die.

But they had waited in vain. The black griffin had covered the blackrobe with his wings and brought his head down toward him, and they had sat back, disappointed. He was merely going to kill him with his beak, and they wouldn't even see it happen. Not even the battle that had preceded it would make up for that.

And then they saw the black griffin move away, and

they looked toward the spot where he had been, expecting to see the blackrobe's mutilated remains. But they were not there. They saw the blackrobe get up and lurch toward the wall, and saw the black griffin glance briefly at him and then turn away. The blackrobe collapsed, either dead or wounded, and the griffin merely sat and groomed himself. They continued to wait, filling the air with savage shouts, but nothing happened. Neither man nor griffin moved.

In the end Darkheart rose onto his paws and walked away toward the gate he had entered by. He tried to open it, and when it wouldn't move he lay down on the sand and went to sleep.

He didn't wake up until the gate opened and the griffin handlers came through and threw a net over him, tangling his wings. He started up and rushed at them, but they expertly avoided his beak and talons and wrestled him into submission. The chains were put back on his wings and legs, more were attached to his collar, and he was dragged out of the pit, screeching and struggling.

Arren, though, did not get up. He lay where he was, unmoving, until a pair of guards hurried into the pit and carried him away.

F alling, he was falling.

There was blackness everywhere, and icy wind rushing past him. He could feel the void pulling him in, pulling him down, faster and faster, and somewhere below him the ground waited, hard and unforgiving. His scream was whipped away in the wind. Blood was coming from his chest, but the drops flew away, straight upward, and he fell.

And then he hit the ground.

Arren opened his eyes and groaned. He was lying on his back on a hard surface, and every inch of him hurt. But there was something warm covering him and a pad under his head, which made him feel safe.

His vision was blurry, but he managed to make out a ceiling above him. It was wooden. Was he in his home?

No. His own ceiling had been different: peaked in the middle and criss-crossed with wooden beams, and beyond those had been the underside of the thatch. And his home didn't exist any more. It had burned down. He had seen it burn. And after that he'd . . . he'd . . .

Memories came rushing back. The chick, the trial, the cage and after that the pit and the black griffin, swooping down on him, its screech ringing in his ears. *Darkheart!*

Fear gave him strength. He sat up sharply, nearly falling over when the sudden motion made his head spin. He felt weak and shaky, and the collar was heavy.

He was back in his cage. It was still daylight, and he had been lying on the floor, by the door. Someone had picked up the black robe and put it over him like a blanket. He shoved it off and rubbed his head. His eyes were aching.

"Hello, Arren."

Arren looked around sharply and saw Bran standing on the other side of the door. "Bran?"

Bran looked shaken. "Yeh all right?"

"My head hurts. Bran, what—what happened?"

Bran nodded at the floor beside him. "Brought yeh some food."

Arren managed to pick up a piece of bread. Chewing felt like the hardest struggle of his life.

Bran watched him. "I came to watch," he said. "At the Arena, I mean. Arren, what *happened*?"

Arren dropped the piece of bread. "Bran, what's going on? Are they going to set me free?"

"I dunno. Arren, I'm sorry for what I said."

Arren shook his head. "It doesn't matter. Are my parents coming to see me again?"

"Don't think so. They ain't lettin' no-one in except guards. Arren, how did yeh do that?"

"How did I do what?" The sound of Bran's voice was making his headache worse.

"Control the griffin!" Bran said urgently. "How'd yeh make it back off like that?"

"I didn't. I don't know what happened. It just didn't kill me."

"What? Yeh didn't do nothin'?"

"Yes. Bran, please, I've got to know. What's going to happen to me now? Are they going to let me out?"

"I dunno," Bran repeated. "I think they ain't decided yet. This ain't never happened before."

"They've got to let me go," said Arren. "I survived, didn't I?"

"Yeah . . . I guess yeh did."

Arren lay back. They *had* to let him go. It wasn't just an empty promise they made to tempt prisoners; it was law. A prisoner who survived the Arena had to be set free. They couldn't break the law. Not when everyone knew about it.

"Guess you'll find out," said Bran. "Eat. They'll come and see yeh soon, I reckon."

Arren nodded vaguely and went back to his food. But he felt much better now. He was going to be released, he knew it. They'd let him out of the cage and send him home. He'd go to Idun and stay with his parents until he was better, and then . . . after that, he would just have to decide what to do next.

Bran looked up at the sun. "Well, I gotta go. Shift's about to end. I'll be back here tomorrow, though. Good luck till then, eh?"

Arren swallowed. "Thanks, Bran. For—well, for being here."

Bran smiled slightly. "Yeh can thank the roster for that."

"You know that's not what I mean, Bran."

"Yeah, I know," said Bran. "G'night, Arren."

He nodded again and walked back toward his post, where two more guards had just arrived to take over from him and his colleague. Arren watched as they disappeared into the cave, and then finished off the rest of his food. There was bread and cheese, but there was an orange as well. For some reason the sight of it put a lump in his throat.

The sun started to sink below the horizon, and he dozed in his cage, too tired to even care about the drop below him any more. Perhaps he was losing his fear of heights.

Voices from the platform woke him. He looked up and saw three people standing by the guard post, talking to the guards. Arren's heart leapt. It was Orome, with Sefer and the woman who had visited him the previous day. He got up, a little shakily, and came forward to meet them. Sefer's weight made the platform creak as the red griffin came to stand on the other side of the cage door; he sat back on his haunches to watch, as Orome joined him.

Orome was looking at Arren with open admiration. "Well, hello, Arren! I have to say I didn't expect I'd ever get the chance to speak with you again. Oh, yes, this is my wife, Emogen. I believe you've already met."

Arren nodded formally to them. "Orome, what's going on? Are they going to let me go?"

"Arren, I really can't tell you how amazed I was by what happened in the pit today," said Orome. "Everyone was. I mean, I've seen what has to have been more than a hundred fights, but I've never seen anything like that. Can I ask how you did it?"

"I didn't do anything," said Arren. "It was the griffin who did it."

"Yes, but you must have done something to make him spare you," said Orome. "What was it? Did you talk to him?"

"Wild griffins don't talk, remember?" said Arren. "Orome, they've got to let me out of here. I survived, didn't I?"

Orome ignored the question. "So, you really didn't do anything?"

"Yes. Can I please go home now?"

Orome shook his head. "Astonishing. There's been a lot of argument about it, actually. Some people are claiming that you used some sort of Northern magic to tame the griffin. You didn't, did you?"

Arren put a hand to his forehead. "Northerners don't *have* magic," he almost snarled. "I don't have any powers, all right? I'm just an ordinary person, and I'm not interested in entertaining anyone; I just want to get out of here."

"You can't be that ordinary," said Orome. "Not if you managed to make Darkheart act like that. He's the most savage griffin I've ever seen, and unpredictable as well. Actually, the only thing you can always expect him to do is kill as many people as he can the moment he's let out. But he's not himself any more. He won't eat or drink anything; he just lies in his cage and does nothing. I—well, forgive me for saying this, but when we sent you into the pit today I wasn't expecting to have a body to retrieve afterwards. He hadn't eaten in days; he must have been ravenous. Which is another reason why I can't believe what happened. I think the crowd was a bit disappointed, though. We've never had a fight that had such a—well, such an indecisive ending. But look on the bright side: you're nearly as popular as Darkheart now. They're calling you the Mad Blackrobe. They all saw how you attacked the griffin like that, with nothing but a spearhead. It was very impressive. And I hope we can see you do it again soon."

Arren gave him a deadly look. "Sorry to disappoint you, but I'm not interested."

"Unfortunately that's not up to you," Emogen interrupted. "You agreed to this."

"I agreed to fight the black griffin and *you* said that if I won I could go free," Arren snapped.

"Yes, so you'll just have to hope that next time you do win," said Emogen.

"But I—"

"The fight was inconclusive," Emogen said in formal, almost faraway tones. "Neither one of you truly won—though since you collapsed and Darkheart didn't, that would in theory make him the winner. A truce—I suppose you can call it that—a truce is not a victory. Your agreement will not be fulfilled until one of you is dead."

"Cheer up," Orome advised. "No matter what happens after this, you're going to go down in history for what happened today. Even griffins are talking about it."

"I don't want to go down in history!" Arren shouted. "I want to go home, godsdamnit!"

Orome gave him a dispassionate look. "Well, that's not my problem. Even if you did somehow manage to make Darkheart lose his senses, you're still a criminal, and as far as I'm concerned, you don't have any worth to anyone except as entertainment. So I'd advise you to be a bit less uppity, Arren Cardockson."

"But it's not fair!"

"Perhaps you should have thought of that before you stole that chick," said Orome. "See you tomorrow."

With that he turned and left, and Emogen went with him. Sefer lingered a moment to peer curiously at him, and then jumped almost lazily off the edge of the platform, making the entire thing shake. Arren, turning instinctively to watch, saw the red griffin's wings open and watched him soar away over the landscape. Vertigo instantly made the ground lurch beneath him, and he fell over sideways, grabbing at the bars to save himself from falling. He hit the bars of the cage awkwardly and, for what felt like the hundredth time, the collar tore into his neck. He let out a maddened snarl of both pain and rage, one which turned into a string of swearwords. It didn't make him feel even slightly better. He lurched upright and staggered toward the door and began to wrench at the bars, trying with all his might to make them break. They shook and creaked against their bindings, and splinters stabbed into his palms, but they would not give. Each one was as thick as his forearm and held in place with metal rivets. The door itself was sealed with a chain, and none of it had an inch of give in it anywhere. Maddened by fear, he tried to squeeze through one of the gaps between the bars. It was far too narrow for his head to fit through, but he persisted anyway, until one of the guards wandered over and shoved him away. He fell onto his back and lay still, breathing heavily, then suddenly grabbed hold of the collar and tried yet again to pull it off. Still it would not come off. Still it weighed him down. Still it hurt. He realised then that it never would come off. He was going to wear it for the rest of his life.

21

Freedom

Night drew in over the city. In his cage behind the Arena, Darkheart dozed. And in his own cage not very far away, Arren slept restlessly; his hands curled into fists, and his legs twitched as if he was trying to run somewhere. His face, too, moved, the forehead creasing as he mumbled in his sleep.

". . . help me, I'm falling, help me . . . falling . . . help me . . ."

Then he was walking along the street toward his home, with Eluna beside him, and Gern there, too, chattering about the latest fight at the Arena. Arren pretended to listen, to humour him. Gern was always hurt if someone complained or looked bored.

Look at that, Gern kept saying. *Look, sir.*

They had reached the door of his home, and the key was in his hand. He put it into the lock and turned it, but the instant the door swung open, flames billowed out and he realised the house was on fire. He backed away, but Eluna pushed past him and ran ahead, straight into the heart of the flames. *Eluna! Come back!*

He ran forward, trying to get to her, but he could not. The door would not come any closer. It was just ahead of him, so close but always out of reach.

Gern was still there. *Sir, look,* he said again.

Arren turned to him. *Gern, help me.*

Sir, said Gern. *Look. You're falling.*

And then he was falling. The ground beneath him vanished and there was nothing but darkness, pulling him down. High above, the black griffin circled, his screech echoing in the night. It grew louder and louder, cutting through Arren's brain, until the world shook with it. The ground beneath him lurched, and he suddenly realised he wasn't falling any more, he was lying on his back and the ground was shaking.

He lay still, heart pounding. The ground lurched again, and he heard something to his left. He sat up, and the sudden burst of pain from the collar convinced him that he wasn't asleep. It was still night-time, and the moon was high in the sky. He was still in his cage, which was swinging alarmingly, the wooden rods that held it to the platform rattling. When he looked up, he saw something huge hanging over the side of the cage. It was moving. He could see the outline of a tail, lashing at the bars, and for a moment, horrible fear caught in his throat. It was a griffin, a dark griffin, it was coming to get him, it was—

"Arren Cardockson?"

Arren looked up sharply. The words had been spoken in griffish, but it was not a griffin's voice. As his eyes adjusted to the gloom, he realised that the door to his cage was open. Someone was standing in the entrance, outlined by the torchlight from the guard post.

Arren stood up. "Who's that?"

The figure stepped forward into the cage. "Are you Arren Cardockson? Speak griffish."

"I'm Arren. Who are you?"

The stranger took hold of his arm. "You must come with me," he said. "And quickly."

"What for? Who are you?"

"Not now!" The stranger dragged him out of the cage, and Arren hurried after him. There was a thud as something hit the platform in front of them; the griffin had leapt off the roof of the cage and landed between them and the guard post. Arren froze. The griffin came toward them, and the stranger went and got on her back. "Get up behind me," he urged. "Hurry!"

Arren pulled himself together and climbed onto the griffin's back. There was only just room for the two of them, but luckily the stranger was slightly built. Arren held on to his waist, and the griffin ran off the edge of the platform and into the air. Almost instantly, she started to fall. Her wings beat furiously, fighting back against gravity; as Arren held on, panic-stricken, she soared clumsily out over the dark landscape and then spiralled upward, away from the prison. When Arren dared to look down he saw Eagleholm laid out below him, a dark, sprawling mass dotted with lights. The griffin flew straight for the centre, already flagging under the unaccustomed weight of two people, and the city got closer and closer as she started to lose height. But she made one last mighty effort and shot forward, the wind rushing past them, her talons grabbing at the air. Ahead, the Eyrie reared up out of the darkness, a great window-studded mountain in the night, coming straight toward them. Arren stifled a scream, and then they hit it. The griffin's talons latched onto the edge of one of the balconies, and she scrabbled up over the side and promptly collapsed onto her side, flinging the two humans off.

Arren picked himself up, wincing. The stranger was already up and attending to his partner. She rolled onto her front and lay still, shuddering with exhaustion. "Go," she rasped. "Hurry."

The stranger opened the door leading from the balcony, and light poured out as he disappeared inside, gesturing at Arren to follow. He entered a large and comfortable-looking bedroom with a carpeted floor and a good fire burning, along with several expensive wax candles. There was a table with a jug of wine and a pair of cups laid out on it, along with a bowl of fruit.

The stranger gestured at a chair. "Sit down. There's time for you to eat something before you go."

Arren sat, staring at him. "Lord Vander?"

Vander was clad in a black tunic and leggings which didn't suit him very well, and he looked a little strained. But he poured out some wine and pushed it toward Arren. "Drink. You look as if you need it."

Arren accepted it without argument; it was sweet and strong, flavoured with exotic spices. "Lord Vander, what's going on?"

"I am setting you free," said Vander. "Ymazu has agreed to carry you away from the city as far as she can."

"But why?" said Arren. "You'll get into trouble. They'll probably lock you up, too, if they catch you."

Vander shrugged. "I am leaving the city tonight as well. My diplomatic mission is finished."

"But if they know you did it—"

"I do not think the Emperor can forge any kind of lasting alliance with this city," said Vander, sitting down and helping himself to some wine. "I have seen enough of your ways by now. The Lady Riona is a fine leader and good-hearted, but she is reaching the end of her reign and her council is plainly corrupt. I witnessed your trial yesterday."

"But why do you care?" said Arren.

Vander smiled very slightly. "I took a liking to you when we first met. I admired your intelligence and your refusal to be ashamed of your blood and background. And your courage in the Arena impressed us both."

"Yes, but why do you care?" Arren persisted. "Why risk your life to save mine?"

"Because I am sympathetic to you," said Vander. "And to the rest of your people. The darkmen are a dying race. Their land is subjugated and occupied, and most of their population live in chains. Despair can destroy a people as no massacre or disease ever can. And though you are not a slave, you have all but been turned into one. You know what it is to be humiliated, to wear a collar and be beaten and locked in a cage like a beast, waiting to be put down as soon as your usefulness comes to an end. It was not enough that your griffin was taken from you and that you were disgraced and cast out from your fellows—now they must use you for their sport."

"You *know* about that?" said Arren.

Vander nodded. "I have heard things, here and there. Lord Rannagon was very anxious to assure me that the city would not have a Northerner advising its Mistress. He told me that it would not be accepted, by him or by the other councillors. And I heard your accusation yesterday and was inclined to believe it. I had already suspected that those in power were plotting to be rid of you, and it seemed far too convenient that you had simply lost your mind. And they would not listen to you. It made me very angry to see. In Amoran, every man accused of a crime may speak out and defend himself, and his claims will always be taken seriously and investigated. The only time a criminal is ignored and punished without fair hearing is when that criminal is a slave. I watched many trials when I was a boy; my master was a judge, and I learnt a great deal about law while I fetched papers and cleaned the floor."

Arren paused. "You mean, you weren't born a noble?"

"No, Arren. I was not," said Vander. He touched his neck. "The marks have faded now, but I have not forgotten that time."

"You were a *slave*?"

"Yes," said Vander. "I was born one. When Ymazu chose me, I was set free."

There was a thump from the doorway and both of them turned sharply, but it was only Ymazu. The brown griffin entered, limping slightly, and sat down by Vander's side.

"Your griffins are fools," she said to Arren, "to only choose nobles. No blood makes one man worthier than another. I chose Vander for his courage and his intelligence, because I knew that he could become great with my help, and so he has done. I liked Eluna. She was also wise in her choice."

"Thank you," Arren said softly. "To both of you."

Vander stood up. "I am sorry for what happened to you. I hope we can meet again, Arren Cardockson, but now it is time for you to go."

"But where should I go to?" said Arren, standing up. "Where can I hide?"

"One of the neighbouring states, perhaps, could hide you," said Vander. "But I advise you to go to the North. Some of your own people still live there free; they will, perhaps, accept you. It is your only hope."

Ymazu stood. "Come," she said, and walked out onto the balcony. Arren bowed low to Vander and followed her. On the balcony, Vander helped him onto Ymazu's back. "Good luck," he said. "And to you, Ymazu."

Ymazu rubbed her head against Vander's dark cheek. "I shall see you again soon, Vander."

Arren held on to the harness fastened around the griffin's neck, and Ymazu took off, flying up and away from the Eyrie with easy grace. She could bear up under his weight without any trouble, and began to circle the city, climbing for height. "Where shall I take you, Northerner?" she asked. "Make your choice quickly."

Arren's mind raced. He would have to find somewhere to hide, of course, but the idea of going to the North almost revolted him. It was far away; even if Ymazu was willing to carry him there, it would take at least a month. On foot, it would probably take six. Assuming he wasn't caught along the way. And, in spite of everything that had happened, in his heart he still felt tied to Eagleholm, where he had spent his entire adult life; it was the only place where he had ever been truly happy and where Eluna's spirit still lived.

But, as the night air cut through his ragged tunic and made him shiver, he saw that there was no way he could stay. There was nothing left here for him, only suffering and death.

His resolve hardened. "I want to go northward. Toward Norton. But first . . ."

"Speak," said Ymazu.

"Do you know where the Arena is?"

"Beside the prison district," said Ymazu.

"Yes. I want to go there before we leave. I still have something to do here."

Ymazu was silent for a long time. "Very well. For Vander's sake. But I will not fight to protect you. If we are discovered, I shall leave you."

"I understand."

The brown griffin angled her tail and flew downward, toward the dark mass of the Arena. There were only a few sources of light down there, and the enclosure behind the pit was completely dark. Ymazu landed neatly on top of the wall, and Arren got down off her back and perched beside her, looking down at the cages. There was a steel net stretched over the top of the enclosure, fastened to the wall where he stood, but the gaps in it were big enough for him to get through.

Arren breathed in deeply. All he had to do was jump down through the net, find the black griffin's cage and let it out. There were no guards down there. Anyone who broke into the enclosure would have to be insane; there was nothing in there to steal, and if they let one of the griffins out they would be killed before they had the chance to remove the thing's chains.

The only question in Arren's mind was how he would get out afterward. If he took the conventional route he would run into guards and locked doors, but the walls of the enclosure were too sheer to be climbed or consisted of bars with man-eating griffins behind them. Anyone trying to use them as a ladder would lose a leg.

Very carefully, Arren began to move along the top of the wall, looking for a loose length of cable or something else that could be used to pull himself back up. He didn't think he could climb a rope, but perhaps he could ask Ymazu to pull one up while he held the other end. If he could only find one.

Ymazu was watching him. "What are you doing?" she asked softly.

"I'm trying to find something I can use to climb out of there," said Arren. "Can you see anything, Ymazu?"

She shifted, talons digging into the wall. "Not from here. Why do you want to go down there at all?"

"Because I made a promise," said Arren. He continued on, putting one foot in front of another and trying to avoid looking at the drop. In his head, words whispered and spiralled. *Wear a collar, live in a cage, wear a collar, live in a cage* . . .

He rubbed his neck, just under the collar. It was horribly swollen. The fight in the Arena had reopened the wounds; he could feel the spikes embedded in his flesh, jabbing at his windpipe as he breathed. Without thinking, he dug his fingers under the collar and tugged at it, trying to pull the spikes out a little way. That made the back of his neck hurt badly, and he swore and yanked his hand away instinctively. But his fingers were trapped under the collar, and the motion pulled his head sideways. Caught off balance, he tried to straighten up, but once again the weight of the collar made him clumsy. He scrabbled desperately to stay on the wall, and then he fell.

He hit the net and fell through one of the gaps in it; a cable hooked him under the arm and he almost managed to save himself by grabbing it, but the cold metal slipped out of his grasp and he dropped into the enclosure, landing with a dull *thump* on the sawdust-covered floor.

Bruised and shocked, he lay with one arm twisted painfully beneath him and caught his breath. Then he got up, quickly looking around for any sign of guards. There was no-one in the enclosure. The griffins lay in their cages, most of them asleep, silent but for the occasional clink of a chain. He was safe. For now.

Arren glanced up at Ymazu and then padded swiftly toward the gate leading out. It was shut, but he judged that he could squeeze through the bars without much trouble. Of course, there would be other gates to get through beyond it . . . No. No escape that way. He looked up at the net. It was more than twice his height, and there was nothing dangling from it that he could grab. Full of fear, he began to make his way around the edges of the enclosure, keeping well back from the cages, looking for footholds he could use to climb back up. But there were none. Though there were some unoccupied cages, their bars were vertical and there weren't enough horizontal supports between them for him to climb. Between the cages there was nothing but smooth, featureless stone.

Arren started to panic. He went to the centre of the enclosure, where the lifting platform was set into the wooden floor, half-buried by sawdust. It was tightly locked into place, and someone had taken the handle off the winch, rendering it useless. He examined the frame holding the ropes attached to the platform. Maybe he could climb that? It didn't look too difficult.

He stepped onto the winch and hefted himself up the side of the frame, grabbing hold of a strut to balance himself. It was hard going but he managed it, and after a brief struggle he got to the top and stood below the net. Perfect. From here he could jump and grab the net, and climb up through it. Then Ymazu could pick him up and get him out of there.

The brown griffin was watching him, and he whispered this plan to her. She listened and then clicked her beak to show her agreement.

Arren breathed in deeply and felt his fear recede. All right. He had an escape route.

He jumped down from the frame, ignoring the brief burst of pain from his legs, and walked toward the nearest of the cages. Which one had they put the black griffin into? It had been near the gate, he was fairly sure of that. Accordingly, he went to the cage set into the wall on the right side of the gate and peered in. It was empty. So was the next.

The third was occupied. Arren stood well back, squinting. All he could really see was the outline of the griffin inside, though a shaft of moonlight had fallen over its beak.

For a long time he didn't move, but then he decided to risk it. "Darkheart?" he whispered.

Silence.

"Darkheart!"

Arren dared to move closer and thump the bars with the back of his hand. "Darkheart!" he hissed again.

There was silence, and then suddenly the griffin's shadow was moving and shifting, and he saw it stand up, its chains clanking loudly in the silence. He moved back quickly, but the griffin thrust its head forward, straining to reach the bars and hissing.

"Darkheart," Arren said again, feeling like a fool. "Darkheart, is that you?"

The shadowy griffin did not move for some time, but then it clicked its beak and moved forward as far as its chains would allow. "Darkheart," it repeated softly.

He recognised the voice. "It's me," he said. "It's Arren Cardockson. I've come to set you free."

A chain clinked. "Arren?"

Arren dared to move closer. "Yes, it's me. Please, Darkheart, you have to be quiet. I'm going to open the door, and then I'll come in and take the chains off. But you have to hold still."

It was doubtful that Darkheart understood all of this, but he paused a moment and then sat back on his haunches. Waiting.

Arren took a deep breath and reached out to touch the door. There was no lock on it, only a pair of huge bolts, each as thick as his arm. He slid one out and then the other, and then slowly and carefully pulled the door open. It swung forward with a faint creak, leaving nothing between him and the black griffin.

Darkheart got up almost instantly and jerked forward, trying to get through the door, only to be pulled back by his chains. He slumped, hissing and rasping in fury.

"Calm down," Arren whispered. "Please, just let me take off the chains."

Darkheart stilled. "Free me," he said.

"I will," said Arren. "I am."

Slowly, very slowly, he stepped into the cage. There wasn't much room in there, and as he ducked under the chain attached to one side of Darkheart's collar he could feel the griffin's feathers brushing against his face. Darkheart jerked his beak toward him briefly, but did not attack him, and Arren, wedged between his flank and the wall, felt his way to the base of the griffin's wings and the manacles pinning them together. The manacles, like the ones he had worn, were held shut by pins. He took them out and opened one manacle, then crawled under Darkheart's belly to the other side, where he removed the other. The chains slid off onto the floor with a muffled thud, and Darkheart's wings opened, beating against the walls of the cage that restrained them. The griffin was becoming more and more restless, impatient to be free.

Arren lay flat on the cage floor and reached for the manacles holding Darkheart's forelegs together. He removed those after some fumbling. "There," he whispered. "You're nearly free, Darkheart."

Darkheart did not need to be told. He raised one foreleg, flexing the talons, then slammed both sets of front talons down on the sand in front of him and let out a deafening screech.

The noise shattered the uneasy silence into a million pieces, waking the other griffins, which started to screech back irritably. Panicking, Arren scrabbled away from Darkheart's flailing talons and flattened himself against the wall behind him, as far away from his hind legs as he could get. "Shut up!" he shouted over the racket: "Darkheart, no! They'll hear you!"

Darkheart paid no attention. He probably hadn't even heard him. He continued to screech, calling his name again and again, and lunged forward against the collar, so hard the walls of the cage shuddered. Arren ran forward and grabbed the griffin's wing, tugging at it. "Stop it! Stop it!"

The wing flicked backward, bowling him over, and his head hit the wall hard as Darkheart continued to struggle and scream. *"Want fly! Want fly! Darkheart!"*

Arren gave up and started trying to squeeze past him, wanting to make his escape before it was too late. But then he heard a sound that made his heart freeze.

Human voices.

There was the unmistakeable sound of the gate to the enclosure opening, and he heard loud footsteps; someone had entered the enclosure. Torchlight lit up the space, and he could hear a man shouting over the screeching griffins. "Shut up! Shut up, godsdamnit!"

It was Orome's voice. When the griffins ignored him, Sefer's screech echoed off the walls, loud and commanding. He did it several more times, and they eventually calmed down.

"All right," said Orome's voice. "That's enough from you lot."

Arren saw the torchlight move and shrank back against the wall of Darkheart's cage. If Orome or Sefer saw that the door was open . . .

And then he heard Orome's voice again, loud and shocked. "What in the gods' names?"

Arren could see him, just barely, standing outside the open cage and staring in astonishment. Sefer was there, too, tail lashing.

"Darkheart, who did this?" said Orome.

Darkheart started to lunge again, trying to get at him. *"Kill!"* he screamed. *"Kill!"*

The shadows of the cage door that were cast onto the floor by Orome's torch suddenly moved. Arren heard the creak of the door, and realised with horror that Orome was closing it. And if that happened he would be trapped inside with Darkheart. He wouldn't be able to remove the bolts again from the inside.

Without even thinking, he threw himself forward. He dived under Darkheart's thrashing wing and seized hold of the collar around the griffin's neck. Darkheart's struggles almost threw him bodily aside, but he dug his fingers in under the collar and reached desperately for the pin that held it shut.

Orome had stopped dead, holding the cage door. "Arren!" he exclaimed.

Too late. Arren's fingers found the pin, and he pulled it out. The collar opened and Darkheart was free. He struggled past the chain still stretched in front of him, and then he charged out of the cage, straight at Orome.

The black griffin's beak hit his gaoler directly in the throat, tearing through skin and muscle like the blade of a huge sword. Blood gushed out and Orome fell.

Darkheart didn't even pause to finish him off. Sefer had rushed to attack him, and he turned and smashed his talons into the red griffin's chest. Sefer reeled away and then leapt back without warning, driving his talons into Darkheart's shoulders.

The two griffins grappled with each other, screeching, and Arren hurried out of the cage and crouched by Orome's side. "Orome? Orome!"

Orome did not respond. He was already dead, his throat torn so deeply that his head had nearly been severed from his body. Arren reached down and gently closed his eyes. "I'm sorry."

He straightened up. Darkheart and Sefer were still fighting, both so intent on each other that they were completely unaware of his presence. He skirted around them and ran for the lifting frame. But even as he stepped onto the winch he heard the shouts, and looked up sharply to see a group of men run through the gate and into the enclosure. Panic shot through him. He started to climb the frame as fast as he could, but the support broke and he fell hard onto the platform, which lurched alarmingly.

The men had seen Arren, and the black griffin. They rushed in, raising the long spears they held. But Darkheart had also seen them. He glanced at them for a heartbeat and then threw himself forward, ducking in under Sefer's beak and hitting Sefer with his full weight. There was a sickening snap as the red griffin's neck broke, and Darkheart wheeled around and attacked the humans now trying to surround him.

Arren watched in horror as they were cut down, their spears utterly useless against the wild griffin's rage. There was no time to try to climb the frame again. He ran around them as fast as he could, and darted out through the gate and into the dark tunnel leading to the pit. One man attempted to go after him, but Darkheart struck him from behind, and Arren heard his scream as he ran.

The door to Orome's office was open, and he ran in and grabbed the sword from the wall. That made him feel a little safer; he stuffed it into his belt and began to search the drawers. He found a ring of keys in one and snatched it, with a little surge of triumph. Then he ran out of the office as fast as he could go.

There were a few torches burning in the tunnel, and he used their light to find his way to the small gate he had seen the day when Darkheart had come to the Arena. He tried several keys before he found one that would unlock it, wrenched open the gate and ran into the passageway on the other side. There were no torches there, but he didn't slow down. He ran on blindly, heart fluttering, and didn't know he'd reached the end until he collided with the door. There he tried the keys, one by one, choosing them by feel until one finally worked. The door opened, and fresh air blew onto his face. He threw the keys back into the corridor, slammed the door on them and ran away into the city.

22

Falling

Arren ran. He left the Arena behind and headed for the market district, where there should be plenty of places to hide. The image of Orome's dead body kept flashing before his eyes, its neck one huge bloodied wound, and horror came with it. *What have I done? What have I done?*

The streets were almost completely deserted at this time of night, but there were still torches burning here and there. Arren stayed out of the pools of light and found a narrow alleyway to rest in. There he sat down with his back to the wall and breathed deeply, trying to compose himself. He had to get out of the city as fast as possible, but how? Ymazu wouldn't be able to find him now, not in the dark, and if he called out to her he would be heard by every other griffin in the city. No. He was on his own now. Ymazu had told him she wouldn't fight for him. Most likely she had already gone back to find Vander. If he could get to one of the lifters and conceal himself on it, then perhaps he would have a chance.

He stood up. No sense in staying here. The longer he stayed in one place, the greater the chance of being discovered.

The nearest lifter wasn't far from the spot where his home had been. He left the alley and loped along the street beyond it. This wasn't too dangerous; the streets were empty.

A screech came from overhead. Arren looked up sharply and saw several griffins flying over the market district. He didn't stop to think; he broke and ran, sprinting down the street and to a crossroads. There he turned right and ran on, his mind racing. He had to keep out of the light, find somewhere to lie low until they had moved on.

He turned and ran down a small side street. Nowhere to hide here. Just blank walls. He burst out of the other end and into another street.

Straight into the path of a squad of armed men.

For an instant both he and they stood dead still, staring in surprise, and then Arren turned and ran away from them. The guards came in pursuit, at least six of them, all armed and shouting to raise the alarm. As he ran, realisation flashed across Arren's mind. *They were hunting for me*. His escape had been noticed; by now every guard in the city must be searching for him.

After that there was no more thought; there was just night, and shadows, and terror. Arren ran as he had never run before in his life, every sense strained to its uttermost, always with the thud of boots and clank of armour following just behind him. The guards were weighed down by their weapons and breastplates—but the collar and the sword in his belt were doing the same to him, and he was still weak from the fight against Darkheart and the strains and shocks of that night. But he didn't feel any pain. All he could feel was his feet hitting the ground, and all he could see was the street ahead of him, the twists and turns and the places where he could hide. He veered off the main street and into an alley; it was narrow and though he got through it easily enough, the guards had trouble following him. It delayed them long enough to give him some ground; he chose a direction at random and followed it at full speed, searching now for somewhere he could hide.

But he wasn't quick enough. This street was well lit by the moon, and he heard the voices of the guards behind him. They were shouting at him, ordering him to surrender.

He paid no attention. There had to be somewhere to go, somewhere to hide, some way to escape, there had to be.

He turned another corner, onto another street. This one looked familiar . . . he turned right and went along it, ducking in and out of the shadows. It was a little darker here, more places to hide. The guards were still on his tail. They were carrying torches, and as they drew closer he could see the light throw his shadow ahead of him. They were gaining on him.

But Arren did not give up. He found an extra burst of strength inside him and sped up, leaving them behind. If he could put enough distance between him and his pursuers, it would give him a chance to hide before they saw where he had gone.

It was working. They were falling behind, tired out, and he felt a kind of wild glee. He was getting away. He'd always had long legs and been well coordinated. He was a natural runner, with none of the stockiness of a Southerner. They couldn't catch him.

And then shouts came from ahead of him. He slowed down, confused, and saw another group of guards come running toward him from the other end of the street. They were heading him off. Arren stopped. He looked back and saw the first group catching up. He was sandwiched between them, with nowhere to go.

No. There was one way to go. He looked to his left and saw a gap between two houses. It would do. He darted through it, scraping his elbows on the wooden walls. Hope rose in his chest. They would be stuck in this gap; it was barely wide enough for him to fit through, let alone them with their armour. He'd made it. He'd outwitted them.

He burst out of the gap and onto—

A stretch of bare planks, jutting out over the edge of the city and into space.

Arren skidded to a halt and looked desperately this way

and that. There was nowhere to go except back through the gap; the houses on either side were built right up to the edge of the planking, and in front of him there was nothing but a sheer drop.

But it was already too late to go back. Arren turned back the way he had come, and saw that the first of the guards had struggled through the gap and was advancing on him, sword drawn. Others joined him, and then spread out to cover the full width of the platform. They had bows in their hands and were already nocking arrows in place.

Arren reached to his belt and drew Orome's sword. Taking it in both hands, he pointed it at them.

The foremost guard came closer. "Arren," he said.

Arren stopped and squinted. "Bran? Is that you?"

Bran raised one large hand. "Please, Arren, don't struggle. Just come quietly."

Arren did not lower the sword, but the tip was shaking slightly. "Please," he said softly, as more guards emerged and took up station behind Bran. "Please, Bran, don't do this. Let me go. Please, just let me go. I'll never come back here; I'll go away forever."

"Put the sword down, Arren," said Bran. "Just put it down."

Arren looked back over his shoulder at the landscape far below him. The wind blowing up the mountainside was icy cold and tugged at him, seeming to invite him to let himself drop. The fear burned in him, and he went toward Bran. The guards drew back their bows, and Bran raised his sword. "Drop the sword!" he shouted. "Do it!"

Arren stopped. He looked at Bran, then at the sword, and then hurled it away. It clattered over the planks, fell from the edge and was gone.

The fear had consumed him utterly. He felt sick and dizzy, and he trembled all over. He lurched away from the edge, holding a hand out toward Bran. "Please!" he said. "Don't let me fall, Bran, I don't want to fall. Help me!"

Bran reached out to grab his hand. "It's all right, Arren, just take my hand, I'll get yeh outta here—"

From somewhere high above, a griffin's cry echoed, and

then one of the guards loosed an arrow. It shot past Bran, narrowly missing his shoulder, and hit Arren square in the chest. He screamed and staggered backward, clutching at the shaft, and then another arrow hit him in the leg.

"No!" Bran shouted, rushing forward.

Everything seemed to happen in slow motion then. Bran tried to catch Arren's tunic, but the bloodstained cloth slipped through his fingers. For a moment, as Arren teetered on the edge, his black eyes looked into Bran's.

Then he fell.

Bran heard his last scream as Arren disappeared into the darkness below, and then he, too, was falling, straight forward, yelling in panic. Hands caught him by the back of his armour and pulled him back, and he crashed onto the planks.

Someone helped him to his feet. He didn't look at them. His eyes were fixed on the edge of the planking where Arren had been. "No," he whispered. "Arren—"

"Come on, sir," said one of the guards behind him. "We've got to get back to the Eyrie and tell them what happened."

Bran turned. "Yeh killed him!"

"He was about to attack you, sir," said one of the guards who had fired. "We all saw it."

"He was askin' me to help him!" said Bran. "He was *scared*!"

The guard shook his head. "He was going to die anyway, sir."

Bran hit him. "That was murder," he snarled.

The guards glanced at each other. "He was only a blackrobe, sir," said one.

Free!

Darkheart struck another human in the chest, almost tearing him in half, and crushed the skull of a second one in his beak. The rest had turned and were trying to run, but he went after them and caught up with them in the tunnel.

There he cornered them and killed them, down to the last man, and when he was done, he lifted one of the corpses and swallowed it whole. He carried the rest back to the enclosure, two at a time, and heaped them up by the platform with the others.

There was no sign of any more guards coming, and he settled down to eat while the other griffins screeched at him from their cages, cheering him on.

"Kill! Kill! Kill the humans! Kill them all, Darkheart!"

Darkheart paid no attention. He tore into a second corpse and swallowed the pieces, savouring the taste of blood. Caught up in his hunger and bloodlust, he completely forgot about his wish to escape and continued to eat, gorging himself on human flesh. So sweet. So soft.

When he was full to bursting, he sat back on his haunches and yawned widely. The sheer amount of food he'd eaten made him drowsy, but he knew he couldn't stay where he was. Other humans would come, and besides, he wanted to leave here and go back to his valley. He got up and trotted through the open gate and into the tunnel; he knew this place. Maybe the gate would open and he could get into the pit. There could be a way out there.

But the end of the tunnel was blocked, and no-one came to open the gate. He hooked his claws into it and tried to pull it out of the way, but it wouldn't move. It rattled when he slammed his body against it, but still did not move, and he turned and walked back the way he'd come, snorting in disgust. There had to be another way out.

Back in the enclosure, he climbed onto the wooden structure in the centre of the floor and reached up to the net that blocked his way to the sky. His perch shook dangerously beneath him, but he ignored it and bit at the steel cables. They were tough and hard, like the chains that had trapped him before, and they wouldn't break. Darkheart hissed and bit down harder, then reared up onto his hind legs and latched his talons into the net, pulling on it with his full weight. The frame beneath him held out for a moment, but then broke. For a moment Darkheart hung upside down from the net, and then he let go and dropped, landing among the wreckage with a hollow thud and a splintering sound.

The net quivered, bobbing up and down over his head, and he looked up at it and screeched his frustration. The other griffins screeched, too, some mocking him and others offering encouragement. Maddened, Darkheart started to demolish the wrecked frame with his beak, knocking down the pieces that remained upright and hurling others aside.

But this was not enough to calm him down; he turned and ran away through the gate again. But the door to the pit still refused to move. He attacked it until he was exhausted, and then lay down on his belly to rest and try to think.

He wondered where the dark human had gone. He had thought of killing it when he had first seen it that night, but when it spoke to him—its voice so calm and strong and unafraid—he remembered what had happened in the pit. The human's presence had calmed him, and he had sat still and waited while it removed his chains and set him free. After that he had been busy fighting the other humans, but what had happened to that one? Had he killed it along with the rest?

He stood up and stared through the gate at the moonlit pit where they had fought. If he could only get through into it, then maybe the human would be there again and would help him get out. Or maybe he would be back in the enclosure.

Darkheart turned and went back, tail swishing. The dead humans were still there where he had left them and he picked through the bodies, looking for the dark one. But he wasn't there. These all had brown fur, not black, and they smelt wrong. He nibbled half-heartedly at one, and then lay down on his belly and sighed.

"Darkheart. Darkheart!"

The sound finally filtered through to him, and he looked up. Aeya was standing up in her cage and was calling to him.

Darkheart watched her for a moment, and then looked away.

"Darkheart," Aeya said again. "I know how you can get out of here."

Darkheart's head turned toward her, and his tail started to twitch.

"There," said Aeya. "The platform, the one you came up on. It has no metal on it. You can break it."

Darkheart stood up. "Where?"

"There, by your talons. See it?"

It was half-buried under the remains of the frame, but he swept the mess aside and peered at the surface underneath. It was bare wood. He gripped it with his claws and they went in deeply, splintering it.

"Stamp on it," Aeya hissed. "Break it!"

Darkheart reared up on his hind legs and then came down, slamming his forepaws onto the platform. It made a loud cracking sound, and a split appeared down the middle. He struck it again and again, until the entire thing shook under his onslaught and the split grew longer and wider. He stopped hitting it and jammed his beak into it, pulling as hard as he could. Having ripped a large chunk of wood out, he began to tear at the gap he had made, levering out great shards of wood with his beak and talons. Growing impatient, he resumed his stamping, bringing his full weight down on it. And then, quite suddenly, it shattered. His front legs punched straight through the wood up to the joints, and then he was struggling to free himself, screeching. His legs came free, and when he looked down he could see the big hole they had left. Cold air blew up through it and onto his face, and joy rose inside him. "Free," he whispered. "Free."

He stuck his beak through the hole. It was too small for him to fit through yet, but he dug the point of his beak into the edge and pulled upward. After a few moments' struggle there was a deafening *crack* and a huge piece of wood broke off, so suddenly that he staggered backward, wings fluttering, the shattered plank still impaled on his beak. He wrenched it off with his talons and returned to the hole. It had nearly doubled in size. He could see the open space through it, and he spread his wings wide over his head and screamed.

"Darkheart! Darkheart!"

The other griffins rose up in their cages, screaming their own names. Some, though, screamed his.

Darkheart glanced back at Aeya. She returned his gaze. "Go, Darkheart," she said. "Fly free."

For a moment he stood there, not moving, and then he went back toward her. He reached through the bars with his beak and touched it lightly against hers. She cheeped softly, like a chick, and then sat down on her haunches. "Go," she said again.

Darkheart stayed there for a time, just watching her. "Aeya," he said at last, and then turned away. He went back to the hole and poked his head through. It fitted, and he thrust his forelegs after it, folding his wings backward to pull himself through. For a moment he became stuck partway, but he dug his talons into the underside of the platform and strained with all his might, until his wings were freed. His haunches and hind legs slid after them, and he fell from the hole.

But not far. His wings opened wide to catch him, and he flew, gliding away from the mountain and on, over the village of Idun. He could see the lake below him, glittering in the moonlight. Above him the stars shone brightly, and among them was the moon, staring down at him. He soared up toward it, not feeling the ache in his body that the chains and the manacles had left.

He was free.

Darkheart circled, his feathered tail turning to balance him, and felt his spirit rise up inside him, hot and vital and alive, like the richest meat and the sweetest water. He could feel the wind in his wings, caressing his face, touching his fur and his feathers. There was the ground below and the sky above, and no chains or humans or cages. He was free.

He flew higher and called out his name as he had never called it before, letting it travel out over the land like a bird. *"Darkheart! Darkheart! Darkheart!"*

He screamed it until he was hoarse, and then flew low over the city, chasing the wind, watching the city's edge rush below him.

And then he heard Arren's last scream rise up from below him.

Darkheart slowed, his wings fluttering to stop him. The scream echoed from the city, like a griffin's call but higher and weaker, and he recognised it. It was the same sound he had heard in the pit that day, when the dark human had rushed at him, clutching a piece of metal in its hand. The same sound it had made when he had chased it and knocked it down.

The name rose up in his head. *Arren.*

Promise me, Arren Cardockson.

Darkheart circled for a time, confused. He remembered how the human had opened the cage and taken away the chains. He remembered the look on its face when they had met in the pit, when he had pinned it down and it had told him to kill it. Darkheart had not understood. Why would it want to die? Why would anything want to die? He remembered how the human had faced him in the field at Rivermeet, how it had shouted out a challenge to him, how it had stayed beside him on the journey to the cages, always watching. He remembered the sound it had made when it had held on to the white griffin's body. That sound no griffin could make.

Arren Cardockson.

Dark human. Dark griffin.

The strange feeling began to burn in his throat again.

Arren Cardockson.

Not knowing what he was doing, Darkheart flew lower, all thought of flying back to his valley forgotten.

He could see the city, all light and shadow, but he did not want to go there. There were cages there, and humans who would trap him again, and other griffins who would attack.

It was not a place for a wild griffin to be. He flew lower, searching the ground at the base of the mountain. There were trees there, all tall and strong. Their smell reminded him of home, and he flew toward them and began to circle, staring straight downward at the ground beneath them. Searching.

He found Arren in the end. The wind carried his scent up to him, and he flew still lower, following it. It led him to a clear spot among the trees, by a heap of tumbled rocks. He landed almost silently on the earth and walked forward slowly, his eyes fixed on the dark shape sprawled not far away.

Arren lay on his back among the rocks, unmoving. The collar around his neck was bent and twisted from the impact, and blood was slowly running down his face from just below his eye, like tears. His eyes were wide open, staring at the moon above, and one leg was twisted beneath him.

Darkheart moved closer and sniffed at him. Arren did not move, and he nudged him gently with his beak. He rolled partly onto his side and then slumped back, but then, as Darkheart watched, he stirred and moaned. He was alive.

The black griffin could see his face moving. One hand twitched, and the eyes blinked, just once, turning toward him. He looked down on the human, and a strange terror entered into his heart. He crouched beside him, so close they were almost touching.

"Arren Cardockson," he said softly.

Arren's mouth moved. He was trying to speak. Darkheart brought his head down closer to listen, and heard him say a word. A strange word. Not one he knew.

"Eluna."

Arren's hand stopped twitching, and his head became still, his face slackening. His shattered chest moved frantically up and down, but then it slowed and weakened until it was barely moving at all.

"Arren," Darkheart whispered.

Arren's eyes turned toward him, and then looked up at the moon, whose light shone down on his face and turned it black and silver. Then they, too, stilled. One moment they were looking at the moon, and the next something behind them, some light that lived on the other side, had gone out.

Quietly, mourned by no-one, watched over by the moon and by the looming shape of the dark griffin, Arren Cardockson died.

23

Risen Moon

Darkheart stayed by the human's body for a long time, unable or unwilling to move. From time to time he shifted slightly, his tail twitching, but then he sighed and settled down again, his great shoulders hunched. His wings and legs hurt, and his neck, but he ignored them. He nibbled at his forelegs, where the manacles had rubbed the scales away and left deep scars behind. There was a bald patch on his neck, too, from the collar.

He looked up at the moon, so bright and cold, shaped like an eye, and felt a deep despair fill him. Suddenly, all his energy had left him, along with his joy in being free. He could fly back to his valley—but he didn't care about it any more. He couldn't even remember it properly, and he did not know the way back. He was lost here, in this place he did not know, with no-one who could show him the way.

He lay down, his head on his talons, and looked at the dead human who had been his only link to home. The one who knew how to open cages, who could appear out of nowhere like a shadow come to life. The one he had known when he was home. The one who wore a collar so much like his own, and who fought like a wild griffin.

"Arren," he whispered.

He pushed at the human's shoulder with his beak, trying to make him wake up, but he had gone stiff and cold and was not like himself any more.

"Free me, Arren Cardockson," Darkheart said.

But Arren did not reply and never would again.

Darkheart looked up at the moon once more. It seemed to look back. A powerful longing rose in his chest, and it was not the longing to be home but the longing for something else, something he did not know or understand. He thought of the yellow griffin with whom he had mated all those years ago, the one with blue eyes like the sky. He thought of Saekrae, her eyes and voice now fuzzy in his memory, and he thought of his two siblings and the warmth of their bodies against his. He thought of the nest where he had lived as a chick.

The longing grew more powerful, and then it moved into his throat. And there, the feeling came back. That burning feeling, that maddening energy. The scream, still trying to get out. He stood up abruptly and opened his beak toward the sky, trying to let it out, but he could not make a sound. The scream caught behind his tongue and would not go, and the feeling grew and strengthened, first a hundred times stronger than before and then a thousand, until his entire body started to shake violently.

He began to run this way and that, darting back and forth and colliding blindly with the rocks all about, and then he fell over onto his side and began to thrash, tearing at himself. Strange whimpers and grunts came from him as he tried with all his might to let the scream out. But all in vain. He stilled and then thrashed again, churning up the soil. The moonlight touched his face, and then something broke inside him.

Light burst out of him. Black light. It was like a hole in the world that outlined every hair and feather, its edges shimmering silver, a darkness so intense that it was darker than the night all around, darker than his fur. It grew in intensity, making his outline ripple and distort, like water. Darkheart ceased his struggles and became stiff, as though dead. Then he jerked upright, not as if he had decided to stand but as if he had been dragged to his paws. His head came up and his beak opened, pointing down at Arren's body.

And then he screamed.

The sound burst out of him like blood from a wound, and it was no griffin's voice, or human's, or the voice of any other living creature. It was like a thousand voices all screaming at once, or like the sound of a gushing torrent of water, huge and fast beyond comprehension. It was a sound that had never been heard in the world before.

And with it came light. It came from Darkheart's beak, pouring out of him like water. The glow around him faltered and then faded, and the light moved out of him and into Arren's body, vanishing inside it and transferring the glow to him. His hair and skin were haloed with the darkness of a living shadow, which made his outline warp and twist before it reformed into its old shape.

The scream stopped abruptly, and Darkheart's beak snapped shut. He slumped onto his belly, panting and exhausted, but unable to look away. He saw the light move over Arren's body, embracing him, and then it began to fade, retreating into his skin and disappearing like water soaking into the earth. Then it was gone and it was all over.

Darkheart's head dropped and he became still, his eyes gently sliding shut. His tail continued to twitch for a time, and then that, too, fell to the ground and did not move again.

The stars began to go out, the moon faded and the first light of the sun appeared over the horizon. As the sky lightened, birds began to chirp in the trees, and in the city above, griffins called their names, announcing their presence to the world. Another day had come, but neither Arren nor Darkheart saw it.

Darkheart woke up slowly, rising out of a morass of dark

dreams. His body ached and he felt strangely drained and weak, even vulnerable. He sat up slowly and yawned, his wings opening wide. It made him feel slightly better, but it was not until he began flexing his front legs to ease the stiffness in them that the memory of the previous night came rushing back. He stopped dead, head darting this way and that to take in his surroundings. It was dawn, and he was sitting among some rocks by the base of the mountain. There was sky above and trees in front of him, and a lake beyond that.

He stood up sharply, tail twitching, and scanned the sky. No sign of other griffins. He could fly away without being seen.

He looked down and saw Arren, still lying where he had been the previous night, and that was when he remembered everything else. The struggle, the scream, the light . . . and the strange and terrible feeling of something pouring out of him and into the human's body, taking all his strength with it.

Darkheart sniffed at Arren, and pushed him lightly with the back of one talon. He was no longer stiff, but he still did not move.

Yet Darkheart persisted. He continued to nudge him. "Arren," he whispered.

And then something happened. A great jolt went through Arren's body and travelled into Darkheart, making him shriek in alarm and back away. It had felt like a single, massive heartbeat—one so powerful it had made his entire body jerk with it.

On the ground, Arren's mouth opened wide and he breathed in a great gasp of air. He twitched once, all over, and then started to breathe again, his chest heaving frantically. His eyes snapped shut as he coughed, but then he opened them again and looked up at Darkheart, and they were alight with life and intelligence and personality. Alive.

The first thing Arren felt when he woke was pain. It went ripping through him in one massive burst, like a giant heartbeat pumping burning-hot blood through his system.

He felt himself jerk violently, and then his mouth opened and he began to breathe. The moment the air flooded into his lungs, the pain disappeared. He sucked it in greedily, and it brought everything back. Light, sound, thought and vision. His eyes opened and he saw the black griffin looking down at him, looming in the sky like a feathered mountain.

He tried to get up for a moment, but then slumped back, trying to think. He didn't know where he was or how he had got there, or what had happened to him. He couldn't even remember his own name.

His hand went to his throat, and touched a cold metal surface. It was scratched and dented, clinging to his neck, and he pulled at it. It came free with a sick, wet sound, and he flung it aside and sat up. He felt strong, and he stood up and dusted himself down. There was an arrow sticking in his leg. He pulled it out and dropped it, then looked around. He was in a forest at the base of a mountain, among some rocks, and there was a huge black griffin sitting nearby watching him.

He looked at it, trying to remember what it was. There was something familiar about it.

The black griffin stood up. "Arren Cardockson," it said.

And then he remembered. It came rushing back in an instant, hitting him all at once. Run, fight, escape, fear . . . and then the fall. He remembered seeing Bran's face as he toppled backward and then fell from the edge of the city. He remembered falling into darkness, screaming, the wind tearing at him, blood crawling up the shaft of the arrow embedded in his body and being whipped away. And he remembered hitting the ground. He remembered the agony that had smothered him as he looked up at the face of the black griffin . . . and died.

When Arren opened his eyes, he found himself lying on the ground. He hadn't even realised that he had fallen over. He got up and patted himself frantically, feeling his stomach, chest and face. It was all still there, just as it had been before. His curly hair, grown quite long over the last few months, the ragged beard that Flell had complained about, the puckered scars left by Shoa's talons, the wound under his right eye. The collar was gone, but it had left a ring of puncture wounds all around his neck. They were bleeding, but they didn't hurt. In fact, nothing hurt. There was no ache in his back, no twinging from his ribs. There was an arrow wound in his leg, but that didn't hurt, either. Nor did the slash on his cheek.

Panic-stricken, he turned and ran away from the black griffin as fast as he could go, dashing into the trees. His wounded leg was weak, but he didn't let it slow him down much. He ran on until he reached a small pool among the trees and there limped to a stop and fell to his knees by the water's edge. He splashed his face and then drank, and it helped to clear his head. As the water stilled, he looked down into it and saw his face reflected back at him.

His own eyes stared into his, and he, too, became still, taking in the face that looked up at him.

He looked the same—and yet different. His face was still pale, with black eyes and a black beard, and black curls hanging over his forehead. He looked dirty and his face was gaunt and thin, making it appear even more angular than before.

It was still his face. But there was something wrong with it. Something he couldn't quite pinpoint that had changed. He did not know what it was, and yet it struck fear into him.

"What's going on?" he whispered. "What's happened to me?"

He felt different, too. It wasn't weakness or sickness or pain, but there was something wrong in his body. He patted himself all over again, searching for some sign of it, and again there was something wrong, but he didn't know what. Something about the feel of his skin and flesh. It was cold, he realised. Colder than it should have been. Then he touched his throat again, feeling the wounds left by the collar and trying to understand why they didn't hurt.

They *did* hurt, he realised suddenly. In fact, all his

wounds hurt. But somehow the pain felt faint and unimportant, without the power to distress him.

He dabbed at the blood on his neck, and once again the feeling of wrongness came over him. It was in his neck, that was it. Whatever was wrong with him was centred around it. He rested his hand on it and kept it there, trying to find it. It was something about how his neck felt to the touch. Something missing.

That was when he realised. It came upon him slowly, like an old memory, and his face slackened gently in horror. He moved his hand and pressed it into his neck, feeling desperately for the thing that was missing, but in vain. He tried his chest, and then his wrists. Nothing. Not a sign. It simply wasn't there any more.

"No," he moaned. "No! This can't—this can't happen!"

He pounded his fists hard against his chest, but nothing happened. He made himself breathe as fast as he could, until his head spun, but still nothing.

Arren began to shake. "No," he whispered. "No!"

There was a noise behind him. He turned sharply and saw Darkheart standing there, watching him in silence.

He got up and started toward the griffin, limping on his wounded leg. "What have you done to me?" he screamed. "What have you turned me into?"

Darkheart drew back a little, confused. "Arren," he said. "You live. You live."

Arren hit him hard in the face. "Give it back!" he yelled. "Change me back!"

Darkheart retreated under his onslaught, hissing. "Arren," he said. "Arren!"

Arren continued to hit him, feeling not the slightest trace of fear. "This is your fault! You monster!" He lunged forward and grabbed the griffin around the neck, squeezing tight, trying to kill him.

Darkheart kicked him, knocking him off and sending him flying. He landed against the base of a tree but got up almost instantly. "Make it come back!" he shouted, snatching up a stick. "Give it back!"

Darkheart said nothing. He sat on his haunches and watched the human, uncomprehending.

"Give it back!" Arren shouted again. "G—" His voice faltered and he fell to his knees, sobbing brokenly. "Oh gods, oh gods, help me, help me."

Something touched his head and he looked up. Darkheart was there, crouched in front of him, the wind ruffling his feathers. "Arren," he said softly.

Arren shoved him. "Go away," he said. "Leave me alone."

Darkheart did not move. Arren got up and walked away from him, but he followed, not taking his eyes off him.

Arren snatched up a rock. "Go away!" he screamed, and hurled it. It hit Darkheart on the beak, and he stooped and picked up a handful of others. He pelted the black griffin with them until he backed away, tail lashing. "Get away from me! Go on, go away!"

At last, Darkheart turned and began to walk off.

Arren took a few steps forward and threw rocks and sticks with all his might. "And never come back!" he yelled.

Then the black griffin was gone, and he was alone. He stood still for a few moments, breathing heavily, and then let the rock he held fall out of his hand. There were tears on his face, making his wound sting, but he felt too drained to cry. He wrapped his fingers around his neck, holding on to it gently. The skin was cold and sticky with blood, but those things did not bother him. The thing that struck fear into him, the thing that made him shake and made his stomach churn, was something that wasn't even there any more.

His heart was not beating.

A rren stayed in the forest for some time, not knowing what to do. He didn't know if he was dead or alive, or even if this was still the real world. Maybe this was the afterlife.

But it did not look like it. It was too . . . real. And in his heart he knew that it was the world of the living. He was dead, but he hadn't left it.

He wandered over the rocks where he had died, and found something lying wedged between two boulders. Orome's sword. He pulled it out and found that part of the blade had broken off, but the rest was still sharp, and the broken edge was jagged, almost barbed. He made a few experimental swings with it, and then put it into his belt.

This done, he went back to hide among the trees. Would people still be looking for him?

Either way, he knew he had to leave. Though where he would go he had no idea.

There was a terrible silence among the trees, pressing down on him, and suddenly he couldn't bear to be so alone. He wanted someone to be there, anyone.

He turned away from the mountain and walked off through the trees, stumbling a little on the slope. Up ahead was Snake Hill, its sides dotted with the houses that made up Idun. He wanted to see his parents again. They had to know that he was all right. He wasn't afraid of being caught. What would it matter if he was? There was nothing left they could do to him.

The sun was well up by now, and plenty of people were up and about in the village. Arren ducked behind houses and other pieces of cover to avoid being seen, slowly making his way up the hill toward his parents' house. He was surprised by how easy it was. For some reason, when he walked his boots made virtually no sound at all. His senses were sharp and alert, perfectly attuned to danger, and he dodged through the village like a hunting cat, unseen and unheard.

He reached his parents' home and went around the back, where there were some crates stacked. He hid behind those until he was sure the coast was clear, and then pushed the back door open and slipped in through it, closing it behind him as quietly as he could. Safe.

He paused there to catch his breath and then walked toward the doorway leading into the main room. He could hear voices coming through it, and called out, "Mum! Dad! Are you there?"

Dead silence fell. Arren entered the room, ducking slightly to get through the door, and there they were, getting up from the table where they had been sitting. His mother froze, staring at him. There were tears on her face, and she was clutching something to her chest: it was the black robe they had given him when he was in prison.

Arren managed a watery grin. "I—uh—I hope you don't mind."

There was silence and then his mother flew across the room and flung herself on him. Cardock was close behind her, and the two of them hugged their son as tightly as they could. Both of them were crying.

"Arren!" Annir sobbed. "Oh gods, Arren, Arren, you're alive, you've come back to me, thank gods."

Arren didn't move. He let them embrace him, feeling their warmth all about him, taking away the coldness in his body. He could feel Annir trembling as she sobbed, and he held on to her as well as he could, feeling a peculiar sense of relief. They were here, they were real, they were alive. He was home.

Cardock let go, his face pale with disbelief. "Arren, how did this happen? Where did you come from?"

Arren looked past him, and his expression changed when he saw who else was sitting at the table.

Bran, frozen in horror.

Arren's hand went to his belt and pulled out the broken sword. *"You,"* he snarled, starting forward. "What are you doing here?"

Bran stood up sharply, knocking over his chair. "No!" he exclaimed. "No, it's impossible!"

Arren pointed the sword at him. "I should kill you," he said.

Cardock grabbed him by the arm. "Arren, no, don't. It wasn't his fault. He came here to tell us what happened. He brought your robe back to us. He said they hadn't found your body—he came to say sorry to us."

Bran's face was blank with terror. "You're dead," he whispered. "You're *dead*!"

"Get out of here, Bran," Arren hissed. "Stay away from my parents."

Bran's hand went to the hilt of his own sword, but he didn't draw it. "Arren," he said, backing away. "There's—in yer chest. Can't yeh *feel* it?"

Arren glanced down and suddenly noticed the broken shaft of an arrow embedded in his body. He grabbed it and pulled it out. The point was sharp and covered with gore; he looked at it blankly and then tossed it aside. Bran moaned softly, and Arren pointed the sword at him again, straight at his face. "Go," he said again. "Get out of here. You were my friend once; otherwise, I would kill you. Get out and don't come back. If you tell anyone you saw me, I'll hunt you down."

Bran stayed where he was for a moment, trembling, and then he turned and ran out of the house as fast as he could go. Arren heard the door slam behind him. He turned away and put the sword back into his belt. "Mum, Dad, I'm sorry," he said. "I didn't want any of this to happen. I had to come back and see you before I left."

They were silent for a time, watching him with something almost like fear, but then Annir embraced him again. "I thought you were dead," she whispered. "I thought I'd lost you."

Arren held on to her a little awkwardly. "I'm all right, Mum," he lied. "Really. I'm fine. See?" He let go of her and pointed at his neck. "I got that collar off."

Cardock took him by the shoulder. "Arren, you're bleeding."

"It doesn't hurt," said Arren.

Annir touched him gently. "You should lie down," she said. "I'll get some salve."

Arren allowed himself to be led to their bed, and took off his tunic so that Annir could attend to his wounds. She put ointment on his neck and chest and covered them with bandages, then rolled up his trouser leg and dressed the second arrow wound, in his shin.

"There, does that feel better?"

Arren nodded and sat up. "I'm a mess, aren't I?" he said.

Annir was looking at him, her eyes bright with tears. "I don't care how you look," she said. "I've got my boy back, and that's all that matters to me."

Cardock had been rummaging through a clothes chest and now came over, carrying a fresh pair of black trousers and a tunic. "Here," he said. "They should fit you. I've got another pair of boots out the back you can have."

Arren took them and laid them aside. "I should have a wash first," he said. "And"—he scratched his chin—"have you got a razor anywhere?"

Cardock heated some water and poured it into a basin, and Arren stripped off the rest of his clothes, quite unembarrassed, and washed himself from head to toe, rubbing away layers of ingrained dirt. It left him feeling refreshed and strangely relieved, as if he had in some way just begun to reclaim his identity. Once he was clean and had towelled himself off, he put on the clean trousers and picked up Cardock's razor. "Haven't shaved in months," he muttered, and rubbed soap into his beard. Once it was properly lathered, he started to shave it off. He removed the moustache and most of what was on his cheeks and just under his mouth, but he left a thick tuft on his chin. When he was done and had washed what was left, he took a pair of scissors and started to style it, trimming it into a point.

"There," he said when he was finished. "I'm done. How do I look?"

Cardock smiled at him. "You look like a man now," he said. "A Northern man."

Arren shrugged and picked up a comb. His hair was still wet. After months without being trimmed, it had grown almost down to his shoulders and had lost something of its curliness. He trimmed the ends off it with Annir's help, and then combed and reordered the rest. By the time he was done, he felt neat and clean in a way he hadn't for a very long time, since Eluna's death and the day when he had started to let his appearance go. It made him a little sad to think it, but he felt oddly contemptuous toward his past self. Weak and self-pitying, drowning his sorrows in cheap wine. Too naïve to see what was going on, too submissive to fight back.

Well, that time was over now, and he was glad.

He sat down at the table with his parents, and ate the food Cardock offered him. It tasted wonderful.

"Son, what happened?" said Cardock, once Arren had taken the edge off his appetite and slowed down a little. "How did you get out of there?"

"It's"—Arren paused—"complicated."

"Tell us," said Annir.

"What did Bran tell you?"

"He said—" Cardock took in a deep breath. "He said that as far as he knows, you got out of the cage on your own, and that afterwards you went to the Arena and did something. He didn't know what, but he said the word was something bad had happened there and you were being blamed. He said he was going home after a late shift and got roped in to help look for you, and when he was searching the market district you suddenly appeared out of nowhere. They chased you to the edge of the city, and then you surrendered, but you fell off the edge. He said they'd started a search for your body and that it'd be brought here to us when they found it, and he gave us that." He nodded at the robe, which was draped over the back of a chair. "You left it behind in that cage."

"But what really happened?" said Annir. "Was Bran lying?"

Arren was silent for a long time. "No," he said at last. "He was telling the truth."

"You mean you really did fall all that way?" said Cardock. "For gods' sakes, how did you survive?"

"I bounced off the side of the mountain," Arren lied. "And then I landed in the lake. I woke up on the bank."

"Arenadd, that . . ."

Arren looked up anxiously.

"That's incredible," Cardock said at last.

"It was a miracle," said Annir.

"The moon was up when you fell," said Cardock. "The Night God protected you, didn't she? She must have." He smiled, a soft, joyful smile that was most unlike him. "Do you believe me now, Arenadd?"

Arren remembered the moon and how it had shone down on him as he died, and a hint of doubt entered his mind. Had it done something? Had *it* been the thing that brought him back? But if so, why had Darkheart been there? Had he sat there all night watching over him? He felt a little twinge of guilt, but only briefly.

"I think . . . maybe I do," he said. "I mean, I never saw anything, but I . . ."

"What is it, Arren?" said Annir.

"I prayed," said Arren. "To the moon. The night before I went into the Arena. I asked it to protect me."

"And it did," said Cardock. He leant over and hugged him quickly. "I'm grateful," he said, settling back into his seat, "to the Night God. I've had faith in her my entire life, and now she's repaid me by giving me back my son."

"She repaid both of us," said Annir.

Arren stood up. "I want to stay with you," he said, "and I'm sorry that I can't. There's something I have to ask you. Something I need you to do for me."

"Anything, Arren," said Annir.

Arren breathed in deeply. "I need you to leave here," he said. "Leave Idun. For good."

"Why?" Cardock asked.

"Because if you stay you'll be in danger," said Arren. "And I can't let that happen."

"We're all right, Arren," said Annir. "No-one bothers us."

"You're not in danger now," said Arren. "But you will be. That's why I need you to go before that happens. If I can, I'll catch up with you."

"Arenadd, what are you talking about?" said Cardock.

"Why do we have to go? And why wouldn't you come with us?"

Arren picked up the black robe. "I've made a choice," he said. "And there's nothing you can do to stop me."

He put it on, pulling the sleeves over his arms, and did up the fastenings. It fitted perfectly.

"Thank you for making this for me," he said. "I think it'll be useful." He faced them resolutely. "I'm going to leave now," he said. "But not before you promise me that you'll go. Today. Be out of the village before the sun goes down. Head north, toward Norton, and don't tell anyone where you're going or why. If I can, I'll meet you there, but I can't make any promises. People are going to be after me, and I won't lead them to you."

"But Arren, why?" said Cardock. "Everyone thinks you're dead. If you leave now, no-one will ever chase you."

Arren picked up the sword. "But they will," he said. "By tomorrow, everyone will be after me."

"Why?" said Annir.

"Because tomorrow I will be a murderer," said Arren.

24

The Cursed One

Flell's house was dark and cold when she entered it. Her servants had gone home for the night, but they'd left a lamp lit for her. She picked it up and used it to light her way toward the study, where there should be a fire still burning.

In the corridor, Thrain suddenly stopped. Flell looked back at her and saw that the little griffin had pulled back and was hunched uncertainly against the wall, tail lashing.

"What is it?"

Thrain looked up sharply, then stared in the direction of the study door, which was slightly ajar. The light of the fire behind it flickered around the edges, but there was no sound or sign of anything.

"Thrain?" said Flell. "Is something wrong?"

Thrain hissed, but said nothing.

"Come on," said Flell. She moved on and pushed the door open, and Thrain followed her warily, still hissing.

There was nothing unusual in the study. The fire was burning cheerily in the grate, well stocked with fuel, and a flask of wine and two cups were on the table. Flell frowned when she saw the second cup. She'd given Thrain some in the past, but it was a bad idea, and the extra cup would only give her ideas. She made a mental note to tell her house-keeper not to do that again.

As she set the lamp down on the table, she saw the flame flicker a little and realised there was a cold breeze in the room. She shivered slightly and reached for the wine.

Thrain gave a sharp shriek from behind her. Flell turned in time to see the little griffin streak past her and dive under the table, where she cowered against one of its legs, quivering.

"Thrain? What's wrong with you?"

The breeze blew on her face. She looked up, and then she saw the broken window and went cold. Without look-ing around, she reached to her waist and drew her dagger. The feel of the metal hilt against her skin gave her courage, and she turned slowly, every sense alert for danger.

There was no-one there.

"Thrain," Flell called, still scanning the room for any sign of movement. "Is there someone else in here?"

Thrain hissed again. "Fear," she said suddenly. "Fear. Blood. I smell blood. I smell death."

Holding the dagger tightly in one hand, Flell stepped toward the fireplace. Someone could be hiding behind one of the chairs.

"Flell," said a voice.

Flell almost screamed. She whirled around, dagger raised, and saw a shadow detach itself from the wall and come toward her. It was human, tall and thin, utterly silent when it moved, like a piece of living night.

"Stop there!" Flell shouted.

"Flell," the voice said again. "It's me."

The shape came forward into the light.

A young man, tall and sinewy, most of his body con-cealed by a long black robe. His face was pale, gaunt and angular, marred by a long cut just under his right eye. He had black curly hair and a pointed black beard. His eyes were black, and they were cold and glittering in the darkness.

Flell froze. "Who are you?" she demanded.

The man held out his hands; they were elegant and long-fingered. "Flell, it's me," he said again. "It's Arren. Don't you recognise me?"

And, at last, she recognised his voice. The dagger dropped out of her hand and she staggered away from him. "No!"

"Flell, please, don't be afraid. I'm not going to hurt you. I just wanted to see you again."

"But you're dead," Flell whispered. "You're dead!"

"Flell."

Arren came toward her, his boots making no sound on the floor. She did not move away. She could hear him breathing now; she could see him clearly, see he was real.

He reached out and brushed her face lightly with his fingertips. His touch was cold.

Flell started to shrink away, but then she reached out to him and touched him, feeling his hair and his skin. All real. All still there. "Arren."

He stood there a moment and then pulled her to him, hugging her tightly. She hugged him back; the feeling of his thin body in her arms was so familiar—and yet so strange.

They parted, and Arren looked at her, with a terrible fear and vulnerability in his face. "Flell," he said, "I—I shouldn't have come here. But I had to see you again. So you'd know."

Flell took his hand. "Arren, what happened? How can this be real? Are you—are you a ghost?"

He laughed a sad, hollow laugh. "Do I look like one?"

"No. Well, I've never seen a ghost before. But how did you survive? How did you get back here?"

Arren shook his head. "Where were you?" he asked. "I kept trying to find you, but you were never there. I really missed you. I needed you."

There was no accusation in his voice, but his words cut her deeply. "Arren, I'm sorry. I missed you, too. I wanted to see you, but—"

"It was your father, wasn't it?" Arren said bitterly. "He told you to stay away from me, didn't he?"

Flell nodded. "He asked how you were, and I told him about how I visited you and how I helped you get another job, and how you were coping. He said he was glad you had me helping you, but then he asked me to stay away from you. He said people were afraid you were losing your mind, and he was frightened that you might turn violent and that I'd be hurt. I told him it was all lies. I said you'd never been like that and you never would be, but then when I saw what you did to those men . . . and afterwards, when you . . ." She bowed her head. "I told Father you believed he was trying to kill you, and he said—"

Arren grabbed her shoulder. "Flell, how could you?"

"I'm sorry," Flell sobbed. "I didn't know what was going to happen; I was just scared for you. You were changing; I could see you changing. You weren't like you were before you went away. I was frightened of you. But I didn't know—Arren, what happened to you? You did all those awful things, you killed all those people, you—"

"Flell, I didn't," said Arren. "I didn't kill anyone."

"But everyone *saw* you!" said Flell. "People saw you running out of the Arena, and when they went in there ten men were dead! You let that griffin out of his cage and made him kill them all. You even killed Orome, and Sefer as well! And before then you stole that chick and set fire to your own house, and you said those terrible things about my father right in front of everyone—"

"Flell, please!" said Arren. "Stop it! It's all *lies*. I didn't kill anyone, and I didn't make that griffin do anything. How could I control that thing? It's wild!"

"But you made it spare you in the Arena," said Flell. "Everyone saw it. It knocked you over, and then it just left you alone. How did you do it?"

"I didn't," said Arren. "I didn't do anything. Please, Flell, listen to yourself. I wouldn't do something like that! You *know* me."

"Well then, what did you do?" said Flell. "How did you get out of prison?"

"Flell, I—listen. I'll tell you what happened. Yes, I stole that chick. I won't lie about that. I took it out of its pen and ran away with it. But I wasn't going to hurt it. I thought if I could look after it for long enough it would change its mind, start to like me."

"You can't *do* that," said Flell. "It's wrong."

"I know. I just—I think I lost my mind for a bit. It was so long, and so—after what happened to me, I knew I would die without a griffin. I just wanted my life back."

"Arren, you can't. Stealing a chick wouldn't have made you a griffiner again."

"I *know*. I was going to leave the city, find somewhere else to live and take the chick with me. But I saw the griffins looking for me, and I panicked and ran back toward my house, to hide. And when I got there it was on fire. Someone must have—well, I don't know how it happened. And then I was caught."

"And they threw you in the Arena."

"Yes. I asked to go there. I knew I was going to die, but I wanted to fight Dar— the black griffin. I wanted to kill him. Or at least, I thought if I died fighting, it would be better than just being executed."

"But the black griffin didn't kill you," said Flell. "Why?"

"He was—he *knew* me," said Arren. "He knew my name. He knocked me over and just held me down, and I thought he was going to kill me, but then he—he spoke to me. He called me by my name."

"What did he say?" said Flell.

"He asked me to set him free," said Arren. "He thought I could get him out of the Arena. He said that if I promised to set him free, he wouldn't kill me. So I promised, and he let me go."

"But why?" said Flell. "Why would he do that?"

"I think—I put him in that cage in the first place, didn't I? So he must have believed I had the power to take him out again."

"And that night you escaped," said Flell. "How?"

Arren shook his head. "I won't say. But I got out of there, and I could have just run out of the city. But I knew I had to keep my promise, so I went to the Arena instead."

"Why?" said Flell. "It was suicide!"

"I know. But I just knew I had to do it. Because—"

"Because why? That griffin is a monster! He killed Eluna! What happened to you was his fault, not my father's!"

"But—I knew that, but it was strange," said Arren. "Somehow, when we met in the Arena, when I was looking up at him, I just *knew.*"

"Knew what?"

"Knew that—" Arren closed his eyes for a moment. "I knew we were the same," he said finally, and as he said it he knew at last why he had gone to keep his promise and so sacrificed his own life.

Flell looked bewildered. "The same? How?"

Arren turned away. "I hated that griffin so much I tried to kill him with my bare hands. I blamed him for what happened as much as I blamed your father, but I was wrong. He killed Eluna because he was trying to defend himself. He wasn't even after her, he was after me. And I took his life away from him. Put him into a cage, stopped him from flying any more. I sold him to the Arena. I . . ." He turned back to face her. "I turned him into a slave," he said simply. "A slave living in a cage, wearing a collar and chains. I saw those cages. They were tiny. They couldn't even turn around; they were chained to the walls the whole time. It was inhuman."

"They're man-eaters, Arren," said Flell. "They deserve it."

"No. Nothing and no-one deserves that. When they threw me into prison they thought exactly the same thing. When they put that collar on me, they were thinking, *He's a blackrobe, he deserves it.* When I was sitting there afterwards and thinking about it, I realised I'd done something wrong. And I had to put it right before I went."

"So you let that griffin out of his cage and let him kill all those men?" Flell said sharply.

"I didn't know he was going to do that," said Arren. He bowed his head, forcing himself not to admit what he had been thinking at the time, which was that if the griffin killed anyone, he wouldn't care.

"Arren, the thing is a man-eater! What did you *think* he was going to do?"

Griffins are warriors; they kill their enemies. And so do we.

Arren said nothing.

"So, then what?" Flell went on in an oddly disjointed kind of way, as if each word was hitting a wall. "After that you ran out of the Arena, and . . ."

"I tried to stop him," said Arren. "If I could have—did they catch him?"

"No," said Flell. "He smashed a hole in the lifter and flew away. They were hunting for him all yesterday. He's probably flown back to where he came from."

Arren sighed. "Humans are killing the wild griffins. Taking their homes away from them. Why would anyone be surprised that they're trying to fight back?"

"I saw Bran today," said Flell. "He was going to see your parents and tell them you were dead. He looked terrible. I know he blames himself for what happened. He said he cornered you at the edge of the city, and that you were begging him to help you when some of the other guards shot arrows at you. He said he nearly fell off the edge trying to catch you, but . . . you fell." She looked him in the eye. "And you died."

"Flell . . ." Arren breathed in deeply and reached into his pocket. "I can't stay long. There's something I wanted to give you before I left."

He held it out, and she took it and stared at it.

"Arren—"

It was a small gemstone, jet-black in colour, cut into the shape of a shield. Or a heart. It glittered in the firelight, like Arren's eyes.

"Arren," Flell said again. "Is this . . ."

"Yes," said Arren. "I was—I carried it around with me all year. I kept telling myself that tomorrow I'd give it to you, but I kept holding myself back. It was never the right time, and—"

The shame and longing in his voice reawakened her love for him, and she put her hand under his chin and lifted his head so that they were looking each other in the face. "Arren," she said, "I would have taken it."

"I thought maybe you would," said Arren. "But how could I? I'm so stupid, Flell. I kept fooling myself that I was one of you, that it didn't matter what I was. I knew it didn't matter to you, but it mattered to everyone else. I knew that if I asked you and if you married me, no-one would ever—you'd be disgraced. Southerners can't marry Northerners, even if they are griffiners. I knew that you would do it anyway, and that was when I realised that I couldn't do it to you. It would be cruel, making you choose like that. As long as we were just seeing each other the way we were, everyone would have said it was just flirting. Nothing serious. You'd snap out of it and choose a proper husband. When you stopped seeing me, I knew it was because you were ashamed. So I left you alone."

"No," said Flell. "Arren, no. It's not like that; it never was. I didn't care what anyone said. I love—I loved you. I would have married you no matter what anyone said, including you. I knew you were thinking of asking me. I could see the signs. I kept wondering if I should just tell you to get on with it, but I thought if I pushed you, you'd be hurt."

"I think . . . maybe I wouldn't have," said Arren. "But it doesn't matter any more. Not now."

Flell held out the stone for him to take, but he took her hand and gently curled the fingers around it.

"Keep it," he said. "I mean, if you want to. To remember me by."

"Arren, what are you going to do?" said Flell, clutching it to her chest. "Why are you here? Why are you alive?"

"You won't ever see me again," said Arren. "Tomorrow I'll be gone, and I'll never come back. I came here to tell you I love you, and to . . ." He bowed his head. "I came here to ask you to forgive me," he said. "I care about you and I don't want anything bad to happen to you. I should have stayed away and let you think I was dead, but I had to see you. If you remember me, remember me for who I was when you knew me, because then . . . I think maybe I was worth something then." He took her hands. "Only forgive me," he pleaded.

"You haven't hurt me," said Flell. "There's nothing to forgive."

"Just forgive me," Arren said again. "I never wanted any of this to happen. I spent so long trying to do the right thing, but now I don't know what that is any more. I know what people will say about me. What they're already saying. But it wasn't my fault. Tomorrow . . . tomorrow, I want you to know that I didn't plan it. I didn't want it. Tell them, Flell. Tell them what really happened. Tell them I didn't fall. Tell them I was pushed."

"Arren, I don't understand."

"Only tell them!" he said again urgently. "Tell them it wasn't an accident. Tell them someone pushed me. Tell them Arren Cardockson was innocent. And forgive me, Flell. Just forgive me. One day, somehow, somewhere, forgive me."

He let go of her hands.

Flell was looking at him, full of fear and bewilderment. "What's happened to you?" she said. "You're not my Arren any more."

"No," said Arren. "Flell, something terrible has happened. I don't know what it was. One day, maybe, I'll know. Forgive me, Flell. I love you."

He had been backing away from her all this time, and now he turned and climbed out through the open window. His robe snagged on the broken glass, but he reached back and pulled it off as Flell ran forward to stop him.

"Arren!"

She looked out of the window, but there was no-one on the other side. It was as if the night had simply swallowed him up.

"Arren, please!" she called. "Arren, there's something I—"

But there was no reply. He was gone.

Darkheart was lost. He wandered disconsolately among the trees, not knowing what to do or where he should go. It was daylight now, and he didn't want to take to the air. He was trying to find the human, and humans stayed on the ground.

He followed its scent to the edge of the trees and stood there for a time, looking at the village. It must have gone there, but for some reason he didn't want to try to follow.

He went back toward the base of the mountain and found the place where the human had died and then . . . not been dead any more. He didn't understand how it had happened; he sniffed around the ground there and picked up a strange odour lingering about the rocks, a cold, metallic smell, unlike anything he had ever smelt before. It made the fur stand up on his back.

Darkheart sighed and lay down on the spot where the human had been. Part of him still wanted to go back to the valley, but another part wanted to stay. After having been caged for so long, he couldn't remember his old home any more beyond a few vague images, and somehow the pull it had had for him before wasn't there any more. His longing to go home had changed into a general and hazily defined wish to fly again. And now that he was free and had his wish, he wanted something else, something just as ill-defined and confusing. He wanted something to show him the way, some guide to help him survive in this new place.

The voices of other griffins came from overhead; he glanced up, but all he could see was the underside of the city. If none of them ventured this low, then they would

never see him from the air. He didn't particularly care.
Other griffins held no attraction for him.

He thought about the human instead. The image of its
face was still vivid in his mind, and the sound of its voice,
shouting something he did not understand. *What have you
done to me? What have you turned me into?*

Darkheart shivered. He still felt weak and drained after
what had happened, and he remembered the light and
how it had come out of him and gone into the human. The
scream was no longer imprisoned in his throat. It was gone.
But instead of giving him relief it made him feel empty
and useless, like a heap of bare bones with no meat left on
them. It frightened him, and he hissed to himself.

The fear grew. He was lost in this place that he hated
and feared but felt bound to by some unexplained force; he
felt sick and distressed. He was hungry, but he had no will
to seek out food. He wanted to fly away, and yet he wanted
to stay. He didn't know what to do. He even began to think
of going back to the cage. There, at least, the world made
sense.

He whimpered to himself, a chick-like sound that would
have seemed comical to anyone who had heard him make
it. This place was wrong, all wrong, and now he had lost
the only tie he had to his old home and his old life. He
wanted the human to be there again. It knew how to open
cages. It could show him the way home.

"Arren," he mumbled. "Arren."

After that he slept, woke and slept again. Waiting.

It was not until night came that he finally rose from the
spot where he lay. He walked down into the trees and found
a pool to drink from, the same one where he had left the
human. But it was gone now.

Darkheart looked up at the sky. The sun was long gone,
and the stars were out. The human was out there somewhere. All he had to do was follow its scent.

25

Blackrobe and Darkheart

It was cold in Rannagon's study. He put another log on the fire, hoping that would improve matters. The bark caught and began to burn, giving off a pleasant spicy smell. Once he was sure it was well alight and wouldn't need any prodding, he straightened up and sat down in his chair, looking up at his sword, which hung over the fireplace. It was a beautiful thing, with a long, straight blade and a bronze hilt decorated with griffins. He had used it in battle several times; the blade was notched and worn, and the grip was dark with ingrained dirt and sweat. Kaelyn kept telling him to have it cleaned, but he never seemed to get around to it. Besides, it looked better this way. More honest. Cleaning it would only conceal the fact that it had been used and that it had taken lives.

Shoa stirred beside him. "You will not have to use it again," she said. "Not for many years."

"I prefer not to be too confident too soon," said Rannagon. "Life is always unexpected."

"But planning and foresight can change that," said Shoa. "You know that, Rannagon."

"Yes."

"You did what was right," said Shoa. "For the greater good. One day they will say you prevented the rise of a tyrant."

"Do you expect me to be proud?" Rannagon said sharply.

"I do not see why you should not be," said Shoa.

Rannagon's grip on his armrest tightened. "No," he said. "I'm not proud, and I never will be. I'm ashamed."

"Then you are weak," said Shoa. "Man or griffin should always take pride in doing justice."

"It wasn't justice, Shoa," said Rannagon. "Murder is murder, and lies are lies. What we did was unspeakable."

"The way of a griffiner is hard," said Shoa. "I told you that when you were young and you did not want to go to war. You listened to me, and you became a great warrior."

"That's different," said Rannagon. "Warfare is different. I looked those men in the eye as I killed them—but this time? I wasn't even there. No-one even knows I did it."

"The boy was only a blackrobe," said Shoa. "Why sully your hands with his blood? And he brought it on himself. We did not ask him to steal a chick."

"No." Rannagon sighed. "I should have had him killed. Proper assassination. It would have been quieter. He deserved better. By the end, it was probably a mercy that he died as he did. What did he even have left to live for?"

"Revenge," a voice whispered.

Rannagon froze. "Shoa?"

The yellow griffin stood up and turned around. There was nothing unusual to be seen in the study, but she began to hiss. "I smell something," she said.

Rannagon got up and snatched his sword down from the wall. "Come out and show yourself!" he commanded. "Now!"

Silence, and stillness.

Shoa hissed again, raising her wings. "I smell you," she said. "You cannot hide. If I must hunt you down, I shall kill you."

"Murderer," the voice whispered. It was speaking griffish, and before it had even faded away, Arren stepped out of the shadows to confront them.

Rannagon's mouth fell open. "Arren Cardockson?"

Shoa faltered. She drew back, suddenly losing all her aggressive confidence. "No!" she cried. "No, this cannot be!"

Arren smiled horribly. "When I make a promise, I keep it. I promised I would have revenge on you, and now I will."

"No," Rannagon whispered. "No, this isn't possible! Shoa, what have you done?"

"My curse could not have done this," said Shoa. "The boy cannot be alive." She moved forward slightly, sniffing at him. "And you are not," she whispered to Arren. "You are not alive . . . *Kraeai kran ae.*"

Arren drew his sword. "What does that mean?"

"Okaree smelt it on you," said Shoa, almost dispassionately. "A silver griffin always can. You are cursed, Arren Cardockson. I wove my magic around you and cursed you to die."

"What's going on here?" Rannagon demanded. "How did this happen?"

"I did not do this," said Shoa. "This was another griffin's magic. Dark magic. Evil."

Arren pointed his sword at Rannagon. "You murdered me, Rannagon," he said. "You killed Eluna. You turned me into this."

Fear showed in Rannagon's face, but he started forward, sword raised. "Stay away from me!"

Shoa shoved him aside. "Do not go near him," she commanded. "He is not human any more."

Arren stopped suddenly. "Can I change back?" he asked.

"No," said Shoa. "No, you cannot, Cursed One."

The cold hatred in Arren's eyes faded for a moment, and both of them could see the pure fear and horror behind it. "I have no heartbeat," he said. "I'm dead. You killed me."

"Arren, please," said Rannagon. "It wasn't supposed to happen!"

The look vanished as quickly as it had come, and Arren started to laugh, a broken, discordant sound that had more agony in it than a scream. "You think I care? What difference does that make to me? It's your fault I'm like this,

Rannagon. You killed Eluna, and then you killed me. And now I'll make you join me."

Shoa darted forward, putting herself between the two humans. "If you touch him, I will tear you apart," she rasped.

Arren snarled. "I will have my revenge," he intoned.

"Please!" Rannagon shouted again. "Please, you don't understand! I didn't want you to die! I didn't even want to—"

"But you did it!" Arren roared. "You did it, Rannagon!"

"Rannagon did only as I told him to," Shoa interrupted.

She started to advance on him, and he backed away slowly, step by step. The yellow griffin's eyes were icy cold, full of cruelty.

"Rannagon is weak," she hissed. "He was always weak. I chose him for his mind, but he has no will. Every day I have pushed him to be strong, to choose what is right, to take what is due to him. It was I who made him rise to be Master of Law, next to be chosen as Master of the Eyrie. But his weakness betrayed me. He fathered a bastard and disgraced us both.

"And then you were there. The upstart blackrobe, slipping into our council like a rat, ready to spread your corruption and your evil magic. You had charmed Riona—and so many others—into believing you were not like other Northerners, that the madness was not in you. It was only a matter of time before you duped her into naming you her successor, and became the tyrant that had been inside you since birth.

"Rannagon would not kill his own son. And he did not want to kill you, either, so he arranged for your disgrace. When you survived your journey to the South, Rannagon wanted to leave you be. You could no longer be a threat, with your griffin dead. But I knew you would find a way. I called up my magic, and I cursed you; and from then, I knew I did not need to do anything more. You were doomed to a death as terrible as you deserved."

Arren collided with a table and could go no further. Shoa stood in front of him, blocking his escape, her talons tearing at the floor.

"I'll expose you," he whispered. "I'll tell them what you did."

"Who would believe you?" said Shoa. "A blackrobe, and a murderer? One who was not only insane, but dead? You cannot fight us. You never could."

"I'm sorry, Arren," Rannagon called. "I did what I had to do, I—"

And then it was too late. In an instant, as he looked at Shoa and at the man behind her, the madness closed in over Arren's brain. He dived sideways, rolled and vaulted upright, then ran at Rannagon, sword raised.

Rannagon was fast. He dodged out of the way and swung his own sword, hard, straight at Arren's neck. But Arren ducked it and struck. The broken sword caught Rannagon in the stomach, briefly embedding itself in the flesh before it ripped out, leaving a trail of blood over Rannagon's tunic. Rannagon roared and punched Arren in the face, bowling him over, and then Shoa was there. She lashed out with one wing, knocking Rannagon aside, and then pounced on Arren. He rolled out of the way, got up and ran, darting this way and that to avoid her. But in this confined space there was nowhere to run and nowhere to hide. Her talons hit him, hurling him across the room; he hit a bookshelf and fell to the floor, and when he landed he felt the first true pain he had experienced since his resurrection.

He tried to scrabble away, but Shoa had him cornered now; she rushed at him, beak opening wide.

"No!"

It was Rannagon. He ran forward, pushing past her to get to Arren. Shoa hissed and raised her beak, threatening him, but he pushed her away.

"I said no!" he said again, and she retreated a little, tail lashing.

Rannagon placed his boot on Arren's chest, pinning him down as he tried to get up.

"I want to do this," he said.

But the delay had been long enough. Arren's fingers closed around the hilt of his sword, and he lifted and

swung it with all his might. It hit Rannagon in the leg, so
hard Arren felt it cut through the flesh and strike bone.
Rannagon screamed and reeled away, and Arren picked
himself up, dived under Shoa's beak and ran for the double
doors leading out of the study. He burst out onto the balcony and began trying to climb over the side, but he was
too late. Shoa came rushing out of the study and was on
him, knocking him down. His head struck the wall, and
stars exploded in his vision. He lay half-conscious, groaning, and Shoa's talons slammed down, trapping him.

But she did not kill him. She looked back, hissing, as
Rannagon emerged, limping. "Kill him, then, if you can,"
she said harshly.

Rannagon looked at her, and then at Arren.

Arren looked back, his glazed expression fading away.
"Kill me, then," he said. "Finish it."

"Shoa was right," Rannagon said. "I trusted you once,
but I was a fool. A blackrobe will always be a blackrobe,
no matter where he lives or how." He raised the sword.
"Goodbye, Arren Cardockson."

Arren closed his eyes. He could feel Shoa's talons moving away from his throat, so that Rannagon would have a
clear strike. *Let me die,* he thought. *Please just let me die.*

But then, quite suddenly, as he lay and waited for death
to come, he felt a strange energy rush up inside him. It
was hot and vital and powerful, like fresh blood moving
through his veins. It felt like love.

His eyes snapped open, and he screamed. *"Arren! Arren!"*

"Kill him!" Shoa shouted.

Rannagon moved his feet, balancing himself, and then
brought the sword down as hard as he could.

A screech came from overhead, shattering the night.
Rannagon, caught unawares, deflected his blow at the
last moment. His sword hit the edge of the balcony and
bounced off, nearly wrenched from his grasp. He looked
up and saw the huge dark shape fall out of the sky.

It collided with Shoa with the force of a falling tree,
bowling her over. She smashed through the doorway and

back into the study, and as Rannagon turned, too stunned to even raise his sword, he saw the yellow griffin in the firelight, grappling with a huge black-and-silver monster. The two of them grappled with each other, hissing and snapping their beaks, talons tearing great holes through feather and hide.

Rannagon ran forward. "Shoa! No!"

The two griffins pulled apart and rested a moment, crouched low and snarling. Shoa moved to protect her partner, and the black griffin looked at the door to the balcony and then started toward it, his fight apparently forgotten.

He had seen Arren.

Man and griffin stood a little way apart, regarding each other, and then Darkheart stretched his beak out toward Arren and held it there. Arren reached up tentatively and touched it. Darkheart stiffened slightly, but he did not attack. He sat very still for a moment, and then he came forward and touched his beak to Arren's chest, his claws kneading at the ground. Arren put his hands on the griffin's head, touching the feathers, and Darkheart closed his eyes and purred softly.

But this strange moment of peace did not last. Shoa rose up, spreading her wings. "Be gone, monster!"

Darkheart turned sharply and crouched low, shoulders raised. "Mine!" he hissed. *"Mine!"*

Shoa rushed at him. The black griffin was ready; he reared up onto his hind legs and latched his claws into her chest and throat. Her hind legs came up and kicked him in the belly, tearing off lumps of fur and skin. Darkheart sank his beak into the back of her skull and twisted it, making her scream.

Arren looked past the two griffins and saw Rannagon. He was near the door, sword in hand, obviously torn between fleeing and staying to help Shoa.

"You stay where you are, Rannagon!" he shouted, and ran at him, dodging around the two griffins. Shoa tried to strike him, but Darkheart rammed into her flank, knocking her aside. She landed awkwardly on her side, and he pushed her onto her back, tearing into her belly with his beak and talons. Shoa's claws sank into his head and face, but she had already lost. Darkheart knew how to kill other griffins. His beak ripped through the skin on her belly and the thin layer of muscle beneath, and her bowels slid out, bloody and glistening.

Rannagon started to run forward. "No!"

Arren slammed into him, head-on, knocking him back. Rannagon staggered backward and nearly fell, but he regained his balance and launched himself at Arren.

Orome's broken blade deflected Rannagon's, and Arren drove forward recklessly, swinging the weapon with all his might. He forgot all notion of blocking, or even aiming, and hit Rannagon in the shoulders, arms and chest. Rannagon, panic-stricken, started to retreat.

"Lord Rannagon!"

The shout had come from the other side of the door leading into the rest of the Eyrie.

Someone thumped on it, hard.

"Lord Rannagon, are you all right? Lord Rannagon!"

Rannagon raised his sword. "I'm being attacked!" he shouted back. "It's the—"

Arren thrust. The blade was aimed straight at Rannagon's chest, but before it connected, the old lord's own sword lashed out. There was a loud metallic *crack*, and then Arren was backing away, staring blankly at the shattered hilt in his hand.

The door broke open, and two people and a griffin burst through. Rannagon glanced quickly at them, and it was that gesture which sealed his doom.

Arren ran straight at him, screaming Eluna's name, and hit him in the throat with the hilt of Orome's sword. A long shard of metal still jutted from the spot where the blade had once been joined, and it drove straight into Rannagon's neck, through the skin, through the flesh and into the great vein in his throat. Arren wrenched the hilt sideways, tearing the wound open wide, and Rannagon fell, his sword dropping out of his hand.

Silence reigned in the room for what felt like a long time. Shoa lay dead, her body torn wide open by Darkheart's beak. Rannagon was still moving, but only a little. Blood gushed from his throat in a torrent, and a few moments later he stilled.

Arren, standing over him with the bloodied sword hilt still in his hand, saw the people in the doorway. Erian, with Senneck. And Flell.

Her eyes were fixed on his face. "Arren, what have you done?" she whispered.

Arren threw the hilt away. "I have had my revenge," he said. He stepped forward and picked up Rannagon's sword, and pointed it at Erian. "If you think your father was a great man, then ask yourself why he betrayed me. And ask yourself why even death did not stop me from killing him," he said.

Erian's face was pale and he was breathing hard. "I—I—"

Arren laughed. "And you call yourself a griffiner."

Senneck stalked toward him. "Murderer," she rasped.

There was a movement from behind Arren, and Darkheart appeared. He darted forward and struck Senneck across the face with his talons, violently knocking her aside. She got up and started to hiss at him, but he was larger than her, and his look was murderous.

"Mine," he said, starting toward her. "Mine!"

Arren turned away and went to the fireplace. He picked up a fallen book and held it over the flames until the pages caught. "You should have believed me," he said to Flell, and threw the burning book across the room. It landed on the heap of papers that had fallen from the overturned table, and they caught and began to burn fiercely. A spark landed on a pool of oil spilt by a broken lamp, and flames billowed toward the roof, setting fire to the bookshelf and the tapestries on the walls. In an instant, half the room was ablaze.

Arren pointed at Flell and Erian. "Run," he said, then turned and ran out onto the balcony. Darkheart paused a moment, still watching Senneck, and then went after him. Out on the balcony, he snatched Arren up by the back of his robe and then took off with a single powerful leap, flying up and into the night and taking Arren with him.

Back in the study, Flell tried to go toward her father's body. Erian grabbed her by the shoulder and pulled her back.

"No!" she shouted. "I have to—"

"It's no good," Erian snapped. "There's nothing you can do for him. We have to get out of here."

Flell had to be dragged away by her half-brother. He hustled her down the corridor, shouting as loudly as he could: "Fire! Fire! Wake up! Get out! *Fire!*"

But most of the Eyrie's occupants would never hear his warnings. As the fire spread, burning up through the roof of Rannagon's study and into the level above, there was nothing anyone could do to put it out. Most of the building's interior was wood, and all anyone could do now was run.

As Flell ran, pulled along by Erian's desperate grip, she could hear the shouts of alarm coming from all around. People were waking up, and griffins as well. They were confused, but they could smell the smoke was wafting down the corridor behind them. Senneck ran ahead, clearing a path, and the three of them reached the great council chamber. From there, they made their escape.

When they reached the street outside, Flell looked up and could see the flames billowing out of Rannagon's balcony. They were huge and fierce, burning so high they touched the balcony above it, which was already beginning to catch. Griffins were flying overhead, screeching and bewildered.

She started to sob. "What are we going to do? What are we going to do?"

Erian hugged her. "It's all right, Flell. We're safe."

"But Father!"

Erian looked up at the Eyrie, his eyes fixed on the burning balcony, which was already beginning to crumble. "He'll pay for this, Flell," he said. "I swear it by my father's blood. The blackrobe will pay. If I have to hunt him for the rest of my life, I will."

"And I shall help you," said Senneck.

* * *

That night, the Eyrie burned.

There was no large source of water nearby, no way to smother the flames. They spread through first one floor and then the next, until flames were showing in every window and balcony. There were dozens of griffiners inside, and nearly all of them were asleep. They had no chance.

Flell, standing in the street below, where the other survivors had gathered, could hear the screams. She saw griffins fly up, alone, having left their partners behind in their panic, and then circle overhead, calling for them. Some went back in, but of those most never re-emerged.

Erian was trying his best to help organise the people who had escaped, shouting his explanation to bewildered and frightened griffiners. "The blackrobe did it! He's alive! He murdered my father! Someone has to go after him!"

Many griffiners had already taken to the sky and were flying off in all directions, trying to spot the fleeing black griffin. But their search was in vain. In the dark, a black griffin would be nearly invisible. Arren had escaped.

And Flell cried. She held on to Erian, letting his warm body comfort her, and sobbed as though her heart would break. Thrain came from her house, where she had left her, and rubbed herself against Flell's leg, cheeping her concern. Flell picked her up and held her close, her tears wetting the little griffin's feathers.

Erian put his arm around her. "Flell, it's all right. It's all right. I'm here. I've got you."

"Arren, how could you?" Flell whispered between sobs. "How *could* you?"

"He's evil," Erian rasped. "Like the rest of his kind. He'll die for this."

After a time, Flell stilled and her sobs died down. "Erian . . ."

"Yes, Flell?"

"Erian, I—I'm—I . . ."

"What is it, Flell?" said Erian. "It's all right, you can tell me. I'm your brother, remember?"

Flell stared at the ground. "Erian, I'm pregnant."

A rren dangled from Darkheart's beak, unable to see a thing. He could tell they were high up; the air was cold as ice, and there was a strong wind. The collar of his robe had pulled tight around his neck, half-choking him, but he didn't really notice. Flell's horrified face filled his vision. *Arren, what have you done?*

Far below and behind him, he could see the faint light of the burning Eyrie. It would all be destroyed, he realised. He hoped so.

Rannagon's sword was still clutched in his hand. He thought of letting it go, but something made him keep hold of it. And why not? It was his now. He'd fought for it.

The back of his robe started to tear. He felt himself slipping and grabbed blindly with his free hand, catching hold of one of Darkheart's talons. The griffin's paw twitched slightly, and then he suddenly let go. For one heart-stopping moment Arren was hanging in midair, and then Darkheart wrapped his talons around him and clutched him to his chest, holding him firmly in place with his face pressed into his feathers. They were warm and soft, almost comforting, and he did not struggle. Darkheart wasn't going to kill him. He knew that well enough by now.

They flew on toward dawn. Arren had no idea what direction they were going in, but he knew they were leaving Eagleholm far behind, and that was enough. He slept briefly, lulled by the steady beating of the black griffin's great heart, and when he woke up again it was dawn. Darkheart was flagging; he was flying lower now, and his wing beats seemed clumsy. He began his descent even as Arren woke up, and finally landed in a small clearing in a forest. There he put him down and lay beside him, breathing slowly and heavily.

Arren was stiff and chilled, but he sat up, groaning, and inspected his surroundings.

There was nothing but trees all around, tall and strong, their leaves sighing in the early-morning breeze. Birds sang here and there.

He looked at Darkheart. The black griffin turned his head toward him and looked at him almost placidly.

Arren dared touch his beak, and Darkheart merely sighed.

"Thank you," said Arren. "For what you did. You saved my life."

Darkheart's eyes were alert. "We fly," he said.

"Yes," said Arren. "We fly. Where are we?"

"Arren," said Darkheart.

"Yes, Darkheart?"

Darkheart closed his eyes and laid his head on his forepaws. "Arren," he muttered again.

"Why did you do it, Darkheart?" said Arren. "Why did you come after me?"

Darkheart looked up again. "Mine," he said. "You . . . mine."

"I don't belong to you," said Arren. "I don't belong to anyone. Not even myself. You can't *own* somebody."

Darkheart got up and pulled Arren toward him, covering him with his wing. "Mine," he said. "My human. Mine."

Arren almost pulled away, but then he stilled. "You can go wherever you like," he said. "I won't stop you."

"Home," said Darkheart.

"There isn't one," said Arren. "Not for us. They took our homes from us, Darkheart." He looked up at the sky, searching for any hint of griffins' wings. Nothing. Just a clear open sky, lit by dawn. "They'll be after us," he said softly. "Maybe not now, but soon. They want to kill us."

Darkheart snorted. "I fight. You fight."

"Yes. We can do that, can't we?"

Arren got up and walked around the clearing. He was still limping a little, but he would be all right. Darkheart lay and watched him carefully, not letting him out of his sight.

Arren stopped and looked back at him. The black griffin's presence was still menacing. He was still dangerous. He was still a man-eater. And yet . . .

Arren closed his eyes. What did that matter? How did it make him any different?

"We're murderers," he said, looking up. "Both of us. You and I are the same."

Darkheart seemed to understand. "Dark griffin. Dark human," he said.

"Yes, Darkheart," said Arren, going to him and touching his head. "Both of us."

"Where . . . we go?" said Darkheart.

Arren knew. "North," he said.

It had to be north.

He paused, looking at the griffin. "You don't have a name, do you?" he said.

"Name?" said Darkheart.

"Yes," said Arren. He touched his chest. "Arren."

"Darkheart," said Darkheart.

"No. Darkheart isn't a name. It's a label. They called me blackrobe. So you're Darkheart? Darkheart and Blackrobe, is that what we are? No." Arren touched the black griffin on the head, feeling the silver feathers while he thought.

"Skandar," he said at last. "Your name is Skandar."

Darkheart looked up at him. "Skan . . . dar?"

"Yes. It's a Northern name. A warrior's name. Skandar. Not Darkheart. Skandar."

Darkheart looked thoughtful. He lay down to rest, muttering. "Skandar. Skandar."

Arren watched him, and couldn't help but smile. "Arren and Skandar."

Later, when Skandar was asleep, Arren sat down by the griffin's flank, with the sword on the ground in front of him. He touched it gingerly. It was worn, but sharp and well made. *I'll keep it,* he thought. *I'll need it. One day, when they catch up with me, I'll need it.*

He put one hand to the side of his neck and kept it there for a long time, concentrating.

Nothing. No heartbeat.

I'm the man without a heart.

A cold determination came over him. He pulled the robe more tightly over his shoulders and snuggled against Skandar's flank. North. They would go to the North. There were hundreds of people there who looked like him. He would not be noticed.

I'll find my parents, he thought. *I'll get them to safety. And after that, I'll look for a way to change back. Something that will make my heart start beating again.*

For a moment, he thought of Rannagon. And Flell. And the burning Eyrie. Had he really done those things? Had he?

He looked at his hands. There was blood on them, and more on his robe. *Murderer,* his mind whispered.

"No," he said aloud. "No. A killer survives."

Griffiners were not quite human. Many people said so. After so long living among griffins, they became griffish themselves. And griffins killed. For food, for pride, for revenge. For survival. They did not understand weakness or timidity. His old self—the man he had been—was completely alien to them. Why should he be weak and submissive, always looking to others for approval, always afraid of himself and his own nature? He had killed, and it had been right. Not good, not kind, but right for him. The only way. A griffin's way.

I will go to the North, he thought again. *I'll find a place to hide.*

He looked at Skandar. The griffin's huge sides moved in and out in time with his deep, rumbling breaths, but in his sleep he looked almost peaceful.

And I won't go there alone.

About the Author

"A lot of fantasy authors take their
inspiration from Tolkien. I take mine from
G. R. R. Martin and Finnish metal."

Born in Canberra in 1986, Katie J. Taylor attended Radford
College, where she wrote her first novel, *The Land of Bad
Fantasy*, which was published in 2006. She studied for a
bachelor's degree in communications at the University of
Canberra and graduated in 2007 before going on to do a
graduate certificate in editing in 2008. K. J. Taylor writes
at midnight and likes to wear black.

For news and author contact, visit
www.kjtaylor.com.

**Don't miss
the second book in the Fallen Moon series**

K. J. Taylor

The Griffin's Flight

THE FALLEN MOON, BOOK TWO

Now hated and hunted, Northerner Arren Cardockson
has only one friend: Skandar, the monstrous, man-eating
black griffin. Together, they flee from their enemies,
running for the cold North and the shelter it may hold
for them. When they meet the mysterious wild woman
called Skade, their friendship will be tested—but she
may hold the key to lifting Arren's curse and making his
dead heart beat again . . .

Coming February 2011 from Ace Books

M753T0810